PERFECT
REDEMPTION

PERFECT REDEMPTION

The PERFECT Series

CLAUDIA TAN

w by wattpad books

 by wattpad books

An imprint of Wattpad WEBTOON Book Group

Copyright© 2024 Claudia Tan

Published in Canada by Wattpad WEBTOON Book Group, a division of Wattpad WEBTOON Studios, Inc.

36 Wellington Street E., Suite 200, Toronto, ON M5E 1C7 Canada

www.wattpad.com

First W by Wattpad Books edition: April 2024

ISBN 978-1-99885-496-7 (Trade Paper original)
ISBN 978-1-99025-962-3 (eBook edition)

Library and Archives Canada Cataloguing in Publication information is available upon request.

P1

Cover design by Mumtaz Mustaf
Images © MJTH via Shutterstock
Typesetting by Delaney Anderson

To Irwin, who was my personal bad boy
project—turned husband material.
You're welcome.

PROLOGUE

Jax

Moving to LA, I thought I was doing myself a favor by getting out of town and turning over a new leaf.

Turns out, I only got the "getting out of town" part down.

I've done some fucked-up shit back in my home city, Boston, I'll admit it. Some deranged shit. But I don't like to talk about it. That's what moving cities is for, so I *won't* have to talk about it. Besides, I doubt anyone affected by my actions would want me opening my mouth about it either. So I shut up and try to move on.

But . . . I don't know, I guess a little part of me may have thought that three thousand miles between me and Boston would be enlightening in some way. I thought I'd get swept up in the willingness to change and all the other bullshit that's supposed to make me a better human being. I was open to it. I cracked a little fissure in my armor in case the City of Angels decided I was worthy enough to join the club.

But none of that happened.

I've been here five weeks and I haven't changed. Not even a little bit. In fact, I'm still the same asshole I've always been.

What a fucking disappointment.

Maybe because change is impossible. The people who told me otherwise are liars trying to brainwash themselves along with the rest of the world into thinking that we wake up every day and actively choose our own fate, but that's far from the truth. The reality is that there are plenty of environmental, social, and familial factors that decide what kind of person you end up becoming, and more often than not, it's rarely yourself who's behind the damn wheel.

So, no, I don't believe human beings are capable of change. It's like trying to change the color of your skin or the sky. While I do believe that no one is truly good or bad, I also believe that certain people have an inherent propensity toward doing good or bad things. It's human instinct. So, a snake will always be a snake. A serial killer will always kill more people.

And I will always be as I was.

It's in my nature to be wicked. To destroy everyone who loves me.

And if I have to be honest with myself, I quite enjoy it. There's nothing like the delight of turning someone innocent into a corrupted reflection of myself.

Besides, to be the one who does the corrupting is far better than to be the one who gets corrupted.

Growing up, it's all I've endured. I lost years to suffering under the oppressive hands of my family. My stepdad had tried to break me, to get me to submit to his every whim. But I held on. After years of being on the receiving end of his punches, I became immune to pain. In fact, I even learned how to wield it to my benefit inside the MMA cage. Since then, I vowed to myself that I will never be in that position of weakness again.

So, after more than a month of being here, I've finally come to the realization that seeking peace and forgiveness will never work on me. The evil has already been etched into my soul. I cannot be cleansed.

I've had my sins. I've cheated, manipulated, tricked, fought, and inflicted unimaginable pain on people, including the ones who cared about me the most.

They call me the devil for a reason. The flames of the fire kiss my feet. I burn everything I touch and everyone knows it.

And even if somehow I end up being wrong about my fate, it's not like I deserve change. I don't deserve redemption.

Because you can't redeem someone who has no soul to redeem.

So if I'm not here to change, then what the hell am I still doing here?

Fuck knows. LA isn't as glamorous as everyone claims it to be, but anything beats being back in Boston. Besides, superficial culture aside, I like that you can be anything you want here. Reinvent yourself a million times. Or don't. In my case, I can be exactly as I am and nobody gives a fuck. Nobody that I see reason enough to let in my life anyway.

And that's fine with me.

More than fine, actually.

It's perfect.

ONE

Jax

As I stir awake, I'm no longer surprised by what I see.

A set of unfamiliar walls. My shirt and pants lay crumpled on the hardwood floor. No underwear in sight, only a bottle of Jack Daniel's toppled over the side table, along with a few empty condom wrappers. The lower part of my body is barely covered by the sheets.

Oh, and the women.

The one on my right, a brunette, is naked but sound asleep. She lays on her belly, with an arm casually thrown over my chest. She's okay-looking. A name doesn't come to mind. It might jog my memory if I could see more of her face, but the side of her cheek is mushed against the pillow and she's drooling so hard the tail end of it starts to tickle the curve of my ear.

The sensation of it jolts my body into a sitting position. Fucking hell.

The brunette is still dead to the world when I peel her arm off me and drop it onto the space beside her. Two other girls are passed out on the chaise; the harsh sunlight bearing down through the huge glass window does not faze them one bit. At least they're both clothed.

The smell of weed wafts into the bedroom, filling my lungs whole. Usually, I don't mind the smell, but today it makes me want to throw up.

Or maybe it's the raging hangover. Admittedly, that's the glory and curse of treating alcohol like water. But that's never really been a problem for me. Most of the time, I welcome the hangover. It serves as good punishment for the debauchery of the night before. But I can't say today invites a similar retribution. I can't punish myself for a night I don't even remember, although I can form a vague idea of what happened.

I shrug. *Oh well.*

I push myself off the bed and check for my phone, which is still sitting in the back pocket of my pants. I don't bother to go through my messages or missed calls. The only person who even bothers to check up on me is the absolute last person I want to talk to today.

I slip into my clothes and stuff my feet into my shoes. As I do, I notice that there are some weird scribblings on my left shoe, and annoyance slips into my skin at the audacity of someone drunkenly deciding that a Sharpie looked good with my Nike Airs. Drunk or not, I would never do such a thing to my sneakers. Everything that I own I've had to bleed for, so I won't disrespect my own hard work.

Everyone else's possessions, however, are fair game.

I'm already slipping out of the room by the time I

hear rustling of bodies from the chaise. Morning-after confrontations aren't my forte, and even though most LA girls are heedless with sexual endeavors such as these, I'd rather avoid the conversation entirely if I can.

Typically, I'd expect empty beer cans to scatter the hallway, but I have to remind myself that this isn't some frat house in Cambridge, it's some B-lister's mansion in the Hills with way more money than he'll ever need. After navigating through broken champagne glasses and turning three full corners, I finally reach the floating glass staircase that'll hopefully get me out of here.

I hear vacuuming and the ruffling of trash bags coming from the living room to my right, so I make a left instead once I've made it to the ground floor. I pass by a self-portrait of whom I assume to be the owner of the house, sitting in a chair like a king, decked out in a robe and frills and the whole nine, along with a golden staff. I've seen weirder things than this in LA, but this is up there.

I tuck my smile behind my teeth. I'm not gonna lie, if I had the fame and money, this might actually be something I would do.

I stare at it for a good few seconds, trying to think if this guy and I crossed paths last night. Everything is still fuzzy. I probably wouldn't have come here alone though. It was probably Connor or Watts who brought me, and neither of them wanted to stick around long enough to see where I would end up.

Eventually, I find a gold mirror with spikes poking out of them hanging on one of the walls and use it to quickly fix myself up. The alcohol has paled my skin out to the point of looking sickly. I smooth my hair back and tuck it behind my ears and adjust my wrinkled shirt. I'm not going to risk looking like this if I stumble upon a hot chick my dick stirs for. Once I settle his hangover, I should be back to fully operational again in the next four to six hours.

Which reminds me . . .

My gaze drops to the bar cart in front of me, parked under the mirror. And among the few bottles of liquor sits a nearly full Macallan 18.

Temptation crawls over my skin.

I wouldn't say I'm struggling financially. I've earned my keep from fighting men in underground basements back in Boston. But because I stopped doing that and am currently using LA as my temporary haven, I've been digging a little too much into my savings lately. And that won't get me very far in this city if I'm dropping two grand a night on expensive whiskey.

So, being righteous will have to wait.

I swipe the bottle from the cart and head for the door.

I barely make it a step when I find one of the cleaners staring at me, all confused. She looks to be in her early thirties, curly black hair, wide eyes. Good figure. The vacuum she's using rumbles against the Persian carpet, but she doesn't move.

I'm not opposed to hooking up with older women. They tend to know exactly what they want in bed, which is great. Less work for me since all I have to do is execute.

It's a shame I can't stick around to see if that's the case with this woman.

I glance at the Macallan in the hand, then back at her.

"We're friends," I say.

The woman doesn't look convinced, but doesn't protest either. She definitely thinks I have no clue who I'm referring to when I said "we." I don't let the thought linger either. The last thing I do is give her a sly wink as I slide past her and leave.

The Macallan grows lighter in my hand as I wait for my Uber down the road to take me back to my hotel.

TWO

Jax

The apartment that I'm renting is located on some street in West Hollywood. You'd think that based on the location alone, this makes it a pretty decent neighborhood to live in, but you'd be wrong. I'm nearly seven feet tall and 190 pounds, so I'd like to think I'm a scary fucking dude, having fought many guys in dodgy basements for years, but hell, even going to the store past sundown in this area sparks a kernel of fear inside me that I never knew existed.

That's when I learned my first lesson about moving: do your damn research. I had never stepped foot on the west coast before this, let alone LA, and I was in a hurry to get out of Boston. LA felt like the best option at the time, since I had a few friends here who were perfect to get me acquainted with the nightlife, so I booked the next flight out with no return date in mind. Five weeks later, here I am, stuck in a neighborhood determined to mug, assault, or kill me.

LA truly is a different beast.

It's barely noon now. The summer heat sears my skin as I exit the Uber. I tell the driver to drop me off a street away since I convince myself that walking will help with the hangover. On my left, there's a dilapidated two-star hotel that I've never once seen anyone else but sketchy-ass old men and barely legal girls draped on their arms go into. Beside that is an old strip mall hosting a dry cleaners, grocery store, a Korean restaurant, and a mixed martial arts gym.

I stop at my tracks, lingering outside the gym. I never go in, despite every part of me screaming to partake in a membership. Today, a coach is hosting a group beginner class, I assume, from the way the few of them tackle the heavy bags without the proper techniques to get the most effective exercise in. The guy occupying the heavy bag closest to the window goes in for a hook-hook-body-body combo, and I catch a glimpse of shiny blond hair wrapped up in a ponytail from the student on his right. My rib cage suddenly goes tight and I've lost the ability to breathe. It feels as though I've been struck violently in the chest.

It can't be. Sienna . . .

The guy reels back, throwing an arm out, and then, the blond woman's face comes into view. The fear recedes when I notice that she's much shorter than Sienna, and her eyes are black, not blue like I'd been accustomed to, with a rounder jaw and a thinner pair of lips. I force myself to look away, a hand reaching up to my jaw to ease the pressure building up there.

My mind whirs with what just happened.

Why did I think, even for a second, that it would even be her who's taking a boxing class, *here*, on my street? Why does my mind automatically assume that she'd hunt me down all the way to LA?

She was the one who suggested that I leave.

She was the one who made it clear that I no longer belonged anywhere near her.

A thin trail of sweat glides down the side of my face and I use the back of my arm to wipe it away. Fuck. *Fuck.* Even if Sienna and I are on opposite sides of the country, my mind has a way of finding her in her absence.

Everything, *everything*, always comes back to her.

I don't know if that makes me sentimental or tragic.

***

I'm scarfing down leftovers from yesterday in front of the TV when my phone vibrates in my pocket with "The Imperial March" as my ringtone. I'm not a *Star Wars* fan in the slightest; I just thought I'd be particularly fitting for the caller in question.

"What do you want?" My tone is clipped when I answer.

"You were willing to risk everything for a bottle of *whiskey*? Really, Jackson?" Baxton's voice thunders in my ear.

I flinch at the fact that my dad called me by my old name, despite me correcting him on numerous occasions.

"How? What—?" My body is injected with equal parts panic and confusion as to how he could possibly know that since I left the mansion a mere half an hour ago.

"I have a list of billables by Magnus Stokes. It says here that you broke his refrigerator last night, ordered a bunch of pizzas under his card, and then today, swiped a bottle of his whiskey, according to one of his cleaners," he says as he reads off a list. Anger wraps around his voice again. "What the *hell*?"

Magnus Stokes. Fitting name for someone who has a self-portrait of himself in his own home. Although that's the only thing that seems to make sense here.

"I don't get it." I set my plate down on the coffee table and wipe my bottom lip with my thumb. "Why is it being billed to you?"

"I don't know. Maybe it's because Magnus knows that you're my son and because he couldn't get a hold of you, I'm the next best thing?" My dad blasts out. "Or maybe it's because you refuse to take responsibility for your own actions?"

A muscle pulses in my jaw at his paternal tone, one that quite frankly, he does not deserve to take with me. Despite this, he continues to voice his frustration about my antics all week. It hasn't always been like that. Three weeks before, when he'd caught wind I was here, it was just him wanting to connect again after more than a decade of not reaching out. But the more my social circle overlapped with his and got people talking about what I've been doing, the more my and Baxton's relationship soured.

It's not like I'd been hoping for a happy *reunion*. I hadn't even anticipated a reunion, full stop. My dad had dipped out of my life after divorcing my mom a decade ago to pursue a career in acting, and I haven't wanted to see him since. Especially because he'd decided that erasing his old life from his burgeoning one was the best course of action. And so that meant no contact with me, his then *eleven-year-old son*.

It was heartbreaking, and a big reason why I don't

particularly care about this relationship going down the gutter again. I've dealt with it before; I can do it again.

"Send me the bill. I'll settle it," I press on, my grip on the phone as tight as the collar of my shirt digging into my neck.

A hard scoff echoes through the line. "You're gonna settle ten grand worth of items?"

"*Ten grand?*" I lambast. "For fuck's sake, how many pizzas did I order?"

"It wasn't the pizzas. It was the refrigerator."

A groan rips out of me. Jesus, what the hell did I do to it?

I screw my eyes shut, drawing a breath. I'll just have to bite the bullet and settle the bill. It's either that or have Baxton clean up my mess. And I'd like to believe I have more pride than that.

"I'll deal with it, I swear," I insist.

A heavy breath reverberates through the phone, like he doesn't quite believe me. I don't understand why he wouldn't. I've spent twenty-three years cleaning up my own messes. Ten grand will decimate my savings, but I've been forced into worse circumstances before.

Baxton's voice softens, injected with a drop of pity. "Jackson . . ."

"You *have* to stop calling me that," I say with a groan.

"I'm not gonna call you by the name you give yourself."

"It's as real as any other name," I say defensively.

Baxton isn't aware of the reason why I had my name legally changed. He doesn't know of the horrors my stepdad, Charles, put me through in the underground, to warrant an altered identity. Changing my name was the only way I could fully separate myself from him and the horrors of what he did to me.

Baxton releases a big sigh. "Fine. *Jax.* I'll deal with Magnus. On the condition that you stop with this madness. Going MIA every weekend, partying and fucking till your body gives out? It's not going to end well, I promise you that."

"I don't know what you're talking about. I'm doing fine."

"You just crashed a random celebrity's house, maxed his credit card, and wrecked *and* stole his belongings."

"I didn't say I was doing great."

Baxton sighs. Then, after a short beat. "Have you ever considered therapy?"

Oh god, not this shit again.

"Look, I don't know what happened back in Boston," Baxton continues, his voice taking a sympathetic note. "But you know you can't keep pushing it away."

Divulging what happened back in Boston was not something I had any intention of sharing, with Baxton or anyone else here. He's desperate to know, that's for sure. But he's not getting that information from me. He doesn't deserve it.

"I'm not pushing it away. I'm just moving on." I argue.

"Self-sabotage is not moving on," he barks back.

"Self-sabotage implies that I'm torturing myself when in fact, I've never felt more alive."

A frustrated noise emits from the phone. "Can we at least be honest and talk about what this is doing to you? And find a way forward? It doesn't have to be with a therapist. Just be open to some kind of help," He pleads and I sigh exasperatedly. "I should be done with my last scene by 9:00 p.m. We can grab a late dinner."

PERFECT RUIN

"I'm busy, Baxton." I swipe my food off the coffee table and travel to the kitchen, balancing the phone between my shoulder and my ear.

"Fine. I'll drop by tomorrow."

"I have plans tomorrow too."

"Oh really? What kind of plans?"

"A few meetings. You're not the only one with a packed schedule, Baxton," I lie.

"Fine," he relents, albeit begrudgingly. "But please, keep your head down these next few days? People around me are starting to talk. They think I don't know how to control my own son."

"Right. My bad," I snap, bitterness clogging my throat dropping the takeaway box into the trash can. "The next time I fuck up, I'll be sure to let everyone know it's my own doing, so your reputation as the most unproblematic actor in Hollywood will remain unscathed."

"You know that's not what I meant—"

I don't hear the rest of his sentence because I've already hung up.

The phone skitters across the kitchen counter. I grip the edges of the sink so hard I could very well rip it off. My shoulders curving forward, my face slightly bent as I let loose a strained breath.

I could be nicer to Baxton, I get that. But despising him is a muscle I've trained for years, so it's difficult to let up now. And well intentioned or not, what Baxton wants from me is something I simply can't do. He thinks I'm a cry for help.

I just want to live my life the worst I possibly can.

It's less than a minute later when I claw my phone back. I dial the one person whom I can rely on to get me a good time.

"Hey, Watts," I say smoothly. "Do you have any parties tonight with an open RSVP list?"

THREE

Blaire

My younger brother, Eden, squints skeptically at the smaller kids running about on the kiddie playground.

He watches silently as another boy half his age chases his friend around the perimeter of the park. As the boy rounds the corner, he nearly collides with Eden, but swerves and bumps into his shoulder instead. Eden gives him a dirty look and the boy mumbles a quick "sorry" before picking up speed again.

Eden rolls his eyes and brushes off the dirt from his NASA shirt before returning his gaze to me, this time, punctuated with boredom. "You do realize I'm ten, right?"

"Come on. I thought it would be fun," I offer, nudging Eden with my elbow. "The monkey bars were always your thing."

"Yeah, like . . . a million years ago?" He hurls me a look that says *get with the times, woman.*

Sometimes, I forget that he's not a little kid. Despite only being gone for less than a year, it still rattles me how much of his life I have missed out on.

I steal a quick glance at my phone. Twenty minutes left before I have to return him. A frown tugs at my mouth for a quick second before disappearing.

"How about I race you?" I suggest, looking back up at Eden.

For a moment, his deep blue eyes sparkle with intrigue. Like me, he can't resist a challenge. He plants his attention on the monkey bars that are connected to the top of the slide and lifts his hand up in the shape of an L to gauge the distance between the bars and the ground. He drops his hand and purses his lips contemplatively. "I don't know, B. You might be too tall. You'll just walk to the other side."

"Well, then you'll just have to swing faster, won't you?"

Eden grins.

"You're on."

Seconds later, we're racing up the steps up to the monkey bars. Eden gets a head start and he's already on his third bar by the time I get on the bars. I dangle my feet off the ground, careful to not cheat by walking because I want him to enjoy the victory. Besides, I'm not as agile as a ten-year-old, so he beats me easily. When he reaches the last bar, he practically leaps to the ground, cackling at his victory and proceeds to flip me off for losing.

"Oh my god, don't do that," I say sternly, closing my hand over his to tuck his middle finger down. "Laura might think I taught you that. She already thinks I'm a bad influence on you."

"Eh," Eden says, dismissive, "what she doesn't see won't hurt her."

"Be careful," I tease. "You might actually be turning into me."

"What? That's not a bad thing."

"Try telling that to Laura."

Laura Adams is Eden's adoptive mother. After four years of failing to conceive and another year trying to adopt, Laura and her husband Connor finally got what they always wanted in Eden. I've only met Connor once; he isn't around as much due to the sporadic nature of his job as a pilot, but he's much more likable than his wife, who, unfortunately, is always around, and is highly critical of everything that I do.

To be honest, I don't think his adoptive parents expected that I was going to be a part of Eden's life in this way. In an ideal situation, none of us would have been put in this position to begin with. I suppose it is my fault that we're all here now, since I was sent away to serve seven months in county jail and was subsequently ripped away from my brother.

Serving was torture; not because of the actual sentence itself, but because I was afraid of what was going to happen to my family while I was gone. When I was incarcerated, me, Eden, and my mom were all living in some dirt-cheap hotel downtown. I'd stupidly hoped that by the time I was out, they'd either still be living there or that they'd be close by. However, it took me three months to discover that not only was Eden no longer in my mom's custody, but also that she had skipped town and dropped him in an orphanage like she was returning an item to the store. So when Eden was adopted, the orphanage wasn't aware that he had any known siblings, since my mom failed to disclose that information.

I was equally devastated and relieved to find out he'd been adopted. While Eden was no longer, in the legal sense, mine anymore, at least he was taken care of all those months I was behind bars. At least my mother knew better than to be selfish with him. She and I disagreed with a lot of things, but at the end of the day, we both knew Eden was the best of us, and therefore needed a fighting chance against the life we'd fallen into.

Today is my fourth time visiting Eden. I'm still getting used to the fact that he belongs to someone else permanently now.

Eden and I make ourselves comfortable on the bench overlooking the playground. I pass him a ham sandwich I made at home and he hungrily accepts it, taking a huge bite off the edge and chewing it down. His jet-black hair turns into a mocha-brown shade when the strands catch the late afternoon sun. With his long, straight nose, square jaw, and larger-than-life smile, he looks so much like our late father.

"So, what did you do last weekend?" I ask, tucking in the tag that's poking out of the back of his striped shirt back.

"Mom drove me to Santa Monica Pier and we rode a ton of rides. Got the best score on the High Striker too," Eden details before taking another bite of the ham sandwich. He swallows it down before adding, "We got some churros afterwards. They tasted bad, though."

"Laura told you to call her Mom?" Is the only thing that is stuck in my brain.

"Yeah. She said she doesn't really like to do first names, so we're trying it out."

I feel a painful twist in my stomach. I get that my and Eden's biological mom wasn't exactly the best maternal figure, but it feels like Laura is trying to replace her in Eden's life.

Eden finishes off the sandwich and crushes the Saran wrap into a ball with his hand before chucking it in the trash. "When do we get to do something fun, Blaire?

"Are we not doing something fun right now?"

He looks down on his lap. "You know what I mean. I'm kind of tired of walking around all the time and just hanging out in parks."

I remain quiet. Right. In every ten-year-old's dictionary, doing something fun means doing something that involves spending money.

It's difficult to keep the embarrassment from washing across my face in a red flush.

I don't blame him for wanting those things. I *want* him to have those things. He's had it just as rough as me, so it's about time he got to live a normal life like other kids his age. It just pains me how I can't give him what he needs. It's summer and he's practically stuck babysitting me because I'm too broke to bring him anywhere else.

"Are you still working at Creme De La Creme?" Eden prods.

"Yes," The lie slips right out of my mouth.

"I hope it sticks. You were so sad about leaving the previous job."

My smile wanes. The truth is that I stopped working at Creme De La Creme more than a month ago. They found out about my criminal record and made up some reason to give me the boot.

Unfortunately, I'm used to these things happening. It doesn't matter to them that I have a high school diploma, or the necessary skills to carry the job. All they see is my record, and the possible danger that comes along with employing me. It sucks, and I don't know how to move forward with my life if this is what I have to succumb to every time I apply for something.

"Come here," I say, dragging my brother toward me. My forehead presses up against his and I inhale deeply. "You don't have to worry about me, all right? I've got it figured out."

"Do you really?" he asks skeptically.

"Yeah. I figured out the housing situation by myself, didn't I?"

"That's just because you have Baxton to help," Eden teases, poking holes at my defense.

Baxton Deneris is a family friend of ours with whom I recently reconnected. My dad worked for Baxton as a gardener for a few years, so I was always around his house a lot. When Baxton found out about my situation, he was a big help in getting me settled after getting out of jail. He got me set up in a spare house of his on Melrose, and played a major role in helping me find Eden again. I owe my new life to him.

While I'm eternally grateful to have had someone pick me up out of the gutter like this, Eden's comment elicits a sour feeling in my belly. Everything I've achieved post-incarceration has been because of Baxton. The one thing I want to do for myself, aka, getting a stable income, has been a bust so far.

"If you need anything. Like, anything at all, you let me know, okay?" Eden pouts worriedly. "I know you think I'm too young to help or whatever, but you shouldn't underestimate me."

It makes me smile. "Okay. I promise I won't. And thank you. But I got this."

Eden nods slowly. "Okay."

For a moment, this is all I need. For him to trust that I'll make it work. I'll figure it out eventually.

The moment is undercut by my phone alarm sounding off in the back pocket of my shorts. "Shit." I pull away.

"Already?" Eden groans.

"Yeah." I pull myself off the bench and wrap an arm around his shoulder. "Let's get you back home."

Eden begrudgingly lifts himself off the bench.

The perfectly manicured three-story house with its blue shutters and white picket fence looms directly in front of us, the kind that my parents and I used to live in. However, the idyllic view is ruined by the impatient owner standing on the front porch with a look of displeasure carved into her face.

My feelings of disdain for Laura aside, I admit she's actually quite pretty. Gorgeous, even. She's pushing fifty now, but she doesn't look a day older than thirty-five. Her brown shoulder-length hair is cut into a chic bob, and her dainty mouth holds two rows of perfect, white teeth. She probably strikes fire into men's hearts when she smiles. Not that I'd really know, she doesn't ever seem to throw me those smiles.

When Laura notices both me and Eden, there's momentary relief flickering in those dark irises even as her lips are flattened into an angry, tense line. The line deepens when she notices Eden is happy with me.

Her sharp gaze zeroes in on his muddied-up sneakers.

"Your shoes are filthy," she remarks.

"Oh," he says nonchalantly. He kicks his heels together and shrugs. "We went to the park."

Her chest puffs up with annoyance. "Take them off before you get upstairs."

Eden nods. He gives me a quick wave goodbye before disappearing into the house. Laura watches him leave and when he's out of earshot, turns her full attention to me.

"You're late," she remarks with a chill in her voice.

"Only by eight minutes. We were at the park nearby when you texted."

She shakes her head slowly, in a sign she's not going to tolerate any play that isn't by her rules. "That's not what we agreed to."

My body burns with frustration. This isn't the first time she's tried to pick on any little thing, just to find fault with me. We've been going at it ever since I popped back into Eden's life.

"I'm trying my best here, Laura," is all I can say.

She shakes her head, not believing me. "You know I'm already being too lenient, letting you see him once a week."

"Yeah, for, like, three hours, at your convenience."

She folds her arms across her chest, composure never faltering. "Do I need to remind you that I'm not legally obligated to give you visitation rights? That the only reason why you have them is because Eden *begged* to see you?"

"You know I'm grateful for the arrangement, Laura," I appease through clenched teeth. "I'm just saying, if I have more time with him, I could really see that being good for Eden."

"Oh? And how can you be good for him? By encouraging him to bum out?"

"I have a job, you know."

"Oh, right. Creme De La Creme?" Laura cocks her head sideways smugly. "Funny how I popped in last week to see if you were in, only to find out from your manager that you stopped working there last month."

I swallow hard. I did not see that coming.

Eden will know that I lied to him. Laura will no doubt jump at the first chance to tell him.

"Maybe we should also discuss you mooching off someone else, expecting free handouts from a "family friend"?" Her brows furrow with hardness. I clench my jaw at the mention of Baxton. "Bet your parents would be proud of that. God only knows what kind of arrangement you and that guy have."

Her comment surprises me. Me and *Baxton*?

"Laura, you know that's not the case at all."

"I may not know everything, but I do know that if you're not responsible enough to pay rent, then how am I supposed to trust you with my kid?"

My mouth gapes open.

"That's really not fair."

"What's fair is before asking for more hours with Eden, maybe you might wanna take a good, hard look at yourself and reflect on whether you really deserve it," Laura sneers.

My heart falls out of my rib cage and splatters to the floor.

She's not serious, is she? Surely there's a way to win her over here that I'm not seeing, because she's not an evil woman. No matter how much I would like to villainize her in my head.

But the rationale side of me doesn't win today. Because the last thing she does is make a *tsk*ing sound before shutting the door in my face.

FOUR

Blaire

I head home after dropping Eden off with Laura since I have some time to spare before meeting up with Baxton for dinner. Home is a lovely three-bedroom, two-storey bungalow in Melrose on a rather quiet street with a large yard and a backyard pool.

Yes, my life is a paradox.

Baxton bought the house years ago with plans to flip it and then sell it for a premium. When I reconnected with him after getting out of jail, things changed. The house was nearing the end of its renovations, and Baxton decided to hold off on selling it so that I could stay there until I was able to fully get back on my feet. He never gave me a set date to move out, but, like me, he probably assumed I'd be moving out after a month or two.

It's been more than half a year now.

Although, I'm luckier than most. I've heard stories about ex-convicts getting dropped off on Skid Row the moment they're done serving their sentence. I'm fortunate to avoid such a fate; and that I even *had* a Baxton fighting in my corner for me. My friend Elle thinks that my late dad was the one who sent him to me last year. I love my dad and while I'm grateful for Baxton every second of every day, I know better than to put my faith in guardian angels.

The only person I ever have any faith in is myself.

And if I were to get myself out of this predicament with Laura, I'm the only one who can do it. So, I open up my laptop with a renewed purpose.

Laura's logic was simple enough to understand: if I wanted more time with Eden, I needed to prove that I could be a good example for him, morally and financially. I doubt her entire perspective on me would change overnight even if I held a job—in fact, she'd probably make me work even harder for it than I already do now—but if I kept proving to her that I had my life in order financially, I might just gain a little bit of her trust. And that's good with me for now.

Eden is the only thing I live for. I'd die if I let Laura shut me out of his life for good.

On my laptop (yet another hand-me-down from Baxton), I fired off more emails, along with my résumé, to any restaurant, café, and retail store within a ten-mile radius from where I lived that had a job opening. On the likely chance that I wouldn't be receiving any replies to said emails, I also made an appointment with a job center for next week to see if there's anything I can do to make myself a more desirable applicant. There's gotta be someone there who'd be able to find something for me, even with my record, right? Besides, the job center probably has access to all kinds of databases that'll allow me to cast my net far and wide.

I'm not one to cling on to hope, but it's the only thing I've got.

Although, there is a way I can make the job search much easier for myself.

I could scrub my record off the system.

This was an option I had considered. Theoretically speaking, I could do that. Wipe my record clean so it's like it was never even there in the first place. I went to jail for a non-violent crime and served only seven months, which makes me eligible for expungement. But wiping my record would mean hiring a lawyer to help with my application, and it's a lengthy process with no guarantee of the desired result. The billables would cripple me, let alone the application and court fees.

I could ask Baxton for the money. But that would mean backtracking on the big, fat lie I'd told him, that I had a job and was financially stable. And plus, I don't know if I could ever do that to Baxton. He's given me more than enough to get myself started. I can't ask him for any more favors . . . I won't.

I spend the remainder of my time before dinner scrolling through job websites.

***

Baxton's show, *Heartstorm Hospital*, films its episodes in the Paramount Pictures studio lot, which isn't too far from where I'm staying, so I make the twenty-minute walk there. Baxton is still held up on set, so it's already really late at night when I get there. The show he's filming is a satirical, dark comedy-drama about a group of vampires who run a hospital in the aftermath of an apocalypse and they spend the whole season hiding their devious nature from the survivors. It's unhinged, and a little cheesy, but makes for great TV. A few months ago, it was announced that they were being renewed for a third season, much to the delight of their millions of fans, and production began a few weeks ago.

After signing in at the entrance and retrieving my ID tag, an assistant is there to greet me by the entrance. The name on her tag says Gayle. Her smile is warm, but strained. She looks like she could be my age—probably a film student doing her internship here for the summer—with her dark, wavyhair slicked back into a tight ponytail and her sleepy, brown eyes telling me that she's too underpaid to be this exhausted.

"Baxton is about to wrap up for the day. They're just trying to get the perfect shot for the kiss scene," she informs me when she scoots into the back of the cart with me.

What kiss scene? I want to ask, but I'll likely know soon enough. I've watched the previous two seasons of *Heartstorm Hospital*, and the only budding couple on the show is between the two side characters, Camilla and Edward. If she's talking about a kiss scene between Baxton's character Drac, and his longtime   enemy-slash-hinted-to-be-future-love-interest, Mina, then my interest is immediately piqued.

Gayle taps on the driver's shoulder, telling him there's no one else joining us, and off we go. Even though I've been to set a handful of times by now, I still get this pinch-me moment when the cart drives us through all these different filming sets. My heart quickens when I find that the Brownstone set is closed off today, and I catch a glimpse of Emma Roberts walking out of a subway station, talking on the phone with a coffee on one hand, nearly lost to a sea of extras pretending to be busy, couldn't-care-less New Yorkers.

Once we've reached Stage 9, we hop off the cart and with Gayle's special ID that scans and clicks the door open, we're through. The *Heartstorm Hospital* set is huge. The stage houses most of the indoor sets like the interiors of Drac's office, the hospital meeting room, along with the characters' apartments. When they film outdoors, they usually film at the other premade lots, or lots at the other studios in LA.

Tonight, they're shooting in Drac's apartment. Like his personality on the show, the place is dark and devoid of much character, since he's supposed to come off as a moody, standoffish, lone-wolf type of ancient figure running a tight ship in the hospital. As expected, Baxton is framed as the focus of the shot. Despite him pushing fifty this year, the fine lines and wrinkles gracing his aging face are minimal. He swears he's never done Botox, but looking at him through the director's HD monitor now, I'm not sure if I believe him. His skin looks a little too firm and tight. His blond hair is wind-tossed and damp, like he'd just barely escaped a torrential downpour, and a muscle pulses in his square jaw while his gaze drifts toward Mina, a fellow doctor from the hospital, played by my current favorite actress, Anastasia Lowell.

In this scene, he lets his guard down as Mina ambles over to him, the tension between them heightening. They both look like they've gone through it, their clothes thoroughly soaked in water and blood, but neither one of them seem to care about that.

Mina cups Drac's face in both hands, and with a needy sigh, crashes their mouths together. He clings on to her like she's his only lifeline, arms grasping her hips and angling his face so he can deepen the kiss. The need overwhelms both of them as she wraps her legs around his waist, clinging on to Drac with a familiar desperation only served in soap operas and movies.

"Cut! That's great, guys," the director announces from behind the monitor. "That's a wrap for Baxton for today. Ana, you can head to hair and makeup and wait while we relight the set."

Baxton and Ana are all smiles as they high-five each other, congratulating one another on the scene they just shot. Their assistants arrive with their respective robes and after shrugging them on, they both walk off of set in different directions. I wave at Baxton to catch his attention, and he jogs over to where I am behind the director and the producers.

"Wow. That was . . . intense," I remark.

Baxton, for the most part, does his best to keep it professional, but color sprouts across his cheeks anyway at the explicit nature of the scene. "Hey. Thanks for coming," he murmurs, roping me into a hug and giving me a squeeze.

"No problem," I say, giving a squeeze back. When I pull away, I ask hesitantly. "You know, I'm a Mina and Drac shipper as much as any other fan, but did I hear that this kiss scene's gonna be in the *second* episode of season three? Because I swear the last time we left off with you and Mina, you just killed her ex-lover and she swore she was gonna bury you alive for that."

The features on Baxton's face form into an irritable look. "*Don't* even get me started on that."

Baxton being at odds with the new showrunner, Marshall Tanner, is not a tight-lipped secret around here. Marshall had taken over the role after the previous guy announced that he was stepping down. And by stepping down, it meant he was practically forced to by the studio because, like every Hollywood dirtbag in a position of power, he got Me-Tooed. Justice was served, but that also meant getting a replacement quick to shoot season three, and Marshall Tanner, aka, prince of nepo babies with only two minor writing credits to his name, was called to come on board. So, I'm not surprised to hear that he's already screwing up the pacing of the show.

"Now, I know I said dinner was at Yamashiro's tonight, but I just got told about a club opening I need to attend soon, so change of plans," Baxton tells me. "Do you mind if we get something quick to eat here?"

"Sure."

Near the edge of the studio, there's a little catering area equipped with wooden tables and benches. The food selection is impressive; there's seafood, roast chicken, nicely seared steaks, and even a little sushi display at the end. I fill up my plate with as many pieces of nigiri sushi as I can get, along with some stir-fried noodles on a smaller plate. Baxton waves me over to where he's sitting, and I slide into the bench opposite from him. I barely say two words to him before I'm breaking my chopsticks and plopping the sushi into my mouth.

Baxton watches me devour the rest of the plate with a mixture of concern and interest. He takes a quiet sip of his Coke before asking.

"You had Eden today, right? How was it?"

"It was all right."

The opposite, if I'm being honest. Time with Eden is always too short.

Worry creases across Baxton's forehead. He had once expressed his regret to me once about not getting to Eden before Child Services did, but he didn't even know what happened to me, and my family, until it was too late.

"And is Laura still giving you problems?" Baxton prompts.

"Nothing I can't handle." I don't elaborate further because the last thing I need is Baxton getting involved in that drama. I decide to steer the conversation away from me instead. "Is Harvey around today?"

Harvey Dystel. My one and only love. He plays Dracula's son on the show, and he's positively scrumptious in the role. It helps that the DOP knows it, too, which explains the gratuitous ab shots snuck into episodes at every opportunity. Yes, I'm a whore for TV ab shots. So sue me. A woman's gotta eat.

Baxton forks a piece of roast chicken into his mouth, the curve of his mouth tugging upward in amusement. "He doesn't have a scene today. And like I would even let you near him."

"Why not? You don't trust me?"

"I do trust you," Baxton asserts. "But he just broke up with his girlfriend and he's been looking for an easy lay to get his mind off of it."

"All the more reason why you should introduce me to him. I'm a *great* lay." I smile, flashing my teeth and Baxton rolls his eyes. Sometimes, I forget that he's not so much my friend as he is my unofficial caretaker. "So, the club opening tonight—where is it?"

"Beverly Hills," he informs, reaching over to the next table to steal a box of tissues to bring it to ours. "I'm only going because the club owner is a friend, and a film producer, and he wants me to star in a reboot of *The Addams Family*."

I almost drop my jaw on my plate. If he's starring, that means . . . "As Daddy Gomez?"

"It's a good role." He wipes the edges of his mouth. "And comes with a fat paycheck."

"You know what? Hollywood has sold out its originality, so it's only right you do the same with your integrity."

"That's one way to put it." He grins back, but it's a sad one. With this season of *Heartstorm Hospital* not going the way he'd planned, he probably needs another studio hit under his belt. His new rom-com, *A Fool's Gold*, looks like it could be an entertaining one, but it's far from being Oscar-worthy.

"So how about it, huh?" Baxton nudges me with an elbow. "Fancy a night out of entertaining boring-as-hell TV executives and investors? I'm allowed a plus-one."

"I'm good." The last thing I need is for my inhibitions lowered. I set my chopsticks aside and tent my fingers together. "You can take your son," I offer.

Upon that suggestion, Baxton's expression changes. "A club is the last place he should be right now." His blond eyebrows draw into a hard line.

I set my plate aside. "Right."

I'd heard about his son Jax's entanglement with alcoholism. The binges, the parties, the sexcapades; while it's not uncommon in Hollywood, it's tragic when it happens to your son and you have to hear from everyone else about him being a menace.

I haven't met Jax, nor do I have any intention to. He sounds like a brat acting out because he doesn't get the attention he needs, and the worst part is Baxton is giving him exactly that by policing him.

"Even if I wanted to, I doubt he'd even take my call," Baxton says quietly, pushing the meat around his plate with his fork. "I tried calling him a few times earlier, but no response. I'm starting to get the message that he wants me at arm's length."

I shrug but don't say anything. He doesn't want to hear what I have to say, not when it's telling him the opposite of what he wants to do. But Baxton reads my silence as hesitation anyway. He drops his head sideways and gives me a look.

"What?" He presses me. "You think I'm overbearing?"

I clear my throat and look at him head-on. "I think you can be a little. But, Baxton, he's a grown man. He has every right to make his own mistakes."

"We're Denerises. We don't make mistakes."

"All I'm saying is . . ." I pause so I can mull over how to put this delicately. "Give him some room to breathe. If he's anything like you, he'll get to the place where you want him to be eventually." I doubt I even believed any of the words I was saying, but it was worth a shot.

He nods, staying silent as he thinks about what I've said. "Maybe he needs someone like you in his life. To show him that you *can* overcome tragedy despite the odds stacked against you."

I smile back, but I can't fight the guilt seeping into my veins. Every part of my body compels me to take the lie back, that no, I haven't got my shit together; that, in fact, I'm *barely* keeping everything together, and that I need his help. But my mouth remains shut. I don't care if this lie eats me alive. Baxton has a lot on his plate with Jax as it is; the last thing I need is to add to his worries.

One of the servers comes over to our table and asks if we want anything else, since the set is closing up soon. Baxton and I politely decline, and the server takes our empty plates and cups away.

Later, I follow Baxton out for a quick smoke while he waits for his driver, Cooper, to pick him up. Cooper gets a special permit to drive directly into the studio, that lucky SOB, but Baxton says he'll drop me off back home before making his way over to the club.

As Baxton exhales the smoke from his nostrils, a cart driving by filled with starstruck women yell at him to snatch his attention.

"I love you, Baxton!" A brunette in a blue silk blouse, looking way too old to be acting like an unhinged fangirl, screams. "Can't wait for season three!"

Baxton tilts his head modestly and flashes them a friendly smile. I roll my eyes, feigning a ridiculous grin. The modesty is a front; he can be so full of himself when he's with someone he knows. It makes me wonder if all Denerises—including Jax—possess inflated egos.

Baxton's phone rings and he picks it out of his pocket, just as he's putting out his cigarette. His finger jams on the answer button. "Hey, Nicolas—I just got off set so I'll be heading to Venus—*What*?" A long pause, a mixture of confusion, followed by surprise. Lastly, the most dreaded emotion he possesses lighting up his face—anger. Palpable in the way every muscle in his body grows taut. "I'll be there as soon as I can."

"Wait, what's going on?" I say, taking the signal that it's time to dip and get up from my seat.

"It's Jax." His eyes darken and he gestures for me to grab my stuff. "We're leaving. Now."

FIVE

Jax

It's only 9:00 p.m. on a Saturday and the club is already packed to overflowing with B-listers and influencers desperately pushing their way to get in.

Outside, the VENUS sign blasts in neon purple glow on clubgoers. When we're through the door, the bar is packed with people desperate to pick their poison for the night. The dance floor thrums with the chaotic energy of sweaty bodies pressed up against each other, bouncing and gyrating to the music curated by the DJ on his way-too-expensive setup. Shades of blue and pink and purple flit across the main room from the rotating lights above. The loud music sinks into my blood and sets my pulse racing with nauseating fever.

Clubs aren't my thing—I usually prefer lying back with a beer at my favorite sports bar—but they seem to be all the rage here. I'm a try-everything-once guy, and if I hate it, I'll move on. But not before doing it again for the torture.

I thrived the most in underground fighting basements. The music was less annoying and the crowd was far more interested in watching men batter each other rather than indulging in themselves and their own vanity. I loved fighting. And I was the best at it, which made me love the underground even more. When I was single, it became my jungle of temptation. Women would crowd around me by the cage door and slip their numbers or panties into my MMA robe. There wouldn't be a single night where my mouth wouldn't be latched on some woman's clit. It was a euphoric high that I would try to top with every fight.

So far, this has been nothing short of a letdown.

My eyes move through the room and the people lounging on the leather chairs, most of them tapping away on their phones. The few who are enjoying themselves are laughing and clinking martini glasses. Everyone's trying to be everybody here, and most people would find it hard to tell who's the real deal and who's not. But I can. Fraudsters can spot other fraudsters from a mile away. The slightly off-center logos on their branded bags, the fake drip perched across their necklines, and the heavy LA accents that conceal the otherwise inconsequentiality of their life's purpose. Everything here is a farce, but I would be lying if I didn't find the deception an intriguing game to play.

Connor, Watts, and I are on the main dance floor, but there are more rooms upstairs, their contents concealed by thick, black velvet curtains. *Interesting.*

"Twelve o'clock," Watts spins me around to the direction of where he's looking. "Girl in the purple dress?"

My gaze zeroes in on who he's referring to. A tall redhead swaying beside one of the leather sofas, looking a little nervous to be alone. Either she's waiting for someone or her friends have abandoned her. Either way, an easy encounter. Too easy, almost. Sometimes the easier things seem, the more complicated they actually are. I learned that the hard way from my time with Beth. Since we broke it off, I've been trying to stay away from those kinds of entanglements.

"I'm good. She's all yours, man."

He laughs in disbelief. "What? Are you allergic to girls suddenly?"

"I'm allergic to girls who dance like they have no idea what rhythm is," I say dryly. "You want a drink?"

Watts nods.

The line to the bar has somehow grown since we arrived, snaking all the way down to the other side of the room. I reckon the bar upstairs would have a shorter line, so I make my way up a level. As expected, the queue is much shorter. I peer over the ledge, curious to see what my friends are up to when they're not busy entertaining me. Connor has immediately fucked off with a group of girls headed for the dance floor. Watts is over to the side, talking to a couple of other club promoters. I only know this because they all have the same white tag looped over their necks.

Watts is the embodiment of west LA culture. A podcaster by day, a promoter by night, he's the gateway to all my vices, so I keep him as close to me as I can. He's dull when he's sober, a decent wingman when he's not. Not that I need much help. Connor is . . . there. He's a dickhead and I think he likes hanging around me because I'm his only connection to Hollywood and he's dying to get into the movie industry as a filmmaker. Little does he know that I can't help him with that. But I keep him around because he's a yes-man and everyone needs a yes-man in their life.

Besides, the city can feel so big at times, and I despise being a lone wolf.

"Two gin and tonics," I say when I reach the bar.

The male bartender gives me a glance. "ID, please."

I roll my eyes and break out my wallet from my back pocket.

"Jax Deneris," The bartender reads, drawing out every syllable like he's learning a foreign language. He hands me back my ID, nodding his chin at me. "You Baxton Deneris's son?"

I give an uncomfortable shrug. Usually, I'm never in the mood to disclose my relation to Baxton, but it's been getting increasingly difficult to do so the longer my feet stay dipped into our mutual social circle. It doesn't help that Deneris is such an uncommon last name.

"Yes. Let me guess, you're a fan?" I ask, my gaze boring into his.

The bartender laughs. "Don't know his work enough to be one."

That's a first. Apparently, he's been killing it recently with *Heartstorm Hospital*, his latest TV show that aired on Hulu last year. Not that I've seen it yet. It pains me to give him the satisfaction that I keep track of his acting career.

"I've met Baxton before, though." The bartender pinches two empty glasses off the rack and places them in front of me before pouring in the drinks. "He's friends with the owner of this club."

Of course he is.

That makes me wonder if Baxton will show up tonight. It's entirely plausible that he's on the guest list. Any one of the booths below could be reserved for him. *Fuck.*

Apart from a very awkward lunch that resulted in me having to excuse myself early, I've been blessed to not have crossed many paths with Baxton. So, naturally, I'm saddled with anxiety. I shouldn't be this worried, but dammit, I am. Even though he has no right to be, he's critical of everything I do and it sours my entire mood.

I was hoping to take my time tonight, but it's looking like I'll have to speed run if I intend on having a memorable night.

"In that case," I say, sliding my Amex across the bar with two fingers. "I'm gonna need four shots of tequila. Oh, and start a tab."

***

Three gin and tonics and six shots of tequila later, the devil hibernating inside me finally comes out to play.

My eyes dissect every woman in the club. Only the best of the best will do for me. My gaze skips over the blonds. I've sworn off them. My attention falls on the dark-haired woman standing by one of the taller tables in the middle. She looks impeccable with her perfectly curled hair sitting on one side of her shoulder and her sleek black midi dress. The slit of her dress parts to reveal a set of smooth, creamy thighs. A ribbon choker is tied with a bow around her neck and I picture myself unwrapping her like a present.

There's an air of refinement to her as she laughs at

something the man beside her says, her manicured hand pressing lightly against one of her breasts. She seems like someone important.

Desire sinks its dirty claws deep into my veins.

Beside me, Watts follows my gaze and barks out a laugh. "Oh, I wouldn't if I were you."

"Why the fuck not?"

He nudges Connor with an elbow. "Con, you want to tell him, or should I?"

Connor lets out a chuckle. "No way. I kinda wanna see how badly this could go."

"Have a little faith," I say, handing Connor my half-empty glass of whatever the hell I just ordered. I roll my sleeves up to my elbows and adjust the folds of my collar. *Game time.*

"Oh, trust me, we have faith," Connor says, smirking.

I ignore them and stroll over to the woman. I wait for the conversation between her and the man to end before clearing my throat and announcing my presence.

"And you must be Venus," I say, noting the club's name.

"I'm sorry?" She looks at me, confused.

"Don't be. A beauty like you should never have to apologize," I say smoothly, placing an arm on the table.

"If you think flattery's going to work on me . . ." She lets her voice trail off as her eyes scan me up and down, the light in her irises glowing with what she sees in front of her. Her mouth twitches into a smile. "Maybe it does."

She's attracted to me. A grin slides across my mouth. Now, it's my job to convince her to act on those interests.

She turns to say something along the lines of "excuse us" to the man she'd been talking to and he dips his head down in greeting before walking away. When she's finally free of any distractions, I stick my hand out.

"Jax," I say, and she shakes it.

"Scarlett."

"Beautiful name."

"Thanks," she whispers. "Are you a patron or an esteemed guest?"

"Define 'esteemed.'"

"Invaluable."

"The latter," I say with a sly grin. "But I'm not important in the way that these people are."

"That's not true. You seem . . . familiar to me." She squints like she's trying to place me. "You look like a guy I might know."

"Maybe I'm the guy who brings you into that room and takes you against that stripper pole," I say, eyeing the darkened private room in the corner of the dance floor.

I have no business being this forward. Absolutely fucking none. Usually, I'd give more of a lead-up than this. But I'm eager to get things between us moving. She'll either slap me and call for security to escort me out, or she'll be into the proposition and flirt back.

Instead, Scarlett laughs, like she's half-offended, but half-intrigued. "You're awfully presumptuous to think that I'd let anyone do that, let alone a stranger."

I edge closer toward her. She smells like lilies and pinewood, a stimulating combination.

"I know what I want," I tell her, reaching out to play with the strand of curl. "Do you?"

She scoffs. "Don't be that guy."

"What guy?" I blink innocently at her.

Scarlett steps away from me, forcing me to drop my hand from her hair. "The guy who comes on too strongly. You have to work for it."

"That's fair," I say. "How about I be the guy who asks you to dance?"

I offer her my hand instead, waiting as she mulls over the decision. She wants me. *They always do.* I can already smell the desire. She eventually gives in, allowing me to lead her to the dance floor. My fingertips slide across her palms and her fingers curl into mine. I place my hand around the dip of her waist, fighting the urge to slide my hand even lower. My arms pull her in close so she's flush against my body and I can feel every tight curve of her body as the music transitions to a moombahton song, her hips moving side to side with every beat.

She tilts her head upward to the ceiling, her eyes fluttering closed as she feels the music, and all I want to do is bury my face in her neck and slide my fingers underneath her skirt. Her face is so close to mine that I can taste her breath, hot mint sweetness.

I drop my voice to whisper. "You're intoxicating."

She watches my mouth, entranced. I watch her watch me.

Her brown eyes are pure liquid heat.

She licks her lips and I realize I'm not the only one who's turned on right now. My fingers drift from her back down the curvature of her spine. She shivers in delight. My skin feels hot against the tightness of my shirt and my cock is pushing against the placket of my zipper, ready to burst at the seams. *Come on. Give in. You know you want to.*

We dance like this for a while, but I grow impatient and dip down to start kissing her neck. She moans so loudly that I'm certain the entire dance floor can hear us. I continue trailing a pathway of kisses all the way down to her collarbone until she can't take it anymore and she grabs my face with one hand and brings my mouth to hers. I'm so fucking horny I could rip off my clothes and take her right then and there. It's obvious she's thinking the same thing because she shakes her head and drags me with fierce intent from the dance floor.

"In here. Hurry," she whispers, pushing me into the private room past the velvet curtains.

You don't have to tell me twice.

The room is spacious enough for at least three dozen people, but for some reason, there's not enough space to hold the sheer need of wanting to get inside this woman. Next thing I know, we're tangled up in a fierce kiss again and I'm grabbing her breast in one hand while helping her pull off her underwear with the other. She's undoing my belt and my erection springs free from my underwear. *Thank fucking god.* I shove my pants all the way down to my ankles. I sheathe myself with a condom and spit on my hand for some extra lubrication.

"Hands on the pole. Spread your legs," I order her as I stroke myself.

Scarlett obliges me, spreading her legs to that perfect V I love seeing. There's no time. Anyone could come in and kick me out for the carnality that's about to happen, so I need to do this quick.

Seconds later, I sink into her and there's a collective sigh of relief. Fuck, I love fucking. And I love fucking beautiful women. These exquisite creatures who deserve to be worshipped every second of every fucking day.

I thrust into her and she moans. Shit, what's her name again? Sara? Venus? Fuck it, I'll just call her *baby*.

"Oh, baby," I groan.

"Yes, please. *Ah!*" the woman rasps out.

As I ram into her, her hands keep slipping down the metal pole and her legs threaten to buckle from underneath her. My hand reaches over to grab a fistful of her hair and pull her up so her back is arched against me. Oh yeah. This angle is fucking perfect. Her pussy clenches at my dick and something in me surges and my cock pulses, ready to swim in my release and spill everything into the condom—

A hard tug yanks me back and I stumble backward so hard my naked ass hits the floor.

"What the fuck—?" I yell out.

I don't get to finish my sentence because a hard fist slams right into my face.

SIX

Jax

Minutes later, I'm being dragged into a back alley of the club by four dudes. Large, muscle-defined, could-be-working-for-the-Mafia type dudes. And unlike the bouncers stationed in and outside of the club, these guys are plainclothed and intend to do more than just rough me up a little bit.'

A sucker punch to my gut.

A right hook to my jaw.

A deadly kick to the ribs.

Every instinct in me is begging for me to defend myself. Analyze the pattern. Find the opening. Lock in with a kill. Show them what you're fucking made of.

No mercy. Give everything. Take nothing.

But I'm paralyzed.

Maybe it's the alcohol and I'm sloppy. Or maybe because it's one thing fighting against one man in a cage, but it's another when the fight is coming from all directions. Every time I try to get up, they knock me down even more. I can barely react with my fists before another blow rains down on me. My head lolls against the wet concrete road as I cough up saliva. Or is it blood? A thin trail of it drops down the side of my mouth and splatters in a small pool beside me. Yep. Definitely blood.

"Tell them to stop, Jorgen!" The woman I was fucking wails at the burly man with a shaved head. Oh, I remember her name now. *Scarlett*. The guys keep landing punches in her honor.

Jorgen merely ignores her, instead shedding off his black suit jacket and handing it over to his bodyguard, who's guarding the door. The burly man rolls his sleeves up, and dread immediately sets in with the knowledge of what's going to happen.

He laughs, admiring her fearlessness, and merely pushes her to the side. She stumbles and nearly falls. The bodyguard catches her in the nick of time. "We'll talk about this later when we get home," the burly man snaps, his voice razor-sharp and threatening. "Don't even get me *started* on the fact that you decided to pull this bullshit on my opening night."

As I drift in and out of consciousness, my mind only succeeds in capturing bits and pieces of the couple's conversation.

"Jorgen, we've been through this! I'm sick and tired of you . . ."

"That doesn't give you a free pass to fuck the next guy who offers you attention . . ."

"If you're not going to give me any, then why should I wait around?"

God, they're a bore. I wonder if that's the reason why my ears are ringing, or if it's because of the blood rushing out of my head as it gets smashed against the concrete road.

Despite my blurry vision, I can make out a small crowd forming at a distance, closing off the alleyway. Fear mars their faces, but they're too absorbed with the drama to mind their own business.

LA at its finest.

As the punches continue to rain down on me, Scarlett continues to gives excuses about why she did what she did. But he interrupts her and begins to ramble on about her behavior and how she doesn't respect the sanctity of marriage.

That gets my attention. *Married.* That woman's *married* to this guy. If I could laugh, I would.

Frustrated with the back-and-forth between him and his wife, Jorgen gestures to his men and points to me. "Pick him up," he orders. They oblige him, hoisting me up by grabbing my arms. My legs are jelly; I can barely stand, so they settle for propping me in a kneeling position. Jorgen kneels in front of me, dripping with ego and power. The best kind of opponent. It means they're confident enough to think they've got no blind spots. His hand reaches forward to grasp my chin, smushing my cheeks in between his thumb and fingers.

"Enjoying the beatdown, huh?" he growls. "Perhaps I should tell my men to work harder."

"You can do that," I huff out between tired breaths. "Still doesn't change the fact that I fucked your wife."

A thunderbolt of rage strikes his expression. "Listen here, you little dipshit," Jorgen seethes, grabbing me by the collar and tugging my face toward him. His scowl sinks deep into the wrinkles of his face. "I don't know if you know this, but I'm a big deal here. I can fucking ruin you and nobody will bat an eye about it."

"You can try to ruin me," I say, a tired grin dancing along the edges of my lips. Jorgen's face expression remains passive, but he entertains me, moving his face an inch closer. "But it doesn't matter what you do. I'm already there."

Opening secured. Lock in with a kill.

With a yell, I recoil my head and shatter Jorgen's nose with my forehead.

He doubles backward in horror, crashing onto the ground with both hands covering his face. My head lolls backward, a bloodied grin meeting with the midnight sky. A millisecond of peace, swimming with the stars, before chaos erupts on land again.

"Hold him down!" Jorgen screams, picking himself up and charging toward me with a raised fist. I struggle against Jorgen's henchmen, needing to free my arms, but their grip on me is ironclad. Even my legs are held down this time. I muster an inhale. My eyes pinch shut, bracing for what's to come . . .

But it doesn't arrive.

I open my eyes and Jorgen's no longer in front of me.

"Baxton!" an unfamiliar female voice screams.

I follow the young woman's line of sight. My eyes bulge out of my sockets when I find Baxton holding Jorgen down and slamming a mean right hook into his face.

Holy shit. I honestly didn't know he had it in him.

"Ah, *fuck*!" Baxton rasps, reeling his fist back and shaking out the sting of landing the punch.

"Baxton? What the—get off me!" Jorgen pushes Baxton off of him and climbs back on his feet.

The young woman who had yelled his name earlier runs over to help Baxton up. Who *is* this girl? Baxton pushes himself up, dragging his feet toward me. His gaze fills with a reservoir of misery when he the state that I am in.

The misery turns into anger as he whips his attention back to Jorgen. The woman stands in front of Baxton, shielding him from Jorgen. I admire her loyalty. I wonder what kind it is. The romantic type? I hope not. Strands of her dark brown hair stick to her cheek as she breathes through her mouth, wearing the meanest face I've ever seen on a woman.

"Tell your men to stand down." Baxton huffs out. "That's my son!"

"Your *son*?" A throaty laugh escapes Jorgen. He rubs his mouth, anger twitching his jaw. "Well, that's unfortunate."

"Come on, Jorgen, I'm sure that whatever he did to you doesn't warrant a beatdown like this," Baxton laughs, trying to dissolve the tension between them.

"You really think so?" A hearty chuckle tumbles out of Jorgen's mouth. "I think even your son would disagree."

Baxton's face swivels toward me, searching my face for answers. I don't say anything. I don't need to. His gaze swings to Jorgen, then his wife, who's crying on the steps, her hair disheveled and her makeup smudged all over. Confusion dissolves into understanding. Baxton's eyes flutter shut, fingers going between his temples as he mutters a string of profanities under his breath. I bet he's second-guessing protecting me from Jorgen's wrath earlier.

I should feel nothing, but shame does wind its way around

my battered chest. The last thing I need is for Baxton to get involved. The point was to continue my devilish ways in peace. And now, not only have I colossally failed to stick up for myself, but my dad had to fish me out of trouble. It's a fucking embarrassment. I feel like a kid all over again.

Jorgen's expression maintains the mask of anger. His pupils darken, like he's more than ready for another round of toss-up. Baxton, alarmed, throws a proposition to change his mind. "Look, your men already got some good hits in. He's already down. You want to fuel that crowd over there even more? Bring more of a bad rep to your new club?"

The last sentence steers Jorgen's gaze away from Jax and toward the growing group of people trickling in from the other end of the alleyway. They're cautious, preferring to stay a few feet away. I can pick out familiar faces like a few girls who were mingling on the dance floor, and of course, Connor and Watts, who, instead of feeling compelled to stick up for me, prefer to cower in the corner like pussies.

Jorgen contemplates Baxton's proposition for a moment. He relinquishes a heavy sigh, relenting.

"*Fine,*" Jorgen says through gritted teeth. "But I don't want to see him or you anywhere around here. This concludes all our business together."

"Wait," Baxton's expression is perplexed. "What about the movie—"

"*We're done,*" Jorgen repeats, his voice so loud it travels down the alleyway.

Baxton clenches his jaw tightly, no choice but to accept the fate of their friendship. "I understand."

Jorgen signals for his men to stand down. With glares

thrown my way, they walk back into the club in a single file. Jorgen attempts to seize Scarlett's hand, but she wrenches away, glaring at him. She looks over her shoulder, gaze floating toward my direction and softens with remorse.

I look away and do the one thing that I'd never thought I'd do.

I laugh.

I don't know what on earth possessed me to do that, but I started, and I can't stop. Peels of laughter tumble out of me, punctuating the tension with a misery that wasn't there before. My body doesn't even react when Jorgen stops in front of me and throws spit in my direction.

I just continue wheezing until my ribs feel like they're about to collapse into my lungs. It surprises me that I even have the energy to keep going as long as I do.

Sympathetic to my plight, but realizing that it's better to walk away than fuel the fire, Scarlett hurries away with Jorgen. That's the last I'll see of her probably. It's better that way. The crowd, after seeing that the fight has come to an end, disperses. The pretty woman that Baxton brought looks around and scratches the side of her arm, hesitating to reach toward me. I wonder what I must look like to her. She must think I'm a sociopath. I wouldn't dismiss the possibility.

When my laughter finally dies out, the back alleyway is silent. *Too* silent. The only noises are the sounds of phone camera shutters clicking from the few remaining witnesses and my clouded breaths diffusing into the air. I shut my eyelids, expecting to shut off from the world, but instead, tears spill out in the creases. When I open my eyes again, my face is wet with tears.

Well fuck, this is officially reaching new levels of pathetic.

I try to push myself off the ground and my legs nearly give up on me and my knees buckle. The pretty woman is the first one to rush to my aid.

I'm impressed that she's able to sustain most of my weight as I try to find my bearings with my feet. My gaze travels to her arms, toned and defined, like the rest of her body. Her smell is intoxicating. Sweaty, but with a hint of a rose scent that'll likely be imprinted in my mind for the rest of the night.

It's impossible not to stare at her. The features of her face are made clearer to me now that she's inches from me. Deep hazel eyes, hair as black as onyx. Her chin is small but sharp, and her cheeks are flushed from all the action. The Cupid's bow on her lips is perfectly defined, despite my vision fighting exhaustion, and her mouth moves, but it takes several seconds for what she's saying to reach my ears.

"Huh?" I mumble.

"I asked if you can stand," she whispers.

I shake my head. Usually, I'll shrug the pain off, but this is the first time I'm honest about the fact that my opponent has gotten the better of me.

And the honesty unleashes an anguish within me that I haven't felt in a long time.

Baxton catches my other arm and loops one over his shoulder. "We're taking you to the hospital," he mutters.

I look at him, then at the pretty woman. I drop my head down.

And when they put me in an Uber with them headed for the hospital, I let them whisk me off, no longer having any fight left in me to protest.

SEVEN

Blaire

Jax had broken two ribs. *Two.* The doctors had told us it was going to take eight weeks for him to fully recover.

It was hard to stomach the true extent of Jax's injuries when they were cutting his clothes off to prepare him for the ER. The cuts above his brow and cheek, his busted lip, deep purple bruises marking the entire length of his body. I had never seen anything like it, not even while I was in jail. The wardens always intervened before things got out of hand.

I wonder if Jax had ever undergone such a beatdown before. Baxton mentioned that he was an MMA fighter, so it's possible. But if he was a professional fighter, wouldn't he have fought back? From the looks of it, this body belonged to a person who didn't care whether he lived or not.

Baxton has been here every day. Most of the time, Jax is sleeping off his injuries, which means there isn't much for him to do, so Baxton just sits by the windowsill and watches TV.

The flowers are heavy in my hand as I back away from the glass mirror. I didn't know what to get Jax, so I decided to pick some stargazers from my backyard and arrange the bouquet myself. I got the skill from my dad, who used to do it for Baxton when he really wanted to impress on dates. My hands aren't as crafty as Dad's, but it'll do.

I knock on the door and I hear Baxton's muffled voice saying, "Come in."

"Hey," I say hesitantly as I step into the room.

"Hey." Baxton shuts off the TV and rises from the windowsill. He ambles over, wearing a friendly but sleepy smile. Today, he's in a plain white shirt, jeans, and brown loafers. Lately, he's been less casual with his outfits in case the paps find him, so it's refreshing to see him looking rather normal, at least for LA standards.

"These are nice," Baxton notes when I hand over the bouquet.

"Thanks," I say, not wanting to tell him I made the arrangement myself.

Jax doesn't seem like the type of person who'd appreciate flowers and a get-well-soon card, but I thought it was better than coming empty-handed. And to be perfectly honest, I only got him something because I didn't want Baxton's gift to be the only one in the room. Casting my disdain for Jax aside, no one deserves to wake up feeling like nobody cares about them.

"Crap," Baxton mutters when his phone starts ringing. He glances at the caller ID and groans. "Watch him for me while I take a work call?" He gives my shoulder a pat and I nod.

"Sure."

When Baxton's gone, the patient room is simultaneously too big and too small at the same time. I force myself over to Jax. His eyelids are closed, his mouth parted open as he snores lightly. His hospital gown had ridden up his torso to reveal white bandages wrapped tightly around his chest. The cuts on his face are less significant than a few days ago, and the bruises on his arms have faded slightly. I pull a stool from the corner and drag it over to his side.

Seated, I lay an arm in the tiny space between him and the edge of the bed. Adjusting myself on the stool, my arm accidentally brushes against his hand and I shiver unexpectedly. It's so cold. I feel compelled to take it between my hands and blow hot air to warm him up a little, but I have to remind myself that he's a stranger to me. Someone who'll probably be gone when he's fit enough to fly back to Boston, resuming his life with no responsibilities for the damage he's inflicted on himself and this city.

And yet, I can't help but feel sorry for him. Perhaps it's because for someone to be this broken, he must have cared deeply about the person who'd inflicted the damage.

Minutes later, the door creaks open and Baxton slides back in. This time, his mood has shifted. His body is stiff, the big vein in his forehead throbbing. He walks past me and sits on the windowsill and releases a loud, frustrated sigh.

"More bad news?" I whisper.

"NBC is gonna run the story about me and Jax at the club tomorrow morning. And there will be more articles to follow."

"Shit," I whisper. *A Fool's Gold* is releasing in the summer. This could spell potential PR disaster.

"I don't know what to do, Blaire." His fingers squeeze the

skin between his brows. "I'm so livid with him that I can't . . ." His eyelids clamp shut and a breath hisses between his teeth.

Irrational anger surges inside me. "You *should* be livid. He fucked up everything for you with just one selfish night—"

Baxton shakes his head. "That's not why I'm angry. I'm angry at the fact I don't know how to get through to him. And I don't know if anyone can." Immense sadness and grief punctuate his eyes. And in that moment, I don't see Baxton Deneris, actor extraordinaire. I see a father trying to atone for his mistakes by making things right with his son. "He's a mere shadow of what I remember him to be."

"It's been a long time since then, Baxton—" I start.

He cuts me off. "I know him. I know his heart, and it's a good one."

I sigh deeply, tenting my fingers together. "You could send him to rehab."

"I can't do that to him."

"Why not? You know he needs it."

"He'll never forgive me for it," he says, like it's not up for debate. He's quiet for a long moment, deep in thought. Eventually, he looks up at me again, eyebrows scrunching.

"I do maybe . . . have an idea," he says reluctantly. "But you're not gonna like it."

I cock my head sideways, curious. Whatever it is, I'm certain that it's because Baxton has his heart in the right place. And I should be doing my best to support it.

"Tell me," I whisper.

***

Visiting Jax in the hospital, along with Baxton's proposition that day was the more exciting part of my week.

I can't believe I said yes to Baxton. I haven't wanted to think about it because to be honest, I don't think I even know exactly what I'm getting myself into with this favor. I just know that it will put Baxton at ease. And that's just a small price to pay for what he'd already given me. In the meantime, I'm blocking the damn decision out of my head until it's knocking on my doorstep.

I'm focusing on what I can still control, which is cleaning up the house and figuring out a more sustainable way to make money. I signed up for this app where people post odd jobs they need done, like dog-sitting, gutter-cleaning, and window-washing. I made thirty bucks washing someone's driveway yesterday, so that was nice. But the app doesn't get a lot of traffic, which means the listings are sparse, so it's unlikely I'll be able to do this long-term.

The rest of my time was spent waiting for my second appointment at the job center. The first one didn't go very well. The guy that was assigned to me, Ahmed, took one look at my nearly empty résumé and criminal record, grimaced, and spent the next twenty minutes clicking away at the computer with worrying silence. By the end of it, my prospects were bleak, but he told me he was going to email me if I get any offers.

Desperate for a distraction in the evening, I ring up my friend, Elle to let her know that I'm coming over. A half-hour bus ride later, I'm in Lynwood, standing outside a modest, one-story house with a broken white fence and several BEWARE OF DOG signs flimsily nailed onto it. She doesn't even have a dog.

Elle lives with her brother Ben and her dad. I met her and Ben while at the checkout at a grocery store a couple of months ago. They were in front of me in line, trying to purchase thirty four-packs of toilet paper, twenty dish soap bottles, and a new toaster. I watched as Elle pulled a fat stack of coupons out of her backpack and discounted their two-hundred-dollar bill down to eight dollars.

That was when I knew I wanted to be her friend.

I jab the buzzer. The white door grille is already half-open, with the front door creaking wide, allowing the muffled sounds coming from the TV to seep out of the house. I wait outside before letting myself in. A familiar feminine voice yells for me to come in and I slip through the door, shutting it behind me. Elle is seated beside the couch in her wheelchair, her back toward me, her attention glued to whatever is playing on the TV. Even by the appearance of her wavy, chestnut-brown hair, you can tell that she's radiant with beauty. She's got the biggest, brightest blue eyes; a long nose; and a pair of plump lips that'll put any influencer to shame. Her slender body slumps comfortably against her wheelchair, with an arm propped over the handle for her chin to rest on.

"Hi, Ellesmere," I say as I wind my arms around her shoulders from behind.

She cranes her neck to meet my gaze. "Do you have to use my real name? I feel like I'm in trouble or something. And that shit's reserved for the bedroom."

"Ew. Now you made it weird."

"My intention all along." Elle grins.

I laugh, giving her shoulders a squeeze before releasing

them. I walk around her, head swiveling around. "Where's your dad?"

"Passed out somewhere," she says, like it's an inconvenience. We don't stay on the topic for too long. It's not a new occurrence. Elle and Ben's dad has been idle ever since I've known them. Ben's the one taking care of the family, since he's the oldest of the two siblings. It works out since Elle's been studying hard to get into law school.

"How about Ben?" I ask, trying to sound casual about it.

Elle rolls her eyes, then jerks her chin toward the door straight down the hallway. "He's in a meeting. But he'll probably be out in a second, and then you guys can bang it out."

Color sprouts across my cheeks.

Ben and I have been sleeping together for two months, much to Elle's annoyance. It's one thing to hear about your brother and best friend dating, but it's another when it's your brother and best friend are fucking. And she also knows we have zero intentions of stopping any time soon.

I'm fond of Ben. He's funny and sweet, and just overall a good guy. Just my kind of person. And he's decent in bed, which is rare, because half of the men I've slept with don't even know what the clit is for.

"Well," I say, adjusting myself. "That doesn't matter because I came here for *you*."

She rolls her eyes like she thinks I'm lying. When in truth, I've just embellished the truth. I already made plans to come over to see Elle, so I thought why not kill two birds with one stone by seeking out her brother too.

"How's the hotshot in the hospital?" Elle prompts.

Ever since I told her about Baxton's son, Elle treats it like it's the craziest thing that's ever happened to me. She often forgets I'm an ex-convict, which is nice. "According to his dad, he'll live," I say, plopping myself on the sofa.

"You seem disappointed," she remarks.

"I'm lukewarm about it."

"Yeah, what's up with that? He's yummy."

I side-eye her. "Doing some Instagram stalking of your own?"

"You wouldn't paint me a picture, so I had to take the matter into my own hands," Elle says like it's so obvious. "He's like a young Brad Pitt. Very dreamy."

"Yeah, but also tortured," I say, crossing my legs and stuffing a pillow in the space in the middle.

"Those are the *best* kind of dudes," Elle asserts, giving me a look that makes me reconsider my sanity. "You want a drink?"

She disappears into the kitchen for a minute or two and re-emerges with two tiny cartons of orange juice. It's a classic in the Peterson household, because they always get consistent deals for this brand of orange juice.

"This scene gets me every time," Elle says when she adjusts herself back to her usual spot in front of the TV, her eyes glued to an episode of *The Vampire Diaries* as it plays on the screen. Elena is fighting with Damon, and Damon shuts her up by kissing her fiercely. The music swells as she gives in to her affection for this man.

"Unpopular opinion, but they suck as a couple," I say dryly.

Elle gasps, a hand clutched against her chest. "You take that back, madam!"

"I'm sorry but it's true," I protest. "They bring the worst out in each other."

"But they also bring out the best," Elle defends.

"They're toxic."

"What relationship isn't?"

"He's killed people."

"He's a *vampire*."

"Girls like you see all the red flags and look the other way," I point out.

"Girls like you flag everything, even when the reds are really greens," Elle says sourly.

"At least I don't date. I can't count red flags in a man if I don't have one to begin with." I toss the pillow at her. Her hand launches upward to catch it and she hugs it with both her hands.

"Oh yeah? What about my brother, then? You *know* he's got red flags."

"Really? I think he's pretty all right."

Elle rolls her eyes. "That's 'cause your *PC*s for him."

"Only partially."

PC, as in, pussy clench. It's just a little inside joke between me and Elle. We use it to determine whether or not a man's a keeper.

And Ben *is* a keeper. Any girl will be lucky to have him. He's just not someone *I* want to keep. Not because he puts me off in some ways, or that we don't have an emotional connection, but being a romantic is not something that's really been in the cards for me. Love is simply an indulgence I can't afford to maintain, especially when I have much bigger things to worry about.

"That's a relief to hear. Trust me, you don't wanna date a guy who once shat himself on the It's a Small World *kids'* ride at Disneyland when he was seventeen," Elle mentions dryly.

"Hey, in my defense, the animatronics were terrifying," Ben's voice drifts down the hallway. I watch as he emerges into the living room. The twinkle in his blue eyes shines when they fall on me. His floppy brown hair is disheveled, like he's either just woken up or he's ripped out his headset a little too hard and made a mess out of it. I assume it's the latter, which would also explain why he couldn't hear me come into the house.

"It was a kids' ride, Ben. Which means you're a loser." Elle bats her eyelashes.

Ben saunters over to me and plants a kiss on the top of my head. "A *hot* loser who nailed this chick."

Elle swings her attention back to me again. "You see what happens when you choose to sleep with charity cases? Their egos get big and sooner or later they start thinking they're out of *your* league." She inclines her body forward so our faces are close together. "You're better than this, Blaire. Save all the hot chicks from this unnecessary male epidemic."

"Ignore her." Her brother tells me.

"Like you do with everything else around you?" Elle scoffs. "God knows what you're even doing in that room when you say that you're 'working.'" She air quotes.

Ben and I exchange a look. We're the only two people in this household who know what kind of "work" he does behind closed doors.

"I'm trying to figure out how to pay your way through college, *that's* what I'm doing," Ben fires back without giving any context, as usual. Elle rolls her eyes and sinks back into her wheelchair, her attention returning to the TV.

"Can I borrow you for a second?" Ben asks, a hint of a

smile. He holds out his hand to me so he can help me stand up. When I'm on my feet, he pulls me to the hallway.

We're far enough away from Elle's view that I pull his face toward mine and fit my lips onto his. He draws in a sharp breath through his nose as our kiss deepens, but his mouth remains latched on mine, his tongue teasing its way into my mouth. I feel him harden against my leg and a shy smile curves the corners of his mouth.

"Sorry I didn't hear you just now. I was a little busy." He doesn't elaborate, but I understand anyway. Instead of ripping into him about it like I usually do, my fingers climb over his chest.

"Well, are you busy now?"

A smile quirks Ben's lips. "No. Are you?"

I don't want to leave Elle. But I'm also in desperate need of a stress reliever.

"I guess I could spare a bit of time," I whisper.

***

Half an hour later, I collapse beside Ben in bed, my energy completely spent. The springy bed lets out a loud squeak when I fall on the mattress. I cringe. I suppose Elle already knows what we do in here, so the bed sounds aren't unexpected. I would bring Ben over to where I'm staying instead, but I feel a little weird about hooking up with men under a roof that isn't technically mine, especially when I told Baxton that he can pop by whenever he likes.

Ben's haggard breathing fills my ears, an arm locking over my waist to pull me toward the side of his body. He tips my chin up so our gazes connect, and he smiles softly at me. I smile back at him, but not for long enough because Ben drops his mouth.

"You good?" he asks. "I didn't hurt you, did I?"

I shake my head, pulling my shirt back down. "No. You didn't."

"Then what is it?"

"It's nothing."

"No offense, Blaire, but you don't seek me out unless you're *not* fine."

My heart clenches with guilt. "That's not true."

"I've made my peace with it." Ben shrugs, stretching his arms out to the length of the bed. "As long as it always ends up like this, I'm not complaining."

I muster a weak laugh.

"Is it about the job search?" He asks. "Do you have any leads yet?"

"So far, nothing."

"I'm sure you'll find something."

"Yeah, that's what everyone says. But it's been *seven* months, Ben." Frustration wends its way down my body. I push myself into a sitting position and wrap my arms around my knees. "And I can't keep living like this. Day in, day out, bumming out, barely able to afford my groceries. It's starting to affect my relationship with Eden. I'm *so* ready to do something with my life. Anything. The whole thing just sucks."

Ben nods quietly, the weight of him resting on his elbows.

"You know I can always help with that if you need me to," he says.

I purse my lips inward.

"You mean Portia can help," I note sourly about Ben's boss.

"I don't get what your problem is with her," Ben groans. "She used to be your friend."

My front teeth dig into my frown.

Portia Lopez, whom Ben has been working with for the last few months, was my cellmate while I was in jail. She is a handful to say the least.

A runaway since she was fourteen, she spent her formative years in and out of a bunch of gangs until she got arrested for assaulting a police officer at eighteen. Once out of jail, she worked as a drug mule until she got busted for transporting cocaine, in which she ratted out everyone under her chain of command to get a lesser sentence. She finished serving her sentence this spring, and now she's taken control of the very same drug operation herself. Ben's been working for her, helping her manage the business finances, among other things I'm not too clear about. I only found out about them working together when I bumped into Portia as she was leaving Ben's house one time and I've been uneasy about their working relationship since.

It's not because I'm passing judgment on what Ben chooses to do to make money. I'm the last person to do that. Besides, I've seen people in worse circumstances do desperate things to make ends meet. So, whatever keeps him and his family afloat. Rather, it's his boss that I'm worried about.

My feelings toward Portia, along with our friendship, are dubious at best. She's nice to you when she wants something from you, and if you get on her bad side, you're enemy *numero uno*. I, thankfully, escaped that fate once we were no longer cellmates. While I'm grateful for everything that she did for me then, Portia is a part of my past—one I'm desperate to move on from.

"She still thinks very fondly of you, you know," Ben tells me. "I could ask her if she's hiring."

"And what? Be one of her brainless henchmen?" I laugh way harder than I should. When I realize my mistake, my mouth curls inward with regret. "No offense."

"Um, offense was taken." Ben leans forward, a serious look falling over his features. "Portia and I are trying to build something here. And it's not as bad as you think. She may not be honest in what she does, but she's just doing whatever she can to survive."

"You know what I mean. The entire operation could be busted. You might end up in prison. And if I'm part of that, I might just end up there with you." My throat tightens at the thought of us both getting incarcerated. Elle not being able to see her brother. Me not being able to see mine. *Again.* "A one-time incarceration is a mistake, Ben. A *two*-time incarceration is a serious behavioral problem."

"Mistake or not, you're carrying the weight of the label for the rest of your life—you already said so yourself. Unless you want to do something about it," Ben states, rubbing his bottom lip with his thumb. "The job isn't that bad. And the money's good. More than you were earning at Creme De La Creme. You'd be able to pay rent. You might even be able to expunge your record. You always said things would be easier if you did, and now, here's your chance."

I look down on my feet, my brain soaking up all his advice. What Ben is saying is ludicrous. Do bad to do good.

"You don't have to do it for long," Ben adds. "Maybe just enough for you to lawyer up and scrub that record clean. Then, you can finally live the normal life you've always wanted. Work a normal nine-to-five. At that rate, you might even be able to get Eden back."

That instantly perks up my ears. To regain custody of Eden. I never even considered that possibility, not even once. Being able to support Eden in the way I've always dreamed of, no longer having Laura be his gatekeeper . . . the dream begins to spark a small flame in my chest.

Would it be possible? To get custody like that? It is constantly difficult to stomach that Eden is with another family, but I've been learning to live with it, just like all the other things I lost when I was incarcerated.

What if . . . I didn't have to anymore?

"Look, you know what kind of financial situation my family was in when you met me. We were this close to being evicted." Ben says, his hand finding mine. His thumb smooths over my palm. My mind takes me back to the beginning of the year, when Ben told me that his father couldn't keep a job longer than a few weeks due to his severe insomnia. Ben gestures to the walls surrounding us. "And now . . . sure, we still live in this crappy house, but we have a roof over our head and we're no longer late with paying bills. Plus, we're in a good enough place to pay for Elle's tuition fees in the fall. Let her assume what she wants about me, but I know she's grateful that she can afford school."

Ben's right about Elle. She teases him a lot, but at the end of the day, she knows he's the glue keeping their family together. I'm desperate to be that for Eden too. I want to be close to him. I want to be his provider, his support system, everything that he needs.

"You don't have to decide now. But the option is always there for you," Ben says, sensing my dilemma." And if anything, you know I'll be there for you, right?"

"Yeah," I sigh, relenting. "I do."

At the end of the day, Ben means well. He is desperate for me to be happy.

Me too, Ben. I want that for me too.

I crawl over to him and sweep my lips over his. We kiss like this for a while, and when he descends on me again, I feel much better than I did before.

EIGHT

Jax

I get discharged on a Thursday. Five days after the incident in the club.

The doctor said I should consider myself extremely lucky. Apparently, I was very close to puncturing a lung and dying. Even the doctor was stumped as to how I survived. That makes two of us. I was fully prepared for the grim outcome, if it weren't for Baxton and the woman he'd brought with him to save the day.

I don't remember much about how the fight ended, only that I felt oddly comforted by the brunette as my dad raced us to the hospital. The gaps in my memory got the doctor concerned about a possible concussion, but a few tests later, he cleared me of any brain damage.

However, I was told to remain in the hospital until my vitals were stable and the doctor could confirm I was no longer at risk of catching pneumonia. They wrapped me up in a set of new bandages before discharging me, and I've been told to replace them every few days for the next two weeks. Baxton had brought me a fresh set of new clothes from my apartment, so I slipped into those.

My insurance covered most of the medical bill, and Baxton footed the rest of the expenses, much to my protest. But secretly I was thankful. I still had debts from last week's shenanigans I had to settle.

Baxton didn't have much else to say when we walked side by side to get his car in the parking lot. A big white Tesla—I roll my eyes at the predictability of the car choice. He's usually chatty when he sees me, whether it's to complain about my behavior or to express concern about what I'm doing with life, but this time, his mouth is pulled into a tight frown.

"I'm taking you home," Baxton says quietly when he pulls out of the parking lot.

"Back to my apartment?"

He doesn't answer me. He goes wooden, his shoulders snapping stiff.

We don't talk for the remainder of the journey.

***

The car pulls into an unfamiliar house in Melrose. Baxton parks in the empty driveway and gets out of the car. I follow him, unsure of what else to do because this certainly isn't his house—or at least the Hollywood Hills house that I'm acquainted with when I visit him.

We wait in the car for a few moments, until the front door

to the house opens and a woman pops out. My heart stutters in recognition.

That's the girl that Baxton had brought to the club.

In an instant, the memories come pouring into my mind. Warm, maple-brown eyes asking if I could stand up. Smooth skin sending all my nerve endings on overdrive as she held my hand while we raced to the hospital. Her worried face hovering over mine, caressed by the moonlight.

Today, she loses the fringe by wearing her black hair in two French braids, emphasizing the youthfulness of her facial features. She's wearing a black tank top, and the same worn-out sneakers that are practically falling apart at the seams. But damn, does that top look good on her, cupping her tits in a way that drives me insane. I'm a sucker for a good work of art, and she is it.

The girl's gaze connects with mine, just as I scroll back up to her face.

She scowls.

I gulp.

Guess I wasn't as discreet as I thought.

When the surprise of seeing her again eventually fades, I'm left to question why we are parked in her driveway. And why Baxton has gotten out of the car to pull out my luggage and bags from the trunk.

"Baxton, what's going on?" I hop out of the front seat. Baxton continues ignoring me and walks my stuff over toward the girl. Now, I'm even more alarmed. "Wait—what the hell are you doing?"

Baxton stops long enough to whip back around and say, "You're gonna be staying here. For as long as you're in LA."

I did *not* hear that right.

"This is Blaire," he says, gesturing to the young woman. "You're gonna be staying with her."

My brain works overtime to integrate this information. Blaire. Her name is *Blaire*. It suits her so well. Apparently, I'm gonna be more familiar with that name moving forward because I share a place with her now?

I recoil at the idea, my head unable to wrap around it. "You're fucking with me."

"Does it look like I'm in the mood for jokes?" Baxton flashes me a deadpan look.

"I'm not living with some stranger I don't even know!"

While I'm a big fan of how hot Blaire is, I'm an even bigger fan of my solitary life, the one I had when I was living back in my apartment.

Baxton merely ignores me and turns to Blaire. "Could you help me with his bag?" he asks in a gentle tone that he never uses with me.

Blaire clambers down from the front steps. She grabs the handle of the luggage. I walk forward and clamp a hand over her wrist.

"Leave the bag," I warn.

I expect her to shrink in fear, but her chin juts out in a stubborn pose. "I don't listen to you."

She snatches her hand from me and gives the luggage a hard pull toward the front door. The wheels run over my left foot and I wince.

"I don't understand why this is happening," I mutter to myself, shaky fingers pulling at my hair.

"Why?" Baxton echoes sharply, shocked at the audacity of

my question. He reaches into his back pocket and pulls out a few rolled pages of what looks like a bunch of articles stapled flimsily together. He flips through the pages while reciting the headlines: "Baxton Deneris and son Jax Deneris scuffle during opening night of Venus; son of actor Baxton Deneris attacked at club opening and the details are gnarly; fight breaks out with Baxton Deneris, his son and club owner during opening night over affair with club owner's wife." He rolls the articles back up, gripping it hard with a fist. "Do you see the media shitstorm you've caused?"

"Let me read that," I snatch the pages from him, my eyes scanning through the contents with lightning speed. "Okay, maybe this seems bad . . . but this will blow over in, like, a few days, right? Isn't that how the media works?"

"Then what's next, huh? What's the next headline you're gonna give me? You gonna sleep with a celebrity's wife? How about a DUI? Maybe even serve prison time?"

I slap the roll of papers at this chest. "You're being dramatic."

He snatches the papers from me and holds it up in front of me, wielding it like a weapon. "I'm being *practical.* You have zero self-control, and quite frankly, I'm sick of it. And as long as you're here in this city, you're a liability to yourself, and to everyone around you."

Blaire appears at the front door again. She leans against the doorframe with her hip, her arms crossed over her chest, watching the argument unfold in amusement.

I clench my jaw tightly. I didn't want my face heating with shame. Not in front of her.

Baxton tucks the pages back into his pocket and blows

out a breath in a sad attempt to thin out his anger. But he's a Deneris, and we don't squash out our anger. We use it as ammunition to get what we want.

"I'm gonna give you two options."

My shock manifests in a sharp laugh.

"Option *one*: You're going to therapy and you're cutting out alcohol." He looks me dead in the eye again. "And Blaire will make sure you won't step a toe out of line."

He can't be serious.

But Baxton's glare holds strong.

His cold, unrelenting eyes meet with mine. I gulp.

Sweet baby Jesus, I broke my dad.

"You said there were two options," I say softly. "What's the second one?"

Baxton swallows hard.

"I'll send you to rehab," he squeezes out.

A breath dies in my chest. Admittedly, rehab is a much worse fate than any of the options laid out in front of me, and Baxton knows it too. I'll lose any ounce of freedom I may have. There will be nurses and doctors monitoring my every move, I won't know how long I'll be forced to stay there for.

I stay quiet. Retreating.

Baxton's attention drifts toward Blaire, his gaze softening. "Blaire, I trust that you'll take care of things?"

She gives a hard nod. "I'll try my best."

"You know what to do. I'll check in with you again tonight." He gives a curt wave, and she waves back in farewell as Baxton walks back to the car.

Panic flutters in my chest.

"Baxton, just wait. Wait, please," I gasp desperately, jogging to the driver's seat. By the time I get there, he shuts the door in my face, a pained expression gracing his face as he puts the car in reverse. "What the *fuck*, Baxton!" My hands are in my hair, my mouth dropping open in horror as I watch him pull out of the driveway and onto the street.

He can't just abandon me here and not expect me to get back to my own apartment. Does he not realize I can just call a car?

I head toward the front door with a newfound determination. "Where are my bags?" I demand to Blaire.

"At the foot of the stairs."

I breeze past her and into the living room. The furniture has a midcentury-modern flair to it, sporting taupe velvet sofas, Persian carpets, and wooden paneling spanning throughout the house. This screams Old Hollywood to me, which seems more like Baxton's style than Blaire's. I may be wrong, but she seems more like a minimalist to me.

I find my bags just as she said they would be, sitting in a neat pile under the steps. I grab the duffel bag with one hand and tug on the luggage with the other. I breeze past Blaire without a word and get my phone out.

I feel her smug gaze on me when she voices my very predictable plan out loud, "You can try to get an Uber back, but you'll find the locks to your apartment have been changed."

What?

I whip my attention toward her. "Baxton can't do that."

"You're right. He can't," Blaire says. "But your landlord can. And he's more than willing to give you the boot in exchange for a signed autograph of Baxton Deneris and three months' rent paid in cash."

Fuck. *Fuck!*

Cursing under my breath, I exit the Uber app and drop my phone into the duffel bag. Blaire leans her weight on one hip and folds her arms across her face, taunting me with her smugness as she watches me order a cab.

God, she's so hot, torturing me like this.

Every part of me is screaming to turn this conversation around, to see what's the fastest way I can get her into her bed. I've no doubt she'd be a great lay. She may look sweet on the outside, but she's got a devilish side to her under that under much simpler circumstances I wouldn't be opposed to picking apart.

But if only she weren't a big deterrent to my plans here in the city.

I lower my phone. "What does Baxton have on you?" I take a few confrontational steps toward her. bitterness clogs my throat. "Are you his girlfriend or something?"

Blaire recoils, her expression twists in disgust. "God, no. Why does everyone keep assuming that?"

Relief flits through me momentarily. But that still doesn't answer any of the big questions I have about her.

"How do you know Baxton?"

"I'm a friend," Blaire merely says, leaning both her arms against the back of the couch behind her.

I squint. "He's forty-nine. You look half his age. You're not his friend."

Blaire looks away. "I don't need to tell you anything."

"You do if you want me to trust you."

"I don't need you to trust me. I just need you to not give me any trouble."

"Well, I'm not exactly designed to do that," I reply rather proudly. "Come on. Tell me, or else I'm going to think the worst."

She drops her temple onto her fingers, massaging the skin there.

"He was a friend of my dad's," she admits. "A long time ago. And he's helped me out a lot since then. And that's all I'm gonna say about it, all right?"

"And this is your house?"

"No. It's not," Blaire's voice drops in volume, like she's somewhat embarrassed. She tucks a stray look of hair behind her ear. "It's one of Baxton's many houses."

"That you're renting from him . . .?" I urge her to finish the sentence.

"Not . . . exactly."

"So, you stay here rent-free."

Blaire doesn't answer. She curls her shoulders upward into a shrug, not in confirmation, but not to refute my words either, like the answer lies somewhere in the middle.

Frustration coats the inside of my throat.

"So let me get this straight: you don't pay rent. And you've been living here for a while now. And your dad is 'a friend of' Baxton's." I make air quotes. Even saying the statement out loud sounds ludicrous. "Yeah, I'm not buying it."

She steps daringly toward me, cocking her head sideways and glowers. "Or maybe you're just not familiar with concepts like 'empathy' and 'an act of kindness,' so I suggest you look those up."

I chuckle, finding it endearing that she's naive enough not to assume that everything comes with a price, especially in LA.

"Come on, just admit it to me: either you're involved with my dad, or you're some kind of leech—"

"I'm not!" Anger surges through Blaire, her words clanging around the living room. I clamp my mouth shut. She throws her hands up in frustration. "Actually, you know what? I change my mind: I don't care if you stay here or not. I'm not obligated to be your babysitter. Trust me, I would rather be doing anything other than this. But I'm doing this as a favor to Baxton because I care about him a lot, and therefore, I feel compelled to care about *you*. But truthfully, I don't. Not even a little bit. Because you're too selfish to know what you've got, and you're more than happy to run it all into the ground. And I don't fuck with people like that." A fierce arm whips toward the door. "So, if you wanna go now, I won't stop you. In fact, be my guest. Go and make my life easier and *leave*. At least that will take the burden off my shoulders."

I'm rendered speechless.

She doesn't wait for me to say anything, though. Probably because she knows I can't. Instead, she just turns around and storms up the stairs, leaving me and my bags in the living room.

NINE

Blaire

What. A. Fucking. *Prick!*

I shut my bedroom door behind me and dig my hands into my hair, trying to catch my breath. What an entitled piece of shit. The nerve of Jax to assume those things . . . he thinks I'm sleeping with Baxton to get free rent? Are you fucking kidding me?

I'm well acquainted with Jax's type; I was just really hoping that I was wrong about him. After all, during my conversation with Baxton at the hospital a few days ago, I got the feeling that there was something inside Jax that was worth saving. Guess I was wrong.

Still, guilt beats in my chest. Considering I just told Jax to get out of the house, I'm not sure if that statement still rings true.

He's not gonna do it, I assure myself. There's nowhere for him to run. Not in that physical condition anyway. The only reason he wants to leave is to spite Baxton. But he won't go through with it. Soon enough, he'll realize this is the best and only option he's got.

I don't bother checking up on him downstairs. There isn't any need. Because, just as I expect, about five minutes later, I hear the loud thumping of luggage wheels being dragged up the stairs, followed by the door down the hallway snapping shut.

A delighted smile spreads across my face.

***

I see none of Jax in the evening—I assume he's probably in his room resting—so I take my sweet time in the kitchen to prepare dinner. Dinner is *aglio e olio* with leftover shredded chicken, garlic, and some fresh parsley I picked from the garden. Many people think it's a simple dish to execute, but the way the dish shines is in the details. Add too little water and your pasta dish will end up dry. Wait too long to combine your pasta water with the olive oil and you'll end up burning your garlic. Put the temperature too high and your emulsion will end up separating. Patience and right timing are what gets you the best results when it comes to food.

After I'm done plating, I carry my dinner upstairs and catch up on some correspondence in my room while digging into my food. There's not much, except for an email from Ahmed from the job center. I hold my breath, hoping for good news.

Hi Ms. Sullivan,

Unfortunately, no viable job leads have come up since our last meeting. I took the liberty of sending your résumé out to businesses we have worked with in the past to see if there is any interest. But I have to stress that due to your lack of education, as well as the nature and timing of your conviction, there is a strong chance that we might not yield much results.

I apologize that there isn't better news. I will keep you posted, of course, with any more updates.

Regards,
Ahmed Faris
WorkSource Center

My chest constricts. Everything hurts more than it should. I can feel the spark of hope that'd I'd desperately bottled up slowly fizzle out.

What the hell am I going to do now? I could focus my efforts on one-time jobs, like from the app. But that'll only get me so far. I can't go back to school without drowning myself in debt. And I can't get my record expunged because I simply can't afford to. How am I supposed to fix all my problems if I don't have a job that'll get me the money to do said fixing?

I bury my face in my pillow and scream.

At least I have Eden in two days. I already have our time together planned out and have saved all week just for this. Already feeling the twinge of excitement beginning to lift my mood, I pick up my phone and dial Eden's number.

"Hey, you," I greet when he picks up the phone. "How's it going?"

"Awesome. Did you know that Stanley Kubrick tried to take out an alien insurance policy when making *2001: A Space Odyssey* to protect himself against any possible losses in case aliens were discovered before the release of the movie?" Eden blurts out through the phone.

"Are you watching a documentary right now?" I speculate.

"Just finished," Eden voices proudly. "Isn't it crazy? Like he actually believed that shit."

"*Language*, Eden!" Laura shouts from a distant corner of the room. There's never a moment where she isn't around, monitoring our calls.

"Sorry," Eden says while stifling a laugh, and I can already picture him rolling his eyes away from her view.

"It *is* a cool fact," I say in assurance. "And I'm on Kubrick's side. After all, you gotta believe in aliens if you're gonna be making movies about them, you know? That's what makes the movie so iconic."

"I guess," Eden mutters. "But, I mean, you still can do stuff that you don't necessarily wanna do. Doesn't mean it's not going to be good."

"Yeah, but it's better when you're passionate about it," I volley back. "Stick to what you believe in."

"Oh yeah?" There are sounds of movement as he gets comfortable on the couch. "What do you believe in?"

I take a couple of moments to think about my answer. With everything that's happened to my mom, and Mrs. Adam's skewed perception of me, there's no answer that resonates with me as deeply as the one I tell Eden: "The truth."

"That's really boring, Blaire."

"What? It's the only thing that matters," I say amused. "What do you believe in, then?"

"Lots of things. Bigfoot. Yeti. A pot of gold at the end of rainbows. Cereal-fried onion rings."

"Cereal-fried onion rings?" I choke out.

"Best thing I had all summer," Eden drawls, making a chef's kiss sound.

"Okay. We'll hunt for them on Saturday, then," I smile. "Speaking of, I've got a full day planned for us. I've just secured tickets to see the first Star Wars movie at one of those hipster theaters, and if you want, we can catch a bus to Griffith afterward. They're doing the free public telescopes thing, and I think it'll be cool to check it out."

I expect some excitement coming from him, but instead, he goes silent for a beat.

"Um, right," he mumbles hesitantly. "About that . . . my dad just told us he got a big raise at work so Mom suggested that he take tomorrow off so we can all fly to Orlando to see Walt Disney World."

"Oh," I say, feeling my chest deflate with hurt and disappointment. "I thought I was going to see you on Saturday. Is Laura there?" I'm sure she's hovering close by, listening in on our conversation.

"Yeah."

"Can you pass her the phone, please?"

"Okay," Eden's voice trails off with uncertainty. "Hold on."

I hear him bounce off the couch and mumble something to Laura. After some back and forth between her and Eden, she sighs and takes the phone. I hear shuffling and the sound of a door closing, like she'd gone to another room so Eden won't overhear, which not only confirms my suspicions that she already knows the reason why I want to talk to her. It heightens my anger because that means she could've been the one to inform me about me not having Eden this weekend.

"Hello?" Laura's uninterested tone prickles in my ear.

"Eden just told me you guys were heading off to Orlando tomorrow. I thought we agreed last week that I was going to have him this weekend."

"Yes, there's been a slight change of plans. Jack doesn't get a lot of time off and you know . . . with Eden going off to space camp next week, we wanted to do something nice for him."

"I'm sorry: *what?*" I snap myself into a sitting position on the bed. "Eden hasn't told me anything about space camp."

"We were planning on surprising him on the Orlando trip," she explains.

I try to remain composed. "So how long is this space camp?"

She pauses, like she isn't sure if she even wants to tell me.

"A month."

"A MONTH?" I clear my throat and lower my volume, but the irritation is still palpable in my voice.

"Oh, don't be so dramatic: it's not like we're shipping him off to the military," Laura scoffs patronizingly. I want to scoff. It's hypocrisy at its finest. She and I both know that if I pulled this kind of stunt on her with Eden, she'd be flipping out and cursing me all the way to hell.

"The only time I have left with him till then is on Friday, and you're conveniently flying him out of state then," I say through a clenched jaw. "Do you think I'm that stupid?"

I see what she's doing here. She can't outright refuse me or my visits because that would mean upsetting Eden and her husband, so she's trying to work around them.

"I have no idea what you're talking about," Laura says, feigning ignorance. "Besides, Blaire, it's *space* camp. What do you want me to do? He's excited about it. I'm starting to think that you just don't want to see him happy."

"Of course I want him to enjoy space camp. And you know I can't afford to send him, or I would," I argue back. "Look, I just want to be treated fairly. You can't stand there and tell me you've been fair. I only get three hours of the week with him. And I've tried hard to respect that. But not only do you deliberately choose to disrespect the rules you yourself have set up, but you also refuse to give me any notice or ask for my input about big decisions concerning him."

"No offense, Blaire, but your feelings about this arrangement are not my responsibility to coddle. I'm his legal guardian now. Not you," she snaps back.

"Well, if I'm not seeing him for a month, can I at least see him tonight?"

"It's getting late and he needs his rest," she explains.

"Fine. How about tomorrow morning?" I say determinedly.

"Morning doesn't work for me."

"It doesn't have to work for you. It just needs to work for *him*," I assert.

"It's just not a good time. We'll probably be doing some last-minute packing."

"How about right before you head off to the airport? Can I see him then?"

"I don't think it would be appropriate."

Not appropriate? I want to laugh. Even her excuses are getting sloppier.

"Seriously?" My anger spilling out of my throat and through the receiver. "What the *fuck*, Laura?"

She gasps like I just shot her in the chest. I'm surprised by how reckless my anger has become; Laura has always gotten on my nerves, but never to the point where I've found myself cussing her out directly.

"You know, if you're going to use that language with me, I'm going to have to hang up on you!" Laura warns.

"I'm just trying to meet you in the middle here," I snap, frustrated. "I've compromised with you on endless occasions when it comes to my brother. Why can't you extend some compassion to me?"

"BECAUSE YOU DON'T DESERVE IT!" she yells.

My mouth hangs open in shock. I can feel the phone in my grip slipping.

Laura is breathing hard as she tries to collect herself, but the rage has already clung to her stern but steady tone. "People like you don't deserve compassion, Blaire," she adds. "You are no longer his family, Blaire. *I* am. Real families *support* each other. And the truth of the matter is that your incarceration is the reason why Eden's with me in the first place. You failed to put him first, Blaire. That, to me, tells me everything I need to know about your ability to take care of *my* son."

I keep quiet as the tears spring in my eyes. My jaw hurts from grinding too hard to prevent the tears from spilling over.

I close my eyes and let out a slow exhale, the realization dawning on me that no matter how hard I try, I will never be able to get in her good graces. There's simply nothing I can say that'll make her change her mind about me.

"I'm done being civil with you," Laura sneers. "You will see him when *I* say that you see Eden. And based on how you've been treating me lately, I'll be re-evaluating when that will be, if it will ever happen again. Goodbye."

When she hangs up on me, *I climb back onto the bed and curl up in the sheets.* The tears run down my cheeks before I realize that I'm crying. Strands of hair cling onto my wet face and I make no attempt to push them away. My heart feels like it's been cleaved wide open. I sink into bed and hope to never come out again.

The grief pours out of me in tears, clouding my vision. I ruminate on all my failures, on how I must look to my dad right now. An utter disappointment, most likely.

I got myself into crime, got myself caught, and broke my family apart. And I continue to allow Laura to walk all over me, when I should've stood up for myself more. Now, I've allowed her the opportune moment to cut me out of the equation completely.

I don't know how long I lie there for, but it's long enough for the anger to seep into my bloodstream, a swirling storm of insecurities and anxieties . . .

No.

The word detonates in my mind, rendering everything else irrelevant.

I can't allow myself to feel sorry for myself. It's not an option. Not when it comes to Eden.

And there's one option I haven't explored yet. Haven't been *willing* to explore.

I've lost Eden once; I won't lose him again.

And this time, I'm not just coming back for a slice.

I'm coming back for the whole damn pie.

Ben's words float back into my mind, the picture he'd painted for me of my life with Eden. A good life. A secure life. A life where our family, or what's left of it anyway, will be whole again.

My fingers are already punching in Ben's number.

"Hey," I say, the clarity in my tone and vision becomes clear. "You let Portia know I'm down to meet her as soon as tomorrow."

TEN

Jax

It's the night of the finals and I'm in the MMA cage, tearing through my opponent, Kayden, with my fists.

He's struggling to stand up, stumbling as he absorbs the weight of my hits. Blood streaks across his teeth and brow. His guard is completely down. Good. Time to deal the final blow. The ravenous crowd pushing against the sides of the cage demands it to be so. Time to end this, once and for all. I reel my fist back and launch it toward his face.

Except where my fist was supposed to meet his jaw, it meets someone else's.

Sienna.

My fists recoil back just as I watch her crumble to the ground. Time and space come to halt. I watch in slow motion as her head hits the floor. Her body stills, and all the air in my lungs is vacuumed out of my lungs.

My knees buckle and send me crashing to the ground. The blood in my body has gone cold. My hands dig in my hair so hard I feel like I could break through my skull.

The crowd has gone deathly silent.

Nothing can prepare me for this. There have been some crazy fights in the underground, but this, this is something else entirely. The fight has transcended the realm of entertainment. This is reality, with cold, life-threatening repercussions.

Everything next happens in slow motion.

A scream of anguish from Kayden rips through the air, silencing the crowd. My terrified gaze falls on him. He scrambles over to her, nearly stumbling while he's at it, and hovers over her face, which is red from the force of my own hands. When I first met Sienna, I was sure she was made of fire and steel. But in this moment, she's malleable and sinking into someone else's arms in an awkward manner as he frantically searches for signs of life in her face.

A firm hand lands on my shoulder, forcing me to look up. The same blue eyes that I saw snap shut minutes ago, are now looking down at me, quiet fury carved into her face.

"S-Sienna . . ." I choke out, the tears painting my cheeks.

The ghost of Sienna kneels in front of me and grasps my jaw so hard I'm certain she's going to shatter it. Instead, she turns my face toward her body.

"Look at what you did to me, Jax," she growls and fear drops into my stomach. "Look."

I don't want to look. I don't but she grips my jaw harder and my eyes snap open again and my heart plummets out of my ribcage. Her face is leached of any color. Her lips are blue. Her body is unmoving. Lifeless. I'm too afraid to check her pulse to see if my worst fears are confirmed.

How did it come to this? How did I allow my obsession with victory to destroy the one *person who had loyally stood by my side? It wasn't too long ago that I swore I would burn the world down for her. Not only have I done that, I made her a casualty too.*

I'm crying now. Downright hysterical. I didn't think my body was capable of producing tears. If I could drain my body of all its water, I would.

"I didn't . . . I didn't see you coming, I swear, on my life, you know . . . you know I wouldn't have-" The words tumble out of me in between the wretched sobs. *"Sienna, please . . ."*

A stern line folds over the ghost's lips as her emotionless gaze meets mine again.

"You'll never change your stripes, Jax. And I hope you never do." Her hand runs down my cheek, caressing it with a kind of unsettling affection. A calm before the storm. Her mouth twists into a slow, wicked grin. *"Because monsters like you are always bound to meet their end."*

I propel myself out of bed, drenched in sweat.

It's just a dream, I tell myself, *it's just a dream.*

But my heart isn't entirely convinced. Because it, along with my mind, is well aware of the truth. My dreams are a reflection of past events. Dramatized, but as honest and grim as it can get.

This has been a recurring dream for a while now. Usually, I'll force it out of my mind, but it's been a particularly challenging time, having just been released from the hospital.

I suck in a breath, and release through my teeth. In, out, in, out. Hoping that I can expel Sienna out of my system the same way I'm expelling the pain that accompanies my rapid breathing. I press my hand on my chest to stabilize my breath, but the fire continues to spread across it. Instinctively, I press on my ribs, only to find the pain expanding like a band across my chest.

Ah, fuck! I double over.

Okay, okay, broken ribs and a bad dream don't go well together. Fucking noted.

The pain is paralyzing. I force myself on my back again, remembering the coughing and breathing exercises the doctor had recommended I should do. To be honest, they don't really work on me, but at this point I'm willing to try anything. I press a hand against my chest and inhale through my nostrils, then push out the breath through my mouth. The same fiery feeling manifests in my chest again and I wince. I resume the breathing exercises. Breathe in, out. Breathe in, out. And nothing. Everything still hurts.

I drop my hands to either side of me in defeat.

Recovery shouldn't be any different than all the other times I've ended up in hospital from my MMA injuries. Sure, I am in the worst shape I've ever been in twenty-three years, and I should expect some bad days and good days with my condition, but I always managed to keep bad days away.

Maybe I'm not as strong as I thought I was.

I pinch my eyelids with my fingers and groan. Sienna's haunting words to me in my dream come seeping back.

Mustering the strength, I use my arms to haul myself up into a sitting position on the bed, then grab the glass of water sitting on my bedside and pop some painkillers into my mouth.

I spend the next ten minutes sitting around, waiting for

the painkillers to kick in. But the longer I wait, the more I'm convinced they don't work. And now I'm just pissed off because I've spent way too much time relying on other people's advice when I'm the only one who knows my own body the best. So I slide off the bed, chuck on a shirt and jeans, and leave my room to go looking for a better alternative for my pain. The only alternative I can rely on.

When I reach the kitchen, my breath halts painfully in my lungs as I find Blaire leaning her body over the marble kitchen counter, her hips swaying like she's enjoying her sandwich a little too much. I don't want her picking up on me checking her out like yesterday, but all I can think about now is my hands clinging on to that ass while my lips latch onto her neck.

How about maybe not pissing off your already pissed-off father by seducing your new roommate . . .

I shuffle past her silently and can feel her gaze boring into me. I don't acknowledge her, instead focusing on my hunt for that bottle of gin I stashed in the cabinet beside the refrigerator last night. When I don't find it, I rummage through the rest of the cabinets and drawers, under the assumption that I'd misremembered where I put it. But again, nothing. I whip back around, only to find Blaire staring back at me, this time, with the faintest smile on her lips. My gaze locks in on her like a missile.

"Where is it?" I snap.

She doesn't reply to me immediately. She draws out the silence as she finishes the last bite of her sandwich, licks her fingers clean of the peanut butter. Her tongue swirls over her thumb slowly, and my jaw tightens, refusing to acknowledge how that minute action gets me so fucked up.

"I threw it away." Blaire says in the end. "Along with the rest of your alcohol."

The rest of my—?

I rush over to the living room and check on the sofa, where I specifically remembered nursing half a bottle of whiskey before heading to bed, and swear a string of obscenities when I find that it isn't where I'd left it.

My body spins back toward her, annoyance flaring in my skin. "What the hell, Blaire? Where is all the alcohol?"

"I told you. Garbage disposal has them as we speak."

I mutter a frazzled curse as my brain soaks up all that information. How did she know exactly where all the bottles were? I thought I'd been extremely careful last night, making sure she was fast asleep before heading downstairs to hide everything.

As if reading my mind, Blaire says, in a rather bored voice. "All alcoholics have a stash. I wasn't born yesterday."

"Did Baxton tell you that?"

"Baxton told me to do whatever necessary to get you sober. And step one of sobriety is to detox."

"Detoxing is the whole point of drinking, smartass," I say through gritted teeth.

Anger tugs at my chest. Forcing me to live with a hot stranger, that I can get behind. But having her police my every move? This is a step too far, even for Baxton.

Blaire rolls her eyes. "Can you stop being such a baby? If you have a problem with it, take it up with your father."

My arms cross over my chest as I suss her out, trying to make sense of her involvement with Baxton. It still confuses me how she fits into all of this. "Are you getting paid for this gig? Because I'll pay you double to leave me alone."

"I don't accept bribes."

"Don't consider it a bribe. Consider it a one-off payment to return my privacy."

"You *do* have privacy," Blaire counters. "You have your room, and you have this house. Whatever you do on these premises, I couldn't care less about it as long as it doesn't involve alcohol. As for outside . . . if you don't want to go back to Boston or rehab, you're gonna have to do what I *say*. And that means going to your therapy sessions and your doctor appointments."

I shake my head vehemently. Not the shrink who's supposed to be magically talking all my problems away. "I can't do therapy."

Blaire narrows her eyes. "You can't?"

"I *don't* do therapy," I correct myself. "I don't like talking about my issues to someone I don't know."

"Just out of curiosity: do you even have anyone you *do* know that you talk to about your issues?"

My first thought is *what kind of question is that?* But then, I realize Connor and Watts aren't exactly the type of people that I'd open up to. I don't think I've ever had someone I regularly shared my feelings and struggles with. I try to summon a reply, but only a weak breath falls out of my lips.

A smug smile tugs at Blaire's mouth. "That's what I thought. You have a problem, and you know it, and instead of doing something about it, you surround yourself with a bunch of enablers to stay busy enough to ignore the fact that it's consuming your whole life."

My jaw clenches, my cheekbones probably looking like sharp glass.

"I don't have problems, darlin'. Only solutions. And two bottles of them are missing from this house as we speak," I growl back. Just then, a feeling pinches in my head, the pain so vivid and sharp. "And now this conversation is giving me a headache. Fuck. I need a hit," I mutter, heading toward the stairs so I can retrieve the pot.

Usually, I only take it when I can't sleep, or if my dick needs some extra sensitivity when I'm having sex, but if I don't get anything in my system to sort out this migraine, I'm not going to like how I'll act around Blaire. I already *don't* like how I act around her now. She pulls a kind of hostility out of me that I don't usually wield unless it's on an opponent on the other side of the cage.

"Yeah, you're not gonna find the *pot* either," Blaire says, following me up the stairs.

"What—?" I swing back, my jaw clenched so hard as the conclusion formed in my brain. She wouldn't have. Because if she did, she'd have to sneak into my room to get it while I was asleep, since I have it stashed in my bag.

Oh, but she would.

A fresh bolt of anger whips through me as I stare her down with the wrath of the devil. "What else? Is there anything you'll be taking from me? My clothes? My phone? My *sanity*?"

"Like I said, I don't care what you do as long as it doesn't involve your vices." Blaire edges closer to me, but this time, leaning her weight against the counter, her fingers clasping in front of her. "Look, the more resistant you are to the process, the longer you have to stay here, and the longer we're both stuck together in this house, miserable and wishing we were anywhere else. I don't know about you, but I have big plans for the summer that don't involve planning your murder, and I'm sure you feel the same, so it'll be nice if we can co-inhabit this place in peace."

A raspy chuckle leaves me. "Well, I don't plan on murdering you, darlin'. It's too much work."

"Well, I'm glad you think I'll be too smart to get murdered by you."

"I meant the cleanup would be a *hassle*. Not that I won't be able to do the job well," I seethe.

My mind cycles through Blaire's advice. Blaire probably means that the sooner I get my act together, the faster I can resume my life unsupervised.

But really, what if I can just . . . pretend to get better?

Show Blaire that I'm making real progress and get her to place her trust in me. Soon enough, I'd be able to slip back into my old ways—minus the part where I'm careless about it—and she won't be any wiser. That way, we both get what we want. I get to wine, dine, and fuck in peace, and she gets the house back to herself.

The prospect of falling back to my cunning ways elicits a spark of excitement inside me. I've always excelled at the art of deception. And fooling Blaire will be no different.

"You know what? I think maybe you have a point," I say, a resigned breath falling out of me to sell the ruse. "Moving out of this house as quickly as I can is a pretty good motivator to get sober."

Blaire reels back, surprise coloring her cheeks.

"So . . . you're gonna let me be your babysitter?"

"Babysitter?" Disgust drips in my tone. "Call yourself a sponsor and I'll agree to whatever you need me to do."

"Sponsor it is." She sighs at our newly established term. "Now that we got that sorted . . ." She clicks on her phone to check the time. "That means we can get to our agenda of the day."

My eyebrows draw low. "Which is . . ."

"That I already scheduled an appointment for you to see a therapist in the afternoon."

For fuck's sake.

"You'll find Dr. Fisher is a reasonable and intelligent woman who has worked with many recovering alcoholics," Blaire explains. "Oh, and I'll be personally escorting you to her office myself with Baxton's car so you can't flee."

"Are you ever going to tell me what we're doing with more notice so I can plan my days?" I say with a grumble.

"And give you a chance to back out of it? No way." Blaire says, patting me on the shoulder. She walks past me and into the living room.

"In two hours, you got me? We'll meet here at 12:00 p.m. sharp," she announces before plopping herself on the couch and turning on the TV.

I return to my room. The stress is eating me alive, so I'm desperate for a hit. The first thing I do is check the duffel bag. For some reason, I was hoping she was lying about throwing everything out. But of course . . . Blaire was right. Not even a smidge of weed left. My rolling paper, grinder, and small stash of tobacco are also nowhere to be found.

ELEVEN

Jax

A babysitter, I mull the words over in my head as I take my seat in the waiting room of the therapist's office. It's fucking humiliating.

I want to laugh at the irony of it all. Jax Deneris, the most coveted MMA fighter in the underground, needs a goddamned babysitter.

I should've dragged my sorry fucking ass back to Boston while I still had a chance.

I glance around the room, hoping I'm not alone in my own predicament. There are a couple of therapists working in the same center, so the waiting room is packed with people anxiously waiting for their appointment. A couple sits beside me on the sofa, looking tense and cold toward one another. On the opposite side sits an anxiety-ridden teen girl with hollow eyes in a suspiciously long turtleneck, despite the weather pushing seventy-eight degrees outside. An office door opens and the therapist ushers out a patient before calling the teen girl's name. The girl rises from the seat and scurries into the office as if terrified she'll be seen, and the door closes.

"You should be up next," Blaire reminds me as she approaches the newly vacant seat.

After checking me in with the receptionist earlier, she went to get two lattes from the coffee machine by the washrooms. Now back, she hands me a cup and places her own on the glass coffee table, then checks her phone.

So far, she's done that six times since we left the house. I'm surprised that I've kept track.

"You're anxious to leave," I observe, taking a sip of the latte. The coffee is acidic, but I swallow it down anyway, desperate for the caffeine.

Blaire slips the phone back into her pocket and gives me a glance over. "I have plans."

"As my sponsor, doesn't your life kinda revolve around me?"

"You wish, Deneris."

And yet, my curiosity gets the better of me.

"These plans . . . do they involve a guy of some sort?"

Instead of choosing to engage with me, Blaire releases a big, dramatic sigh.

"What?" I ask.

"Can we not do this?" she grumbles.

"Do what?"

"Stick our noses in each other's business."

I shift uneasily in my seat. "Just trying to make conversation."

She ignores me and plucks out a lifestyle magazine from the rack beside her. I get the hint that she just wants to be left alone, but a part of me wants to prod further. She's already seen me at my worst, and I barely know anything about her.

"At least tell me how old you are," I say.

Blaire flips through a page, contemplating on withholding that information.

"Twenty-one," she says eventually.

"Didn't expect you to be younger than me." When she doesn't ask me about my age, I decide to offer up the information myself. "I'm twenty-three."

She scoffs, her attention still planted on whatever column she's apparently reading. "Twenty-one and twenty-three are practically the same age."

"You're a baby. You're barely old enough to drink," I tell her, another follow-up question popping into my mind. "Are you in college?"

I didn't expect that to be a trigger for her, but apparently it is, because she dramatically closes the magazine and shoots me the deadliest glare. *What did I just say about your questions?*

Oo-kay.

She's a tough nut to crack, but I've dealt with worse.

"Jax Deneris," the receptionist calls out minutes later. "Dr. Fisher is ready for you."

Blaire picks herself up from the seat and tucks the magazine back into the rack. "I'll be back to pick you up in an hour."

"It's not daycare," I remind her. "I think I can manage an Uber home."

"I'll pick you up," she insists again in a tone that tells me that I shouldn't say stupid things. She opens her mouth, probably to say something smug, but the words don't arrive. Instead, she slams her mouth shut, and a look of apprehension crosses her face. "Good luck in there, all right?"

I watch Blaire silently as she swipes her coffee from the table and aims a warm smile toward the receptionist before leaving the building altogether.

"Jax?" the receptionist repeats, looking at me weirdly. "Dr. Fisher is waiting."

I glance at her, then toward the ajar door to Dr. Fisher's office. A pair of slender, crossed legs sits in view, and a black clipboard balances on the ball of one of her knees. Panic swells in my chest, along with a repeated chorus line of "I'm not ready" persistently attacking my mind. My feet instinctively shuffle back.

Yeah, there's no fucking way I'm walking in there.

Putting in the work isn't part of my plan.

Keeping the appearance of it is.

I refocus my attention back on the receptionist, trying to appear as calm as I can. "Bathroom break. I'll be quick."

I don't bother noting her response before jogging down the hallway, past the coffee machine. Just as I'd hoped, there's a fire escape past the three bathroom doors. I descend the steps and shove open the exit door to get outside, the remainder of my anxiety shriveling away like polymer under the summer heat.

By the time my session with Dr. Fisher has started, there's already a pint of beer in my hand from the nearest bar.

TWELVE

Blaire
Six Months Ago

There's a new inmate sitting on the top bunk where it was empty this morning.

I was already aware that I was gonna get a new bunkie after the old one made bond yesterday. I'm happy she's gone and can no longer terrorize me. Apart from her daily taunting, she was always using my deodorant and hairbrush without my permission. And if I had to hear about her brief music career as a DJ one more time, I'd gladlyuse the razor blade she stashed behind the wall to slash my throat.

I'd been hoping for at least one night of peace before being forced to interact with a new cellmate, but as evidenced by the fact that I've ended up here, luck has never been on my side

The first thing my eyes linger on is my new cellmate's auburn hair. Like firelight pouring down her shoulders, catching the light in different shades of red. It's a shame our yellow top and blue pants uniform makes the color of her hair stick out awkwardly. Her eyes are a seaweed green, and there's a natural flush to her face that colors her cheeks and the tip of her nose. When she sees me, she grins knowingly.

Naturally, my guard is immediately up.

"And here I was starting to get lonely," my bunkie coos, hopping off the bunk and landing on both her feet with ease. She leans against the steel bed frame and looks at me like I'm about to be her latest fixation.

The expression on my face remains unfazed. I wasn't gonna spill anything about where I've been to a stranger. "Who are you?"

"Portia. You must be Blaire." She sticks her hand out. She's suave about it, which makes it feel like I'm interviewing for a job, and I feel compelled to impress her. I shake her hand and she drops it back to her side. She looks me up and down for a few beats longer than necessary, and discomfort coils around my spine. I'm suddenly acutely aware of the weight of my head balancing on my neck, and all the hairs standing on the back of my arms. Eventually, her gaze is back up on me, an intriguing gleam in her eyes. "I hear my new bunkie's a menace."

So she was aware of where I'd been.

"I don't know what you heard, but it was my first time in confinement and I was just trying to not get my teeth knocked out by some girl's tray," I mutter, brushing past her to wash my hands in the sink.

"Why'd she start the fight?" Portia asks.

"I accidentally elbowed her while I was getting lunch," I explain. "She thought I was trying to pick a fight with her."

She shrugs, her hands shoved into the pockets of her pants. "It's unfair, isn't it? Rules never work the same way here." I stay silent, unsure of what to add. Portia tips her chin toward me. "Did you know some prisons will fund hormone replacement, but won't provide dental beyond pulling a tooth? Not that I'm against it in any way, but you'd think oral care would be an essential service of similar importance. Guess I learned the answer the hard way." She opens her mouth and using her finger, she pulls one side of her mouth aside so I can see the awkward space in the back in between two teeth where a third was supposed to be.

"You've been here before," I observe, looking back up. "For what?"

There it is again. That trademark sly grin of hers.

"I'll trade that secret if you give me one," she purrs.

"I don't keep secrets."

She walks in a slow circle around me. "You should. Especially in here. Secrets are the best form of currency."

I thought ramen noodles were, but okay. "So, following that logic, why should I trade you my secrets, then?"

She lets the silence stretch for a while before admitting. "Because I like you."

"You like me?" I want to laugh. "You only just met me."

Portia's grin widens, She strolls over to my box of items that I keep under my bed. All my essential things. My clothes. My tampons. Toiletries. Shoes. Hooking a finger inside the box, she pulls it out in the open. "You disinfect your things," she notes and I'm stumped. "Don't deny it. I can smell the bleach. You must have swiped it from the infirmary. Why do you bother?"

"Because I like to be clean?" I say flatly.

"No, it's because you don't wanna die," Portia asserts. "You know how bad it gets in here. Inmates catching diseases left and right. Rodent infestations. Bed bugs. You're not going to take your chances. Why? Because you're a survivor. Whether you want to be or not." She edges closer toward me, fingering a loose strand of my hair. "Well, lucky for you, I'm one too."

She pulls away, far enough for me to see her give me a stern once-over.

"We're gonna be here for a while, so you need me as much as I need you, So, if you keep my secrets, I will keep yours."

"I don't know . . ." My voice trails off.

"How 'bout I'll start? To break the ice?" she muses.

I stare at her, watching her silently but curiously. She takes my silence as an invitation to speak.

"I'm here on drug-trafficking charges," she states.

"Then, why aren't you in prison instead?"

"The DA told me I would get a lesser charge if I helped them catch some of the guys in my chain of command here. So I did," she says without an ounce of remorse. "Before I got here, I was running deliveries across state lines. Oregon is actually my home state. I miss it. Had a lake house and everything. But I had the misfortune of getting caught here so . . . whoops." Portia shrugs. "Your turn. Tell me why you got sent to confinement."

Her words put a knot of dread in my throat.

Portia is already the most interesting bunkie to have stepped foot in this unit. Playing by her rules may work to my detriment.

Or may make life here more convenient.

I'll take my chances.

"Okay . . ." I inhale a sharp breath. "For some reason, I'm an easy target amongst the other inmates, which means I've been to the infirmary more than a few times now. It also means I have the nurses' routine memorized. So whenever the nurse isn't looking, I use a tampon to soak up the bleach. And when I get back here, I squeeze it into this container. "I nod to the container that's half full of liquid inside my box of supplies.

"Smart." Portia nods, impressed.

"So . . . we're friends, then?" I ask.

"Friends." Portia grins, sticking her hand out for me to shake.

The next day, in exchange for some of the bleach, Portia got the inmate who fought with me sent to confinement for three days.

***

I have one hour to myself before I have to see Jax again and resume my sponsor duties, so hopefully this isn't going to take long. At least I have Baxton's car this time around to shave off some travel time.

I decide to park the car a few streets away and walk the rest of the way there. I dig out a couple of coins from my pocket to give to the veteran sitting on the curb outside of my destination. He grunts at me and counts the coins in his palm. I hope he has enough for whatever he needs today.

As I look up at the plain beige walls of the building, I can't help but feel my nerves running wild. A lot of the people living here were previously living on the streets and were relocated, which is a good thing, depending on how you look at it. On one hand, at least they're off the streets. But because there aren't any rehabilitation programs to keep them out of crime, these buildings end up as hellholes for drugs and drinking. I was lucky enough to escape that fate. If I want to keep it that way, I need to be careful with what I'm willing to agree to today.

A middle-aged woman walking her dog comes out of the building I'm heading into. She doesn't bother to hold the door open for me, but I manage to squeeze my way through and slip into the building without needing anyone to buzz me in. I take the stairs two at a time, making it to the fifth floor with a burning sensation in my thighs. The smell of weed floats through the air as the perpetrators lounge by the stairs, eyeing me with interest as I swerve past them. House music hums down the hallway, growing louder until I make it to the last door on the right.

I curl my fist and pound on the door three times.

A woman's voice yells something incoherent to another girl and they exchange some muffled words. The music softens to an acceptable volume, and I hear footsteps coming closer. The chain on the door rattles as the door opens an inch, and a girl wearing two long braids pokes her face through. She's probably around my age, if not younger.

"Name," she says flatly, her gaze boring into mine.

"Blaire," I say. Her eyes narrow even more. I roll my eyes, my impatience wearing me down. "I'm here to see Portia."

The door slams shut and I hear her muffled voice yell, 'You know a Blaire?" A few seconds later, there is a rustle of the chain lock and the door pulls open.

The first thing that hits me is the smell; if I thought the stench of weed in the hallway was bad, it's basically a cannabis nursery in this apartment. There are bricks of them, along with boxes shoved against the walls, and pills and powder strewn across a few of the surfaces. The windows are boarded up with cardboard, so it's mostly dark, save for the fluorescent overhead lights. I'm relieved to find that there are only three people around, unlike the picture Ben painted about most nights, where there were at least a dozen or more people occupying the space, smoking up and playing cards. This afternoon, a bong is out, shared among a lanky guy I don't recognize and a woman whom I definitely do.

I watch silently as the girl who let me in shuffles into the kitchen to feed the cat. Not sure what she's feeding it with, but it sure doesn't look like cat food.

"Well, look who's back. Been a while since you came around." Portia grins slyly, setting the bong on the coffee table in front of her and rests her elbows on her thighs, cocking a dark brow at me.

She looks a lot different than the last time I saw her six months ago. Her long auburn hair is chopped off, leaving her with a straight bob. At least she didn't stay the same petite size she did in jail; she's jacked now, with more muscle around her arms, face and hips. But some things never change; a Cheshire cat grin and viper-green eyes eager to unlock everyone's secrets.

My gaze makes a sweep of the room. "Ben's not around today?"

"He's doing some on-location work for me," Portia tells me, leaving it at that. "Sit." She gestures toward the stool and I oblige, lowering myself onto it.

Portia leans over to the guy beside her and mutters something in his ear. He shrugs, swiping the bong and shuffling into the next room before shutting the door behind him. The girl with the cat immediately senses that we need privacy, nods at Portia, and makes herself scarce.

"So," Portia starts off, leaning forward and resting her arms on her thighs, "what do you want?"

"You already know what I want," I mumble.

"Yeah, but I want you to say it," she says, her gaze pinning me helplessly. "Come on, it's only polite."

I set my jaw tight, despising the power politics. It was all she played while we were cellmates, and I spent half my time admiring her for it to get what she wanted and the other half despising it for when she'd use it on me.

She raises an amused brow. *Well?*

"I need a job," I admit through clenched teeth.

"Good girl," Portia murmurs, a pleased smile forming on her lips. "So, I take it you got the rude awakening that the job market did ex-cons dirty?"

"I need the money," is all I say.

She doesn't ask me anything about my current living situation. Good. It's better she doesn't know about Baxton. If she knew I'm connected to someone of his caliber, she would ask more questions I'm unwilling to answer.

"I appreciate what you did for me while we were cellmates," I make sure to add, to butter her up. "You made my life way more bearable than it could've been."

"Wouldn't hurt for you to say it once in a while," she grumbles, her eyes shining as she meets my gaze again. "I like you, Blaire. I've missed you. A lot. Not a lot of people have the stomach to survive in this city, but you do. You really were one of the good ones. But even goodness has its price. So . . ." She weaves her fingers together and tilts her head. "Why come to me now?"

Here it goes.

I lay out the general plan. "I need to get my record expunged, so I can get a proper job and win custody of my brother."

She hums. "Fair enough. What do you wanna do then?"

"All I know is that I don't wanna deal."

"That's fine with me. I'm closing up shop anyway. Too many mules trying to hustle me, and in this economy, I'm playing the loan shark more than getting back what I'm owed. Hence, all this." A lazy hand gestures to the dozens of boxes. She holds a finger up, the signature grin appearing on her mouth again. "I have another job. It's not long-term, but it'll be enough for you and me to get what we want. Wait here," she instructs before getting up from the couch and going over to a corner of the room that's littered with boxes and miscellaneous items. She grabs a big, black duffel bag and brings it to me. She unzips the bag and pours all the contents onto the coffee table. Jewelry, diamonds, and dresses spill across the surface.

"What's all this?" I say, rifling through the mountain of items.

"Just a small portion of what we got from a house near Rodeo."

"Like . . . from an auction?"

"Don't be ridiculous," Portia scoffs.

And then, the answer hits me like a freight train.

"You *stole* this?" I ask, baffled.

"Yes. And honestly? Easier than it looks." Portia shrugs. "The surveillance part is what takes the longest. But once we know their routine, we're usually in and out of the house in ten minutes."

I'm unable to register the shock. That's probably what Ben is helping Portia with.

I can't get over the fact that all of this in front of me was stolen from somebody's house. I sift through the items: lots of necklaces, rings, branded clothes with tags still on them. This is crazy.

"How long have you been doing this?" I whisper.

"Not long. This was yesterday's loot," Portia points out, her fingers energetically running over the items. "We're in need of one more crew member, though. An extra set of hands. That's where you come in."

I shake my head, refusing to believe what she's asking of me right now.

"You're talking about burglary. That's a *felony*," I gripe.

"Only if we get caught," she says determinedly. "Besides, a stint like this can't go on for long, or the cops will catch on. I just need to do it enough to get out of this hellhole."

"This is insane," I breathe.

My brain struggles to soak up all that information. There's nearly a hundred grand worth of items in front of me. My stomach turns. Surely it can't be as easy as Portia says it is. There's a catch . . . right?

"You simply can't beat this kind of money, Blaire." She laughs heartily, her eyes shining with invisible dollar signs. "One night yields up to a few hundred G's if we're lucky. If you're in, we'll split the profits evenly between the four of us. So, you do the math."

My mouth goes dry when I think about it. One house like that? I could arm myself up with a lawyer the very next day. With an air-tight plan and a good team, we could do this. We *could*.

"Four of us? Who's your crew?" I ask.

"Me, Ben, and my buddy, Whiskey, who's done her fair share of burglaries herself. She's gonna be our muscle."

My throat feels tight as I weigh the pros and cons of participating in this. On one hand, I could get everything I have dreamed of. On the other hand, I could end up in federal prison.

Soar through heaven or fall so hard from grace I'll never recover from it.

This wasn't exactly what I had in mind when I arrived here, but if I was being really honest with myself, I doubt I was going to leave empty-handed. I *need* whatever Portia is offering. Clearly making an honest living is not in the cards for me right now, and I'm running out of options.

And yet, a dilemma strikes my brain. The same moral dilemma that struck me while I was in a similar position nearly a year ago. My jaw clenches in reproach. Noticing this, Portia rolls her eyes.

"Oh, come on. Don't give me that look. You cannot draw the line at *theft*, Blaire," Portia mutters, frustration darkening her irises. "Not when that was the reason you went to jail in the first place."

There it is.

What I'd feared all along.

Repeating the same mistakes I made all those months ago.

I swore to myself I was going to be better after I got out of jail. I wasn't going to go back to my old ways. I couldn't hurt *Eden* again. I'd already lost everything once.

But this opportunity might just be your chance to get it all back, the little voice in the back of my head whispers in retaliation.

I lift my chin up, fixing my gaze back on Portia. "How many houses are you planning for?" I manage in a somewhat steady voice.

"Two. And then we're out."

"And how do you pick the targets? What makes your plan foolproof?"

"We have Ben hack into the two security firm databases and pick the targets from there, based on what security features they have, and whether it's possible to work our way around those features. Then, he jams the signal to the security cameras. He's also our lookout when we enter. We take what we can fit into a duffel bag, no more, no less," she explains. "We work smart, and we work fast. We'll be in and out of the house in less than ten minutes, and we'll be long gone by the time the cops arrive."

At least this isn't something that's been hastily put together. There's a lot of thought in the process, and there's a solid plan there. And if Ben is in on this, it must mean he trusts himself, and Portia, enough to get away with it. There's too much at stake for him too.

It's just two houses, I rationalize. All I need to do is to be smart and to not get caught. I'm not gonna be doing this forever. Just twice.

After all this, I won't go near Portia again. I'll move out of Baxton's place. Pay him back somehow. Get a proper job. Fight to get Eden back. Make sure he has the best upbringing money can buy. I'll make it worth it. Not just for me, but for Eden, for Baxton, for everyone that I know.

Do a little bad to do a lifetime of good. Karmically speaking, that all balances out, doesn't it? It has to.

Just two houses.

Just *two*.

And I'm out of this. *Forever.*

"Well?" Portia says, a twitch of her lips. "What do you say?"

My gaze connects with hers, swimming with defeat.

With a weak nod, I take her hand and shake it.

THIRTEEN

Jax

I didn't go overboard at the bar this time because I didn't want to reek of beer back at the therapist's building. I kept it simple, only nursing two Bud Lights and only lightly flirting with the bartender. Her name was Abby and she wrote her number on the back of my receipt. She was pretty and had an easy smile. I tipped her generously and made a mental note to text her when I got back.

I was worried I might be late and Blaire would wise up to the fact that I skipped my session, but lucky for me, I'd already been waiting for her for a good fifteen minutes.

"Sorry I'm late. Got held up," Blaire mumbles cryptically as I yank the front door open and slide into my seat. When she pulls out of the parking lot, her eyes are pinned on the road. She bites down on her lip as a worried crease digs deep into her forehead.

"All right, lay it on me," I say in an attempt to intercept her thoughts. "What's going on?"

She shifts in her seat, but her grip on the steering wheel doesn't ease.

"Nothing," she mutters.

"Sure looks like something."

She gives me *the* look and swings her gaze back to the road, her expression impassive. I sink into my seat. *Fine.*

We spend the rest of the car ride in silence.

***

The next two weeks were uneventful, since Blaire and I avoided each other the best we could. For someone who doesn't have a full-time job—other than keeping an eye on me—she sure is busy. She gets more use out of Baxton's car than I do. She's usually out early in the morning, sometimes as early as 6:30, doing fuck knows what, but she always returns home before dinner to ensure I don't attempt to escape to some party or club. I don't know what gave her the idea that I can't dip into any of my vices during the day, but whatever prevents her from looking too closely.

I did manage to sneak out one time in the middle of the night to buy a bottle of gin, and I thought I'd hid it well too (in the garage behind some old boxes). But the next evening, when I returned from my evening walk, I found Blaire standing at the front porch greeting me with the bottle in hand. I watched, half shocked and half impressed, as she emptied the contents right in front of me with a vicious gleam in her eyes.

Fucking hell. She's good.

And I hate to admit that I enjoy her torturing me like this.

Blaire is a sexy woman and she knows it. She wears her confidence like a second skin, and she's got both the mind games and the sex appeal to go with it too. Every time she walks, there's a subtle sway to her hips that gets me fucked up. And *god*, I love staring at her tits. I don't do it often, but when she's not looking, my gaze instinctively gets pulled toward them. It's a good day when she wears a tank top. I fantasize about how I'd take my time licking her nipples, my tongue flicking over her sensitive buds and watching as she squirms from under me. Tits are the best part of a woman. They're god's forbidden fruit, and she's got 'em.

It's impossible to *not* want her physically.

What a shame . . . with her being so aloof with me.

Besides, my chances with her are more than slim. I heard she has a fuck-buddy whom she frequents. I overheard them talking on the phone the other day by accident and it's the first time I've seen her get a little flustered over someone. I think his name is Ben. It's not like me to care about who Blaire's fucking, because hell, she can do whatever or whoever she wants, but for some reason, it does grind my gears that it isn't me.

Tonight, I'm itching to get out and socialize with anyone other than Blaire. Baxton checks in on me once in a while, but my messages to him are sparse since I don't appreciate him putting me in this impossible predicament. The blood in my veins screams for alcohol, and my dick is begging for an easy lay. I need to chase the high again. I've been in this goddamn house for too long with only my right hand to keep me company. And the only woman in my periphery is hell-bent on keeping me locked up in here.

I stick my fork into the lasagna on the dining table and squeeze my eyes shut, forcing the sexual frustration away.

"I'm heading out," Blaire's voice drifts into the dining room. "I won't be back till late."

I peel my eyes open and find her rushing down the steps from above me in an all-black outfit. A ribbed top, distressed jeans, and the same pair of dirty Converse. She always has her hair down, but tonight is the first night that I've seen her wear it in a tight bun. I have to admit, she looks pretty like this. Don't get me wrong, she looks pretty all the time, but her hair up like this highlights the sharpness of her eyes and the natural curve of her jaw.

"What do you mean late? It's *already* late. It's past midnight." God, being on house arrest is making me lose my cool factor. The monochrome outfit is enough for me to keep poking the hornet's nest though. "Why are you dressed up like you're about to commit a crime?"

Her body freezes at the base of the steps.

"Don't say that," she mumbles, kneeling down to adjust her shoelaces. "I'm just heading out with a friend. I'll be back in a few hours. Don't wait up."

All right then.

"Also, one last thing." She stands up and walks in my direction at the dining area, then sticks her hand out to me. "Pass me your phone. I need to do something quick."

I bark out a laugh. "No offense, darlin', but I don't know you like that."

"Neither do I. Which is why this is important."

My eyebrows furrow, perplexed. I can usually read people very easily, but her mind is an impenetrable fortress.

With her hand still out, she cocks her head sideways. *Well?*

I sigh, digging through my pocket for my phone. "Let me guess: Baxton's orders?" I ask dryly, unlocking the phone with my ID and dropping the device into her palm.

"Not exactly." She taps away on the screen.

I peer over to get a better look and my face twists into a scowl. "Did you just download a *tracker* onto my phone?"

"Yes," Blaire confirms, switching to her phone to link our devices together via the app. "Because I know you, and the second I'm out of here you'll be in some club going way overboard, and next thing I know you'll be passed out in a dumpster and I'll have to help Baxton clean up your mess. *Again.* So I need to know that you'll be home by the time I come back."

"This is ridiculous," I mutter when she returns my phone back to me. "What if I just want to go somewhere and hang out?"

"I don't trust you enough to do that completely sober in the middle of the night," she says with a cold shrug. "Just . . . stay at home, okay? Put on a Netflix show or something. If you're craving a drink, there's leftover juice in the fridge."

"How considerate," I mutter. My gaze falls onto the app that's been left open on my phone. I wonder if I'm able to gauge her location like she's able to do mine, but when I scroll through the settings, I find out that she's set it to one-way only, which further deepens my annoyance. "If you get to track my phone, it's only fair I get to track yours."

Laughter spills out. "No."

"Why? Afraid I'll find out a dirty little secret of yours? News flash, everyone's got them. You're not that special."

"Aw, nice dig. But you're not getting my location." Blaire swipes her house keys off top of the shoe cabinet beside the door. "I'll see you when I get back," she says, her expression softening with guilt. For a second, she looks like she's about to apologize for putting me in this predicament, but instead, she purses her lips inward and adds, "Just . . . stay out of trouble, okay?"

I mutter an *I'll try* and she rolls her eyes before slipping out of the house.

The silence of her absence is immediately felt throughout the house. The night wraps around me and sinks into my bones, making me so queasy that I'm in no mood to finish the rest of my lasagna. I swipe the bowl from the table and chuck the leftovers into the trash. Then, I look around the living room, wondering what I should do for the night. Heading to bed when I'm not tired doesn't seem appealing. And if I don't do anything, I'm sure the constant ache in my chest reminding me that I'm weak and breakable will only increase.

A shiver compresses down my spine.

Yeah, no. Screw this.

A distraction is needed, ASAP.

My hip is against the kitchen sink when I pull up my phone again and rifle through my contact list to find the bartender I'd met two weeks ago. We've texted here and there, and I remember her saying that she was off tonight. When she answers my call, I make the offer.

"Hey, you. I'm having a house party tonight. You keen?" I tell her, making sure to add, "Oh, bring booze, and everyone you know."

FOURTEEN

Blaire

We enter through the back gate.

Portia gets out of the car first and gives me and our third accomplice, Whiskey, a large, beefy woman with black hair, the signal that we're clear. I lean forward and smack a quick kiss on Ben's cheek. He's our getaway driver and will stay with the car. He grabs my hand and squeezes it hard, like he's reassuring himself of my safety.

"Be careful, all right?" he whispers.

"Always."

Begrudgingly, he lets go of my hand and I slip out of the car.

The house we're planning to burgle is on a quiet street with very little traffic, about a house down from where Ben has parked. It's a Spanish-style home belonging to some B-lister; a sweet rig in Beverly Hills. It's also the perfect target since, as we learned from the next-door neighbor when pretending to be a delivery service with an important package, he's always out of town this time of year.

Portia is the first to step on to the property. After snapping the lock on the gate using a pair of bolt cutters, she gently pushes it open wide enough for me and Whiskey to pass through. Come to think of it, I don't think Portia ever told me how her and Whiskey are acquainted, and I doubt I'll ever find out. Whiskey seems to go out of her way to maintain distance and anonymity, given her real name is obviously not a brown liquor beverage.

It's fine. I'm not here to make friends either. I'm here to do what I agreed to do and leave

Do it for Eden, my heart beats the mantra until it fuses into my bloodstream. *Do it for the life you deserve.*

A surveillance camera attached to the right-hand corner of the Spanish-tiled roof captures our every move as we cross the lawn. We anticipated this, and keep our heads down, ski masks pulled tight over our faces. One of the four cameras is installed on the back side of the roof, overlooking the yard. There are two more at the front door that I know of, courtesy of my surveillance on early-morning jogs. It's easier to spy on houses, I realize, when you're pretending to be a curious neighbor interested in fascinating architecture.

What most people don't realize, and I learned this from another inmate while I was serving my time, is that surveillance cameras aren't actually designed to deter crime. They exist to provide evidence after the fact. It's easy to avoid any chance of being ID'd by the camera as long as you keep your face covered and work fast. In and out in eight minutes, Portia had stressed.

That included a two-minute cushion, in case anything went wrong.

We scurry across the lawn and reach the house.

"Alarm?" Portia hisses into the walkie-talkie.

No less than five seconds later, the walkie-talkie filters out a "clear" from Ben.

I steady my breath as Portia picks the back-door lock with a picker stuffed in her front pocket. After a couple of seconds, I hear a *click* as she opens the door without the alarm going off. A small sense of relief washes through me, but I remind myself not to have my guard down. The alarm system could reboot any time, so we're not in the clear just yet.

The house, I recognize, is as immense on the interior as it appears on the outside. Luxurious paintings adorn every wall. A single artwork here is probably worth millions. It's a shame they're too bulky for us to carry out of here. Even if we could somehow smuggle them to a gallery, art dealers are notoriously good detectives.

We've been instructed by Portia to take only what we can carry that won't leave a trail, things like small electronics, jewelry, and cash if we're lucky enough to find it. That rules out TVs, furniture, and safes. Everything else is fair game.

"All right," Portia says, her intense green eyes pinned on me and Whiskey. "Whiskey, you take this floor. You can also keep a lookout. If we've got heat on our tails, yell. I'm not beyond using this if I have to." She lifts her hoodie up above her waist to flash the gun tucked into the front pocket of her jeans.

"Portia, what the hell," I hiss. "You said we weren't bringing weapons."

"You said *you* weren't bringing a weapon. I decided not to discourage your stupidity," Portia hisses back. She faces Whiskey. "You know the drill. Anything you find, you dump in here." Her hand goes under her thick hoodie and pulls out two compressed nylon duffel bags. She unzips one of the bags and throws it on the floor, then turns to me, still clutching the other. "Let's head upstairs."

We take the steps two at a time and beeline straight to the master bedroom, into the shared his-and-hers walk-in closet. It's massive, overflowing with designer labels, red-bottomed shoes, and handbags with every designer logo you could think of. It's fitting for Hollywood royalty, or at least people wanting desperately to fit in with Hollywood royalty.

"Jackpot," Portia whispers, barely containing the excitement in her voice. She peels open the top drawer of a clear chest of drawers, illuminated by elegant, white LED lighting. She swipes a Patek Philippe watch, dangling it in front of her. "Look. This alone could pay for your lawyer's retainer."

I say nothing. Reveling in the theft is the absolute last thing on my mind. I'm here to do my job so I can get out of here as quickly as I can.

Portia smirks as she chucks the watch into the bag. I pull the rest of the drawers open and mindlessly scoop up the contents and dump them into the duffel bag. Necklaces, watches, rings—I pour them in like liquid gold. My chest is tight and bile rises up in my throat. I want to say I feel the dirtiest I've ever felt, but Portia certainly wouldn't be a sympathetic ear, and I frankly can't afford to indulge such a sentiment right now. Not when we only have a few minutes to finish the job and get out of here.

The duffel bag is just about stuffed to capacity when Portia's watch beeps in warning, signaling that it's time to get out of there. Right on cue, Ben buzzes through the walkie-talkie, telling us to pack up. I zip up the bag and haul it downstairs, where I find Whiskey heaving a half-full bag over her shoulder. Portia takes one look at it and purses her lips with dissatisfaction, probably wondering why her duffel isn't full to the brim like ours. We go back through the sliding door and Portia snatches the bolt cutter from the top of the gate before closing it behind her.

We throw the bags into the trunk and Portia jumps into the front seat while Whiskey and I slide into the back.

"All good?" Ben asks nervously, his hands planted firmly on the wheel.

"Yep. Let's haul ass."

Portia doesn't have to say it twice. Ben releases the hand brake and speeds out of the neighborhood, tires screeching against the road. The old car rattles, jerking us side to side as we weave through the residential back roads before sneaking onto the main road, merging seamlessly with the rest of the cars.

Portia peels off her mask, wiping the sweat glistening on her forehead with the back of her hand, and lets out a howl of excitement, clearly drunk off the high. Whiskey joins her, banging her fists against the window screaming, "Yeah! YEAH!!" Meanwhile, my body slumps against the back seat, a combination of shame and exhaustion overcoming me.

"What did I tell you, Blaire?" Portia exclaims as she swivels her head back to face me, a giddy grin curving her lips. "So easy even your brother could do it."

At the mention of my brother, I release an unsteady breath, trying to calm my ragged nerves.

"Did y'all get anything good?" Ben asks, eyeing me in the rearview to see how I'm handling all this.

Portia echoes with a loud cackle. "Blaire, show him our loot."

Wordlessly, I drag the duffel bag over the rear seat and unzip the top. Ben turns his head to the right and catches a glimpse of the glinting jewelry. "Damn, guys. A hell of a step up from the last time."

"Hell yeah, it is," Whiskey affirms in her gruff tone, patting Portia on the shoulder. "We'll hit the pawn shop first thing tomorrow."

I watch Ben smile, unable to hide his excitement as he drives. Portia turns the volume on the radio up and stretches her legs and arms over her seat, basking in her success. Whiskey takes the duffel bag from my lap and combs through the contents, smug and satisfied.

And despite their pleased looks, all I feel is guilt and discontent.

***

Portia insisted on getting dropped off first so we could stash the loot at her place, so it's about half past one when Ben offers to drive me back home. As we near Melrose, I insist on getting dropped off a couple of streets away from Baxton's. Ben wanted to drive me to the door, but I told him that I needed the walk. He reluctantly obliged after I told him I'll text him when I made it home.

Honestly, I just didn't want Jax to see him, or see me, for that matter, and start firing off questions, and I simply don't trust myself not to break down sobbing at the first sign of his interrogation. I wouldn't put it past him to get all judgmental with me about it.

Oh god.

I actually *care* about what Jax thinks of me.

Rock bottom, meet Blaire.

I feel nauseous. There's a stabbing, burning need for oxygen in my lungs that is as sharp as a thousand needles piercing my chest. My body is slick with sweat that rapidly becomes cold on my skin with the night chill. I so desperately want to roll over and curl into a ball, but I can't, especially not here in the middle of a neighborhood wearing all black, teary-eyed, my hair a disheveled mess.

The night air steeps me in its cool quiet, and I suck in a deep, crisp breath.

If my dad was looking down on me now, seeing what my life has become, he would be shaking his head in disappointment. He always had big goals for me that I wanted to achieve. I remember being fourteen when I told him that I wanted to be a chef. I told him that the lunch he was eating at Baxton's, prepared by his private chef, was mediocre at best and lacking in nutritional value. The next morning, I woke up early and prepared a chicken, pear, spinach, and celery sandwich for his lunch and snuck it into his bag. Later, I received an alert over the intercom school that I had an urgent call from my father. Turns out, dad had loved the sandwich so much that he couldn't wait until after school to tell me. After that, I made all his lunches for the next four years. I had big plans to go to culinary school, run my own kitchen, and maybe even open a restaurant.

Resignation and hopelessness intertwined themselves with my soul.

Perhaps I don't deserve clinging on to those dreams. If the universe had a finite number of good things to bestow on to people, there's no way I would make the cut. Because if my moral code could bend as easily as it did tonight, then what kind of person does that make me?

There's no coming back from what I did tonight. Absolutely none. I've made my choice, to not take the higher road, and I'll have to live with the guilt for the rest of my life.

My hand reaches up to wipe the tears skittering down my cheeks. I feel so lost in my own thoughts that I almost walk head-on into oncoming traffic. I'm jolted out of my trance when I feel the rush of the cars whizzing past me. The wind catches my hair, spilling it all over my face and catching on my mouth and my lashes. My hand desperately pushes most of the strands away and tucks them behind one ear.

My vision clears and the first thing I spot is a police car parked a couple of yards away from me. I squint and see that there's no one in there. My body relaxes. Okay, at least nobody saw me. But there's no chance it's an abandoned car. The cop could be around, patrolling the neighborhood—

"Hey! You there," The officer calls out to me from behind.

Fuck.

I freeze, my mind kicking into gear.

Should I greet him? Pretend I'm just walking around? I do live here.

All I need to do is act cool.

Cool cool cool cool.

But . . . what if he senses something is off and he IDs me? A girl wandering around alone at one o'clock in the morning, not far from the site of a burglary that he may or may not already have received an alert about? I'll be behind bars before they even prove my guilt.

Yeah, not so cool.

"Lady?" The officer's tone grows suspicious and sharp. "Turn around."

Fear lodges itself in my throat. Indecision runs laps in my mind.

What do I do? What *do I do*?

Fuck! Fuck! Fuck!

"I said *turn around*!" the officer yells.

The aggression in his voice is enough to jerk me forward..

My feet launch me into a sprint toward the houses, and I don't look back.

FIFTEEN

Jax

"Two martinis, coming right up!" Abby yells drunkenly. She squints to find the bottle of gin amongst the sea of liquor bottles sitting on the marble kitchen counter and when she does find it, she squawks out an "Ah!" and pours it into the cocktail shaker.

"You're off the clock, you know that?" I coo, coming up behind her and landing a strong arm around her waist. I'm fucking hammered from being fed too many shots by women I don't know, so I sway a little as her back makes impact against my chest, and I lean into it, pretending I'm just grooving to the Drake song that's blasting through the TV speakers.

"But I like making drinks," Abby says, messing my hair up with a hand before giving the cocktail shaker a tough shake. "Do you want anything?"

"A gin and tonic, with a splash of you. And make it strong,"

I whisper, grazing my nose against the curve of her neck. She smells nice, a fresh body-wash scent coming through, but Blaire smells like lavender and pinewood, and I prefer that scent.

Abby laughs seductively, breaking me from my thoughts. "Be careful what you wish for." She turns around to grab my face with both hands and molds her lips over mine. *Well, okay.* Our tongues curl over each other greedily, and with us being so out of it, and I'm sure that people watching us.

"Leave some for us, Jax!" A blonde shoots from across the room. She has an arm over another girl's shoulder, both of them are in their bikini tops and shorts, grinding to the steady rhythm of the music. Their bodies are touching, breasts pressed up against each other, and they're both looking over at me, giving me a sly wink.

Fuck, I love women.

When I gave Abby a free pass to invite whoever she wanted to invite, I didn't expect to host a party for nearly two dozen people. Apparently, Abby's in her third year of college in UCLA and president of the contemporary dance club, which explains the hordes of mostly hot, eager-to-connect juniors. Most of them are women, with the exception of a couple of guys. I played beer pong with a few dudes on the patio table outside, and now they're cannonballing into the pool, and dragging some of the girls in with them.

I was in the mood to entertain myself in other ways, so I made an effort all night to interact with the rest of the guests. So far, I've already made out with two of the women, one of which has already tried to lure me into my bedroom.

This party has quenched my thirst for female

companionship, but I must admit I feel guilty for indulging the way I do. Maybe it's because I'm going behind Blaire's back to do it. While I've technically found a loophole in her logic of me staying at home, I don't feel great about committing such debauchery under the roof we share.

Abby sighs against my mouth, reeling my attention back to her. A hand drifts down my chest and her index finger traces the outline of my cock, which now stands semi-erect. I groan because there's nothing more I really want right now than to get inside this woman, but the thought of Blaire coming home and finding my drunk ass ramming sloppily into some woman has me second-guessing the decision.

I hate that despite Blaire being not physically present, she still plagues me like a stubborn scar. I see her shaking her head in disappointment as she watches a few girls trying to climb onto our rooftop. I see her lounging by the sofa with a rum and Coke, irritated by the loud volume of the music. I see her seething from outside through the kitchen window as I shove my tongue inside Abby's mouth. Damn, even as a manifestation of my subconscious, she still finds a way to be disappointed in me. I squint again, prompting the last ultra-realistic vision of her to go away. And yet, Blaire is still by the window.

Wait, what?

I'm not dreaming.

There's a sense of urgency in her expression as Blaire mouths for me to come outside. *Now.* She exclaims with urgency.

My mouth peels apart from Abby, prompting a confused look from her.

"What's wrong?" she asks.

"I'll be right back," I say to her rather absentmindedly.

I slip through the kitchen door and step onto the grass. Sure enough, Blaire is crouched against the wall in her all-black garb. She's breathing hard like she's just competed in a 100-meter sprint and her jet-black hair is in a state of disarray. What catches me off guard is the terror in her eyes, an emotion I thought she was incapable of feeling.

"Look, I'm not even going to ask why you have invited a harem over to our house," Blaire mutters. "And I'll explain everything later. But just . . . cover for me, okay?"

"Cover for you? What—?"

"Shit!" Blaire sinks lower against the wall while looking over my shoulder, tucking her head into her hands. I follow her gaze to find a cop in uniform trudging toward the front door of our house. He's short, burly, and from the looks of it, doesn't appear to be on a casual patrol around the neighborhood.

I glare at Blaire. *What did you do?*

She avoids my gaze. The terror tensing her entire body is enough for me to take this seriously.

Swearing under my breath, I straighten up and slip back inside through the kitchen, then jog toward the front door. The doorbell buzzes twice right as I swing the door open, plastering the friendliest grin I can muster.

"Good evening, sir. How can I help you?" I say smoothly, holding the door open with an arm. The cop dips his head at me in greeting, but his expression remains serious. "Is the music too loud? I'll tell my friends to keep it down."

"It's not that," he clarifies. "I'd like to ask you a few questions about a young woman. She's about five foot six, possibly in her early twenties, and has brown or black hair. And she's wearing an all-black outfit. Has she come around here recently?"

"Did you get a look at her face?"

"No."

I'm tempted to breathe a sigh of relief. At least they aren't aware of how Blaire's face looks, which makes her more difficult to track.

"Mmmm." I frown. "It's gonna be hard for me to help you there."

He cocks a wary brow. "You sure you haven't seen her? She disappeared as soon as I neared your house."

"I don't know what to tell you, Officer." I shrug, crossing a leg over the other as I lean against the door casually. "There are a lot of girls that come in and out of here, as you can see. It's hard to keep track."

Right on cue, an excited squeal coming from one of Abby's friends pierces through our conversation.

The cop cranes his neck in an attempt to see past my bulky figure blocking his view of the occupants inside the house. "You don't mind if I come in and ask your friends, do you?" He takes a challenging step toward me.

I should tell him no, but it would only serve to heighten his suspicions. Better to play along and hope nobody saw Blaire enter through the house.

"Go ahead." I swing the door back to allow the cop to walk through.

The cop adjusts the hat sitting on his head and with his index finger curled over his belt loop, he stops in the middle of the living room and promptly yells, "All right, quiet down now!"

Seconds later, the music lowers in volume. The few girls mingling about in the living room, including Abby, immediately stop what they're doing. It takes a few seconds for the rest of the girls outside to realize what the commotion is all about. They quickly put on their clothes and pile into the space, droplets of water smacking against the marble floor.

"Good evening," he says in greeting, scanning each and every single one of their faces. "I have reason to believe that there is a criminal on the loose around this neighborhood, and I need your cooperation. Has anyone in here seen a young woman pass through here around five to ten minutes ago? Brunette, early twenties, five foot six?"

Someone laughs and makes a face at the woman next to her, as if saying *is he serious?*

"You're gonna have to be a little more specific than that," another woman says, gesturing to the eight or so brunette girls standing around in the living room.

"She was wearing an all-black outfit. Just recently came around here."

There are a lot of murmurings among the women, but most of them shake their head no.

"Looks like you got your answer there, Officer," I say, leaning against the wall with my arms folded around my chest.

Please be satisfied enough to leave. Please—

The cop is aggrieved with the response. Determined, he glances over his shoulder and says to me, "Mind if I look around?"

Instead of swallowing the huge lump in my throat, I try to relax my shoulders.

"Go ahead."

Blaire better be listening in on what's happening and smart enough to secure a good hiding spot right now.

With his hands behind his back, the cop slowly makes his way around the living room, then walks outside to the outdoor pool area through the double doors. The room blankets with an uncomfortable tension. Meanwhile, my heart is pounding so fucking hard that it rattles my brain. I don't want to avert my gaze to the kitchen door, because then I'll give it away. So I remain as passive as I can, clicking my tongue at the roof of my mouth in boredom as I pretend to slip into the role of a playboy desperate to resume his pleasure-seeking activities, which isn't that far from the truth.

The cop scans the perimeter of the backyard, eyes lingering on the bikini top strewn over one of the lounge chairs before clearing his throat and walking toward the side of the lawn with the shrubs where the kitchen door leads to. He stops just a few feet shy of the door, peering through the darkness. His gaze lingers for a moment.

Panic clutches my chest hard.

There's a beat that seems to stretch on for hours, and then he turns around and walks back inside, disappointed.

I don't realize I'm holding my breath until it comes out of me in a huge exhale.

The cop takes his hat and wedges it in between his arm and the side of his body. He gives me a stern but apologetic look. "Sorry for halting your evening. Have a good night."

"You too, Officer."

I walk him down the steps and watch soundlessly as he strolls onto the main pathway. When he reaches the end of the road, I hear his walkie-talkie buzz with a low male voice. "We need backup for a possible code 4-5-9 down at 240 S Wetherly Drive. Anyone to respond?"

"Those damn house burglaries," the cops mutter under his breath. He responds something unintelligible back into the walkie-talkie, makes a hard right and disappears.

I suck in a shocked breath. Wetherly Drive isn't too far from here. A ten-minute drive maybe . . .

Suddenly, the puzzle pieces of what Blaire's been up to snap into place.

The cool mask that I'd once worn crumbles away, leaving a simmering, quiet rage. Once I'm certain the cop is gone, I head back into the house.

"All right. Party's over. Everybody out!" I announce.

Groans and multiple exclamations of "are you serious?" punch into the air. I shrug, too worked up to care about their feelings. They begrudgingly collect their things and drag themselves through the front door.

"Buh-bye," I say flatly, waving the women along to get the lot of them to leave faster. "Leave. Scram."

"What about me?" Abby asks when she approaches the door, caressing a hand along my arm. "You're gonna kick me out too?"

"I'll call you," is all I say.

She tries to go in for a goodbye kiss but I turn my head so her lips meet my cheek instead. The rejection registers on her face and she reels back from me, dejected. I watch soundlessly as she jogs toward her friends and leaves in one of their cars.

My anger reverberates throughout the house as I slam the door shut. Seconds later, the kitchen door opens and Blaire pokes her head through, and slips back into the house. Relief trickles through her as her muscles cording her body relax. Little does she know that the battle is far from over.

I lean an arm over the kitchen pillar, my gaze narrowed at her.

"You robbed a house tonight?" I accuse, my voice scarily calm.

As I look at her, I'm desperate for my theory to be proven wrong. For her to tell me that I haven't been living with a goddamned *criminal* for the past week. But instead of being met with confusion, I'm met with guilt, laid bare across her features.

"It's complicated," Blaire whispers.

"Complicated?" I huff. "What's so complicated about my question? You either committed a crime or you didn't, Blaire."

"Can we talk about this another time?" she pleads.

I grit my teeth. The nerve of this girl to dismiss me when I just lied to a fucking cop for her.

"No. We're talking about this *now*. I don't give a fuck about your rules anymore. You owe me the truth," I snap, intercepting her path toward the stairs. Her hands drop to her sides, her jaw tightening with annoyance. "Did you or did you not come back from burglarizing a *house*, Blaire?"

Her shoulders stiffen from the accusation. I can almost see the gears in her head kick into motion as she has an internal debate about whether or not she should answer me. Eventually, she sighs, rubbing a thumb over her bottom lip like she's not going to like the taste of candor that's about to come out of her.

"I did," she confesses.

Despite her guilt being so transparent, her admittance still knocks the wind out of my chest.

"So you're a thief. And a fucking terrible one at that," I mutter, looking her up and down. "And something tells me this isn't your first run-in with the law."

It's starting to make sense now, just why she's so guarded about her life, why she doesn't want my nose up in her business. Although, other things don't add up. If she's been doing this for a while now, why is she so thrifty with what she spends her money on? You'd think that she would splurge on food and clothes more than what she typically does. I swear the soles of her Converse are about to tear off any second now. But, more importantly, I still don't understand how Baxton has managed to get himself involved with a criminal. Unless . . .

"Baxton doesn't know, does he?" The question hisses out from between my teeth.

Shamefully, Blaire shakes her head no.

I huff out a laugh. "Okay. Wow." My hand rubs over my mouth. "You have quite the nerve to do something like this under his roof when the only reason you're staying here is because of his kindness."

"It's not what you think," Blaire warns carefully, but the desperation undercutting her tone is clear. "I didn't mean to come off as betraying his kindness in any way. Like, I said it's more complicated than that."

"Well, maybe he should be the judge of that." I jerk my phonephone out to dial Baxton's number. Blaire's eyes bulge out of their sockets and she lunges forward to clamp a hand around my wrist.

"Wait, no please," Blaire begs. "He can't find out."

I cut her a glare. "It's funny how you think that when you've just admitted to a felony to his *son*."

"Please don't tell him," she chokes up. Her hands clasp together begging me for silence. "*Please*, Jax."

"I just did you a favor by not ratting you out to that cop," I say with a huff. "Now you want more favors from me?"

"Baxton can't know. Nobody can. I just . . ." She pinches her mouth with her hand and inhales sharply, her shoulders sagging. When her gaze meets mine again, there is a pained look on her face. "Look . . . I've been to jail before, all right?"

"Good for you. At least that'll make the transition easier when you *go back*," I snap.

"Just listen to me," Blaire appeases. But it's difficult to even look at her. A hand whips over my face, taking a minute to process this. What the hell was I thinking—sticking up for this woman? I barely even know her. And now, I've become an *accomplice* to her crimes.

This is ridiculous. Anger claws up my body, fiery and scorching hot. Anger at myself for allowing myself to get wrapped up in her business.

"*Please.*" Her voice comes out of her as a desperate, strangled choke. "Hear me out."

"I don't know if I want to hear you justify *robbing* someone, Blaire!" The words come out sharp and thick with anger. And you can't expect me to feel sorry for your current predicament when you've clearly been in it before."

"It is *because* of my past predicament that I'm here!" Blaire cries out. Every muscle in my jawline goes taut. Her body is trembling, like she's on the verge of tears. She turns away from me, blowing out a breath to collect herself. She swallows her pride and looks back at me, this time, a miserable expression carved into her face. "You're right. I cannot explain away

PERFECT RUIN

what I did. There is nothing I can say that will ever justify it because I know what I did was truly terrible. I *feel* terrible. But I don't know what else to do about it. And I don't expect you to understand because you've probably never been in a position like mine before. I've done all I possibly can to leave my mistakes in the past, but that label sticks with you for life. And the irony of it all is that I'm trying to build something better here." There's sadness in her gaze, which tugs at my heart. "I was going to use the money from the robbery to expunge my criminal record. So I can get an actual job and fight for custody of my brother before his stepmom can successfully cut me out of his life. I just . . . I just want my old life back."

I open my mouth, then close it, too stunned to speak. I had my suspicions that she struggled with money, but I had no clue just how bad her financial situation was, and how her criminal record was affecting every aspect of it.

Still, there are so many questions circling in my mind. What did she do the first time that got her in this mess? Was the crime that she was involved in the same crime she's fallen into again? Why aren't her parents in the picture? Why isn't her *brother*?

Curiosity swells in my chest, but I force it back inward, not wanting to bombard her with questions about her life story. It doesn't matter anyway, at least not for now.

Blaire straightens herself up, the frown still apparent in her voice. Her shoulders loosen after being stiff as a board, and she rounds them back, pulling her chest forward. She stares at me head-on. "So, you can judge me all you want for what I did. Hell, get in line. I don't feel good about it. If I could choose a different path, I would. But I'm trying to do something meaningful with the scraps I was given. I don't get the privilege to fuck up my own life while running away from whatever problems I have. So if you could exercise a little less judgment and a little more empathy to what people outside your little bubble go through, that would be really nice"

Her words hit me straight in the gut.

She's right, I will never understand what she's been through. And I do believe her when she says she feels like this is her last resort. For those reasons alone, all I want to do is pull her into my arms and hug her, because the pain pouring out of her is too much to bear, even for me.

"Blaire . . ." I start off, feeling my shoulders sag from sympathy.

Blaire shakes her head, her teeth clenched so hard it threatens to break her jaw. It's almost like she's trying hard to keep the tears at bay.

"I'm heading to bed," she mumbles. "Just, please don't tell Baxton. He's one of the only people who makes me feel like my life is actually worth living. I'll be gutted if he ever finds out what I've chosen to do with it."

Defeated, she gently nudges me out of the way and ascends the stairs to her room.

SIXTEEN

Blaire

When I wake up the next morning, there's a low thrumming in my head as everything that happened last night slowly seeps back into my mind.

Oh *god*. Jax knows. He knows everything.

A wave of humiliation crashes through me and I groan loudly. I wasn't supposed to get him involved. And now . . . everything's just a big, complicated mess.

I peel away the blanket and drop my feet down to the floor. My legs tremble from the nerves and my stomach churns with acid. Would Jax really turn me in? After how terribly our conversation went last night, I won't be surprised if a SWAT team is waiting outside my room.

Braving a steady breath, I drag my ass out of the bed and peer out the doorway to my room. I can see Jax's door is left ajar. I push it gently with my finger, the door creaking when I peer in. He's not in his room. My nerves are on fire as I trickle down the steps on my tippy toes.

My heart buoys when I swerve toward the kitchen, only to find Jax hunched over the stove in nothing but his joggers. The smell of sizzling bacon fuses into the air. Tension courses through my body, turning my shoulders to stone and my spine to iron. He doesn't acknowledge me, instead choosing to keep humming and pushing the bacon around with his spatula. I decide it's useless to keep standing awkwardly in the corner, so I shuffle toward the kitchen.

I'm unable to stop myself from peeking over at him. His blond hair is unkempt and messy; it suits him. His body is massively sleek, with powerful muscles spanning across his shoulders, chest, and back. A fighter's body. I wonder if it's all natural or if he's on steroids. Based on what I already know about Jax, he'd probably see steroids as an easy way out. Jax is proud about himself, but there is usually merit to the things he boasts about.

Regardless, I'd be lying if I said checking out his physique wasn't making me feel less nauseous about what he's going to say to me today.

Jax clears his throat, catching me staring at him.

I drop my gaze immediately. The glass that I've been filling up is overflowing with water. My neck heats up and I switch off the tap.

Jax simply jerks his head in the direction of the refrigerator. "There's milk in the fridge if you want."

I empty out the glass and pour myself milk instead, then slide into a seat around the dining table while he finishes cooking. It's a couple minutes later when he shuts the stove off and divides the grilled bacon between two plates. He picks the plates up and heads over to where I'm sitting.

"Here," Jax mutters, shoving a plate of scrambled eggs, bacon, and French toast toward me before taking a seat. "Eat."

I take the plate eagerly. "Thanks," I mumble, cutting myself a small piece of French toast and forking it into my mouth. I chew a couple of times before swallowing and I wipe my mouth with the back of my hand, remarking, "Wow, this is bad."

Jax glares at me. "Didn't think you knew what good food tastes like. All you ever have is instant noodles."

"It's an incredibly versatile dish if you have the right ingredients," I say with a knowing smile. Catching myself slipping, I drop my mouth into a neutral line, almost forgetting the giant elephant in the room here.

My teeth scrape against my fork when another bite of the bacon enters my mouth. Jax sets his plate to the side and purses his lips inward, all while weaving his fingers together in front of him.

"I'm not going to tell on you," Jax whispers, meeting my gaze. "To the police or to Baxton."

I pause mid-chew.

"Really?"

"Yeah . . ." his voice trails off and his hand goes up to scratch his chin. "I had the whole night to think about what I wanted to do. And as much as it would probably benefit me to turn you in, I'd rather not do it. Not because I have much of a moral code or anything. It's really because . . . I know a thing or two about being backed into a corner and needing to do everything you can to survive, even if it means turning your back on what you believe in," he mumbles cryptically.

I blink in confusion, wondering what he's been through. Granted, his life back in Boston is unfamiliar to me, but I always assumed it was a rather easy one, with the generous child support payments Jax's family had received. Perhaps I was wrong about him. About everything.

"So, does that help?" Jax weaves his fingers together in front of him.

I nod willingly. "Thank you. I really appreciate it."

"How much do you need?" He asks. "To expunge your record and start the custody battle?"

I shift uncomfortably in my seat. "Thirty grand to start."

He nods for a moment, taking the information in.

"And after . . . last night, do you think you have that money?"

I nod again.

"So, what would you like from me, then?" He eyes me expectantly.

"I don't want anything from you."

"Except for my silence."

"I guess . . . yeah."

"Okay, then," Jax says, laying an arm over the back of his seat as he angles himself better in my direction. "Like I said, I ain't gonna pretend like I'm some righteous person. So, calling you out yesterday for what you did was hypocritical of me." A muscle pulses his jaw in discomfort and he uncrosses his legs, only to cross them over with the other leg this time. "I'm sorry for judging you as harshly as I did last night. It wasn't fair."

I suck in a breath. Jax doesn't look like the kind of guy who apologizes easily, so this must be new to him. I'm glad I get to be on the receiving end of this rare moment.

"Thank you," I breathe. "You were justified in your opinions, but thank you."

He nods his head, staring down at me with a somewhat conflicted expression, like even he's not sure what to make of his own opinions on me. A mixture of disdain and sympathy, probably, which doesn't exactly go hand in hand. I don't like being pitied, but if that means I get to stay away from prison, then I hope the feeling stays rooted in his mind. A part of me wonders if that's the only emotion that's driving him to apologize, or if there's something more.

"One more thing," Jax adds, lifting an index finger up. "But before I lay this whole matter to rest, I'm gonna need something from you."

"Okay."

"I'm gonna need your phone." He holds his palm up toward me expectantly.

My automated response is to tell him no, that he's not allowed in my business, but I relent, feeling like I owe him this for the huge favor he's doing for me. "You're putting a tracker on my phone, aren't you?"

"Yes. But not because I want to even out the playing field between us." Jax says, holding out my phone toward me to unlock my face ID, and proceeds to link our phones together. "Okay, maybe it's a little bit of that. But more importantly, if you're going to keep doing what you're doing, I need to know that you're doing it safely."

I hold in my surprise. Jax cares about my safety? I was under the assumption that he would be much happier if I got run over by a bus.

"I'd like us to start over, Blaire. Really," Jax says when he hands my phone back to me. "You don't have to like me. Hell, you're not on my favorites list either. But I think it'll make life more bearable if we try to be civil with one another. I don't know about you, but I actually want to enjoy my summer."

"That's fair." My mouth twitches into a thin smile. "The only reason why I was so harsh on you was because I didn't want you to see that side of me."

"Well, you've already seen more sides of me than anyone has ever seen in their time knowing me, so . . . I think we're okay."

For some reason, I like that I'm the only one who gets to see those facets of him. But I'm not the only one he has to answer to. My smile wanes.

"You know I still have to keep you accountable, right? Baxton still wants updates about your progress, and I still have an obligation to him. So it'll be a lot easier if you don't make my life hell by dodging all the help he wants you to get."

Jax purses his lips inward and nods tightly.

"Okay."

"Okay?" It's weird to hear him be so agreeable with me.

"Yeah . . ." He draws the word out, like he despises admitting it out loud. "I suppose you're right about me self-sabotaging. And that there might be better ways to deal with my issues. You said yesterday I'm in my own bubble. I think . . . . I'm ready to step out of it."

"Really?" I whisper. "You're not saying that because you feel trapped and desperate, are you?"

"It may have started out like that, but you have to admit, those things do help as motivators to, you know, 'do the right thing.'" She air quotes dramatically.

"You know that means no more antics. And no more loopholes."

A faint smile crosses Jax's lips. "I know."

I want to believe what he's saying is real. That he really is ready to confront his issues head-on. I just hope putting my trust in him doesn't blow up in my face.

I stick my hand out, my mouth quivering into a faint smile. "Truce."

"Truce." Jax slides his hand over mine.

His skin is rough and callous, and when his thumb brushes ever so slightly against the inside of my palm, a foreign feeling spreads over my arm. I look up to find him staring at our locked hands, an unreadable expression slathered across his face.

Jax avoids my gaze, removing his hand from mine and dragging his breakfast plate back in front of him.

"By the way," I start off as I watch him eat. It's the only thing I can do since I'm done with my food. "You know you can actually leave the house, right? I mean, I'll still have to come with you, but if you want to do something other than therapy and physio appointments, I'm not stopping you."

"Good to know. But for now, I'm alright being a homebody. Other than the occasional jog, I don't have much else going on for me.""

"Really? I find that hard to believe. Didn't you use to do MMA?"

Every muscle in his jawline goes taut.

"I did." The way he squeezes out the syllables denotes a sore topic.

"Maybe . . . you can ease back into the sport," I suggest.

His head gives a tough shake. "No. That part of my life is over. Besides . . ." He gestures to himself. "Need I remind you that I can barely breathe, much less fight?"

"But you can have sex just fine?" I lift a wary brow. I doubt he was on his best behavior last night during the party, if him locking lips passionately with a woman in the kitchen was any indication.

"I haven't slept with anyone since I left the hospital," Jax remarks.

"Wow. Must be a record for you."

"You'd be surprised to know that I actually have self-restraint, darlin'." Jax scoops our empty plates and stands up from his chair. But not before his heated gaze scrolls up and down my body. "More than you know."

I sink back into my chair, heat creeping up my skin.

SEVENTEEN

Jax

A few days later, Blaire has taken me to see the therapist again.

With its clinically plain white walls and tall, leafy plants and their "It's okay to be not okay" posters, the only feeling I get here is tense and unwelcoming. It's also impossible to avoid the female receptionist watching me like a hawk today, ensuring that I don't skip out on my session this time.

"You promise you'll cooperate," Blaire hisses when she notices the deep frown on my face as my eyes scan the room.

The scent of her lingers in my nostrils as she's near me. She smells like rose and geranium, like she's been out in the garden again. Yesterday, I watched her nurture the baby tomato and basil plants she's started alongside the already existing flowers. I spotted a few familiar flowers—those damned pink ones were the only things I stared at while I was still in the hospital. It amazes me how even then, before she really knew me, she wanted to show that she cared.

Goddamn her and her annoyingly big heart.

"Jax?" Blaire shoots me an expectant look.

"What?" I say, trying to remember what she just said to me. "I *am* cooperating. I came here willingly."

"Really? Because your eyes are glued to the exit."

Instead, I shift uncomfortably in my seat. "I wanna be here, Blaire. That doesn't mean I have to *like* it."

"It can't be any different than the last time. Unless . . ." She adds with a knowing look. "You have something to admit to me about your previous session?"

A look of confusion masks over my face. The last time I was here . . . *oh.* Blaire's words drip through my mind with slow, chilling realization. Of course she knows I skipped out. Why am I not surprised?

"How?" I whisper.

"I knew as soon as I got back home and Baxton made me call the office to double-check since they didn't fax him the bill for the session," she explains to me, a coy smile on her face. "Why do you think I put the tracker on you?"

"Because you're just that obsessed with me?"

Blaire's gaze bores into mine. "It's because you're untrustworthy."

"And yet, I'm here. I kept my word." My eyes narrow at her. "Besides, if we're talking about lack of trust, you might wanna take a look in the mirror, thief."

Blaire's smile wanes.

"Fair enough," she admits, almost unwillingly. "But I still keep my word. Maybe you should consider doing that too. I'm gonna take a wild guess and say that it might even be the first time you'll prove yourself reliable."

She lets me sit with that for a moment. A muscle twitches in my jaw as I clench it.

The longer the words marinate in the back of my brain, the more I begin to consider that she might be right about me.

There has never been a time in my life when I haven't turned my back the moment things got difficult. In the MMA cage, I could fight till it was my last breath, but outside of it, if I couldn't crack the problem, I'd deem it unsalvageable.MMA had always been my priority and so naturally, everything else came second to it. Even my relationships. That was what happened with Sienna, then Beth, and I allowed both my relationships to perish in the worst way imaginable. I was selfish then, and I continue to be selfish now. I rarely consider anyone's feelings but my own. So, what does that make me if the only thing I stand for is myself?

I promised Blaire that I was going to try to rise above this. I promised *myself*. Put all my effort into recovery, for *real*. I didn't know if I truly meant what I said at the time, but now . . .

Maybe I do want it to mean something.

"Jax Deneris," the receptionist calls out. "Dr. Fisher is ready for you."

Fuck.

"Well, look at that," Blaire says, rising out of her seat. She tugs on my arm and guides me toward Dr. Fisher with a hand on my back. "Come on, you can do it. I believe in you."

My gaze returns to her. Her usual smug expression is replaced by a sincerity that I've only seen her wear when she confessed to the burglary. Blaire isn't lying for the sake of getting me into a therapist's office.

She genuinely believes in me to get better.

It would be easier if she didn't, because then I wouldn't have to feel guilty about possibly letting her down.

The biggest fight of your life has just arrived. No more self-destructive thoughts. Just discipline and drive.

The therapist greets me at the door. "Hi, I'm Dr. Fisher." With a hand over her clipboard, balancing the end of it on the side of her hip, she adds, "Should I call for backup in case you plan on fleeing our session again?"

"I'll be on my best behavior today. Scout's honor."

Dr. Fisher turns to Blaire for confirmation.

Blaire smiles. "He's willing to give it a try."

Dr. Fisher folds her lips inward. "Then let's get started."

Blaire bids us goodbye and returns to her seat out in the lobby. With that, Dr. Fisher closes the door behind us. I dump my ass onto the chair adjacent to Dr. Fisher. The clipboard now balances delicately on one of her thighs.

"So, your friend Blaire briefed me on what you've been going through, but I'd like to hear it from your perspective," she starts off.

"All right," I say, resting my elbows on my thighs, my hands linking together nervously. "My name is Jax, and I'm originally from Boston. I came to LA because I wanted a fresh start."

"From . . .?" she inquires.

I ease back into the chair a little bit. "I don't think I'm ready to talk about why I needed one so badly but . . . what I do realize now is that I've been dealing with things the wrong way."

"Well, the first step to recovery is acknowledging the problem, so that's a good start," Dr. Fisher says, scribbling on her clipboard. "We don't have to talk about what you're not ready to talk about. Just tell me what you feel comfortable with. We'll discuss how you feel about it, and how we can help you move forward. But with that said, it's not always going to be this easy. You've got a long road ahead. But just know that you'll come out of this so much better than you were before. You may not know this, but you've got quite a few people rooting for you."

"Thanks, Doc," I whisper, unable to stop the smile from climbing up my lips. "I think . . . I'm rooting for myself too."

I feel it in my bones that I'm telling the truth.

***

"See? That wasn't so hard, wasn't it?" Blaire prompts, skipping backward, facing me as we both make our way back to the car. The evening sun casts harsh shadows of us on the ground. There's barely any vehicles left in the parking lot since I had the last appointment of the day.

"It was awful," I groan, keeping my hands shoved in my pockets. "But . . . not the worst thing I've ever done."

"Good." She grins, pleased. It inspires a warm feeling in my chest that I get to be the one to put that smile on her face. We reach our car and she wrenches the driver's seat open. "Let's go home, then. I'm starving."

"We're out of groceries," I point out. "Also, I'm sick of eating at home."

"Where do you wanna go, then?"

I take a moment to think about it. "How about I take *you* somewhere for a change?" I suggest. "What are you craving?"

She takes a long pause to answer, like it's been a while since she's been asked that question.

"Tacos," she says in the end.

"Tacos? Okay." The first thing I ate when I landed in LA was Mexican food. Tacos are one of my favorite things to eat. "I think I know a good spot. Let's go."

Thirty minutes later, we end up at a taco truck on Vine Street. We get fish tacos and a chicken burrito to share. All the tables propped by the side of the truck were occupied by dinner-goers, so I drive us up to Griffith Observatory, a place I like to visit sometimes for evening hikes, back before I could cover four miles in thirty minutes without setting my lungs on fire. Thank god we have a car at our disposal.

By the time we make it to the top, the sky has turned to an inky blue, with a silvery crescent moon surrounded by a softly glittering blanket of stars keeping it company. Blaire and I both begin scarfing down our food and trying not to make a mess of the vehicle. I turn up the radio and flip through the stations until AC/DC drifts through the car at a steady volume. I roll down the windows to allow the wind to sneak in and cool our faces.

Right in front of us is the most gorgeous view of LA, with mansions perched on rolling hills and long, wide, straight roads stretching out toward the wall of skyscrapers in the far distance. You can feel the energy pulsing and shuddering through the streets.

"This is surprisingly good," Blaire marvels as she takes a huge bite of the burrito. She hands me my half of it, but I turn her down, preferring to watch her tackle her half first. For someone as small as her, she sure can eat a lot.

"Did you not trust that I was going to find us a good spot?" I ask her, taking a large sip of my Coke.

She snorts. "You've only been in LA for like, what, five weeks? That's hardly enough time to explore every pocket and corner of the city. But brownie points for knowing that the best type of food here comes from the food trucks."

"What can I say? I'm acclimating."

Blaire's smile widens, somewhat pleased. And then something flickers in her eyes, like she's unsure if she should be feeling like that.

Outside her window, there's a ridiculously huge pair of golden angel wings propped up by two long metal bars, and an Asian couple takes turns posing and taking shots with the wings.

"I bet it's different here than in Boston," she says, watching with intrigue as the guy snaps probably over a hundred pictures of his girlfriend, but when it's finally his turn to be in front of the camera, his girlfriend takes about two pictures and calls it a day.

"Definitely different," I agree. "For starters, we don't pay eighteen dollars for a smoothie."

Blaire groans, like she's heard that all before. "Erewhon is a whole different state of living. Your dad probably shops there."

"Good. That makes it much easier for me to make fun of him."

"You know, he's not as bad as you think," she tells me, her mouth quivering. Her caramel eyes take on a faraway gaze. "He's actually one of the best people I've ever met."

I tense my jaw. All I've been hearing ever since I landed in LA was people telling me how amazing Baxton is. I wonder what would happen if I told people how *un*-amazing he was when I was still growing up.

As if Blaire has read my thoughts, her expression softens. "He really, *deeply* cares about you," Blaire insists. "If not, he wouldn't have taken such extreme measures to get you sober. It was either this or rehab, and he wanted to give you a chance to work on your issues on your own."

I stay quiet, because deep down, I'm well aware that I could've ended up in a way worse situation than being on house arrest with a very hot sponsor.

"I'm trying, Blaire," I whisper, my eyes connecting with hers. Taking in the beautiful features of her face. "I really am."

She gives a thin smile. "I know you are."

I shift in the driver's seat, getting comfortable as I angle my body toward hers. "How about you? What about your family?" Blaire's expression denotes a sore topic, and I can already feel her willingness to share slip away from my fingers, so before she shoots me down, I decide to start with something easy. "Tell me about your brother, at least."

Blaire's eyes soften. "Well, um," she starts off, "his name is Eden and he's ten. He's amazing, and smart and truly the better one of us," Her eyes remain the same, but her mouth changes. Her lips fall into a disappointed frown. "It's been hard reconnecting with him after I got out of jail. I want to make up for everything that I couldn't give him. I want his life to be better. He deserves that."

My chest deflates with tenderness. With all the bad that she's done, it's not for herself, but righting some of the wrongs she did. It doesn't dismiss what she did, but it makes the crime a little easier to stomach.

"He's lucky to have a sister like you," I whisper after a while. She seems surprised to hear me say that, which makes me assume that no one—not even her own family—has ever said that to her before. "To be honest, I've never had anyone look out for me like that. I always had to do it myself. And that kind of thing can fuck you up."

Blaire nods in agreement. "I get what you mean. Ever since my dad died, it's all I had to do. Survive and take care of the people closest to me. I didn't have space in my mind to do anything else." She toys with the straw scraping against the plastic lid of her drink. "Now that I have money, it feels weird. Like I could splurge on a seven-dollar taco and not have to worry about saving half of it for tomorrow's lunch."

"That reminds me. Now that you can splurge on yourself more, you need to eat better," I start off. "I'll tell you what. Tomorrow I'll get us groceries for a really nice home-cooked dinner."

She makes a weird face. "And have you cook it? No way."

"Come on. I know my chef skills are a little rusty, but let me do something at least," I sound whiny, but I don't care. I'm desperate to be of use around here. "I mean, look at me. Does it *look* like I can do anything else?" I gesture to my weakened body, the bandages underneath my shirt wrapped tightly around my torso.

Blaire's eyebrows dip low on her face. "Jax Deneris," she says in a skeptical tone. "Are you feeling a little . . . *useless*?"

I groan. "Do you have to use that word?"

"How else would you put it, then?"

Fair point. "It hasn't been easy for me, okay?" I say with a frustrated breath. "Before this, I was an MMA underground champion. To go from that to this . . ." I sink against my seat. "I don't know how to do anything else."

"You are doing something. You're recovering."

"Well, it doesn't feel like it."

Another wary look from her. "You are doing your breathing exercises, right?"

Upon the mention of the exercises, I shrink into my seat. Her mouth drops into an annoyed frown. "Jax."

"Before you say anything, I *have* tried. They just don't help with the pain."

"That's because you need to do them consistently, dumbass," Blaire rightfully points out. "You promised me the self-sabotage was going to stop."

"It has." I assert. I haven't drunk a drop of liquor for a few days now, and I haven't bothered to top up my weed since she threw out my last stash.

"So, what are they?" Blaire asks. She jerks her chin at me, schooling her expression into a look of resolve. "What are the exercises?"

"Coughing and deep breathing exercises."

"I wanna see you do them," she demands.

"I'll do it at home."

"You won't. It doesn't take long, does it?" She pins my eyes with her own. "How many times?"

"Twenty coughs. Three rounds. Every day."

"Show me," she instructs.

My jaw clenches in annoyance, but I bite the bullet and do what she says, otherwise I'll never hear the end of it and our night will be ruined.

Blaire brings her legs up to her seat and crosses them, watching me curiously. Soon, the car fills up with the noise of coughing and choking coming from me. If anyone walking by heard us, they would think we're doing some wild foreplay up in here.

Blaire counts the number of times I've elicited a loud cough and makes me redo them if she doesn't think the cough is strong enough. Seven . . . eight . . . nine . . . ten. She allows me a fifteen-second rest before the next round of coughing. By the time we're done with all the rounds, I'm laying back against my seat, clutching the side of my chest hard as I desperately try to catch my breath. My ribs wail in pain with every inhale.

"There," I say breathlessly. "Happy now?"

"Not yet. How about deep breathing? I wanna see that." I roll my eyes and pull in the air through my nostrils. She shakes her head, disappointed. "You're not doing it. You're not breathing."

"Well, call the fucking coroner."

She ignores my note of sarcasm. "You need to breathe deeper. Feel the air as it expands your chest, let it linger for your ribs to adjust to the pain, and feel the breath as it leaves you," she instructs me, and I do it again. But my chest is so tired from all the coughing that I can only muster short spurts of air.

Blaire shakes her head. She turns off the volume of the radio and starts clearing the empty cans of Coke in between us and lays them on the floor. "Pull your seat back," she instructs.

"What?"

"Just do what I say."

I yank the level down and kick my feet backward, allowing the seat to move with me. As soon as I put it into the new position, Blaire lifts a leg over the handbrake and climbs right onto my seat.

"Whoa, whoa whoa," I say, whistling out, my hands going up as she wriggles into a comfortable position on my lap. Fuck. Fuck. *Fuck*. My cock is not going to like this one bit. "What the hell are you doing, darlin'?"

"I want to feel you breathing. So I know you're actually doing it right," she says irritably. "Relax. If I wanted to make a move on you, you'd know."

"I don't know what your definition of making a move is, but sitting on my lap is an obvious telltale sign that you want to fuck my brains out."

Her laughter heats my blood. "Now why would I do that? Without your brain, you're just a useless chunk of meat."

"A ridiculously *hot* useless chunk of meat," I correct her.

"Come on," she urges, pressing a hand onto my chest. "Ten long and deep breaths. Ready?"

I nod weakly.

"One," she counts.

Staring at her hand, I inhale a lungful of air, wait for a few seconds before expelling it. Pain shoots through my ribs, but it's not nearly as painful as the coughing was.

Blaire hums, pleased. Her hand presses more against my chest. "Two."

I inhale again. Making sure to take in enough air to expand my chest, holding it, and exhaling the breath out from my lungs.

"Better. Three."

With every breath the pain arrives, but each coming in duller than the previous time.

"Four."

My eyes remain glued to her hand on my chest. Her hand

applies the slightest bit of pressure when I would inhale, and the pressure recedes after I exhale; it's almost like she's doing the exercise along with me. I can hear her draw in the same breaths I do, her mouth rounding to a perfect O shape.

"Five."

Her hand is so small on my chest, I realize. Just like the rest of her. I don't know why, but my hand reaches up and closes over hers. If I had it my way, the thin fabric belonging to my shirt would disappear and I'd be feeling the skin of her palm all over my damn chest. But I'll settle for this.

"Six . . ." A breath dies in her chest.

I look up at Blaire's face, asking her if this is okay. Our gazes lock.

She doesn't answer me. But she doesn't pull her hand away.

"Seven . . ." Her voice is barely a whisper now.

Fuck, why haven't I realized she looks so good like this, sitting on my lap, palm laid flat on the skin above my heart? It's like she's promised herself to me.

Fuck, where were we again?

Eight? Seven?

Blaire stops counting. Her gaze is still on mine, tracing the features of my face like she's seeing them in a new light. I swipe my tongue over my bottom lip, watching the movement her eyes make. My heart is pounding so hard that I can hear it in my ears.

Instinctively, she adjusts herself on my lap, like she herself is uncomfortable with the way her body responds to our locked gazes. Her squirming on my lap sends a lazy jolt through my cock, causing it to thicken behind my zipper, and my tongue runs along the edge of my top teeth.

I'm no longer doing the exercise.

I think I've even stopped breathing altogether.

The car is quiet. So quiet.

Her eyes watch my mouth. Silent. But curious.

I'm watching her mouth too. Her lips part, but no sound comes out. Her eyes are wide and searching mine, and she's breathing fast, so fast. Fuck. I want to pull her toward me and close my mouth over hers. I want to swipe my tongue against the seam of her lips and drown myself in the warmth of her burning, searing kisses. I want my mouth on her throat, her breasts, her stomach . . . everywhere, until the taste of her overrides every other flavor in my palate I've ever had the displeasure of tasting.

Our heavy breaths meet in the tiny space between us.

"*Blaire*," I hiss out. I lean in, our lips a hair close to touching—

She pulls away.

Rocketing out of my lap, she climbs off so fast that the back of her head hits the roof of the car. Embarrassment overtakes onto her face as she readjusts herself and settles down back into the front seat.

We're not looking at one another. Our eyes are glued guiltily to the front of the car.

EIGHTEEN

Blaire

I spent the rest of the week throwing myself into finding an attorney and getting my expungement documents in order. It was a process that took a lot of sorting and reviewing of information with my attorney, but it was a good distraction from what had almost happened with Jax in the car. It would have been a terrible, *terrible* mistake. For the first time, Jax had shown me his tender side and like a starved cat, I pounced on him, nearly taking advantage of him while he was at his most vulnerable. What kind of sponsor does that make me?

I shouldn't be entertaining anything with Jax. He's mentally and physically weak right now, and if I slip up again, I could jeopardize any progress he makes. I've been failing miserably at being a decent human being lately; I don't want to fail at the *one* thing I promised Jax I'd be to him. So, I'm starting fresh from today. No more crossing anyone's boundaries.

And no more trying to sleep with a recovering alcoholic, no matter how much my PCs for him.

Tonight, my fingers drum patiently against the white tablecloth of the table that seats two people. I'm wearing my best garb—a black halter top maxi dress with a very modest slit on the side, a relic belonging to my high school homecoming that I'm surprised even fits me after all these years. It's the only dress I have that fits the dress code of this high-end Italian restaurant, and I think my date tonight wouldn't accept anything less.

The restaurant has no overhead lighting, just antique lamps hanging on the walls, casting a dim light onto the space. Burgundy wallpaper compliments the velvety carpet flooring, which is gentle on my heels. I'm the last person who'd believe I belong here, amongst the hunky bartenders with rolled-up sleeves mixing cocktails behind the antique bar and flashes of Cartier bracelets against bar patrons' wineglasses. but I have to try.

I fold my arms over the table uncomfortably and adjust the shawl on my dress. I thought my date would appreciate the modesty.

"Blaire," a woman calls my name sternly, prompting me to look up at my dinner guest.

"Laura," I greet in a calm tone I'd never heard myself use before. "Have a seat."

Eden's adopted mother is wearing a rather nice outfit today; a gorgeous silk blouse paired with some black slacks and a pair of black heels. Simple and elegant. It's almost shocking to see how well put together she looks. Maybe she's always been that way and I didn't know that because I've been too hyper-focused on the usual scowl she greets me with.

Normally, Laura wouldn't be my first pick as a dinner guest. But my attorney, Mr. Hewitt, advised that even if the judge grants me my expungement, it could take years to build a custody case against the Adamses. We would have to collect a mountain of evidence to prove that I'm better fit to care for Eden.

Even before bringing on Mr. Hewitt, I was well aware this was going to be a long fight. And I am willing to do it, but in the meantime, it's important for me to still maintain a relationship with Eden. And since my visitation has been up in the air since Disney World, I need to be able to rectify that with Laura ASAP.

"What would you ladies like to order?" The waiter comes around our table with an easy smile as he pulls his notebook and pen out.

"The grilled cod for me," Laura says flatly, not even glancing at the waiter as she hands over the menu.

"I'll have the same," I say to the waiter, handing my menu over with a pleasing smile.

"And for drinks?"

I glance at her. "Are you okay with wine?"

"I suppose."

"Perfect," I say, then smile at the waiter. "Then, a bottle of your finest red, please."

I can feel Laura's skeptical gaze burning into my face like a heat gun.

The waiter nods and disappears into the kitchen with our order.

"This is fancy," Laura comments, leaning a casual arm over her armrest while looking straight at me. Her implicit meaning is not lost on me: *are you sure you can afford it?*

"Yes, indeed," I say, tilting my head up. Laura hides her surprise, slipping back into the cool mask that she always wears.

"How is Eden?" I ask smoothly.

"Fine," Laura says, adjusting the napkin on her lap. "He just got back from space camp yesterday."

"Did he have fun?"

"I believe he did. He couldn't stop bragging about how he walked in zero-gravity on a Boeing 727."

"Well, that was a lifelong dream of his. That, and living long enough to witness the invention of edible cell phones."

"That boy." Laura shakes her head in dismay. "Most things he says never make sense to me."

"I think wanting to know the flavor profile of a bionic chip is very progressive," I say in his defense. "You know him, always looking for a way forward."

Laura purses her lips into a frown, the double meaning not lost on her.

"Look, I know we both got off on the wrong footing," I start off, tending my fingers together. "And what we're doing is only hurting the person we're both trying to protect. So, I would really like a chance to make things right between us."

And because I can't bear the thought of not seeing him again, I almost want to add, but stop myself. Being emotional isn't going to get her to allow me to visit him again. Being practical will. And to gain her trust, I'll need to play her game, at least for a while. Until I'm ready to pull the rug out from under her.

"Well . . ." Laura's mouth quivers, and a dash of guilt flickers in her eyes. He did say he misses you," she admits, her jaw clenching as she does.

My mouth twitches into a smile.

If she's willing to admit that, it means I've got a small chance to change her mind.

Just then, the waiter returns with the bottle of red I asked for, along with two glasses. He pops open the cork and glances between the two of us.

"Who would like to try the wine?"

Before Laura can answer, I gesture towards her, "She will." The waiter nods in acknowledgement.

"But how can I possibly trust you now, Blaire?" Laura furrows her brows at me as the waiter pours a little bit of wine into her glass. "You lied about being unemployed."

"That won't be a problem anymore."

"And why is that?" She eyes me skeptically. "You have a job now?"

I nod tightly. "One that pays well. We can talk about what this means for Eden."

Laura cocks her head sideways, wondering if it's all true. I hold my head high, meeting her gaze fearlessly. She needs to know I'm serious about courting her, and that I'm not backing down when it comes to Eden.

When she senses the honesty in my words, she inhales sharply.

"Ma'am?" The waiter beckons her.

Laura's gaze snaps towards the waiter, then to her wine glass, remembering that she'd been assigned the taste-test. She watches me with cold, unrelenting eyes as she swirls the liquid around the glass. It feels like a test to see if I've made the right call with the wine.

She tilts it to her mouth and takes a sip, like she's weighing the worth of giving me another chance and equating it to the worth of the wine.

Her lip curls in when she swallows, barely hiding the satisfaction of how good the wine is. She nods to the waiter to fill the rest of her wine glass, followed by mine.

"You have my attention," Laura says to me." Let's talk."

***

"So, I told her that all has been good with my finances lately, and I've been more proactive than I've ever been," I recall to Ben a couple of days later as we walk into his room.

I let myself fall onto the bed, my back hitting the pillows. It's been a while since I visited Ben and Elle; lately, it feels like there's no other plane of existence but in that house with Jax.

"Anyway, it took a lot of wine, a lot of flattery, and a lot of sucking up to Laura, but by the end of it, she said I could resume visiting Eden again," I tell him.

"Wow." An exhale from Ben as he lies on the available spot of his bed beside me. He turns to me, his head propped against his elbow. "That's amazing, Blaire."

"I know, isn't it?" I say, feeling the burden I'd been carrying these past few weeks finally float away and disappear into the abyss. "Things are really starting to shape up. With the court hearing for my expungement scheduled for the end of next month, everything's going according to plan."

My prospects for getting my record expunged were good, according to Mr. Hewitt. It did help that I had sought one of the best expungement lawyers in all of California and paid him handsomely to expedite the process. The faster this is settled, the faster my life can return to normal.

"I told you working with Portia was a good idea." Ben grins lazily.

"Yeah. I mean, it's not the best idea, but the money's helping," I say, fingering the edge of his pillow quietly.

"Tell me about it. I just finished clearing my dad's medical bills from a year ago, which means we're finally debt-free."

"Wow, really?" My gaze snaps up at him excitedly. "That must be a great feeling."

Ben nods, a grin slathered across his face. "Now, I can actually focus on Elle's college fees, and maybe starting my own IT business once all of this is over."

Finally, putting his skills to good use. I always knew he was meant for better things. "Isn't it weird that we have to do all this just to get some level of normalcy in our lives?" I ask.

"Yeah. It sucks. But . . . is it weird I don't feel bad about it?" Ben says with candor. He brushes a lock of hair covering my eyes and tucks it behind my ears. "Like, the people whose mansion we robbed—they're gonna cry about their stolen stuff for one day, but they're not actually gonna *miss* those things. You and I both know they can easily replace every one of those items without any struggle. It's fucked up, I know, but that's how I deal with it, okay?" His expression morphs into a tender one as he looks at me. "We deserve to be happy, Blaire. Without regrets, without anything holding us back. Just try not to beat yourself up too hard about it, okay?"

I suck in a breath, hoping Ben's words reach into the deepest levels of my body. "I'll try," I whisper.

He smiles back, then leans toward me to fold his lips over

mine. I reel back, blinking away the surprise of his affection.

"Oh, um. Wow," I say, my fingers running over the seam of my lips.

Concern writes itself across his features. "Sorry. Are you all right?"

No. But I should be. Kissing used to be the most natural thing in the world between me and Ben. Now, I don't find myself seeking his lips as much as I used to. Right now I crave his friendship more than the physical aspect.

"I'm sorry," I say remorsefully. "I can't."

He shakes his head. "That's fine. I'm sorry. I should've asked."

Now I feel bad that he feels bad.

"No, I mean, I want to . . ." I start off, then stop myself again. *Did I? Did I really want to? Why did I say that?* I adjust myself, lifting my upper body into a sitting position, my feet dangling off the bed. "I'm just not in the mood today."

Something flickers in his eyes, like he wants to prod more, but he holds those words back. Instead, he nods tightly, a thin smile crossing his mouth. "Of course I do, Blaire."

I smile back, but I'm silent.

Ben doesn't say anything either. I stare at my sneakers uncomfortably.

"Do you wanna just *put on a Netflix show*?" Ben suggests.

I shift uneasily on the bed. We've never once just put on a Netflix show. His suggestion might be an innocent one this afternoon, but a part of me doesn't want to take that chance.

"You know what?" I say, shooting off the bed. "I'm good. I think . . . I'm just gonna head back."

He blinks at me. "But you just got here."

"Yeah, I'm just you know . . . busy. With Jax stuff," I mumble, leaning down to pick up my bag and loop it over my shoulder. "You know how it is. If I don't keep an eye on him for more than an hour, there's no knowing what he'll do."

"Okay," Ben stretches the last syllable out, while giving me a suspicious look. "I'll see you soon, then?"

"Of course." The thought of kissing him on the lips again doesn't sit well with me, so instead I settle on a quick smack on the cheek. "Thanks, Ben, for everything."

Back at the car, a string of curse words fly out of my mouth before I even have the chance to shut the door. I slam my forehead against the wheel, my mind reeling from the possibility that I—and my heart—might just be royally fucked.

NINETEEN

Jax

I must be itching for something to do around the house because I've been on a roll this week.

The breathing exercises and the physio sessions must
be working because my body feels more capable now than
it used to a month ago. I still haven't touched MMA or any
other sports yet, nor have I felt the need to. I've come to the
realization that I'm just as useful on a domestic level.

So far, I've organized the kitchen and the pantry twice,
cleaned the gutters and the pool, and organized all of Baxton's
boxes in the garage. That last task took a full day since
there was over a decade's worth of stuff in there that needed
organizing or getting rid of, like the three full boxes of rusted
woodworking tools, from a time I assume he had a sudden
passion for the hobby.

I've realized that before Blaire had moved in, Baxton

had essentially used this place as a temporary storage unit for luxury purchases and memorabilia that he'd collected from previous sets. I recognized a walnut gun from when he played a gunslinger in some pirate movie, but the rest of the props are unfamiliar to me. Most of the things he'd taken were small, easy-to-pocket items that likely wouldn't be missed, like accessories. There were dusty folders filled with call sheets and old pictures of him with crew members and fellow actors. His smile is wide, infecting the other occupants of the photo with a similar excitement.

The first time I saw him on television, I was flipping through the channels for something to accompany me while I ate the dinner I made from whatever my mom hadn't left rotting in the refrigerator. By that time she just started dating Charles, my soon-to-be stepdad, so she wasn't around a whole lot. Good for me because it meant I could do whatever the fuck I wanted. Bad for me because it meant I could do whatever the fuck I wanted.

It was past midnight, so there wasn't a whole lot of shit to watch, but a particular movie had caught my eye. It was one of those old-timey Westerns that was cheaply made and by no means career-defining for the actors in it. I can't remember what the plot of the movie was, mostly because it was forgettable. The only thing I can vividly recall was that my dad played the villain who refused to give back all the money he'd stolen in exchange for his son. A cruel, heartless smile crept over his lips as he turned to the boy and said that his life was worth as much as the used cigarette stuck to the bottom of his boot.

I was convinced that the reason Baxton was able to play

that role perfectly with such little compassion was because he was that kind of person in real life.

It's funny. Peering into these boxes and piecing together the life he'd made in LA, I never once pegged him as a sentimental guy, since he'd so easily had the ability to leave me in Boston under the less-than-loving care of my mother, while he fucked off to the other side of the coast. Maybe he's only sentimental with things he deeply cares about, like his acting career. Or people he hadn't screwed over yet.

I try not to feel offended about my lack of presence in these boxes. After all, he left me a decade ago and I've—for the most part—made my peace with it. I wouldn't allow him into my life now if I wasn't over it in some capacity.

And yet, it takes everything in me to stomp out the seed of frustration growing in the pit of my stomach as I shove the last of his memorabilia back into the box and slap the top of it over with tape.

***

Tackling the front porch became task *numero dos*. Blaire had done a splendid job landscaping, but ever since I came into the picture, her time has been split between being my therapy and physio chauffeur so the backyard could use some proper care.

I start off by watering the struggling plants. I'm reminded how unforgiving the Californian heat can be by the elderberries lining the sides of the driveway, which have seen better days. At least the lower maintenance aloe vera plants are still doing fine without my help. Next is settling the weeds growing in between the cracks of the driveway. There wasn't a weed puller anywhere and Blaire had hogged the car for the day, so I had to make do with my own hands.

Just picture it: Jax Deneris, on his hands and knees, in a pair of bright yellow gardening gloves, ripping out weeds from the driveway.

The world has gone mad, truly.

I toss all the weeds into a trash bag and spray down the driveway with a hose, getting rid of all the dirt and smaller weeds I didn't pick up on. The sun is hanging low in the sky by the time Blaire pulls into the driveway with Baxton's car. I make sure to hose down the car just as she's about to step out of it. Luckily for her, the car door shields most of the water.

"Good evening, darlin'," I muse.

"Ah!" Blaire groans, shielding her eyes with her hands like my half nakedness is burning devil signs into her corneas. "Don't you ever put on a shirt?"

I lower the hose, my eyes narrowed into slits. "It's hot out."

Confusion wraps itself around my head. Usually she's rather indifferent to me walking around the house half-naked. At times, she enjoys ogling when she thinks I don't notice.

"Just put on a shirt," she mumbles, her gaze scanning at the driveway. "Wow. It's looking . . . nice."

"Nice? Are you kidding? My work should be on the cover of *Architectural Digest.*"

She rolls her eyes, fighting a smile on her face.

"Are you almost finished?"

"Pretty much." I turn off the tap and wind the hose back up.

"Good. 'Cuz I wanna bring you somewhere. Somewhere kind of important to me."

I warily arch a brow. "Really?"

She nods. "I could sure use the company."

A warm feeling tucks itself in my stomach.

***

We arrive downtown. Blaire pulls up at an unfamiliar redbrick building on a street that's filled with tents. Outside, there's a long queue of men, women, and children snaking out of the building all the way down the block. Simple, blue letters that are painted on top of the door read FAMILY RESOURCE CENTER.

"You brought me to a soup kitchen?" I ask as she grabs my hand and leads me into the building.

"Yeah," she admits. "I try to come here when I have time to spare."

My eyes widen with surprise. I don't know what I assumed she did in her spare time other than rob houses, but spending it volunteering at a homeless shelter was not something on my bingo card. But it does makes sense. She's so incredibly selfless when it comes to other people.

"You should've told me this was what you've been doing," I tell her when we reach the start of the line in the cafeteria, where people are waiting with their bowls and utensils for the volunteers to bring out the big metal trays of food.

"You didn't ask. Besides, I don't like to brag about it. I just like giving back," Blaire says, a reluctant smile tugging at the corners of her mouth.

We head into the kitchen, where there are plenty of other volunteers in aprons cutting up vegetables and searing poultry over stoves. It's busy with orders being barked from all across the kitchen and volunteers hauling trays through the doors.

"Anyway, I wanted to bring you here because you said you were struggling with feeling like you had a purpose," Blaire tells me, handing me a hair net. "So, I thought maybe this is something you might be interested in. Think you're up to try?"

"You know I'm always up for a challenge, darlin.'" A slow grin spreads across my lips. She slings an apron around my neck and when I'm done attaching mine, I help her with hers.

"Don't be nervous. They'll make you feel right at home," Blaire assures me, then calls out to the rest of the volunteers occupying the kitchen. "Hey guys, this is Jax! Anyone needing extra help, let him know."

I wave a hand, and I receive a few friendly smiles in return. A tan-skinned man in his forties approaches me and Blaire, his apron caked with flour and sauce.

"Hey, you made it!" the man exclaims, roping Blaire into a hug so huge her feet lift from the ground. She laughs when he sets her down and tucks her hair behind her ears.

"I brought new meat." She hooks a thumb in my direction. "This is Jax."

"Hey." I stick my hand out. "Thanks for having me."

"Thanks for coming to help out." The man gives my hand a firm shake. "I'm Dave. I run the family resource center with my partner, Marie." he says, pointing to a curly-haired woman who's busy stirring a big vat of soup while delegating duties to the other volunteers. Dave's gaze swings back to me. "Can you cook?"

"Enough to survive."

"Good enough," he says with a smile. "You can help chop

up the tomatoes and put them in the vats on the stove. When you're done, you can help serve."

"Got it." I go over to Marie, who pulls me into a friendly hug and prepares a chopping board for me beside her.

The next two hours pass by in a blur. I make polite conversation with Marie and discover that the reason they opened a resource center here is because both her and Dave used to be homeless. They'd lost their jobs during the recession and it took years for them to get clean and find proper work again. But they never forgot where they came from, and any time or dime they could spare went toward this place. They've been in operation for nearly three years now, relying mostly on donations from NGOs and the community.

Their story was inspiring. Growing up, I was at least lucky enough to have a roof over my head, and even though my mom and I had suffered financially after Baxton left, I can't possibly imagine what it would be like to be homeless. Luckily, I had enough sense to take all the fight money Charles had stolen from me before I left that place. It was enough for rent and food, but even with rations, I knew it wasn't going to last me for long. So I found work in an MMA gym and hustled hard. I graduated from community college and kept working. Kept fighting. I was one of the lucky ones who was dealt a handful of shitty cards by life and made it work. I know there are many others who don't have the luxury of getting out the same way I did.

After chopping up all the tomatoes, Marie allows me the honor of stirring the sacred vat of soup that apparently no other newbie has the opportunity to do. I thank her graciously, and help haul the soup to the serving station, where they are already starting to serve people. Blaire pokes her head out and smiles at me. I watch as she returns her attention back to the person in front of her, asking them if they'd like beef or chicken today. Her shoulders are relaxed and overall, she looks more at ease. She's been glowing recently. The only time I ever see her like that is when she's come from a call with Eden, which has been happening more frequently now.

I swipe a ladle from the back of the kitchen and go to work at the serving station.

Around nine, the line had dwindled, so some of the volunteers were back in the kitchen, cleaning up. I head to the washroom to freshen up and join some of the residents who were still eating. I squeeze into an empty seat with a plate of cookies we served for dessert and munch on them while I watch people sink into their food and chat with their friends.

"Hey," the blond-haired boy opposite me looks at me curiously. He couldn't have been older than sixteen. He has on a black beanie and a gray hoodie that has a few holes in one sleeve. "You're new," he observes.

"I'm Jax."

"I'm Carl."

"Did you come here alone or with family?"

"Family. My mom's eating over there." He points to an older blond lady three tables away, chatting with a few other women. He stares at my face for a few moments before fixating on the words printed on my shirt. "Universal Fighter's Gym," he reads aloud and slowly. "Are you a bodybuilder or something?"

I look down at my shirt. I was in a rush to leave the house so I just threw on whatever shirt that was clean. It didn't occur to me that I still had this. It was my old gym back in Boston, before I left it to fight in the underground. My stomach twists with guilt when I recall my time training there. My and Sienna's boss, Julian, while hard-headed and tough, had always been good to me. I wouldn't be nearly as disciplined of a fighter without his mentorship. It was one of my many regrets, to have turned my back on him and the integrity of the sport.

"No. I am—*was* an MMA fighter," I say, correcting myself.

"Wow," he breathes, somewhat in awe. "Like . . . Muhammad Ali?"

"Close. Muhammad Ali was a boxer and boxing is one aspect of MMA."

"Cool. Were you a good fighter?"

I grin slyly. "I was the best."

"I don't believe you."

"It's true," I insist.

"Prove it." He jerks his chin at me. "Show me some moves."

"Like, right now?"

"You're done with your food," he taunts, gesturing to the empty plate in front of me that's no longer filled with cookies. "And I'm done with mine."

I look around. "We're in the middle of a cafeteria."

"There's an empty hall next door that nobody ever uses."

I push the plate to the side and fold my arms across the table, giving him a suspicious look. "Why do you wanna learn MMA?"

"I like learning new things," Carl mumbles.

I call bullshit since I was around his age when I got roped into the danger and thrill of MMA. And I didn't do it just to "learn something new."

"Yeah, no. I'm not going to teach you MMA so you can beat other dudes up," I mutter.

"What if I need to defend myself? It's a dangerous world out there. Do you know homeless youth are nine times more likely to be victims of violent crime?"

I cock an eyebrow. Even if that stat is true, his intention to learn MMA might not be so innocent. But regardless, who am I to starve someone willing to pick up the sport? My history with MMA might have been a contentious one, but it doesn't have to be for others.

"Okay. Fine. But I'm only teaching you MMA defensive techniques," I mutter.

He rolls his eyes. "That's boring."

I shrug. "Then, forget about it."

I turn over to the person beside me and start striking up a conversation with him. We only get past introducing our names before Carl runs over to me and cuts me off by laying a hand on my shoulder.

"Fine," he sighs. "But I want you to teach me now."

TWENTY

Blaire

After I've helped clean up in the kitchen, I search for Jax in the cafeteria, but come up short. Eventually I catch a glimpse of a small crowd of kids poking their heads through the doorway connecting the cafeteria to the once-derelict hall. I weave through to get to the front.

The chairs are stacked in a tall pile and shoved into the corner of the massive hall. Amidst the empty space, Jax is teaching Carl how to do a shoulder-slip move. Then they get into some kind of mock fight. Jax towers over Carl, pretending to be the aggressor, while Carl dodges him by pushing his left shoulder down to evade Jax's punch. He lets Carl get used to the movement, adding some kind of catch-up step to change it up, then makes him move forward and backward in a repeated motion.

I'm unable to hide my smile. I have known Carl and his mom

for a while now. They've been on the streets since they left Carl's abusive dad a couple of months ago. His mom's been trying to get into a woman's shelter, but there are very few in the city with vacancies to take in more people. Carl's been feeling down about it lately, so he's definitely a kid in need of a distraction.

"Nice," Jax remarks to Carl. "You have pretty good reflexes, dude."

"I knew it," Carl says with a proud huff of his chest. He doesn't stop repeating his movements, eager for his body to get used to the techniques.

"What's going on here?" I announce my presence in the hall. Both Jax and Carl whip their attention toward me. Carl drops his arms to his sides.

"Hey," Jax says with a nervous smile. "I'm just teaching Carl over here some defense techniques. I hope you don't mind."

I can't believe he would think I'd mind about something so beneficial to the community as this. "If anything, I'm a little upset that you didn't include the others."

I gesture to the dozen or so children and young adults peering through the doorway from behind me, looking at Jax expectantly. Jax and Carl exchange a surprised look.

"All right," Jax says, gesturing to the kids. "Come on guys. Whoever's interested in learning, find a place and partner up."

The rest of the kids get up to speed with basic MMA techniques. After that, they get into pairs, taking turns being on offense. After a while, Carl runs off to help a pair that's struggling to learn the moves, which leaves me and Jax to carry on a one-on-one session.

"You can't hit like this, Blaire," Jax says when he watches me curl my fists and lifts them up to my shoulders.

"This is how I've always done it."

"Your thumb needs to be outside of your fist. Like this." He takes my hand in his, which sends a wildfire of goosebumps across my skin. He goes behind me, his chest pressed against my back and pushes my feet wider apart with his foot. "Your feet . . . like this. And your hips . . ." His hands wrap around them, steadying them, and I bite my lip hard, trying to stay focused. "Stay forward. Keep it controlled. That way when you punch, it'll give you better leverage."

I could melt with the heat of his body so close to mine.

"And striking combos?" I whisper, peering up at him.

Jax's voice slides into my ear. "Remember what I taught you. And don't forget to switch it up. Never let them know your next move."

I nod, smiling. He positions himself in front of me rather than having his chest against my back, and I immediately miss his warmth. Damn, MMA is an unexpectedly steamy sport. He readies into his stance opposite me, a lopsided grin worn across his face. "Ready?" he asks. "Try to aim for my head."

"Okay." I prepare myself into my stance again and propel my fists forward. He dodges my shots easily, slipping from left to right. We do this for a while, me jab-cross-jabbing and him anticipating which side I'm gonna throw my next punch at.

"This is amazing!" Dave exclaims when he strolls into the hall, prompting me and Jax to halt our mock spar. He's practically bleeding with happiness as he watches the kids learning to defend themselves and having fun together. "This is the first time I've seen the kids so enthusiastic about something. Blaire, where did you *find* this guy?"

"Oh, at the back of a club somewhere," I murmur, grinning up at Jax.

"You should come by more often. Keep teaching the kids," Dave says to Jax. "It'll be good for them to be proactive in their safety. Plus, a lot of them don't have much to do around here anyway, and learning MMA could give them something to look forward to."

Jax nods, taking him up on the offer. "I'd like that."

"And keep bringing Blaire here too. She's been so busy lately. Lord knows we need all the help we can get." He pats a hand over my shoulder. "Donations are usually sparse this time of the year. But our Blaire over here saved us by donating a big sum a week ago."

Jax gapes at me. Color blooms on my cheeks.

I probably should've told Dave to keep that to himself. Hopefully eight thousand dollars would keep them afloat for a few more months, at least until Christmas, when people are feeling more generous.

It was approaching nine, so Jax decided to end the MMA session, *with a promise* to resume it again next time. Dave and I thought it would be best to have Jax cap the class for kids over fifteen years old and keep the maximum number of students to twelve. Jax told Dave that he plans on bringing proper MMA gear next time and donate it to the business, so the kids can learn the sport safely. He may not want to admit it, but he has a generous heart.

After closing up the center, Dave gave us doggie bags for some of the leftovers. We stayed for a few more minutes chatting, discussing plans for the MMA class before he sent us on our merry way.

The air had cooled significantly, evaporating the sweat buried in my hair from mock sparring earlier as we walked to the car. I sneak a glance at Jax, smiling. His excitement about teaching the kids is infectious; I haven't known him for long, but I have a feeling he never usually gets that way. Which means tonight was a success.

"Every day is a surprise with you, isn't it?" Jax whispers as he glances over at me. "One day I come home to you hiding from a cop, and the next I'm following you to a family resource center, teaching kids MMA."

"Never let them know your next move," I say, quoting what he said earlier.

A car whizzes by, so close to the sidewalk, a couple of inches from where I'm walking. Jax lays a hand on the curve of my back and guides us to switch positions, so he's the one walking beside the road and not me.

A fuzzy feeling wraps itself around my body.

Jax's hands are shoved in his pocket. The mood has changed; his brows are furrowed and the easy smile on his face has worn off. "On a serious note, Blaire, can I ask you something?"

"Sure."

He pauses for a beat, "It looks like you have history with some of the people in that resource center."

My mouth quivers.

"I do."

Fearing where this conversation is heading, my first instinct is to shut Jax down. But maybe he deserves to know. Maybe I want him to know. After all, I was the one who brought him here, knowing full well what can of worms it might open. And for the first time in a long time, I'm okay with that.

I'd always assumed Jax would be my worst critic, given the privilege that he had, but now he might actually be my biggest ally.

"Okay." He fidgets with his hands, swallowing hard, then he stops in his tracks. "If I'm wrong about this, I'm gonna sound like a dick, but I just have to ask . . ." His gaze sweeps over mine, paralyzed with worry and fear. "Did you used to be homeless, Blaire?"

Slowly, I nod in confirmation.

"Oh. Wow." Jax smooths a hand over his mouth, swallowing down the revelation. Before I know it, his gaze is back on me again, glinting with curiosity. "How did you end up on the streets?"

"You got an hour or two?"

A tender smile graces Jax's lips. "I'm all yours for however long you want me, darlin'."

I bite down on my lip, hiding a smile. He never spares a chance to flirt with me. It's both infuriating, but welcome at the same time.

There's a brightly lit park situated on the opposite side of the road, so we both head there. I place myself on the wooden bench overlooking the slide, and Jax slides into the spot beside me. He shrugs off his jacket and places it over my thighs, which are barely covered by my denim shorts. I have every mind to wrap the jacket over my body and sink into it, already feeling vulnerable with what I'm about to tell him, but I decide against it. This isn't something I should be embarrassed about. I should embrace as much of my story as I possibly can, no matter how fragmented and painful it is.

"When my dad died, things weren't easy for me and my

family," I start off, picking at the loose skin of my thumb. "It wasn't easy before, but his unexpected passing made things a lot worse. My mom took my dad's passing the hardest. She stopped going to work. Stopped doing anything, really. She spent her days at home looking out the window, hoping she would find my dad tending to the garden like he always did. She was no longer capable of taking care of Eden in her state, which is when I had stepped up. Dad didn't leave us with much, so I had to drop out of college and work to keep us afloat. I became the main provider of our family. I was a kid taking care of another kid and an unfit parent. Soon, it became all too much for me.

"We couldn't afford the mortgage, so it didn't take long for debtors to repossess our house and the car. We crashed at my mom's friend's place for a few monthswhile I figured out a plan. But my mom's idleness was making things hard for her friend, who was struggling with the upkeep of three new guests in the mix, and it wasn't long until the burden became too much to bear and we were politely asked to leave. We had nowhere else to go. No one to turn to. Both my parents were only children and my grandparents passed away when I was little. So we were out of options."

A chill zips down my spine when I recount the day we got some sleeping bags and found a spot in the park to settle. It felt like such a punch in the gut, to go from having everything we ever needed to nothing at all. *It'll only be temporary*, I swore as I tucked myself further into the bag to hide from the vicious bite of the winter chill. *I'll get it back again. I'll get it all back.*

I didn't.

To me, the worst part of being homeless wasn't the

unwarranted fights or the hunger. That I could get used to. It was being treated like you were invisible that was the unbearable part. To watch as people's eyes moved right over you, their guilt deflecting their attention elsewhere so they could feel better about themselves and move on with their lives.

Living on the streets was difficult. The daily grind of life was constantly overshadowed by the constant worry about where to sleep. Was it safe? Were we trespassing? Could I leave my belongings there if I needed to get something to eat? It was exhausting. Every day I had to fight to find some kind of enemy—be it bum-rushes, malnutrition, my declining mental health. It was never-ending, the kind of torture where letting your guard down for even one second meant life or death.

"Where was my dad when all of this happened?" Jax asks, confusion twisting his expression. "There's no way he wouldn't have stepped in if he knew about your situation."

"He didn't know. My dad stopped working for Baxton after he got the *Heartstorm Hospital* gig and moved to the Hills. Dad wanted to find work closer to where we lived. That was a year before he died. By then, I'd assumed my dad, and my family by extension, was a forgotten memory."

"And when you were on the streets, was that where you um . . . fell into crime?"

I nod slowly.

"I think when you're around people who do shady shit all the time, you start to think it's normal and if they can get away with it, so can you," I say, staring straight ahead into the mossy darkness. "Times were tough for us. I wanted more, for Eden, for my mom. There was a hostel nearby that was going for thirty dollars a night, and I knew that was the only way I could guarantee their safety every night. But affording the hostel was another thing.

"So, I stole," I admit shamefully. "It started out small, shoplifting a few essentials. Then food or medication when we got sick. Then alcohol and cigarettes to sell on the street. Then I got more desperate, and I had to do more." My eyes flutter closed as the memories pour back into my mind. I hated how my past felt dirty on my skin, and I loathed how I had fallen back to my old pattern even more. "I fell in with a group of desperate kids like myself. We started breaking into cars, stealing whatever we could pawn off. One night we fucked up, breaking into a car owned by some detective. We got caught for larceny and I was the only one old enough to feel the full extent of the law.

"I remember the fear that consumed my body as I got handcuffed and sent to the station—not of what was awaiting me in county jail, but rather what was going to happen to my mom and Eden now that I couldn't take care of them. I cried myself to sleep in my cell every night, knowing that I let them down.

"But thankfully, I got out early on good behavior, so I only served seven months," I mumble, a solemn look on my face. "When I got out, your dad was the only one who greeted me at the gate. According to Baxton, after he caught wind of my dad's passing, he tried to contact us to see if there was anything he could do to help, but we had moved out of our house by then. It wasn't until he learned that I'd been arrested that Baxton finally put together the pieces of what happened."

"So that was when you moved into the Melrose house." Jax connects the timeline together.

"Yeah," I murmur. "Baxton gave me some money, a phone, and a laptop so I could look for jobs and prep for interviews. Any spare time not spent applying for jobs, I was searching for my brother and my mom. I spent months following any leads and scouring the streets for any sign of them. Eventually, I found a woman who used to share her food rations with Mom when I was away. After I'd been arrested, my mom decided she'd had enough. She dropped my brother off at an orphanage and left with a boyfriend who had a ticket out of the city. We haven't heard from her since. I think the responsibility on her shoulders when I was gone finally broke her."

Growing up, I always knew Theresa wasn't the best mother in the world. Having two kids was more of my dad's plan rather than hers, and she loved him enough to put up with us. But I never thought she'd be capable of abandoning us in the way she did.

"Fuck." Jax withdraws his hand from the small of my back, a distressed look on his face. "I'm so sorry she was a terrible mother, Blaire. She should've been the one to pick up the pieces, not you. You were just doing what was best for your family."

"Yeah, and look where it got me," I say with a huff. "My dad's gone, my mom's god knows where, and I lost my brother to another family. I don't know . . . it just seems like no matter what I do, or how good my intentions are, I always find a way to fuck it all up."

"That's not true. You haven't fucked this up. Those people in there"—Jax jabs a finger in the direction of the resource center—"they depend on you. They care about you. And they're still operating *because* of you. Don't allow yourself to discount all the good you've done because of some of the bad."

"Okay." I choke on a dry laugh. "If you say so."

"Blaire," Jax snakes a hand around the curvature of my jaw, forcing my gaze to connect with his. He's so close that I can feel the warmth of his breath skidding over my skin. "You're one of the bravest people I know. That's what I like about you. The fact that you're still here, and you're still going, is an achievement that shouldn't be understated."

I nod, wanting desperately for the words to reach me. Because I'd like to think that with enough time and effort, I can earn my place in this world that had broken me once before.

Jax's lips twitch upward, his hand trailing up to my temple. "Besides . . . there's only room for one self-saboteur in our house and I'll be damned if I let it be you."

This time I crack a smile. My forehead rests against him. I never imagined that he would be the breath of courage that I need, but I'm happy that it's him.

"Thank you, Jax," I whisper, looking up at him. "Really."

"Thank you, too, darlin'," Jax whispers back, gratitude pouring out of him and wrapping me up in it. "For letting me into your world."

TWENTY-ONE

Jax

I meant every word I said to Blaire. What she went through was admirable, and what poverty forced her to do did not make her a bad person; just a flawed one, like everyone else.

And I've never wanted her more than I do now.

Besides, I didn't think her past would help put my present into perspective, but it did. Everything I had—even if I had to do it all myself—was a massive privilege. Even my recent stint in LA, drinking my liver off, not giving a fuck about anyone else, became something that only someone privileged could afford to do. Blaire couldn't afford to spiral. It was live or die for her, and nothing else.

I thought she might need a little cheering up after a heavy conversation last night, so I spent the whole day preparing something special for her. A little gesture to show her that I'm proud of her for overcoming her hurdles.

It's 7:00 p.m. when I hear the car pull into the driveway. I'd just come back from the shed to put all the tools back as Blaire opens the front door.

"Hey, darlin'," I muse, leaning a hip against the dinner table in greeting.

"Hey. Sorry, it's been a long day," Blaire exhales, dropping the keys into the bowl sitting on top of the shoe rack. "I had lunch with Elle and then I spent the rest of the day doing prep work with my attorney for the expungement hearing next month."

God, I love that she updates me on her day without a second thought now.

"Sounds fun," I remark.

"It was awful, actually," Blaire sighs. "The prep-work part. Not the lunch-with-Elle part. That was fun. She's got some wild stories about her Bumble dates, one involving a horse shed and an interesting use of the riding crop."

"I think I can fill in the blanks myself. But I'd love to hear about it anyway." My mouth twitches upward. "Have you had dinner?"

"Mr. Hewitt ordered takeout." Her gaze scrolls up my body and lands on my face, her expression twisting into a perplexed one. "Why are you covered in grass and dirt? More landscaping? You didn't touch my garden, did you?"

"Oh, I wouldn't dream of it. But I did make some upgrades to our backyard."

Blaire cranes her neck to check out the backyard from here, but groans when she finds that the doors to the patio have been covered up by curtains.

"No peeking," I wag my index finger side to side.

"How else am I supposed to see your upgrades?"

"You will. But first, let's go for a swim. It's a warm evening and I think we should take advantage. What do you think?" I suggest.

"Oh, yeah." Blaire breaks into a smile. "I'll go change."

Blaire heads upstairs to change into her swimwear. I'm already in a pair of shorts fit for swimming so I jump into the guest bathroom to rinse off the grass dusting my hair and chest.

When she creeps back downstairs, she's wearing a navy-blue bikini with a matching-colored sarong tied around her waist, her dark hair loose around her shoulders. My heartbeat skitters. Her smooth, pale skin seems velvet to the touch.

"Are you ready?" I say, hurrying her through the living room excitedly to get to the backyard. I dare say it's my best work yet. A hand remains over her eyes as I guide her through the patio doors and down the steps onto the lawn. "No peeking."

"You're rushing me. If I don't peek, I will fall," Blaire mutters.

"I've got you," I murmur, tightening my grip on her hand. Having her skin on my skin is enough for me to combust into flames. "Stay here," I say, rushing over to the pool area to flip on the newly installed switch.

"Okay, open your eyes," I instruct.

Blaire's eyelids fly open.

"Oh my god," she whispers when she sees it.

I can't help but smile smugly to myself. Hanging all over the patio and above the pool are rows upon rows of gorgeous string lights. A beautiful, warm glow floats on the surface of the water, refracting light onto the blue tiles at the bottom of the pool.

Blaire laughs in disbelief. "What brought this on?"

"I wanted to thank you. For everything that you've done for me since meeting you. For sharing your story with me yesterday." I shrug, feeling embarrassed to say it. "And I don't know. Feels like you needed a bit of a pick-me-up, so . . ."

"Jax, this is . . . really nice," she whispers, her gaze darting back to me.

"Care to swim under the stars tonight, darlin'?"

Blaire nods, grinning from ear to ear.

I hop into the pool first, the cold water attacking my skin and shocking my body. But soon enough, the water feels like a second skin. Meanwhile, Blaire has opted for the other method of descending slowly into a pool, the water seeping into the fabric of her bikini as she maneuvers herself into the water to get used to the temperature. When she's submerged to her shoulders, Blaire tilts her face up toward the sky, her dark hair splaying all around her on the surface of the water.

Blaire exhales with relief. She allows her arms and legs to float, suspending herself between air and water. I chuckle to myself. This is the first time I've ever seen her look truly relaxed.

"Jax, I don't ever wanna leave," she groans.

"You don't have to." A breathy chuckle from me as I swim over to her. "This is your home. You can do whatever you want."

We spend a few minutes like this, floating on our backs, drinking in the stars. Later, I swim toward the edge of the pool, Blaire follows me, folding her arms over the edge and resting her chin. Her eyes squint at the view.

"Jax?"

"Hmmm?"

"Did you try to mow the lawn today?"

"Yeah. What about it?"

"You missed a patch." Blaire points to the small patch of land wedged between the fence and the shed where we house the gardening tools.

I whip my head toward the direction of where she's pointing. "No, I didn't. I went over the whole thing twice."

"Look!" Blaire exclaims, my gaze falling on another spot near where her garden is. "And you missed another one there! Also, did you cut while the grass was wet?"

My mind cycles back to earlier in the afternoon. It was raining, and I couldn't afford to wait until it was dry since I wanted the yard to look perfect before she came home. "Yeah why?"

"There are huge ruts left by the mower wheels. See? Over there," she urges, pointing to the rows of tire marks in the middle. "There's probably wet grass sticking to the underside of the cutting deck. Did you check? Cuz that's gonna be annoying to get rid of."

"I just assumed it was normal," is all I can say.

Blaire makes a *tsk*ing sound, voicing her disapproval. "Well, this won't do. My dad would have never approved of this. D-minus."

"Whoa whoa whoa, D-minus?" I say incredulously. My chest broadens boastfully. "My work, though a little patchy and uneven, still deserves a better grade than a D-minus. Take it back."

"No way."

I cannot believe she's so smug about it. Sure, she knows more about yard work than I do, but she hasn't been at home enough to put in the actual work.

I whip my hand across the water and splash her face.

Blaire gasps, pebbles of water rolling off her face. "Oh my—*Jax*!" she sputters out. The look on her face. My back falls against the water, unable to control my laughter. "You know what? I *do* take it back. You get an *F*."

I straighten up, tensing my jaw. "Blaire Sullivan, that better be an F for fan-fucking-tastic."

"No, it's an F for fuck-you-for-questioning-my-grading-methods," Blaire snaps, pushing water toward my direction, completely soaking me. I spit the remaining water out.

"Right, this calls for retribution," I proclaim.

I stalk toward her and grab her waist, turning her so her back is against my chest. Blaire thrashes around me, trying to get me to loosen my grip, but it doesn't work, my strength overpowering hers. Finally, she jerks away from me hard, but this time she slips, gripping my wrist and submerging both of us into the pool.

"JA-GGGRHBBB!" Is the only thing Blaire can muster out before her mouth fills up with water. She's thrashing at my chest and I want to laugh, but my mouth is also clogged up with water. It's weird that I love how mad she gets at me. She's a beautiful, reckoning force of nature and all I want is to get caught up in the blaze.

Eventually, Blaire's feet kick up, propelling herself to break the surface. She gasps for the biggest lungful of air.

"That was not . . . *funny*!" Blaire goes to slap me against the shoulder, but her hair is stuck to her face and covers her eyes, so she ends up missing and smacks me lightly against my neck.

"It's a little funny," I'm laughing even harder now, but I decide to put her out of her own misery by pushing her wet hair aside so she can finally see. "Blaire, it's fine. You're fine."

"I hate you," Blaire whispers, but her face sinks into my hands when I cup her cheeks.

"No, you don't," I shake my head. My chest is moving up and down in shallow breaths. "You don't, darlin'. Not even a little bit."

I lean in, our foreheads closing in together, our noses grazing. I'm breathing hard. I can feel my pulse beating in my neck. She inhales me too, a tortured expression on her face. I break out into chills at the feel of her hands as they travel from my shoulder blades to my neck, drawing me close.

Oh fuck, I've just lost my ability to breathe.

She wants this. She wants me.

The confession is on the tip of her tongue. It's written across her face.

Come on, Blaire. Put me out of my misery. Please.

"Jax . . ." she chokes out. "We-we can't . . ."

"We can," I breathe, our mouths nearly touching. I cup her chin and tilt it toward me. "Fuck, baby, we *can*."

"No, we can't. And you know why."

I drop my hand from her chin. "I actually don't."

"What about *Baxton*?" Blaire makes an aggrieved noise. She grabs my hand and oh god, that was a mistake because my hand wants to reel her back into my chest and smash our mouths together. Blaire forces my gaze back to her. "Listen to *me*. What if Baxton finds out about us? It would kill his trust in me. I'm supposed to be taking care of you."

"But who takes care of you?" I retort, frustration sinking into my chest like an anchor. I just don't understand how we can spend so much time together, and she still doesn't realize what a phenomenal pair we can be. Unless it's her ego getting in the way of what she wants. I reel back, my perspective on the situation as clear as day. "Right, I see how it is. You're scared."

"About your dad kicking me out when he discovers I haven't been keeping my boundaries with you?" Blaire yells back. "Of course I'm scared!"

My throat tightens as my brain soaks up her rationale. She thinks I want her because I'm in a physically and emotionally vulnerable position? If that's the case, she's never been more wrong, because after I met her was the first time, I felt like I could finally breathe.

Blaire hands lift up in surrender. "I'm sorry, all right? I can't do this with you. There's just too much at stake."

She wriggles her way toward the pool ladder. Frustration burns her body when the water doesn't allow her to walk any faster than she wants to.

I'm not letting her get away.

I let the water swallow me whole as I swim in her direction and pop right back up in front of her, hindering her path to the ladder. Blaire bounces back, surprised.

"You're not really scared because of my dad," I tell her straight on, like I am ripping off a bandage, too quick to even think about what I am saying. "I don't know how he would react, but I doubt it would be terrible. You're scared because you feel a lot for me and you don't know what to do about it."

Blaire reels back, but I don't allow her to retreat, drawing her closer to me with a strong arm. Her breathing hitches. "It's okay to feel scared, Blaire. This shit is all new to me too. You think I like feeling like this? Like you have a chokehold on me like no other? I *hate* not being in control, and you know it. But, for you, I'd give it all up because that's how much you fucking mean to me. At least I'm not afraid to admit that out loud." My voice softens and I whisper, so softly but with so much certainty, my bottom lip trembling. "You're not just anyone, Blaire. I want you because you're the best goddamned thing that's ever happened to me, and I think we can make each other miles happier than if we're both alone."

I've spent the past month overcoming dozens of fears about myself and the people around me, and it has liberated me in a way I never thought possible. Sure, there are going to be bigger hills to climb, but *I'm* ready for whatever comes. Whatever this is between me and Blaire, is something I'm ready for.

I don't wanna lose this fight, but if Blaire isn't ready to fight for it, then I have no choice but to let her go.

Blaire opens her mouth to speak, but no words fall out. Nevertheless, her body language is clear. Her gaze refusing to meet mine, her lip trembling with nerves, I've already lost this fight before it even began.

"Okay," I swallow the rejection down, clenching my jaw in reproach. "Okay, I get it."

"Jax—" Blaire starts off.

"It's fine." I shrug. "Let's just forget about it okay?" I clench my jaw. "I'll be fine."

I won't. It'll hurt like hell, not being able to touch her, but I'll respect the decision she's made about us. We don't have to be together for me to care about her deeply.

"It's getting late," I mumble. "Let's get out of the water."

She nods quietly, wrecked with guilt.

A heavy breath gets stuck in my throat. I don't want to look at her anymore, so I turn my back on her and walk myself toward the pool ladder. The silence stretches for too long between us until I hear a string of obscenities slip from her lips.

"Wait," I hear Blaire say. "Just . . . wait."

"What?" I say, annoyed.

I whirl around, and in a span of a heartbeat, she's already swimming toward me. Her eyes are on fire, and every molecule of heat is directly aimed at me. My body throws itself into high alert.

I don't get a breath out because she winds her arms around my neck and brings my mouth to hers.

TWENTY-TWO

Jax

My entire chest nearly collapses from the weight of her kiss.

Goddamn.

She kisses me firmly and without restraint. Hands buried in my hair, she takes everything she can get from me. There is nothing light and innocent about this kiss. It's wild, greedy, and all-consuming. Tongues collide, teeth clash, and mouths devour. Damn, she kisses *good*. I've always imagined how her lips would taste—and the real thing doesn't disappoint. She's sour, sweet, bitter, tangy; hell and heaven all rolled into one.

I tighten my grip on her waist, my hands roaming around her, my fingers itching to get rid of the flimsy fabric of a bikini. She growls softly when my fingers splay against her skin, gripping it like I want to be permanently fused with her. In response, she takes the opportunity to suck on my bottom lip, then bite it.

It hurts but I couldn't care less. I'm so fucking delirious from the pleasure of it all that I'll let her do anything she wants to do to me.

Let her destroy me.

She already fucking owns me anyway.

Aching to be closer, I grab the back of Blaire's thighs and lift her up, forcing her legs to wrap around me. My fingers graze from her spine down to her ass and grip on the tight muscles there. I'm itching to slide my cock inside her. I'm rock-hard thinking about how easy it would be in this position, her legs wound around my hips, me pumping into her as she slides up and down my dick. It'll be so easy, so effortless, especially in the pool.

One of my hands find its way under her bikini top, my index finger grazing the nipple there. She moans and *fuck me,* if that isn't the most beautiful sound to ever exist in the world.

Blaire's mouth rips away from mine and suddenly it's by my ear, her heavy breath skimming the outside of it. My heartbeat is erratic as I'm thinking she's gonna tell me to fuck her in this pool, but she whispers to me something else.

"Like I said," Blaire breathes, "I'm not scared."

What. The. *Fuck?*

"Blaire . . ." I say, unable to register it all. "What—"

But she's already hauling herself out of the pool, swiping the towel resting over the sun lounger, and wrapping it over her body. She stops just shy of the doorway into the living room and her head turns a little to the side. Her thumb runs over the seam of her bottom lip, like she's remembering how amazing that kiss felt. Her gaze meets mine, softening. She looks at me for what feels like an eternity.

Kiss me again, goddammit. Kiss me and let's finish what we started—

"Goodnight, Jax," Blaire whispers instead.

No. No—

The last thing I notice is a slight twitch of her lips upward before she makes her way up the stairs.

I bury my hands into my wet hair, feeling like my entire world has ruptured.

***

I couldn't sleep the whole night.

I spent fifteen minutes trying to take care of my blue balls, and the rest of the night up in my bed, thinking about that goddamn kiss. It's not in my nature to have my thoughts revolving about one stupid kiss, but fuck, Blaire has left me in such a state of chaos that I'm this close to starting a riot over her.

I can't believe Blaire would kiss me like that and leave me ruined. Absolutely fucking ruined.

I hate it. Because I want *so* much more where that came from.

The thought alone keeps me tossing and turning for hours. At some time during the early morning, I hear Blaire's bedroom door creak open and the soft pattering of steps down the stairs, followed by the sound of the main door shutting. I'm tempted to run after her and demand to know where we'd left things, but the logical side of me forces me to stay put and give her some space. If there's anything I've learned about Blaire in the past month, it's to know when to step back and let her do her own thing. I force the frustration aside. Restraint is a muscle I've been exercising a lot of when I'm with Blaire.

I do eventually get some rest from Blaire's torment. By the time I've slipped into an undisturbed slumber, the doorbell rings, stirring me back awake.

I groan and turn away, stuffing a pillow over my face, hoping that it's just a delivery man who has enough sense to leave whatever package on the front door and leave me alone to be dead to the world.

But the doorbell buzzes for the second time. Then a third.

By then, I'm already up and annoyed as hell.

Who the fuck is awake at seven in the morning? A disgruntled neighbor? A nosy pap? Or . . . is it Blaire? Hope blossoms in my chest. Perhaps she forgot her keys and she's eager to finish what we started back in the pool. I haul my ass out of bed quickly, l put on a shirt and hurry down the stairs to look out the front door peephole.

It's a *kid*.

He looks young. About ten years old, maybe. Short, with long, thin arms and protruding ears. His black hair falls over his face, covering his eyes, as he moves his head left to right, second-guessing if there's really anyone here after all. *Shit*.

The kid takes a deep breath, then rings the doorbell for the *fourth* time, his other hand clutching tightly to his red backpack. He waits at the door impatiently, his body bouncing on the balls of his feet. He stares down at his sneakers, then looks up at the door again, this time a frown falling on his lips.

Well, shit. Part of me feels bad for him, but what the hell am I supposed to do? I don't even know the kid. And I'm supposed to let him in?

"Blaire!" The boy yells, pounding on the door three times with his fists. "Are you in there?"

Eden. As soon as the revelation falls upon me, I mentally slap myself for not realizing it sooner. They both have the same inky, jet-black hair, wide, hazel eyes and straight, sharp nose. Even the way he's standing right now, with his weight shifting from one leg to the other as he waits, is so Blaire-like.

What the hell is he doing here? I don't remember Blaire mentioning that he was coming to visit.

I unlock the front door and open it. Eden's eyes grow wide.

"Hey," I say, my voice still heavy with sleep.

He squints at me. "Are you Jax?"

"Yeah."

I guess Blaire's been talking about me to him. I wonder how much he knows about me, and what Blaire has probably left out.

"I'm Blaire's brother," Eden says, sticking his hand out.

I shake his hand awkwardly for a few seconds.

"Is Blaire around?" He peers through the crack in the doorway, curious. "Where is she?"

"Blaire's not home right now," I tell him, scratching my head. "Did you get here by yourself?"

"No," he seems annoyed by that. "My mom's in the car. Over there."

At the end of the driveway I notice a red car with a very irritated-looking middle-aged woman perched in the driver's seat. Upon noticing the exchange Eden and I are having, she pops the car door open and steps out, adjusting her long-sleeved blue blouse that looks like it came straight out of an '80s magazine. Her black heels click annoyingly against the driveway and up the stairs as she scrambles to the front door. "Excuse me. What's going on? Who are you and where's Blaire?" Both her hands cling on to Eden's shoulders as she stands behind him, looking at me like I've greatly offended her with my mere presence at my own house.

"I'm Jax. Blaire's roommate." I introduce myself to Eden's stepmom.

She stares at me with a mixture of judgment and irritation.

"Laura. Blaire didn't mention she had a roommate," Laura says, tendrils of impatience snaking through her. "Why is she not around? We agreed three days ago she was going to have Eden till the evening. If she didn't even bother to show up back home—"

"No, she's here." The lie shoots out of my mouth. "She just overslept. I'll wake her up."

"You go do that," Mrs. Adams hisses, tightening her hold Eden's shoulder. "We'll be waiting outside."

With a polite smile, I shut the door behind me and punch in Blaire's number as I go upstairs so I won't be overheard.

"Come on, come on. Pick up," I say to myself, waiting to get through. Hoping she's not in prison or dead in a ditch somewhere.

She answers the phone. "Hello?"

I release a huge sigh of relief. "Blaire—where the hell are you?"

"I'm on the way back from Ben's. Why?"

Jealousy plunges a knife into my gut.

So she goes and kisses me, then decides to sneak out of the house and spend the rest of her night with *Ben*?

A muscle throbs in my jaw. As much as I'm dying for more

answers, there are more important things to discuss.

"I don't know if you remember, but you have Eden today. Him and Laura are outside the house as we speak," I tell her.

"Yeah. But I wasn't supposed to have him until . . ." The realization dawns on Blaire when she finds out what the time is. "*Shit*. Time just flew for me. Just tell Laura I'm getting ready upstairs or something. You can just let Eden in."

"I'll try, but I doubt she's gonna let go of him that easily unless she sees you walk out that door."

"Just try, okay?" Her desperation filters through the phone. "Whatever you do, don't let him leave with her. I'll be there in ten." And then she hangs up.

I drop my phone back into the pocket of my joggers and compose myself before heading back downstairs for the second time and greeting them at the door again.

"Blaire's upstairs getting ready." My voice is smooth and calm as I say to the both of them, "Eden should be fine to wait in the living room."

As predicted, Laura jerks Eden backward defensively. The motion is so abrupt that Eden nearly stumbles.

"I can't do that," Laura mutters. "I need to speak to Blaire first before I leave."

Eden's annoyed gaze swings up. "You can do that when you pick me up later."

Laura's attention whips toward him, incredulous. "I'm not leaving you alone with a complete stranger."

"I'm not a stranger. I told you I'm Blaire's roommate."

"I don't care if you're her roommate," Laura's gaze darts back to me, cold and unrelenting. "I'm not leaving my son alone with you."

"He won't be alone. Blaire is upstairs right now getting ready."

"Then, we'll wait until she comes downstairs."

Even Eden senses the unnecessary aggression permeating this back-and-forth. He steps in between me and Laura, an irritable look slathered on his face. "You have that conference to go to, remember? You're already late," he says, turning his wrist to show her the time on his watch. "I'll be *fine*. I survived a month without you at camp. It's not that difficult."

A sigh pulls out of Laura. "That was different."

"Fine. If you can't let up on me because you think he's dangerous, here's my active location," Eden mutters, pulling out his phone and sending a live map containing his coordinates. "If Jax kidnaps me in Blaire's own home, then you and the cops will know where to find me." He's already shooing Laura off the front porch by swatting his hands. "Now *go*. Off to your conference. I'll see you later."

Laura steps back with uncertainty. "But—" she protests.

"It'll be *fine*!" Eden exclaims, already shimmying his way through the front door of the house. I step to the side to let him come in.

"Tell her to call me when you see her!" Is the last thing we hear from Laura before Eden slams the door shut.

When she's finally gone, Eden slumps against the door and looks up, letting out a long exhale.

"She's really something, huh?" I say to Eden.

"She's suffocating," Eden mutters. "But I've endured worse."

Eden looks around the house, noticing the lack of Blaire occupying the space. Eden looks at me expectantly, his hands tugging on the straps of his backpack. "So where is my sister?"

"On the way back from her . . . friend's place," I say with a cold shrug.

"Hmmm. *Friend*," Eden drawls out, catching the hesitation in my voice when I mention the word. He passes me, doing a little stroll around the living room. He nods his head like he's thinking *not too shabby*.

Nervousness creeps up on me. The last time I've ever felt like this was during my first underground fight, and that was nearly seven years ago.

Teenagers I can deal with. They're easier to relate to, and they usually don't mind me having no filter around them. I've never been good with kids. They're needy and ask for too much.

"So . . . you want some milk?" I ask awkwardly. "You wanna watch some television?"

Eden sends me a look that genuinely has me questioning my intelligence.

"I'm not five," he says sharply.

"I didn't say you were five."

"But you're treating me like I am. You can't bribe me with food and entertainment to keep me occupied." He places his backpack on the floor and climbs onto the sofa, crossing his legs and resting his arms on his knees. "I'm actually ten, you know."

"Okay. So, what do ten-year-olds like to do, then?"

"Well . . . I was going to wait until Blaire got here, but I guess we can use it now to kill some time," Eden mumbles, unzipping his backpack.

He digs both his hands in and pulls out a console of some kind, along with two controllers and what looks like a racing game cartridge.

"Fine." I roll my eyes. "I guess it'll help kill some time."

***

Ten minutes later, the little turd manages a *Mario Kart* sabotage so sneaky that he completely snubs me from ranking on the podium.

"You cheated!" I accuse, throwing the controller onto the space on the sofa beside me.

Eden laughs, basking in the glow of his victory. A victory he did *not* deserve.

"How the hell did I cheat?" He blinks at me innocently.

That look might work on me with his sister, but I'm not falling for it.

"You used the lightning shell on me!" I blast out. "I was in a vulnerable place."

"What are you talking about? You *were* first place," he argues back, but there's no mistaking the smile clearly meant to mock me for being a loser. "I had to level the playing field somehow."

"I want a rematch."

"Don't be such a baby."

"Rematch," I hiss out, the substantial need to prove myself that I'm just as good a *Mario Kart* racer as I am an MMA fighter roaring in my veins. *"Now."*

A laugh pops out of Eden. "Fine. But if you lose again, you can't call foul."

"I won't. Because I won't lose," I hiss again through gritted teeth as I balance the controller between my hands, laser-focused on the TV. We choose our players and I let Eden pick our racecourses. We're halfway through the second course when I hear the rattle of keys outside, followed by the door opening.

"Hey, guys," Blaire's smooth voice rings throughout the house.

Eden immediately smashes the pause button. Thank god because he's still whooping my ass in the rankings and I need a damn breather. Fuck this stupid game.

"Blaire." Eden dumps the controller and pushes off the sofa and runs over to give his sister a hug. Blaire tightens her arms around him, her face lighting up like fireworks on the fourth of July.

"Hey, E," she breathes, half standing, half crouching down. Her face is buried against the crook of his neck and she inhales deeply. "Oh my god, I missed you so much. You have no idea."

"I missed you too," he murmurs.

"How was space camp?" she asks.

"*So* much fun. I met a lot of cool people there. We learned what it's like to live onboard the International Space Station. Oh, and I got to feel what it's like to float in zero gravity. It was so weird. It was like floating in water without the sensation of water on your skin, you know?" he blurts out excitedly, as if he had a whole list of things he'd been dying to tell her. "We also got to eat freeze-dried food. Tastes so much worse than I thought."

"Well, it's only gonna get better from here. You ready for me to beat your ass at the High Striker?" She mock-punches her brother in the arm.

Eden peers up at her. "We're going to the Pier?" Blaire nods and he breaks into a wide grin. "Yes!"

"Go pack up. I'm gonna get ready," she tells him. Eden nods, rushing over to the TV to unplug his console.

When he's all packed up and waiting impatiently in the front seat of the car, I turn to Blaire.

"Hey," I say.

"Hey," she says.

The look we exchange is loaded with much more meaning than either of us intended. I'm tempted to ask her about the kiss right now, but I figure I'll save it for later, when it's just the two of us and we have more time on our hands.

"Looks like you have a fun day planned," I say instead. "I hope you enjoy your day with Eden."

Blaire passes me a quizzical look.

"What do you mean? You're coming with us," she declares.

Surprise colors my features. "You want me to come?"

"Yes," Blaire says, hiding a smile. "Will you come?"

Something tells me she doesn't often bring men to spend time with her brother. At least this means she doesn't completely hate my guts after what happened between us last night.

"Sure," I say, trying to play it cool. "I've got nothing better to do. It'll be fun."

"Okay. I just gotta grab my purse."

When she disappears into her room, I can't help smiling to myself.

Fuck, I'll do anything for this girl.

TWENTY-THREE

Blaire

As planned, Jax, Eden, and I end up at Santa Monica Pier around midday, indulging in every possible ride with a loop in it and gorging on carnival food. At one point, Eden was carrying an armful of hot dogs, churros, and pretzels as we strolled between the rides, games, and hordes of people.

We saved the best for last. I did my best on the High Striker, hitting a score of 650, which isn't too bad. Eden got ten points higher than me, resulting in a good thirty seconds of mocking before Jax swept in, cracked his knuckles, and got to work snagging the highest score of the day. Eden's jaw fell to the floor when the puck nearly shattered the bell, prompting a bewildered look from the carny.

After that, Jax became the coolest thing to ever exist for Eden, and I easily replaced Jax as the third wheel. To be honest, I didn't really mind. It warmed my heart to see them bonding.

Eden always craved a brother when we were growing up, so it's nice to see Eden clinging on to him like that. They talked about MMA, and Jax indulged him in some signature moves that he wielded in fights as we strolled on the boardwalk. Jax ended up performing something called a rear naked choke, pressing his elbow against Eden's neck. I have a feeling I'm gonna have a stern call from Laura tomorrow about Eden's sudden interest in taking MMA classes.

Later in the evening, we head down to the beach. We find ourselves a nice spot, enough of a distance away from the many pockets of tourists, but near enough to the ocean to enjoy the view of the sunset. I lay the towel down on the sand and take off my shoes, stretching my feet out in front of me and propping my elbows up behind me. While Jax jogs away to go grab us some water, I pull Eden into the crook of my arm and he leans into my side. We stay like this for a while, enjoying the sound of the waves crashing against the shore and the seagulls scavenging for food amongst the inexperienced tourists. Eden turns to me unexpectedly, contentment reaching his eyes.

"This is nice, Blaire," he whispers to me.

"It is."

"Thanks for the awesome day." He smiles giddily at me. "I'm really happy you have a job now."

I can only nod and smile back. When he turns away, I can feel my body shriveling with embarrassment and guilt.

All this time, he was under the impression that the reason I was able to afford the day today was because I managed to find work again. In a way that is true, but it's not work I'm proud of. I still owe Portia one more burglary soon, and I can't talk to anyone about it. I'm still recovering from the burglary from three weeks ago. My court date for expungement is coming up, so hopefully I'll be through with this web of lies soon.

"Got the waters. Four dollars a bottle. Can you believe that?" Jax approaches us, rolling Eden a bottle. "Also, I saw some kids' volleyball down the beach. Heard they're looking for another player."

"Really?" Eden asks, wide-eyed and nervous. Jax nods, pointing to the few of the three teenage boys a mile down the beach who are kicking around a soccer ball that has seen better days.

I nudge him, smiling. "Go. I think it'll be fun."

"All right." Eden pulls himself off the sand. He turns to Jax. "You wanna join us?"

"I'll join in a bit," Jax suggests.

As Eden makes his way over to the other kids, Jax plops himself down beside me and twists open his water, gulping down the liquid greedily. I stifle a laugh when it dribbles down the side of his mouth, droplets splashing down his arm.

"Eden looks like he's having a lot of fun," Jax jerks his head in Eden's direction.

"Yeah . . ." My smile wanes, still unsure of how to reconcile my guilt about lying to Eden about where my money is coming from. He thinks I'm an honest person making honest means, but it's far from the truth. My stomach flips sharply. My gaze pivots straight ahead, not wanting Jax to read into my dilemma. But it comes out of me anyway. "Jax, do you think we're all predestined for a certain kind of path?" I ask vaguely instead.

"That's a random segue." Jax hurls me a puzzled look. "What's wrong?"

"I'm sorry . . . it's just, Eden was talking about my job, and I lied to him about it, and I don't know . . ." I smooth a hand over my forehead, aggrieved. "I've always wanted to be the one to give him everything he ever wanted, you know? And yeah, I've done some bad stuff in my days, but I also always thought that what I did was just circumstantial and things would be different if I weren't on the streets. But now, I'm not so sure. It feels like I make the wrong choices all the time. And I still do them anyway because. . . I'm an inherently bad person," I admit, quietly picking away at the grains of sand clinging on to the side of my leg.

"That's not true, Blaire," Jax says, scooting closer to me. "You're not a bad person."

"I am," I whisper, feeling the emotion welling up inside me. "But it's like . . . I can't do anything else but *be* that person. And I'm just doomed to make the same mistakes over and over again."

Jax points a finger toward Eden. "You fight for the people you love. You fight for the people who can't fight for themselves. You fight because of some fucked-up system that labels people like you as deviants, and you fight because you will not let that ruin your life," he whispers, a crack audible in his voice. "That's a braver cause than anything I've ever fought for in my entire life. And trust me, I've done some cowardly stuff myself."

I blink a few times, pulling my gaze up to Jax's eyes, wondering what he meant by that. He's looking back at me too, but I get the sense that he isn't seeing me. It's that look that I'm already familiar with; one that has him wrestling with an avalanche of guilt.

Jax's guilt about his past was something I've never had

any interest in prying into, mostly because I was perfectly fine making the wrong assumptions about it and judging him for it. But now that I care about him, more than I allow myself to admit, I wonder if he will allow me to know what's been haunting him. And I suppose this is as good of a time as any to try.

"Is this about what happened in Boston, Jax?" I whisper, almost a plea. "Can you tell me what happened?"

Jax's jaw clenches in reproach. It's a while before he sighs. "I hurt someone there. A lot," he admits.

It's obvious he wants to say more, but his mind struggles with the words. I close my hand over his, glancing at him tenderly. "You can tell me."

Sadness drips into his face. "Her name is Sienna. She's my ex-girlfriend. She's the one I hurt." His throat tightens. "It was a very tumultuous relationship. I was the one to blame for it turning out like it did, really. I was selfish. Too focused on my own ambitions. And I couldn't give her what she wanted, which was my vulnerability. She took it very hard. It caused a lot of strain between us, until one day . . . we just couldn't take it anymore."

My mind struggled with the information. Jax in a long-term relationship? It's hard to picture at first, but as I thought about it more, it made sense; there's no way he would be as broken as he is if love didn't play a huge factor in his destruction.

Jax lets out a self-deprecating laugh. "I felt fucking stupid afterward. Like, *of course* I fucked up the only good thing I ever had. Of course it was me and my ego and my selfishness that turned her away. I decided eventually that I should just stop trying. Stop caring that much and just switch everything off. She said I wasn't capable of love anyway, so I swore I'd believe that. I decided to become the worst possible version of myself. I became the person that she thought I was all along. So . . .' He swallows hard before admitting his crime. "I had an affair. With her sister."

I'm at a complete loss for words. Of all the things I imagined Jax running from, it wouldn't have been an ex-girlfriend. And to betray her by getting with her sister . . . a chill shudders down my spine.

"There's no excuse for what I did," Jax asserts, noting my horror. "It's disgusting, and really fucked up. And it still haunts me to this day." His eyes were a pool of misery. "After Sienna found out what I'd done, she swore her revenge on me for ruining her life. We kept torturing each other, in the MMA ring, and out of it. It was driving me crazy. Drove her crazy too," Jax tells me, looking down at his feet. "Until one day, I was fighting in the ring against her boyfriend at the time. I was looking forward to fighting him. I gave it my all too." Jax swallows a lump down his throat. "But what I didn't expect was for Sienna to step in the ring to save him just as I was about to deliver the final blow . . ."

All the air rushes out from my lungs. Despite us being in an open area, I feel the world slowly closing in as my mind fills in the blanks for me in that sentence.

"Oh god." I clamp a hand around my mouth.

"My fate was sealed," he croaks out. "I was a monster. That's all I was. That's all I'll ever be."

"It was an *accident*, Jax." The words rush out of me, tightening my grip over his hand. "You can't blame yourself."

"Yes, I know that. But the whole thing could've been

avoided if it weren't for me and my complete and utter selfishness." The sorrow in his expression never went away. "I promised her I was never going to hurt her in *that* way. I've broken a lot of promises to her before, but I knew, or at least I thought I knew, that was the one promise I would die keeping."

"Did she make it out okay?" I whisper, unsure if I even wanted to know the answer.

"Yes. She recovered." Relief floods into my core. "We spoke for a bit after everything went down. But it was evident she needed space from me. Everyone did. I left because I couldn't handle the guilt. Clearly, until now, I didn't do a good job dealing with it," he mutters with a self-deprecating smile. It washes away from his face just as the waves in the ocean recede, and misery takes root instead.

My brain works hard to make sense of what happened.

I don't know how to feel. I don't even know what to say. I don't think there's anything *to* say. What Jax had done in Boston clearly warranted the backlash he'd received. I just wished he'd owned up to it sooner. Instead, he'd buried it under mountains of weed and alcohol because he couldn't deal with what he'd done.

But that man he just described to me—the man who had done all those things back in Boston—doesn't feel like the Jax I know. I recognize the remorse and the guilt that he harbors. A month ago, he probably would have allowed himself to get swallowed up by it all, but now, it's clear to me that he intends to do something about it.

Jax takes my hand in both of his, cupping them gently. "You said that you're doomed to make the same mistakes over and over again. If that applies to me, that means I'm destined to be what I've always been and there's no chance for redemption."

"There is a chance for redemption. There *is*. You just have to find it," I insist, adjusting our hands so our fingers intertwine. I need him to know that our lives aren't so different after all; in fact, they seem inextricably linked. "I've seen the potential for goodness in you, Jax. I see it every time I bring you to therapy, I saw it when I brought you to that resource center, and I see it when you're with me and when you're with Eden. You. Are. Good. You just need to embrace that side of you. Because it feels like you're constantly at war with a version of the person you think you're meant to be versus the person you *really* want to be. I can only hope that you're rooting for who's actually winning."

Jax flinches, flexing his fingers. He's still staring at our linked hands. This feels way more intimate than it's supposed to be, but I don't shy away from it. It feels nice. It feels *right*. Like two last puzzle pieces slotting into place.

"You're tough, Jax," I murmur. "You're probably invincible when you're in that ring. But when you're out of it, you're just as human as I am. Everyone makes mistakes. Maybe you and I just have to right more wrongs than ordinary people."

Jax's lips twitch into a smile. "There," he whispers, giving the back of my hand another soft, delicate brush with his thumb. "Looks like you answered the question about predestination yourself."

I lean back, forehead creasing. "I did, didn't I?" I say, surprised by myself.

Jax nods. "Life doesn't get to choose who we're meant to be. We carve that path on our own. I didn't used to believe it, but I do now," he tells me. "Before, I thought I had a prophecy to fulfill to be this villain, but . . . I don't want to be that guy anymore. I fucking hated that guy. That guy couldn't keep himself accountable for anything. You made me realize that I was the only one holding myself back all along. That there's a little space for a better version of me. I want to work on that. However improbable it may be."

"That's good. Don't be afraid to take the leap, Jax," I whisper, my hand reaching to the base of his neck and stroking the skin there. "Only then you'll realize how far you can actually fly."

He inhales my words and smiles. It's a confident smile, one that promises he's more than just words now. He's a man of action, a man of progress.

And dammit, does progress look so good on him.

If it's working on him, I sure hope it does on me too.

TWENTY-FOUR

Jax

We are too tired to make dinner when we get home from the pier, so Blaire orders us takeout from a nearby Chinese restaurant. After dinner, Eden and I manage to sneak in one quick game of *Mario Kart* before Laura's car arrives at our driveway to pick him up. It's bittersweet watching Eden and Blaire say their goodbyes. Blaire clings on to Eden tightly, her sorrow carved into the frown on her face as she's forced to let him go.

Blaire's attention is glued to the window until Laura pulls out of the driveway with Eden. When they're gone, she turns around and leans against the glass, a look of somber contentment on her expression. Her gaze falls to me, and the smile disappears at the realization that it's finally the two of us. I glance at her with equal confliction.

I'm not usually a man who wants answers, but this time, I'm desperate for her to say something, anything, that'll address the kiss, and the words we exchanged on the beach earlier.

"Today was really . . . nice," Blaire says, a faint smile on her lips.

"It was," I agree, remembering how unexpectedly open we were to one another about our struggles. She pulled something out of me that no one else has been able to crack open.

"I think I'm gonna head to bed," Blaire announces as she hugs herself tightly, discomfort tensing her body. "Got an early day tomorrow."

There is a thrum in my chest, a compulsion to say something, anything, just so I can keep her talking to me a few moments longer. Even if it means saying something stupid.

"Going out with Ben?" I ask, hating the sharpness my voice takes when I do. But I can't help myself with her; the thought of her running back to him the morning after we kissed was a major slap in the face.

Blaire frowns at my tone. "No. I've just got a bunch of errands to run."

"Right. Okay," I inhale. I step away from the stairs, giving her a chance to leave first. "Good night, darlin."

Blaire doesn't say anything. As I feared, I'd soured her mood. Clenching her jaw, she strides past me, a steely expression on her face, and up the stairs.

Then, she halts in her tracks. Her entire body swings back and she stalks back down, her eyes narrowed into slits toward me. This time, the anger is palpable, both in her expression and voice. "Just FYI, not that I need to provide an explanation, but I didn't go over to Ben's to sleep with him."

"I didn't say that you did."

"You didn't have to. It's written all over your face."

My hands fall to either side of me. "I'm sorry. You're right. It's none of my business."

Her hand drags down her mouth, frustration leaking out of her like an open wound. "I went over to end things with him, okay?" Her gaze meets mine with full force. "It didn't feel right to keep our arrangement going."

Pink tints her cheeks. She looks away, closing a hand over her face, feeling the warmth there, like she's embarrassed she just admitted that.

"Blaire." I grasp her hand.

She shakes her head but allows me to draw her close. She's still shaking her head when our bodies are mere inches apart.

"Don't look at me like that," she whispers.

"Like what?" I ask incredulously.

"Like you want to kiss the fuck out of me for telling you that," she groans. "It's not helping."

"Really? Because I believe I'm speeding up the process."

"That's not why I told you that."

"Then *why*, Blaire?" I insist. "You mean to tell me you ended a few-months-long-friends-with-benefits situation on a random Tuesday morning because you *felt* like it?" I shake my head in dismay. "You can't hide your heart from me forever, Blaire. It speaks to me in a language that only I can understand."

Blaire opens her mouth, but she doesn't speak. Only a struggling breath falls out. She glances away, embarrassed. She's retreating, I can feel it.

But I'm not gonna let her go without a fucking fight.

"Let me ask you this one more time, and please, tell me the truth: what the hell are you so afraid of?" I use my index finger to tilt her chin upward so our eyes can connect. I want to see exactly how I make her feel, because she won't give it to me otherwise.

Her face pinches with conflict, telling me she knows exactly what I'm talking about. Her shoulders tense and her eyes flutter shut, a sign of defeat.

"I'm afraid because you were not who I was supposed to fall for. You were not in the cards. Nobody was supposed to be," she whispers. "What if what you feel for me is fleeting, Jax?" she says, glancing up at me desperately. "I don't want to be temporary in your life."

I laugh, because my heart knows it to be false. The second I met her at the club, I'd fallen for her. I fell for her strength and kindness, and her willingness to help everybody, even a complete fuck-up like me. Being around her this month only made me realize I wanted her even more.

"You won't be temporary, Blaire. I'll make sure of it," I say, determination coursing in my tone.

"But how do you know that?" she moans.

"Because you're it for me," I growl. "I knew it even before Baxton had told us we were gonna be living together. You hear me? You're fucking *it*."

"You said I needed to take a leap. I am willing. I want to."

My hands are cupping her face, and she shivers against my touch. My lips hovering over hers. "So, take the leap with me, baby. *Please*."

Blaire whimpers, like a plea, and oh god, I can't fucking take it anymore. Before I can think twice, I bring her face toward me and cover her lips with mine.

The kiss *obliterates* me.

I bury my hands in Blaire's hair and she presses her hands on my chest,. I grasp her face in my hands to deepen the kiss. My tongue thrusts into her mouth in a deep, punishing stroke and she gasps when my hands clamp on her hips as I continue to devour her.

There's nothing subtle about the way we're kissing. It's pure starvation.

My heart is pounding so loudly that my heartbeat slams into my head like a drum. I can't get enough of her. Several weeks of sexual tension has finally led to this and holy shit, it's so fucking worth it. It's worth all the arguments and sweet torture. I'd endure it all again if I could replay this moment again and again.

My mouth continues to dominate her, passionate and frantic. Her hands bury themselves in my hair, holding me captive. Hot and sweet, she teases me with that tongue, tasting me in the same way I'm tasting her. Most days, I let her call the shots. Not tonight.

I grasp her chin and lick a path from her neck to her ear. I suck on her lobe and she clings to me, losing herself in the sensation. The desperate moan that escapes Blaire's lips sends a surge of adrenaline through my cock.

God fucking *damn* her.

There's no way I'm stopping this now. I just can't.

Her hands run up my arms, dancing over my biceps, and I cradle her face and angle it in a way that allows me to lavish the skin there with soft, open-mouthed kisses that'll surely get her going.

"Oh," she gasps, groaning as I suck on her skin. *"Oh."*

There's that sound again. My *god*.

I feel like I've won the fucking lottery every time with that sound.

She smells good, but tastes even better. Her buttery-smooth skin makes it easier for my lips to glide across. She gives a slight intake of breath.

"I hate what you do to me," she whispers.

I smile against her collarbone. "Do you want me to stop?"

She shakes her head, guiding my face back to hers.

I chuckle against her lips. Back to work, then.

I heave her up and she takes the opportunity to wrap her legs around my hips. There's no time for the bedroom, not with what I plan to do to her right now. My lips find hers again and I carry her to the kitchen table, propping her at the very edge of it.

Part of me thinks we should slow down, take our time, savor every inch of our bodies, but tonight, I'm greedy. I'm selfish. I want her, all of her, all at once, and if I don't, I'll fucking die.

The soft whimper that escapes her mouth when my thumb runs over the seam of her lips suggests to me that she feels the same way. She looks at me, pouting, waiting for me impatiently.

I bestow a light kiss on her lips before helping her out of her clothes. I leave the tank top on—I'm saving that for later—but I slide her jeans along with her panties down, then fling them somewhere I'm 90 percent sure we'll never see again.

She smiles, biting her lip as she parts her legs, her ankles digging on the edge of the counter. Seeing her spread open in front of me like this is breathtaking. *Erotic.*

She's a masterpiece and I'm motherfucking Monet.

I lick a finger and drag it across her opening, getting her

ready. But Jesus, she's already dripping wet, shivering at my touch. A growl leaves my mouth. I don't know if I'm gonna last, but I'm gonna have to try.

I plunge the finger inside Blaire and she moans so loud it echoes throughout the entire house. I work another finger inside her and curl them to hit the spot that has her chanting my name like she's in church and I'm God. She rocks against my hand, taking everything that I'm giving her. She bites her lip, never breaking eye contact from me I fuck her with my fingers, her eyes are blazing with unadulterated lust.

I need to taste her now or I'll lose my fucking mind.

Slowly, I remove my fingers from her warmth. I lower myself onto the ground. She is the only woman in the world I'll proudly get on my knees for.

"What are you going to do?" Blaire breathes, watching me curiously.

"What people do on tables," I say as I get on my knees, so I have better access to her pussy. "Eat."

I drag the tip of my tongue across her clit, tease her slowly, adding pressure when needed. My tongue swirls, poking and prodding, pushing and pulling. Her hands dig into my hair, encouraging me to *keep going. Don't stop. Don't ever stop. Right there. Please, Jax. Oh, yes.*

Everything that comes out from her mouth is a prayer demanding retribution. When she moans my name, my cock twitches every time, desperate for the friction. I could very well take her against this kitchen counter right now, but I'd rather see her lying comfortably against a bed while I fuck her senseless, because she's not gonna be getting out of it for a long time.

I curve my arms around both of her sweet, juicy thighs and grip them for support as I feed off her. She tilts her face upward, her mouth parted in that perfect little O while her hands grasp my hair. I don't stop doing what she wants me to do—lick, tease, blow, kiss, flirt. My tongue is performing a series of dances, relishing every inch of her.

She tastes like everything I ever dreamed of and everything that I thought I would never have.

Her skin buzzes from my licking. I eat her up like she's my last meal and I'm ravenous for her, for any part she will give me.

"Jax, I'm going to . . . I'm going to . . ." she croaks out.

"That's it, baby," I growl against her skin. "Be a good fucking girl and come for me. And don't hold back."

She moans loudly, my name escaping her tortured lips, and the last of her restraint falls apart. I watch her as she comes undone before me, and I want to sear the image of her coming into my mind forever because that was the most beautiful thing I've ever seen.

I get up from my knees and fit my lips over hers again, my hardness pressing against her slick wet pussy. The only thing separating us is the thin fabric of my pants, which I'm ready to tear off when the time calls for it.

Blaire groans, deepening the kiss, her legs wrapping around my waist and her arms sliding around my neck. She kisses me roughly, her lips greedy, her hands tightening around my neck, like she wants me so bad, and she never wants to let me go.

"Where to?" she whispers against my lips.

"My room," I gasp out, lifting her butt off the counter and walking her up the stairs.

Our lips never once part as I bring her up to my room. I infiltrate her mouth again like I pictured doing in all my fantasies, my tongue driving against hers, tasting her in my mouth. Her hands stroke the back of my neck, her hips grinding harder against my erection, moving slowly up and down the fabric of my pants. Even when we're together like this, she lives to torture me. I'm barely holding on.

I break away from her kiss long enough to whisper, "Keep doing that and it's going to get really embarrassing for me."

She laughs quietly. "I want to make you come."

"You can do that when I'm deep inside your pussy," I growl against her ear, biting it softly. "I promise."

I kick the door open carelessly and when we're both inside the room, I press Blaire up against the wall, latching my mouth on to her neck, my lips leaving hot, scorching kisses all the way down to her collarbone. She moans loudly in response, clinging on to my shoulder, her nails digging into me and scraping against my skin, the pain turning me on even more.

I press another fiery kiss on her lips before peeling myself her body to remove my shirt. Her hands roam from the top of my chest gently, down to the abs, all the way to the navel.

"Is this okay?" She peers up at me. "Does it hurt?"

"Not anymore," I whisper.

"Good." She smiles satisfyingly. "Take me to bed, then."

I chuckle, obliging her by carrying her to the bed, then gently lay her down on the mattress.

She stares at me, biting her lip as I quickly kick my shoes off, then unzip my pants and step out of them, leaving me in just my underwear. I help her out of her top, then her bra. When she's completely naked under me, she grins, her eyes challenging me to do something about the current state she's in.

"I love your tits, Blaire," I whisper. "Fucking obsessed with them. I've been wanting to do this for a long time now."

I dip my head down and latch on to one of her nipples, and she cries from the pleasure of it all. My teeth graze her nipple and she thrashes beneath me, squirming, her hands digging deep into my hair to prevent me from doing anything else other than worship her body.

"Oh my god," she moans. "More, Jax. *More.*"

I twirl her soft peaks with my tongue, slowly but surely, so she can feel what I'm doing to her. She whimpers a plea to keep going and I do, sucking and licking her rapidly hardening nipples. They're so sensitive that a mere flick has her thrashing around like live wire. My ego grows, knowing that I'm the one doing this to her. It's been a dream of mine to taste her here and now that I have, I don't ever want to stop.

My hands have gone fucking AWOL. I'm touching her everywhere, all at once, until I'm not sure where I'm touching, but as long as I make her feel really good, I honestly don't give a fuck anymore. She moans, then sucks on my bottom lip and runs her tongue along it. *Damn this sexy girl and her ability to undo me.* A cross between a breath, a sigh, and a groan escapes my lips when she reaches in between us to palm my erection through the fabric of my underwear.

I love the way her hands feel on my body, touching my chest, her fingers dancing over my pecs, outlining each one, her thumbs sliding over my lips.

I want to memorize the way she responds to my kisses and my touches. I want to remember the sexy sounds that she makes when I'm exploring her body with my hands and fingers. And I want to capture the pure, unabated hunger carved on her face when I slide out of my underwear, allowing my erection to slide out.

She licks her lips when she sees the length of my cock. Her elbows dig into the mattress behind her, and I grin wickedly, knowing all too well what's going to happen next.

I reach over my drawer to grab a condom, but Blaire grabs my arm and shakes her head. "I'm on the pill," she whispers. "And I just got tested. I'm clean. Are you?"

"I'm clean too." I don't skip out on getting tested regularly.

"Then, fuck me bare, Jax," she says, looking up at me with doe eyes that gets me rock-hard all over again.

I chuckle softly. "As you wish, darlin'."

I grab her leg behind the knee with my right hand, joining our lips together once again, after feeling that she's wet and ready for me, I thrust inside of her. She gasps so loud inside my mouth and I immediately still inside her.

"Did I hurt you?" I ask, crippled with worry. "Are you hurt—"

"No." She shakes her head. "You feel good. *Really* good. Please, don't stop."

A grin slides across my lips. I do what she says. I don't stop. I thrust into her deeply, my groans matching hers, filling the entire room. Her knees fall open as she holds on to my body, her fingers digging into my butt to encourage me to keep going. Her lips part, and the sounds that come out from her mouth sing in my ears like fucking heaven.

"Fuck, baby," I pant, my cock plunging in and out of her. "You feel so fucking good."

"Please, Jax, please," she moans. *"Harder."*

I dive into her, harder, faster, pushing in as deep as I can go. She moans in pleasure, her body clenching and unclenching beneath me each time I push in and out of her. Her breasts bounce with every thrust I make, and her hands clench around my arms, clinging on to me for dear life as I rock my hips into hers.

If this isn't nirvana, I don't know what else is.

My breaths go shallow and my mind is foggy. My brain threatens to shut down completely as my cock loses itself in her body. Her eyes roll back from the pleasure and each time my name escapes those lips of hers, I soar higher and higher. I can feel her nipples brushing against my chest, her hands tightening around my back, her gasps filling the air, forming precipitation on my lips.

Blaire, Blaire, Blaire, my heart is pounding her name so loudly I can almost hear it. She shivers under the heat of my skin as I glide my palm up her arm. I moan her name and roll my tongue over her nipple, my mouth knowing and tasting her.

"Come with me, darlin'," I whisper against her ear, groaning as I dive into her at an increasing speed. She yells my name from the top of her lungs, her body shuddering uncontrollably beneath me as the climax hits her.

"Fuck!" I scream, joining in on her cries.

Pure, red-hot ecstasy radiates through my body, convulsing with pleasure. I come so hard I forget how to breathe. Stars flash behind my closed eyelids as the orgasm crashes through me. She spreads her legs wider apart as I grab her hips and slam into her one last time, completely losing it.

When our climax subsides, heavy panting echoes around the room. She's still shaking from the aftershock. I fall onto the mattress beside Blaire and angle my head so I can see her. I pull her into my arms and kiss her bare shoulder. She shivers slightly, her eyes fluttering close. I chuckle when she reaches down to pull the blanket that I've thrown off the bed to sheath both of our bodies.

"Don't tell me you're tired already," I murmur, the back of my hand gliding down her arm.

"No," she half says, half yawns, and I chuckle loudly.

"Darlin'," I say, thumbing her lips. "This is just the beginning. I'm going to be the best you've ever had. And I intend to fulfill that promise."

"Promise fulfilled," she breathes.

"Not yet. I want to give you everything tonight. I want to taste you. Everywhere. I want to fuck you on every single surface imaginable. If you'll let me, of course. Unless . . ." I run my finger over her clit, eliciting a shiver to run through her body ". . . you're done for the night."

"Are you kidding?" she snorts, winding her arms around my neck. "Bring it on."

And I do.

TWENTY-FIVE

Blaire

I wake up with my head and arm dangling off the foot of the bed.

What the hell . . . ?

I prop my arms underneath me and blink rapidly, getting my vision back into focus. The bed is completely unrecognizable from what I remember it looking like before. Part of the headboard had collapsed, making it lopsided. Not only is the blanket nowhere in sight, but so are the sheets; just like us, the mattress is completely naked. I tilt my face upward, groaning, only to find my bra hanging from the overhead lights.

Memories of last night slowly begin to trickle back into my brain, so vivid I force my eyes shut from being overwhelmed.

I lost count of the number of times we had sex last night.

I remember him driving into me the second time while

I was perched on the edge of the bed. And I barely recovered from that before he pulled me up and had me pinned against the wall, pushing into me recklessly from behind. It was quick and dirty sex. And it didn't stop there. He bent me over the desk in his room and took me swiftly again. I got my revenge, tackling him to the bed and riding the both of us to exhaustion until we were too tired to move.

He kissed me good, like I was experiencing my first kiss all over again. He kissed me breathless, stealing all the oxygen from my lungs. He kissed me dizzy, making my whole world spin off its axis. He kissed me ferociously, like he had made up his mind about me and he wasn't backing down from it. Not now, not ever.

And let's not even start with the monstrosity that he packed in his pants. It's a miracle how I'd managed to withhold from him for so long. God, Jax's cock is a masterpiece. It was like it was specifically designed to make me spiral off the edge. I've been really missing out these past few weeks and it pisses me off to no avail. My PCs at the thought of wanting more from that came from.

Oh god.

I'm truly lost.

My gaze travels to the unmoving lump beside me. One of Jax's arms is thrown over my torso as he sleeps on his chest. His mouth is parted, snoring lightly. With a cautious finger, I poke Jax's shoulder, testing to see if he's really out of it or not.

My poke doesn't stir him.

He's still dead to the world.

I roll my eyes, and shift my weight to the other side, still reeling from what we'd done here. It's embarrassing, and quite frankly, pathetic, how much of myself I've surrendered to Jax. He fucked with my mind, my feelings, and now . . . he fucked me. Hard. *Good.*

My heart pounds as I stare up at the ceiling. Last night was based on raw, burning emotion. I need to be rational about this now.

Slowly, I remove Jax's arm from my body and drop it onto the available space between us. Then, with my arms, I push myself up into a sitting position. I try to bend my legs.

Oh my god, my legs don't move.

I'll just crawl out of bed, then. I use my arms to maneuver away from Jax as quietly as possible. I reach the very edge of the bed when a strong hand grips around my wrist, stilling me.

"Nu-uh," a sleep-heavy voice murmurs, all low and gravelly. "Not happening."

I whip around, horrified to find Jax staring right at me.

"No, I'm just—" I protest.

He doesn't let me finish. He just yanks me toward him and flips me sideways, wrapping a protective arm over my waist.

"Shhh," Jax whispers into my hair. "You're not going anywhere. You belong with me now."

"But—"

"Just stay and let it happen, Blaire," he mumbles, kissing my ear. "Just let it happen."

I turn my head to look at him. He answers me with a gentle, sleepy smile.

My heart clenches from the sight of it. How can I possibly say no to that?

"Okay . . ." I whisper back. "Okay. I'll stay."

It doesn't take me long to fall asleep to the steady sound of his heartbeat.

***

I am in and out of sleep for the next few hours, but when the morning light sifts through the billowing curtains, I stir awake for good. This time, Jax is no longer sleeping beside me. My palm presses over the indent of his side of the bed, wondering where he's gone. My question doesn't go unanswered for long, because a few minutes later, the door opens and a half-naked Jax is standing holding a tray with an assortment of food.

"Mornin'," he says, that southern Boston drawl still not lost on him.

Wow, he looks so incredibly sexy, I could just eat him up.

"Morning." I eye him as he sets the breakfast tray on the bed right in front of me, then climbs back into bed and kisses me tenderly on the shoulder.

"Thought you'd be hungry, so I made you something."

My surprised gaze falls upon the dishes of French toast, pancakes, and fresh strawberries. I'm unable to hide my grin as I drizzle the pancakes with syrup and cut myself a slice. Jax's eyes are on me as I chew, like he's excited for my reaction.

My lips purse into a frown as I swallow the bite. I push the tray to the side and rub my hands together contemplatively. "Jax, what did I say about your cooking?"

"That I should keep doing it every day?" he asks sheepishly.

I fight off a smile, my nose grazing his. "You're down bad for me, aren't you?"

"Am I? Because you're the one who can barely work."

I give him the stink eye. "And you didn't think to help me?"

"I wasn't about to aid you in your escape from me," he says, a sly grin twitching on his lips as his fingers pinch one of my hardened nipples. The wave of pleasure nearly catapults me off the bed.

"Oh . . ." I murmur, burying my face against his neck as he rolls my nipple between his fingers. "Mmmm, Jax . . ."

My head lolls to the side, and he takes advantage of that, licking the lobe of my ear and then all the way down my neck. When he reaches the base of it, he stops, mouth hovering over my skin. "You, know, I would love for you to not call me that anymore."

"You don't want me to call you Jax?" I ask, a little dazed.

He nods. "Call me Jackson."

I lift my head up so I can look at him. "I thought you hated being called that." I never really understood why.

Jax shakes his head. He pulls away far enough so he can cross his legs and rest his arms over his knees. "Before I was overreacting. I don't think it sounds half bad," he murmurs. "Jax is a forged identity. A buffer. A mask. When I put it on, I'm someone else. Someone who nobody should ever get close to. But when you're around . . ." He leans forward to cup my cheek with a steady hand. "Suddenly, I don't feel the need to be an outcast anymore."

My mouth forms a gentle smile.

"Jackson," I say, rolling the syllables with my tongue. "Jack-son. Jack*son*. Wow. That's gonna take a little getting used to."

"Don't worry," Jax whispers, tilting my chin upward to kiss

the tip of my nose. "We have all the time we need. I'm here for as long as you want me."

His words make my heart flutter. If someone told me a month ago that Jax would be committed to anything other than a bottle of Jack Daniel's, I would have simply laughed in their face.

"This . . . us . . . was a good decision, wasn't it?" I say, my lip quivering.

The feeling of uncertainty is so foreign to me, but it always seems to manifest when I'm with Jax. Not that I don't trust him. I do, with all my heart. I simply don't trust myself to not ruin a good thing.

"Of course, darlin'," Jax coaxes. "As you know, my reputation for making good decisions precedes me . . ." He lays me back down onto the pillows and climbs over me, a mischievous grin dangling on the edges of his lips.

I lose my breath just thinking about where else on my body I'd like him to kiss with those lips. As if he's heard my thoughts, he dips his head down and lays a trail of kisses from behind my neck down to my throat. His tongue rolls down the column of my neck, leaving a delicious shiver in its wake.

Before this, I wasn't even aware that my neck was my Achilles heel, but he knows exactly how to work it; the most sensitive spots to kiss. In just one night, Jax has learned a plethora of things about my body that no man had ever bothered to learn.

"Didn't you say that you had some errands to run?" Jax mumbles against my skin, a hand slipping in between my thighs to part them for him. He grins slyly when he feels the slick wetness pooling there again.

"Oh, I think I can afford to do them a little late," I whisper, feeling his hardness press up against me.

Jax chuckles, nudging his cock against my entrance.

"A *lot* late, darlin'," he clarifies, just as he enters me again.

TWENTY-SIX

Jax

"Cough for me," the doctor instructs, holding a stethoscope against my chest.

I do as he says, pushing the air out through my mouth. He asks me to repeat it, and I do, giving a couple of coughs until he tells me it's okay to stop.

He makes a *hmmm* noise, and I try to decipher the inflection of his tone in my mind, wondering whether it's a good or bad sign. I'm nervous. Usually, Blaire tags along with me to these doctor appointments, but I figured it's time for me to go to them myself. I would like to bring home some good news to her.

He removes the stethoscope from both ears and lays it over his shoulder. "Tell me if you feel any pain," he says, pressing three fingers against the left side of my ribs. "Here?"

"No."

"How about here?"

"No."

"Hmmm," he hums again. Again, I'm left unsure if it's a sign that I'm doing better or worse. I adjust my shirt as he wheels his chair back toward his computer.

"There are no signs of lung infection," the doctor tells me. He types something on the computer, his mouse making some clicking noises. He turns to me again, the glasses perched on his nose slipping as he tips his head down. "You've been doing your breathing exercises, right?"

"Yes." I nod. "Forty minutes a day—twenty when I wake up, and another twenty before I sleep."

"And you've been keeping healthy?"

"I jog every morning. And I just started teaching an MMA self-defense class for kids. No grappling or anything, though. I haven't been doing anything intense." *Except for sex*, I almost wanted to add.

Ever since the first night—and morning—we'd spent together, Blaire and I have been careful to not put my body through more strain. I protested at first, but knew it was necessary for my recovery. So we decided to hold off on sex until today's doctor's appointment.

It was difficult to go through the week without having sex with Blaire. I was creative enough to unleash my sexual frustration in other ways, mostly by going down on her. My face and tongue are very well acquainted with her pussy at this point; they might even actually be friends. But I'm eager for more than that. Which is why I need the doctor to give me the sign-off.

His fingers fly over the keyboard again, an expressionless mask over his face. After an uncomfortably long pause, he adjusts his glasses and mashes his lips together in a pleased smile. "Well, Mr. Deneris, I believe you're on track to make a full recovery. Based on what I'm seeing, you're good to resume your normal routine." He glances at the screen again, reading off something from an earlier report. "You mentioned you were an MMA fighter, right? You should be in the clear to start training again, should you wish to resume the sport."

"Thanks, Doc, but I'm good," I say, having zero intentions to return to fighting. I ease back against the chair.

"Oh, and by the way, you are also in the clear to travel," he makes sure to add. "I imagine it has been difficult, being far away from home."

I shake my head. Going back to Boston had not once entered my mind. At this point, it's barely an afterthought.

***

By the time I return home, it's almost evening. The smell of Mexican food wafts from the kitchen and greets my nostrils. Blaire is wearing one of my shirts, paired with my favorite black booty shorts, and her hair is tied up to a ponytail. Even when she's barely making an effort, she's gorgeous.

Her hands are expertly plating a salad from a wooden bowl when I wind my arms around her from behind and kiss her shoulder.

"Hey." I nuzzle against her neck. She smells like sour cream and cayenne.

Her body immediately relaxes. "Hey," she looks over her shoulder and smiles. "I made tacos and quesadillas." She spreads her arms wide open in a *ta-da* moment.

"Wow," I say in awe, leaning over the kitchen counter.

There's a plate filled with half a dozen hard-shell fish tacos, laid horizontally on top of each other. On the other plate rests four quarters of a perfectly grilled quesadilla, complete with oozing cheddar cheese. My stomach churns with hunger.

"Can I?" I point to the tacos and Blaire smiles, nodding. I claw a taco into my mouth. "Holy shit," I say when the first bite hits me.

"Like holy shit, it's good? Or holy shit, I should never touch a cooking pan again?"

"It's good. *Really* good," I say with a wide grin as I swallow the bite down.

There's a perfect amount of crunchiness and passion and flavor to it, balanced well by the acidity of the sauce and saltiness of the fish. I've tried making Mexican food at home before, and I've learned enough from it to know that not a lot of cooks would be able to nail this balance.

The dishes she'd been cooking for us have all been hits. You can always tell when something is made with love, and Blaire's heart is full when it comes to food.

"Remind me again why aren't you in culinary school?" I ask, grabbing a piece of quesadilla and popping it into my mouth. "I think LA City has a good culinary arts program."

"I know. I used to be enrolled," she admits.

"Really?" Surprise colors my features. "It's a good program. Have you ever thought about re-enrolling?"

She seems to be weighing her response. "I think I'm past that point in my life where I'd consider going back to school."

"Nonsense. You're never too old to go back to school."

"It's not my age. It's just that . . . I've got bigger things to worry about now. College is for people who are trying to figure themselves out. I think I've got a good grip of who I am, and what responsibilities I have."

Her response makes me frown. Sometimes I wish she could experience what it's like to not have the weight of the world on her shoulders.

"Anyway,"—she steers the topic of conversation elsewhere—"how was the doctor's appointment?"

I don't like her avoiding this college thing, but I know better than to keep pressing her about it.

"It went well, actually," I say, wiping the corner of my mouth with my thumb. "He basically said I could do whatever I wanted now."

"I thought that's what you were already doing." An amused gleam appears in her brown eyes.

"But at least I have the permission," I say, sharing her amusement. "He said I can train again if I want to."

Blaire sets aside her plate and tents her fingers together in front of her. "You know, that's not a bad idea. You should take up training again. Don't you miss it?"

"I like teaching. It's more fulfilling than whatever I used to do."

"Training can be fulfilling too, no?"

"Maybe. But not to me."

Blaire frowns. I don't get why she's upset about it. Fighting was what got me into the whole mess with Sienna and Kayden in the first place. I can't bear the thought of hurting another human being in a similar way. The sport brought out the worst in me; I'm not allowing it to have that control again. Better to steer clear of getting into the cage, and instead use my knowledge to arm others with the skills.

"Okay." Blaire drops the subject of training for now. "What else did the doctor say?"

"He mentioned I'm free to travel again if I want to," I tell her.

"Oh." She leans her back against the sink. "Right." She pouts, nibbling on her lower lip.

"What?"

"I guess we haven't really talked about it, have we?" Her gaze meets me head-on. "About you going back to Boston. I mean all this . . ." She gestures to the space around us. "Was supposed to be temporary."

"There's nothing to talk about," I say with a laugh, trying to diffuse her worries. "I'm not going back."

"You're not?" She holds in her surprise. I stare at her blankly, unsure of what she wants me to say. "Jax, you've been here for like what . . . almost two months now? Don't you have family back home? Friends who miss you?"

I squint at her. "My mom and my stepdad are dirtbags. My friends aren't really friends. They were more like people who only cared about what they could get from me. I don't really have anyone I really care about in Boston, Blaire."

"Well . . . how about Sienna?" she asks.

An itchy feeling crawls up my spine. "What about her?"

"Don't you want to see her again?"

Her question catches me off guard. Truth be told, I haven't thought about seeing Sienna since all that has happened. All I was focusing on was getting the hell away from her.

"I don't think she wants to see me," I say earnestly.

Blaire shakes her head. "That wasn't what I asked."

I suck in a breath. "I think it's best if we leave things as they are. Besides, she is my past. And I'm hers too. She deserves to live a good life, without me in it. I just want to start over fresh. Here. With you."

Her bottom lip sticks out. "Are you sure?"

"Yes, I'm sure," I murmur, strolling over toward Blaire and taking both of her hands in mine. "Come here, darlin'," I whisper, guiding her away from the kitchen and toward the living room. I pull her onto the couch beside me, a gentle hand stroking her thigh. "LA is my home. *You're* my home," I murmur, cupping her cheeks. "We've built something special here, don't you think? In this house? I'd personally like to see it through," I say, gesturing to the space we're in right now. Throw pillows and blankets that we'd bought together from Target decorate a once bare living room.

"Okay. I'm just worried," she whispers. I've learned whenever she says that, she's struggling with the vulnerability of showing how she feels in that moment.

"The hell I'm going anywhere, baby. You're stuck with me," I whisper back.

Her body softens and she smiles. Lately, she's been smiling a lot because of me, and I love it. I love knowing that I can make her happy. Cupping her cheek, I catch her lips in a kiss.

She sighs against my mouth, kissing me back fervently. I curl my fingers over the hem of her shirt, jerking her close, until we're flush against each other. Every time our mouths fuse together, it's electric. My body buzzes to life with her kiss.

"Jackson?" her whisper blankets me, making me feel fuzzy and warm.

"Hmmm?"

"Now that you got the green light from the doctor . . . can we fuck?"

I chuckle against her mouth. "I was definitely getting to it."

Grabbing her hand, I guide her toward the sofa.

Blaire crawls into my lap, hungrily exploring my mouth. I'm desperate for control this time, my mouth conquering hers in a blistering kiss that dissolves all of my sanity. I run my hands down the curve of her spine before my fingers dig into her waist. Her hands slide underneath my shirt to stroke my bare chest. Christ, her hands feel so good on me. I'm not a sensitive guy, but her touch always has me going rock-hard in an instant.

Pulling Blaire's shirt up, I yank her bra down to expose her tits. I pull one beaded nipple into my mouth, suck hard, and almost get a contact high. Her skin tastes divine, and her nipple is the best thing my tongue has ever wrapped itself around. I flick my tongue against her other nipple and she whimpers loudly, lost in the pleasure of it all.

"Jackson," she moans, one of her fingers teasingly gliding up and down my zipper before toying with the metal tab. I've suddenly lost the ability to breathe. "I wanna touch you."

"You've got two minutes to do what you want before it's my turn," I growl in her ear.

Blaire only answers me with a wicked smile. My cock twitches with excitement. Freeing my cock from my underwear, Blaire's hand fits around the base, starting with slow, punishing strokes.

The back of my head drops against the sofa, my eyes unable to keep themselves open. Goddamn, she really knows how to get me all fucked up. She makes sure to rub the sweet spot on the tip of my cock with her thumb, while not forgetting to toy with my balls. And there she goes, moving her hand along the shaft, applying the right kind of pressure, and a shudder of pleasure overtakes me.

Meanwhile, I can't take my eyes off her. She's staring at my cock and licking her lips, like she's hungry for more. But the ache in my balls warn me that the second there's any kind of suction on my cock, I'm going to explode.

I grasp her hand, stopping her movements on my cock.

"Time's up," I hiss out impatiently. "Get naked. On your hands and knees. *Now*."

Blaire licks her lips, a roguish grin on her face. She doesn't need to hear it twice; in fact, she does exactly as I say, shimmying out of her clothes and undergarments, and bracing herself on her hands and knees on the sofa. I kick off my shoes, underwear, and jeans, and pull my shirt up with a sweeping motion. I've waited for this moment all week, and I'm not waiting any longer.

"Lift that gorgeous ass for me, baby," I growl, stroking myself while Blaire perks her ass up for me. "I'm gonna fuck you on every surface and in every room in this house. Do you want that?"

"Yes. Please," Blaire croaks out.

She didn't need to tell me twice.

I sink into her, an inch at a time, hissing at every fraction of movement. She's hot and wet and so damn *snug*. Blaire's muffled moan against the sofa cushion is the motivation I need to fill her up completely.

"Oh," Blaire groans when I begin moving inside her. Holy

shit. Sex always feels good. But with Blaire, it wasn't just better. It was different. It made sense. It was perfect. "Oh, yes, baby, just like that."

I give her hair a hard tug upward so her upper body is flush against mine, arching her like a bow and drawing my hips back. The back of her head is pressed up against my forehead, her beautiful tits bouncing with every hard thrust. A delicious shiver tears through my body as our bodies slap together like this. I like seeing her like this. Completely at my mercy. The angle is different now, as I ram into her, our bodies slapping together with a punishing rhythm, my arm holding her captive against me. With each trust, I feel my balls tightening and tingling, my dick throbbing and pulsating.

I pull her mouth next to mine, dragging it across her check, and groan into the shell of her ear. She moans, getting off on the sound. She clenches around me and exhales loudly, thick with enjoyment.

"You love it when I fuck you like this, baby?" I growl in her ear. I don't get a response, only a hurried breath. *"Say it."*

"Yes, I love it," Blaire groans.

I tug her hair backward until her head lolls against my shoulder. I kiss her roughly, my fingers finding her clit between us and rubbing in circles. Each pump of my cock into her primed me for detonation.

"Oh, Jackson," she moans. "Oh, *yes.* Right *there.*"

"Fuck," I say, gripping her belly, my movements becoming more frantic. Meanwhile, she's clutching the armrest hard, like having a physical handle on something will help. The sensation is too intense. I can feel her shivering in my arms, which means she's close. I want to watch her come.

"Jackson, I'm . . ." she starts off, then flinches, and every muscle in her body tenses like she's having a stroke. She clenches around me so hard that my body feels like it has to join her. It hardens like stone, and I begin to break apart.

When it's over, we both collapse onto the couch. Blaire's hair is splayed across my chest. I chuckle to myself.

"What?" She grins up at me.

"If I had to choose between your food and sex with you, it would have to be this."

She rolls her eyes, offended about the ranking. "Who said you had to choose, idiot?"

That made me chuckle even harder.

TWENTY-SEVEN

Blaire

The next day, I hop out of the car, pushing my way through the front door of the café and find Elle tucked into a corner booth by the window, texting and smiling at her phone. There are already a few plates of pastries sitting in front of her. Her wheelchair is folded neatly and rests against the pillar beside her. We'd planned this brunch two weeks ago, but Elle had been busy with her fling-of-the month while I'd been wrapped up in my own little bubble with Jax.

I figured it was time to break the news to Elle that, for the first time since meeting her, I have officially acquired a boyfriend.

"I'm sorry I'm so . . . late." My words come out in short spurts of breath as I rush toward her table.

I decide it's best to omit the reason why I couldn't make it in time, which involves a superhot quickie in the bathroom, followed by fifteen minutes of trying to find my underwear while Jax begs for me to stay home for lunch. Instead, I drop my bag onto the table and slide into the seat in front of Elle.

"You got here by yourself?" I ask.

"Ben dropped me off," Elle mentions, tucking her phone away. She's all dolled up today, with pink glittery eyeshadow on her lids and wearing a rather cute, white floral dress with puffy sleeves. She watches me lift the menu and browse through the fifty-something food options as she gives her tea a stir. "I took the liberty of ordering for us because I'm starving. Two soy lattes, an almond croissant, strawberry tart, and some other pastries. And also I can't stay long because I have a coffee date with a B-lister I met off of Hinge in half an hour and you never seem to have anything going on in your life anyway so I'm sure our brunch will be short—"

"I'm dating Jax," I blurt out. "And worse, I might be falling in love with him."

Elle stops talking because her jaw is already on the floor.

I admit, the announcement could've waited until our order arrived, but I've just been feeling too over the moon that it feels like I'm on a slippery slope, and if I don't discuss this ASAP, I might just fall and crash into the deep end without a second thought.

"Damn." Elle whistles low, her arms folded across her chest. Her front teeth sink into her bottom lip contemplatively. "I missed out on a lot.?"

"A little," I say with a weak laugh.

"Okay, give me a second. I'm gonna text him I'll be late," she says urgently, pulling out her phone from her bag. "But the second I'm done, you better spill everything. And I mean everything, *capisce*?"

A wry smile tugs on my lips.

"Capisce."

***

"I wanna be happy. I do. God, I *am*. So happy," I say with a sigh, toying with the straw in my third sangria of the hour. The alcohol has already worked its way into my system, and there's a light buzz filling my head. "I never thought I'd ever say this, but I'm high on Jax-mania. But I just can't help feeling like it's a little too good to be true, you know? Like in the end, this is gonna end up hurting me. It's just a matter of when."

I've completely been sucked into Jax's orbit, infected with some kind of disease and he's the cure for it. I can't even look at him for long without getting shy. It's bad. It reminds me of a time when my innocence wasn't yet corrupted by all the things that had happened to me, and it makes me feel uneasy. Unguarded.

For the first time in my life, there's someone other than Eden whom I hold close in my heart; someone who has the ability to wreck me from the inside out.

Elle rolls her eyes. I can't tell if she's buzzed as I am—probably not, since I'm a lightweight—but even if she is, she hides it way better than I do because she reaches forward and pinches me really hard in the elbow.

"Ow!" I shriek, cradling my arm as the sting reverberates down my hand. "What the hell was that for?"

"There. You're hurt," she declares. "You couldn't stop *me* from doing that, could you?"

"You're completely missing the point."

"No, *you're* missing the point, Blaire," Elle argues, a serious look painted across her features. "The point is you can never know who's gonna hurt you or when you're gonna get hurt. Only that the pain liberates us rather than kills us." She speaks so eloquently here that I often forget that this trashy-TV-show-obsessed fan has an IQ score of two hundred. Her hand reaches forward to cup mine, and her tone is earnest when she adds, "You have something rare with Jax. Don't get wrapped up in survival mode, otherwise you'll forget what it's like to actually live."

I sink into my seat, her words settling down into my mind like a warm blanket. She's right; I'm so concerned about how it's inevitably going to end that I might just miss out on enjoying these precious moments with Jax. And if there's anything I should have hope for, it should be for this special thing I have with him.

"You're right," I say with a sigh.

"I'm always right." Elle puffs out her chest proudly.

"Yeah, you are. Goddamn you," I say begrudgingly. Elle lifts up her sangria glass and does a little shimmy as she sips on it.

I continue to gush, telling her about my firsts with Jax, like our first date and for our first hookup (Elle was not surprised to hear that that came *before* our first date).

I manage to steer the conversation to Elle, was curious to find out about her brief fling with a famous social media influencer, which was a wild one. It involved a manipulative ex-girlfriend at Elle's doorstep at three o'clock in the morning, shouting expletives at her from the front yard and a hidden paparazzi cam hidden in Ben's car. That was a doozy, and I'm personally glad that relationship is over.

There's one last thing I'd been dying to ask her about, my heart beating rapidly when I do. "How's Ben?"

The amusement in Elle's expression wears away. She sets her glass of sangria down, her eyes getting a little glassy, and I'm unsure if it's from the copious amounts of alcohol we've consumed, or the complicated emotions attached to her brother mixed with the awkward situation I put her in when I ended things with him.

"Uh, he's all right," Elle says, though something tells me she's stretching the truth a little bit. A sigh pulls out of her and she slumps her chest forward. "He just misses you. Not in like a sexual way, but you know."

I nod wordlessly.

"I miss him too," I whisper.

After I kissed Jax the first time, I was riddled with guilt about liking it a lot more than I should. That was when I knew that whether or not I ended up with Jax, it was no longer a good idea to keep seeing Ben in an intimate way.

Ben took it hard, of course. It surprised me how hard he took it. Our arrangement was always casual, and he always emphasized that we could end it any time we wanted.

But in a way, Ben knew the end was coming. I wasn't exactly subtle in avoiding his physical touch. I probably should've ended things with him much earlier, but I'd been hoping my feelings toward Jax were simply an anomaly in my brain. But the feelings were here to stay, and it didn't feel right anymore keeping Ben in the dark about them.

"I just think it's better if we don't talk for a while, you know?" I say to Elle. "He didn't admit it to me then, but I got the feeling that . . . well, feelings were involved on his end."

"Yeah, I knew about that." Elle's mouth stretches out into a thin line. "Honestly, it's a good thing you guys aren't talking. He needs the space. To be honest, I was expecting this to end sooner or later. If not for Ben catching feelings, then it was gonna be you doing your whole cold-feet spiel."

I blink at her. "I do that a lot, do I?"

Elle huffs out a laugh. "You may think you're an emotionless husk, but you're the most emotional person I know. It makes getting advice through to you a lot harder. But you know I love you in spite of it."

My heart compresses with appreciation.

"Oh god, I freaking missed you." I throw my arms across the table to hug her. Elle laughs when they only meet halfway. Whatever, it's the thought that counts.

"See what I mean?" Her face breaks into a ridiculous smile. "I missed you too. At least we'll be seeing more of each other in the fall, since the UCLA school of law building isn't too far from here . . ."

It had slipped my mind how close Elle's fall term is closing in on us. I guess it never really felt real to me since affording Elle's tuition was always a point of contention in the Peterson household, but now that it's happening, I don't know how to feel. Left behind is a feeling that comes to mind.

Elle notices the shift in my mood. She leans forward, an earnest expression in her gaze. "Study with me, Blaire. I know you said you didn't want to go through it again, but you can try."

I frown. "UCLA doesn't have a culinary arts program."

"It doesn't have to be UCLA. It could be anywhere you want. It could be LA City again, for all I care."

"But it's already July. Admissions are long closed by now."

"There's always the spring term."

I shake my head, dismissing the notion in my mind. I shouldn't be entertaining this. My college days are long over. And besides, I can't do that; not to Eden. He's the single most important thing right now. All my energy and funds should be directed toward him.

"I wish I could but . . ." I find myself saying. "I've got more urgent matters to put my money toward. You know Eden still needs my full attention. And building a case to fight for custody isn't cheap."

Elle stares at me with a conflicted expression. "All that may be true, but you're forgetting the most important bit." A hand reaches over to clasp over mine, and she stares at me with a somewhat conflicted expression. "I know you think you don't deserve it after you went to jail, but I don't want you wasting your years away wishing you had gone back to college. It was robbed from you once, and I don't think I could bear to witness you do that to yourself."

My heart lodges in my throat. She's probably right. All of my points are just excuses to tell myself that I'm undeserving of this experience. I just can't seem to admit it out loud. I have to think about Eden. If I had to choose between either of us to build a strong future for, it's always gonna be him.

"I'll . . . think about it, okay?" I whisper.

Elle's eyes remain the same, but her mouth changes. Her lips curl into a wavering smile. "Okay."

Desperate to diffuse some of the tension between us, I make her a promise. "I know this isn't a good consolation, but I swear I'll be there to pick out all your dorm furniture and give the stink eye to your new roomie who thinks she's gonna replace me as your best friend."

Laughter spills out of her, bright and warm.

"If she's smart enough to get into UCLA, she'll know there's gonna be no competition." Elle smiles tenderly at me.

**

By the time I get home, it's 4:00 p.m. and I'm still reeling from the two jugs of sangria I shared with Elle from brunch. I stumble through the French doors to find Jax working the yard with a lawnmower in nothing but a pair of jeans, his powerful, muscled body glistening with sweat as he pushes the mower through the last patch of grass toward the far end of the fence.

I can't believe this man is mine.

Jax's face perks up when he notices me walking over toward him, and he shuts the mower off. "Hey, darlin'," he murmurs when I'm nestled against his chest.

"Hi," I squeak out, grateful to be in his arms again.

He catches my lips in a swift kiss before releasing me. He gestures to the neatly mowed grass around him. "This is looking much better than the last time, no? I waited until there was less heat during the day, like you said, and only cut about a third of the length of the grass to let it grow more evenly this time."

"To be honest, I wasn't really paying attention to the grass," I coo, biting my lip mischievously as I find my fingers dancing up his naked chest. It would be be cruel not to have this pressed up against my back, like right this instant.

My cheeks grow a flush. *My god, is this me or the sangria talking?*

Jax catches my chin with a finger, grinning wildly. "My, my, Blaire Sullivan, am I turning you into a sex fiend? Do I need to get you on some therapy program? Put *you* on house arrest?"

"House arrest might actually make things worse," I whisper. "Whatever else can we do while we're locked up together?"

He lets out a raspy chuckle.

"All right. Come here," he says in a tone suggesting that *we need to rectify this immediately*, weaving his fingers into mine and tugging me toward the pool area, abandoning the mower.

He sits himself on the sun lounger and guides me on top of him. I lay my hands on either side of his shoulders, wondering what he's going to do to me. A sense of thrill and anticipation buzzes in my brain and travels down my body. Both of his rough, calloused hands get a feel for my upper body, snaking underneath my T-shirt.

"Tell me about your brunch date with Elle," he murmurs, his nose grazing the curve of my neck. Oh *fuck*. He's not taking his time today; he's on a mission and gunning for what yields him immediate results. He lays a trail of kisses, then licks my earlobe. I let out a soft moan.

Jax's hands stop moving. His lips graze my ear.

"Answer my question, darlin."

I see what game we're playing here.

I nod smally. "My brunch date with Elle was good. We had a lot of cake," I say, and Jax returns to worshipping my body with his hands and his mouth. I feel the urge to tell him about Elle asking me to go back to college, but Jax would probably get in her corner and it would ruin the whole mood, so I decide it's better to omit the thought and instead focus on Jax and his talented hands.

"What else, baby?" His lips graze my jaw.

His fingers work the latch of my bra, allowing easier access to my breasts, which became destination number one for his left hand. The other works the buttons on my denim shorts. My breathing hitches. I try to make sense of anything but Jax, but it's impossible, not when his hand is so close to where I want it to be the most.

"We also had way too much sangria," I whisper.

Jax chuckles, his thumb grazing one hard nipple. "That explains the wine breath," he whispers against my neck. Then, he starts to roll the hard peak between his fingers.

"*Oh,*" the sound bursts out of me, a mixture of satisfaction and surprise. My thoughts begin to fade away as I focus on the pleasure of it all. My hands claw at his shoulders, a sigh seeping from my lips. "Jackson . . ."

"Continue your story," he demands, lifting his head up to meet my gaze. Defiantly, I shake my head no.

Jax stops what he's doing. I whine in frustration. "Please."

"Continue. Your. Story."

Jax isn't going to budge, and I'm too impatient to play this game with him, not when I'm determined to get what I want. Silently, I give him a nod. He returns to my neck, pleased. His right hand has successfully slipped inside my pants, past my underwear. "What is Elle up to?"

"She's currently on a date with an actor who used to be on

Gossip Girl . . . ah—" I let out a moan so loud our neighbors can probably hear it when he dips a finger inside me, all the while his other hand continues to palm my breasts. *"Please."*

"Which one?" Jax asks innocently, ignoring my desperation.

"Huh?"

"Which actor?"

His finger slips in and out of me, sending my mind spinning off axis. "I don't know . . ."

"Did you tell Elle about me?" Jax prompts, grazing my nipple with his thumb again. I don't know how he's able to do all that while fucking me with his fingers in complete synchronicity, but it works, and my body can't take the overwhelming sensation. My hips move against the rhythm of his finger. "What did she say about me?"

This time, I'm the one who pauses, doing a double take. "You care about what Elle thinks of you?"

"Of course. She's your best friend and I need the BFF stamp of approval. Every guy knows that's the one to gun for," Jax tells me with such seriousness. Massaging a response out of me, he adds a *second* finger in. "Tell me, baby. Tell me if I got the stamp."

"Yes," I say weakly. "She thinks you're good for me."

"Only for you, baby," he whispers, pleased. "Only for you."

His fingers shift against me, finding that swollen heat.

"Oh . . ." I moan out, my eyes squeezing shut as I savor the sensation. "Oh!"

His head is squashed against my chest, breathing hard too as he works his fingers hard. My nerves burn with pleasure as the heat spreads through my pussy. My hips ride his hand shamelessly, chasing the orgasm that's rising through me.

"Don't stop," I rasp, pushing my pussy into his hand.

He chuckles against my shoulder, pushing his fingers in and out like a pleasure machine. His entire face drips with lust. "That's right, baby. I love it when you fuck my hand. So hot. So *fucking* hot."

"*Oh, yes—*"

I don't know why those words are the thing that do it for me, but they do, and the orgasm ripples around his fingers, traveling down my body in a wave of shivers. White stars blink behind my eyes as all the air rushes out of my lungs. Jax's hand flies over my mouth unexpectedly, muffling the sound of my moan as I cry out, jolting against him. When the high subsides, he quickly removes his hands from my body and helps me button my shorts. He's quiet. Concerned.

"Jackson?" I whisper, suddenly worried that I did something to upset him.

"Don't panic," Jax says calmly, but the fear in his eyes tells me a different story. "But I heard someone come through the front door."

A mixture of confusion and apprehension flits through me. Who would just show up at our house-

"Anyone here?" Baxton's voice rings throughout the living room, loud and clear as he shuts the door behind him.

My face blanches.

I meet Jax's horrified gaze.

TWENTY-EIGHT

Jax

With quick succession, Blaire catapults herself off the sun lounger, clasping her bra back on and tucking her shirt back into her shorts. I can practically hear the tornado of thoughts ripping through her mind as she racks up a plan to get ourselves out of this situation.

"Okay, I have a plan," she says frantically. "I'm gonna act cool. Pretend I just came home."

"Don't be ridiculous."

"Ridiculous? As opposed to this?" Blaire gestures to her disheveled, just-got-fucked-by-a-hand hair and smudged lipstick on her face. "I'm supposed to be your sponsor. Right now, I look like your whore."

Something about the word *whore* frustrates me. I'm not opposed to the idea, as long as the objectification stays within the confines of the bedroom.

"You're not any of those things. You're my girlfriend," I whisper, leaning down to brush my lips quickly against hers. "We got this."

By the time Baxton manages to find us in the backyard, I'm wheeling the mower back into the shed and Blaire has both her legs up on the patio furniture, pretending to read a gardening magazine that I'd left there this morning.

"Baxton." Blaire looks over her shoulder and smiles at him. She closes the magazine and slides out of the chair. "What a nice surprise."

"What's up?" I say in a surprisingly casual tone.

I dust off the grass from my jeans and walk over in Baxton's direction. Baxton's head snaps toward me, the annoyance palpable on his face. Today, he's sporting a plain white shirt and jeans, as a pair of Ray-Bans rests on his collar. He's usually only dressed this casual when he's out running errands and there's a chance he might run into the paps for a photo-op for that effortless look. When I was younger, I would always see right through them.

"What's up?" Baxton echoes, baffled. "I've been trying to get in touch with you both for days, but no response. Is not checking your phone a Gen Z thing? I thought your generation lived on your phones." A worried frown tugs on his face. "What the hell is going on?"

I try to appear nonchalant. "We've been busy," I say, keeping it vague.

"With what?"

"Housework. Been trying to keep myself useful."

Baxton's gaze swings toward Blaire, expecting a response. Her mind scrambles for a response.

"I . . . uh, you know, Pilates," Blaire blurts out.

A suspicious brow from Baxton. "Pilates?"

"What? I'm trying to keep fit," Blaire mumbles. "It's basically a rite of passage for every LA girl. Thought I should try it out, see what the hype is."

"Well, I'm parched," I declare, saving Blaire from having to spew out more lies. "Coffee?"

Baxton scratches his forehead. "Fine."

The three of us make our way to the kitchen, where I get started brewing a pot of coffee while Blaire picks some mugs out. I pass a steaming cup to Baxton and Blaire and pour one for myself. Blaire hugs the mug in between her hands, leaning over the island. I rest a hip over the pillar and wait for Baxton to speak, because clearly he has something urgent to tell us if he drove all the way over.

I'm hoping it's not another stern warning about something I did. It's not like there's anything he can reprimand me for; I've been a fucking saint lately—I rarely step out of the house, and when I do it's to help Blaire out at the center or to take her on a date. I haven't set foot in a bar or a club in more than a month now. Haven't felt the need to touch a bottle or a joint in weeks.

Baxton lays his coffee down on the island and clears his throat. "Well, if either of you bothered to pick up my calls or read my messages, I was trying to let you know that my upcoming movie, *A Fool's Gold*, will be releasing in theaters in soon and you're both invited to the premiere."

"Wow." My surprise is audible. "Really?"

And here I thought he couldn't even trust me to leave the house alone. Now, he wants to be seen with me in public?

"You really want me there at your premiere?" I say with a questioning brow. "You don't think I'm gonna fuck it up somehow?"

"No. I trust you, Jackson." His tender gaze flickers at me. "I'm really proud of your progress. And I think you'll have fun." He mashes his lips together. "Of course, there will be an afterparty . . ."

"I'll stay away from the alcohol," I tell him.

My mouth quivers into a smile. Goddammit, I shouldn't be as happy about this as I am. I feel ten years old again, desperate for his approval.

"Is Harvey Dystel invited?" Blaire rocks herself excitedly on the balls of her feet. "Do I finally get to meet him?"

"Yes, he'll be there," Baxton says with a dramatic sigh.

"No fucking way!" Blaire exclaims, nearly knocking her mug off the counter. When she realizes her excitement had been way too loud, she clears her throat, straightening herself up. "I mean, it's cool. I'm cool." She shrugs.

"Harvey Dystel?" I eye her. If I recall correctly, he's one of those hunks whom Baxton works alongside on his TV show. Purely as eye-candy—that apparently works wonders on Blaire.

"I believe you said once that he has a cute ass, and you'd like him to . . . do you in every position known to mankind?" Baxton says, hiding a smile behind his hand.

My amused gaze moves toward Blaire. "Is that so?"

"You're exaggerating my words. I believe I said he has a professional work ethic."

Baxton snorts.

I adjust the collar of my neck as the muscles tense. First I had to worry about Ben, and now this actor guy? Jealousy is a string only Blaire knows how to pull.

"So I trust that you both will be there?" Baxton's eyes ping-pong between us.

Blaire nods. "We'll be there."

"Good," Baxton says, pleased. He takes another sip of his coffee before adding, "You'll both need some media training, I reckon. I'll send someone over to go through potential questions you'll be asked. This will be particularly useful for you, Jackson, since you'll probably get asked about what happened last month. And I'll schedule a fitting with a stylist for you both next week. All I need from you guys are your shoe and clothing sizes, and my team will take care of the rest."

"I'll get that taken care of," Blaire tells him.

"Thanks," Baxton says, going over to place his now empty mug in the sink. He rubs his hands together and turns to me. "Oh, and Jackson? A word?"

"Sure," I say, my hands going into the pockets of my sweatpants.

Baxton leads me to the outside patio, and takes a moment to look around. He seems somewhat amazed at how well kept the area is. Dead leaves have been raked, bushes have been trimmed, plants are thriving, and the pool is sparkling. All in a day's hard work by yours truly.

"Well?" Baxton asks, fishing for some kind of explanation.

"Well, what?"

"You know, neither of you are very discreet," he says. "Blaire practically reeks of you. And you keep staring at her like you just discovered that God exists. I didn't want to call it out back there because I don't wish to put either of you on the spot."

My stomach drops.

And here I thought we'd both been so careful.

"Well, um, she's afraid you'll be disappointed in her," I mumble, trying to find the words. "She feels like she's failed at her job."

"Really? Because she got you to quit drinking in less than two months. She's actually done a better job than I would have ever imagined."

"You're not mad, then?" I would have thought I'd be on the receiving end of another one of his fatherly outbursts, ending with him sending me away to rehab as punishment for sleeping with my sponsor.

"You think I didn't think this through? Moving you in with a responsible woman roughly your age, forcing you to spend every waking moment with her, hoping you guys will see in each other what you need to find in yourselves? I'm not stupid, Jackson." His lips quirks into a faint smile. "I may actually be a genius."

Well, then.

He set up the trap and I fell right into it. The worst part is, I've never felt so happy being enclosed in it.

"Just don't break her heart," he warns. "I didn't save her from the streets just for you to destroy her. You have a capacity to hurt just as much as to love. Make sure she's on the right side of it."

I gulp hard, nodding. I have zero intentions of hurting Blaire. She's it for me. I've never felt for anyone the way I've felt about her, so there's no one else I can imagine myself being with.

She's the real deal.

"I'm leaving now, Blaire!" Baxton yells, a hand going into his pocket to retrieve his car keys. "Let's have lunch soon!"

"Sure!" Blaire shouts from the kitchen.

I walk Baxton back to the front of the house, where he gives me a rather awkward pat on the back before slipping into the driver's seat of his Tesla. I watch him pull out of the driveway and disappear down the street before heading back inside. When I do, a worried crease digs into Blaire's forehead, her upper teeth sinking into her bottom lip as she meets me halfway in the living room. I take her hand in mine and lead her down to sit on the sofa with me. She sits sideways, laying both her legs over my lap.

When she registers the expression on my face, she purses her lips.

"He knows, doesn't he?"

"Yeah."

"And he's okay with it?"

"He's actually rooting for us."

Surprise colors her beautiful features. "You think that was his plan all along?"

"It actually was."

"That's weird," she remarks. "But . . . oddly comforting."

It *is* comforting. For him to know that we were perfect for each other without us even knowing it requires a kind of intuition that I didn't think he had in him. Maybe he looks out for me more than I allow myself to believe.

"He cares about you and wants what's best for you, darlin'." I lean over so I'm hovering over her body, sweeping her hair to the side to expose her throat to me. "I'm actually a little jealous."

"Is that so?" She says, a giggle falling out of her lips when mine latch on to her neck. Blaire . . . giggling? That's a first. I can't wait to have more firsts with her. She doesn't let me savor the moment though; as usual, she always has to get one last dig in. "Jackson Deneris, am I the reason why you have daddy issues?"

I stop kissing her neck. "We are *not* going there."

"But I want to. It's fun."

"Okay. Fine. You wanna go there? I'll do you one better: Harvey Dystel."

Upon me saying the celebrity's name, her cheeks turn as red as apples.

"You cannot be jealous of a celebrity, Jackson," she laughs, her hands smoothing over my shoulders. "They don't count."

I lift my face high enough so I can narrow my gaze at her. "Yes, they do. Especially given how close our proximity is to most of them. And two, you know how I feel about sharing you. I don't want to see you eye-fucking him at the premiere."

"Not even to make you a little green-eyed so we can take it out on each other with sex afterward?" she whispers.

"Is that always your goal? To make me jealous?" My chest burns as the words scrape up my throat.

"No. But hate-sex is always better than normal sex," she whispers teasingly.

"Well, I disagree," I hiss out, gathering her in my arms and throwing her over my shoulder with one easy sweep.

"Jackson, what are you *doing*?"

"Settling the verdict." She lets out a laugh and her attempts to beg me to let her go die down when I throw her on my bed once again, climb over her, and close my body over hers.

TWENTY-NINE

Blaire

The next morning, I wake up to a message that makes my stomach drop.

Secured our target for the next house. Meeting next Saturday, 9pm @ my place—Portia

I pull myself up into a sitting position on the bed, staring at the words over and over again. Anxiety rolls over me. I knew this day was going to arrive eventually, I did agree to participate in two of the burglaries after all. I just figured I'd shelf the problem toward the back of my mind for another day.

Anxiously, I glance over at Jax. He stirs in his sleep, but he remains in his slumber. My attention falls back to my phone and my thumbs hovering over the keyboard, trying to summon a reply.

I suppose I should stick to my word and just finish what I agreed to. I've spent enough time with Portia in county jail to know that I never want to get on her bad side. If you were against her, you were a permanent name on her hit list.

Besides, I do need the rest of the money. I still have a monthly payment plan with my attorney that isn't going to settle itself. My expungement hearing is in *three* weeks. I can't do it alone. Representing myself in the most important case of my life would spell disaster.

Things are going well with Eden. I've shown Laura I'm more than capable of taking care of him. If I can prove that I'm a good sister, I could eventually prove in court that I'd be a good parent too. Fighting for custody won't be easy, but the money would help me get there a lot quicker.

But . . . is it worth it? Losing more of myself to this? Playing hypocrite to my boyfriend and my brother, both of whom I'm supposed to be setting a good example for?

"Something wrong?" I find Jax's eyes peeled wide open.

He's lying on his chest, the powerful muscles across his back cresting under his skin. I still can't get used to waking up next to this gorgeous sight. Even now, as we've permanently moved into my room, I don't think I'll ever *want* to get used to it.

I force a smile, clicking my phone shut and drop it back on the bedside table.

"No," I mumble, smoothing my hand over his hair. "Everything's fine. Go back to sleep."

"I'm wide awake now," he says with a lazy smile, despite his voice still sounding heavy with sleep. "Should I make breakfast?"

"Don't you dare." I snort. "I'll do it."

"I'll help you," he declares, slowly rolling himself off the bed. "After I take a shower."

"Want me to help?" I murmur sultrily, desperate to ignite a lusting temperature inside of him.

Jax rises to his feet and chuckles, scratching the back of his head. "Any other day, I would gladly take up the offer, but I need a proper shower this time. Not the kind we usually get up to."

I faux gasp. "You mean to tell me it's not lather, rinse, hand job, and repeat?"

"Maybe for you." Jax winks. "I'll be out in ten."

"Okay, I'll wait out here," I say, and he goes over to my side of the bed to plant a kiss over the square of my lips.

When he disappears into the bathroom, the anxiety slips into my body again. My gaze drifts back toward my phone, Portia's message still left unanswered.

***

It's the time of the week where I get Eden again, and I've prepared yet another special treat for him. Lately, the weather's been getting too hot, even for *mid-August standards*, so I found this cute, hipstery mini golf place located in a new strip mall a few miles away from the Adamses' house.

Loud pop music blares throughout the establishment as Jax and I take a sip of our overpriced mocktails while we wait for the golfers in front of us to clear the next course. Jax doesn't seem to mind; I think it's been a while since he's able to enjoy any kind of drink with a colorful swirly straw.

My gaze scrolls over the dimly lit establishment. Flashy, neon decor is plastered all over the walls with golf puns like LET'S PAR-TEE! and NO IFS, ANDS, OR PUTTS. It's cheesy, but it works with what they've got going on. There are some weird courses in here, like the one where we have to shoot the ball right into the toilet where it pops up on the tail end of it and right into the hole. The context is lost on me, but it's creative.

I set my mocktail down on the high table as Eden passes me the scorecard with a smug look. I take a peek at what's been written down. We've got three more holes left and Jax's score is nearly double mine and Eden's, with Eden having a two-stroke lead over me. There's no way Jax will be able to catch up.

"Looks like we've already got a sore loser," I announce, flipping the card over to show Jax our respective scores so far.

"What? Let me see that," Jax snatches the scorecard, squinting at it. "Someone's been counting my score wrong."

"I assure you, the math is right," I say amusingly, passing the pencil to him. "Feel free to count again if you want."

With a skeptical look hurled my way, Jax takes the pencil from me and prepares his calculations by the edge of the scorecard. When his imminent defeat finally dawns on him, he sucks in a breath between his teeth and slumps his shoulders.

"Aw, poor Jackson," I say, winding my arms around his neck and pouting. "You can't be good at everything, you know."

"Really? You don't know me at all, do you?" Jax mutters and I laugh.

The group in front of us leaves for the next course, leaving it all to us. Eden cracks his knuckles "This is gonna be easy."

Jax stops my brother with a hand and grabs his own club. "Let me show you how it's *really* done, Eden," He drawls, swaggering over to the starting line.

"No thanks. I don't wanna catch your losing streak," Eden

turns to me, rolling his eyes. "Your boyfriend needs to learn shame, Blaire."

"Trust me, I know."

We take our respective turns, with me going last during this round since Jax stole Eden's turn first, too eager to prove that he can do this well. Surprisingly, he does get a better score than me and Eden at this hole, but it barely gives him a leg up with his total score. Eden rubs it in Jax's face, but Jax simply can't help himself.

"I think we should get points for showmanship," Jax declares. "If we're counting that, surely I'm miles ahead of either of you."

"But we're not. We're counting skill, dumbass. Something *you* obviously don't have," Eden jabs.

"Since when are you the official rule-setter huh?" Jax narrows his eyes at my brother. "I think we should also include the level of attractiveness of each participant, ability to capture an audience, and how many times we can Dougie before the ball makes it into the hole."

Eden turns to me, baffled. "Is he serious?"

I shrug, not wanting any part of this. Eden rolls his eyes and argues with Jax about his absurd suggestions.

Tuning out the rest of that argument, I stroll back toward the high table where my mocktail sits, needing a small break from all the bickering. I have to keep reminding myself sometimes that Jax means well, and he only riles Eden up in the way that he does because he's aware that Eden secretly loves it. I can be a doormat when it comes to my brother, but when push comes to shove, us Sullivans love a challenge.

I watch him with a smile on my face when Eden takes

his turn at the last hole, scoring a hole in one by accidentally ricocheting the ball off the tree trunk in the course, causing it to smack against the side of the pit and launching it right into the hole on the other side. Eden throws his fists in the air and yells, even startling himself. Jax pretends to be annoyed as he tallies up Eden's total on the scorecard, but even he can't mask the pride sneaking into his expression.

It's rewarding to see Eden so happy. Knowing that I'm able to provide for him in a way that I'd always longed to brews a sense of contentment in me that I'd been searching for my whole life.

"Did you see that?" Eden sprints over toward me excitedly. "Holy shit. I didn't think I could make that shot."

"I saw it," I say, ruffling the top of his head. "Congrats, E!"

Eden's grin is infectious. "This is nice, Blaire," he murmurs, resting his club against the table. "Thanks for bringing me here."

"Way better than hanging out in playgrounds, am I right?" I nudge him.

I expect Eden to agree, but instead, his lip quivers.

"I never said I hated doing that," he mumbles.

"I know. You didn't have to. I just want to give you an amazing experience," I tell him. "The next time I come visit you, I've got an even crazier day planned for us. Let's just say it involves a road trip, lots of fudge, and front-row tickets to see Cirque du Soleil."

"Wow," His tone takes on a false excitement. "That's . . . something."

"You don't like Cirque?" Maybe it's too wild for him. He's never been a huge fan of theatrics. "How about a day trip to

Joshua Tree instead?" I throw out the suggestion. "I could arrange for us a private tour."

Eden bites down on his lip. He looks over his shoulder, watching as Jax walks himself over from the last course. I get the feeling Eden wants a one-on-one conversation with me, so I gesture to Jax to get us more drinks. Jax stops at his tracks, senses the tension between me and Eden, and nods before making his way over to the bar.

Eden lays an arm over the table, frowning. "I didn't want to tell you because I know you're putting a lot of effort into these things, and I do enjoy them, but . . . I think I need to say it now." He sighs loudly. "I appreciate the gesture, B. All of this. But I think I might have given you the wrong impression."

I hold in my surprise. "What are you talking about?"

"I don't need these crazy experiences all the time, you know." Eden shrugs. "Don't get me wrong, I enjoy it a lot, but it can get a little exhausting sometimes. Last week, our day trip to Malibu tired me out so much I overslept the next day and was late to my tuba class, and Mom wasn't happy with me about that." His eyes meet mine, tender and soft. "The point is, it doesn't matter where we are or what we're doing, B. All I want is to spend time with you."

A frown tugs on my lips. "You say that, but I don't know if you really mean it."

Eden snakes a hand through his dark hair. "I think you sometimes forget that I was with you during those hard times. I was there when Mom got sick and we lost the house. I was there waiting for you every time you and the guys would sneak into the store to steal us something to eat. It was tough times, but . . . I wasn't miserable. To be honest, I was just happy that we were all together," he asserts, then closes a hand over mine. "I really, *really* appreciate what you've been trying to do for me. But . . . I don't need these experiences to feel whole. As long as I've got you, I already am."

His last words break something inside of me.

Tears threaten to spill out of my eyes.

It's true. I often forget that for the most part, what I experienced was what Eden did too. Laura could do many things with him, but she'll never be able to erase our past.

"Oh, Eden," I sigh, pulling him against me tightly, winding my arms around him. "I just wanted to show you that I can give you everything that Laura can."

Eden looks up at me. "I don't need you to be a mother, Blaire. I just need you to be *you*."

The realization that this entire time, I'd been selfish with him, crashes into my chest. I always thought I was the only one who knew what was best for Eden. Going to jail for seven months robbed me of the opportunity to care for him. I wanted a do-over.

But . . . maybe that's not what Eden needs. He needs a loving home and a stable family. He doesn't only need a stable financial situation; he needs a parent who can provide for him and can be stern with him when he misbehaves, to instill good values and morals so he can grow up to be a good, stand-up person.

I can't do that. Not with the situation I'm in with Portia.

I need to learn when to step back.

I need to learn when it's time to let him go.

"I feel like I've failed you somehow," I whisper against him. "Everything I do, I do for you, you know that?"

Eden pulls back from me, just far enough so our gazes can meet. "Take care of yourself first, B," he murmurs. "I want you around for a long time."

A sad smile manifests on my face. This . . . this is the encouragement I've needed. It's enough to find the answer I've been looking for.

Jax arrives at our table just in time with another yellow, fruity mocktail and begins reading off the scorecard. "Okay! So in last place, me as the sore loser with twenty-four strokes, followed by Blaire in second place, with eighteen strokes and Eden, who takes home the cake with just fourteen strokes. What shall be your prize? It'll be our treat."

Eden and I exchange a glance.

"How bout . . ." Eden takes a moment to think. "We just go back to your place and hang out? Maybe we could play in the pool for a bit?"

"Really?" Jax's brows shoot up. "You want that as your prize? You sure don't want to do anything else?"

Eden nods. Jax's gaze lands on me, surprised.

"You know what?" I say, laying a hand on Eden's shoulder. "That sounds like a good plan. I'm in."

For the first time in a while, the knots in my stomach have finally eased.

THIRTY

Jax

"Okay, listen up!" I clap my hands together loudly, the sound bouncing off the walls of the hall beside the family resource center.

New mats line the floor of the hallway, courtesy of me since I don't want anyone getting hurt under my watch. I've attained quite a reputation here now for being the mystery MMA fighter volunteer, and so I'm trying my best to do this the proper way.

"Now that we're all familiar with our slips, here are three easy ways to block a punch in a fight," I say to the eight other kids occupying the space, most of them between the ages of fifteen and eighteen.

Cole is my sparring partner today, and looks excited to punch me in the face, probably because I told him earlier if he didn't stop poking at his food, he wouldn't be allowed in class.

Little does he know he probably won't be very successful at swinging at my face.

"First, you got your parry," I instruct, getting into position beside Cole on the mats. "This is when straight punches are coming in, like jabs and crosses. A parry is to put something in between, like your palm, to stop the blow. Like this." I nod at Cole and he reels his fist back, then launches it right at me, and I deftly block it with my palm. "Second, you got your high guard. Lift up your elbows to your face, bring your forearms together to block punches from coming in." I cue Cole to execute another punch, one that I lift my arms up to my face to block. "Next is the helmet guard. All we're doing is bringing our wrists to our ears like we're answering the phone. We're blocking the side of our head for any hooks, overhangs, or haymakers. Behind the head is a very vulnerable spot. Now since straight punching is the most obvious and aggressive way to assert control, not a lot of people will start swinging from the side, but the experienced ones will, so that's when you have to be extra careful. Know who you're up against so you can formulate a plan in your mind. Make sure you have a strong wrist when you block. If it caves, you're gonna end up injuring yourself more. Lock that wrist and snap those arms into place like so," I order, transitioning from the high guard to the helmet guard, lifting my wrists up to my ears to block them, just as I instruct Cole to throw a left hook. I drop my arms and turn to face the kids. "Now, you guys try."

I pair the kids off and watch as they spar, practicing the three blocks I've taught them. I circle two teenage girls roughly the same age. One of them is more than eager to throw punches, but the other is too focused on memorizing the moves. I see she's already missed out on a couple of hits to the head. "Stop overanalyzing. I can see it in your eyes," I advise, reaching from behind her to lift her guard up. "This isn't a performance that you need to memorize the sequence of. That's not how being in a real fight works. All you're trying to do is stop the strike from landing on yourself. So think with your instincts. Read what your opponent is projecting. There's always a pattern to punches. Keep your eyes open and see where it's coming from, and act accordingly."

She nods, inhales deeply and tries again. Her opponent does a couple of straight punches and it's obvious she's buying time to throw that sudden right hook. The girl seems to catch on to it quickly too, because she's ready for it, snapping her arms on either side of her head to diffuse the blow.

"Nice one," I comment, patting her on the shoulder before going to check on the other pairs. As I do, I can already feel a familiar presence lurking by the doorway, watching me curiously with a proud smile on her face.

"Has anyone ever told you you're weirdly good with kids?" Blaire murmurs against me when I make a detour to plant a quick kiss on her lips.

"Nope. This is a first," I whisper. I'm glad she thinks so, because Eden and I had a rocky start before he easily became one of my most favorite people in the world.

"You think you're gonna be tired after this?" she asks, smoothing a hand round my shoulder tenderly.

"For you? Never."

"Good," she answers with a sly grin. "Because you're not the only one who constantly has surprises up their sleeves."

"I know. That's what makes this relationship fun." I grin back. "Where are we going later?"

"You'll see," she promises.

My gaze lingers on her ass as I watch her walk away from me. It's pretty damn clear that she knows I'm staring at her because her hips do a little swivel as she struts. I hide the grin forming on my face.

I can't believe that girl is mine.

***

"We should get a new blindfold now because this happens way too often," I say, the scratchy material of the Blaire's scarf tied over my eyes, making my skin itch.

At least the car has finally stopped, so whatever it is that we're doing won't be long now. The journey here took fifteen minutes, and the anticipation has been eating me up. I hear her rummage through the back of the car seat for her bag, followed by the sound of her car door opening and her sneakers hitting the gravel a little too hard.

Blaire yanks open the car door for me. I feel her hand clamp around my wrist to pull me out and on to my feet. She weaves her fingers with mine and guides me slowly toward wherever we're going. It's not a long walk from the curbside where we've parked. I feel the brush of someone as they try to make their way around me. Blaire tugs me forward a few more steps before muttering for me to wait there. I hear the sound of a key slotting into a lock, and next thing I know, I'm being pulled through a door.

Her footsteps grow softer and I wonder what I'm supposed

to do now. Then I hear the sound of lights switching on and then I feel her fingers tap on my shoulder.

"You can take off your blindfold now," she says excitedly.

I pull the fabric from my face.

When my eyes finally adjust, the first thing I see is a rather modest spread of gym equipment around me. Racks of weights and kettle bells lie on metal racks on one end along with training benches, and about a half dozen heavy bags float over the floor on the other. The gym is a little scrappy, with paint chipping off the walls and the smell of several-days-old sweat clinging hard on to the mats as I step on them, but there's a kind of familiarity, an immediate sense of ease and calm, that I didn't expect to blanket over me. It reminds me of Breaking Point, the MMA gym that I used to frequent with Sienna. The first place where I trained.

It feels like a lifetime ago that I was there with her. Those were simpler times, when things were still so innocent between us. Since then, our paths have diverged in a way I would have never predicted.

I shake away the tormented thought.

"I found a guy online who was willing to rent me the gym for the night," Blaire lets me know, wrapped up with glee. "Now that you're in the clear to start training again, I thought tonight could be the night. But I don't want you to teach me. I want to see you fight."

I gulp, staying silent as I stroll over toward one of the heavy bags. I clench my fist, digging my knuckles against the bag. Then, in a flash, the bag disappears and is replaced with a person. Someone who's beautiful and kind and loving and consumes me inside out. *Blaire.*

Undulated fear sprouts in my body.

Before what happened with Sienna, I'd never been afraid of anything in my entire life. Not even of her.

Now, fear is all I feel.

It's a disease, attacking my body and paralyzing me in the moments where I feel the most vulnerable. I'm terrified of what might happen if I start MMA again. I'm terrified because it might bring out the demons in me I'd spent all these months taming.

"Jackson?" Blaire whispers worriedly, her voice pulling me out of the rabbit hole.

I shake my head, allowing my arm to fall to my side. "I can't, Blaire." I look up at her, terrified. "You know why."

"I know," her voice is soft and kind when she approaches me. "But you can't let fear win."

"It's not just that. I can't control myself in that cage. When I get in there, I hurt people. People that don't deserve it." My head shakes again, this time more adamantly. "I can't put anyone through it again," I croak out.

"Except that it's not true. Because you *can* control yourself. You're the strongest person I know." Her hands reach up to cup my cheeks. "You got sober. You worked hard to improve your physical health. You got *better*. That's you taking control over your own body. If you can do all that, what makes you think you can't conduct yourself in that cage in a way that truly matters?" Blaire asks, holding my gaze steady. "I've seen how you are with Cole and the kids. You miss being inside that cage. Training them isn't enough for you. You want to fight for yourself."

I say nothing. It surprises me that she has made such keen

observations about me when I'm not looking. Or maybe that I haven't been hiding my real desires about the sport very well. Because I do miss it. Whether I like it or not. I wanted to get into MMA not because of the violence, but because I genuinely loved the feeling of competitiveness and the strive for greatness. But after many years, I lost sight of it.

Perhaps I can find it again.

If she believes in me as much as she does, then it means she sees something in me that's worth fighting for. Besides, it's time.

It's time to step into that cage and shed everything that I've been too terrified to confront.

"Okay." I slide my hand over hers, angling my face to meet hers. "Okay. I'll try."

A smile grows on Blaire's face. "I'll train alongside you."

She jogs over to the shelf beside the counter containing all MMA gloves and goes right back to hand me a pair. White and red. Not my usual colors, but change is long overdue.

When I emerge from freshening up in the men's bathroom, I find that Blaire has already slipped into a pair of athletic shorts and training shoes. I grin. My girl is always prepared.

I climb the stairs into the cage and push the door open. *Take it easy*, I remind myself. I don't know why, but I hold my breath as I step through the door. My eyelids peel open once I'm in and I slowly take in my surroundings—the padded floor beneath my sinking feet, the pillars, the sturdy, steel frames. *Huh.* The hexagonal cage doesn't feel as scary as I thought it would be. Perhaps I'd stewed in fear until it had turned the cage into a bigger monster than it actually is.

But now . . . as I'm here, the cage is just a cage.

And I'm just a regular man standing in it.

Well, not a regular man.

A fighter.

Blaire decides to hang back at the side of the cage, giving me the space I need to do some shadowboxing.

I shake off the guilt crawling up my body and pinching my facial expression. *It was an accident.* I assure myself. *I didn't mean to do what I did.* But unfortunately for me, finding forgiveness for what went down doesn't work when the said person I'd inflicted pain on to isn't here to do the forgiving. Not that she owes me an ounce of forgiveness. Regardless, I force the guilt inward, hoping to reconcile with it another day. I've learned the hard way that the cage is not a place for emotions reign.

I inhale a breath and propel forward.

Jab-cross-jab.   Hook-hook-body-body.   Jab-cross-jab-hook-hook-body-body. Again and again. My feet going forward and backward. Memories of my fights come flooding back to me as I repeat the movements like clockwork. I sift through them and focus on the good ones. And there was a handful of them in the underground. Like the time when I won my first fight. I was a scrawny fifteen-year-old kid forced into the pit by someone who thought I was on the roster that night. And everyone was expecting a bloodbath since the guy I was against was a 150-pound two-time underground-champion beast. It looked like the odds weren't in my favor, so I had to think outside the box. My size was a disadvantage, yes, but it also meant I could be quicker on my feet. I dodged all his throws, waiting for the right time, the right opening. Landing effective strikes along the way. One shot was all I needed to take the fucker down. And it came when he went for the big left hand. I was faster, connecting first with a perfect right hand that came out of nowhere. The fight was over. Just like that.

Those were the things I loved about fighting. The strategy. The quick thinking on your feet. Knowing exactly where to push, and when to pull back. The right combination of moves ending with a satisfying knockout.

It was a beautiful sport to me. Before my control over the fight was taken away from me. Before my stepdad had swooped in and turned the sport into something ugly. Unnatural. Before the seed of violence was planted in me. *No mercy. Take everything. Give nothing.* It was no longer about sportsmanship. It was about what I could reap from the fight. If I didn't win, I was worthless. I had no place in my family. I had no place *anywhere.*

I already lost a dad who had left me with a shitty mom and a violent stepdad. Who was I if I was truly alone?

I carried that mentally for years. I loathed my dad for leaving, because if he hadn't left, none of this would have happened to me. I wouldn't have been forced to fight by my stepdad. I wouldn't have needed to run away from home. Instead of cowering in fear, I placed all my focus on being a winner. A champion. Because everyone in my life has been a disappointment, which means the only person I can count on investing in is myself.

Now, I don't think that at all. I truly believe that there are people who care about me, who want my time and effort and love. So my purpose isn't to win. It's to enjoy playing the sport. It's to test and be tested, over and over again, by a good opponent. It's to fall and break and lose, but always pick myself up every time. And as soon as a fight ends, I'll no longer carry the burden of the result with me. I leave it in the cage, where it belongs.

And I become whole again.

When I'm all burned out from shadowboxing, I strip my gloves off and walk over to Blaire, who's holding up a bottle to me. Her dark hair is a little greasy from the cardio workout, but taking a long break afterward has evaporated much of the sweat clinging to her face and neck.

I plop down and swipe the bottle from her, squirting the water into my mouth greedily. She curls her arms over her knees, glancing around the cage, an unreadable look on her face.

"Hey," I say breathlessly.

"Hey," she says with a grin. "Come on. Admit that you've missed this."

"Yeah," I say with a kind of raw honesty I would never allow anybody else to hear. "I do. I guess I just didn't allow myself to miss it."

"You're so talented, Jackson," she marvels. "But you're not meant to slip into the shadows. No more unsanctioned fights. No more going back to that underground life. Start a new one. Fight the *right* way. Fight the way the sport is always meant to be fought."

"Fight the right way," I echo, enjoying the way the phrase rolls off my tongue.

Blaire nods. "Fight the right way."

"You know what that means for you right?" I prompt, hoping that she understands the weight of what she's saying too. "It means no more going on your midnight excursions."

Blaire teeth digs into her bottom lip.

For so long, I've avoided being too hard on her about her crimes simply because I knew it needed to be her choice to get out of it. But now, I need her to choose. I need her to believe the words she's speaking back to me. Because I don't want to be walking down this road without her. Sooner or later, I might be forced to leave her behind, and that is the last thing I want.

"Yeah." Blaire's expression softens. "Actually, it's something I've been meaning to talk to you for a while now too. I've been thinking about it a lot and I think I'm gonna figure out a way to get out of the deal with Portia."

"Really?" Her decision puzzles me. "Why? I thought you needed the money. What about the custody battle?"

"I think . . . I'm going to let go of that pipe dream for now," she admits. "I need to figure myself out first. I want to be who I think I am—and that is a good person. I want to *earn* it."

"That's a good start, darlin'." A smile stretches over my face.

"I don't know . . . seeing you tonight, how you've overcome everything that was holding you back . . . I want that too."

"You will get that. I believe it." I scoot myself closer to her and wrap an arm around her, pulling her flush against my body. "Hey, look at us," I say, tipping her chin up with a curled finger. "We keep each other accountable, right? No more flirting with the dark side. I'll make sure of it. In fact . . ." I smile to myself when I think about the next words I wish to say. "That is my oath to you."

"Oath?" she echoes. "Why oath?"

"Promises break all the time," I whisper, pressing my forehead against hers. "When you *oath* something, you're bound for life. So, I *oath* it, that I've always got your back."

Blaire smiles. "I like that. I've got your back too."

My lips descend to capture hers. We grin against each other's mouths.

"Hey, Jackson?" she mumbles against my lips.

"Hmmm?"

"Can you teach me how to use the punching bag? I've been dying to try ever since we stepped foot in here."

I chuckle, appreciating her enthusiasm. After so long of hiding this world from her, I'm now more than happy to let her into my world.

THIRTY-ONE

Blaire

As Baxton's movie premiere for *A Fool's Gold* looms closer, the next few days are spent shaking out our lovesick haze and getting back on track to make sure neither of us screw up Baxton's big night. Baxton had already emphasized just how big a deal this will be, but I suppose I didn't realize the sheer scale of it until he sent a bunch of PR guys to our place for media training. Everyone gathered that the spotlight would mostly be put on Jax, since his controversy surrounding the club owner and his wife two months ago, so he bore the brunt of the training.

Still, I need to be laser-focused. And more importantly, I am also desperate for the distraction. Ever since I texted Portia back about wanting out of the next robbery, she's gone radio silent on me, which is definitely not a good sign.

My decision to get out of the deal wasn't an easy one, but it was necessary. The more time I spent with Eden, the more

I realized fighting for custody of him was selfish, and only benefiting me. I'd wanted to take care of him, and had felt like I was the best person to do it. But I never once considered that maybe I'm not the guardian that Eden needs right now. He needs normalcy in his life. And if it has to be the stern Laura Adams behind the wheel, I think I can swallow my pride down. I may not like her parental methods, but she does deliver results, shaping Eden to be a bright, ambitious kid poised for success.

I let that reasoning play in my mind when I stare at my unanswered text to Portia. *This is a good decision*, I assure myself. *This is what Eden really needs from you.*

I pocket my phone and focus on things that need more immediate attention. Like Baxton's premiere. Now that the nightmare PR prep is over, it's time to focus on what we are all wearing to the event. Shopping at Melrose has never been my thing, despite our house being so close to the area. But today, Baxton's stylist has me meeting up with her at some trendy boutique on a street I've never allowed myself to check out since nothing there would've ever been in my spending range. So naturally, I'm a little anxious.

The boutique is spacious, giving off loft vibes with exposed brick and large floor-to-ceiling windows. It's so upscale there are barely any clothes on the racks. Just a big slab of concrete for the checkout and a big, beige sofa sitting in the middle of the shop. How Kim Kardashian-esque of them.

It doesn't take me long to find my stylist, since the other two people in the store are wearing matching black suits and have name tags perched on their chest, and she's the only one in bright colors: a pastel pink flowy blouse, green midi skirt, and matching colored pumps, the style complimentary to her straight, strawberry-blond hair. A pair of large gold loops hang delicately on her ears, and they jiggle when her head turns in my direction.

"Oh hi! You must be Blaire," she chirps, rushing toward the door when I come in. She looks like she could still be a freshman in college. People hustling in LA are truly getting younger by the minute. "I'm Nina."

I shake her hand, smiling. "Blaire. So nice to meet you."

"I've taken the liberty of picking out a few items that I think you'll like, but we can browse through the shop to see if anything else catches your eye." Nina smiles brightly as she guides me toward the sofa, where there is a rack stacked with clothes standing beside it.

"Wow. This rack is really . . . blue." My hands nervously sift through the clothes on the rack.

Most of the items are dresses, with the exception of a sleek, black jumpsuit and a sparkling silver three-piece blazer combo. My mind is overwhelmed. Don't get me wrong, I love fashion as much as the next girl, but I'd rather admire it on people than wear something outside of my comfort zone. And this rack is full of those kinds of clothes.

"Baxton did tell me it was your favorite color," Nina says, watching my eyes glaze over the clothes. "Also, since you and Jax are going to the premiere together, I just picked out colors that are complementary to the color of his suit."

"And what color is he wearing?" I ask.

"All white."

My lips twitch into a smile. My boyfriend does look good in white.

"It was his request," Nina adds. "But as for the color of his bow tie, he'll match it with whatever color piece you plan on picking out today.

"Sounds like a plan." My hands reach for the clothes on the rack again, but luckily, I'm saved from the torment of choosing because minutes later, Elle wheels herself through the door, with Ben trailing behind her, looking like he'd rather be anywhere else.

This morning, I texted her to meet me here since it's been a while since we last caught up. Also, I trust her fashion sense more than mine, which makes her the perfect candidate for today's appointment.

"Sorry I'm late. But fret not, I'm here to save Blaire from her worst nightmare—colorful textiles," Elle exclaims, the sharpness in her tone bouncing off the walls of the shop. She sticks her hand out to Nina, "Hi, I'm Elle."

"Nina," my stylist greets enthusiastically.

My gaze is no longer focused on the clothes in front of me. It drifts toward Ben, who's standing awkwardly behind Elle as she continues her pleasantries with Nina. Ben cuts a glance at me and smiles shyly, but returns his gaze back to his phone.

I gulp. I don't know why I expect him to look any different than the last time we've seen one another, because he's clearly the same person with the same messy brown hair and blue eyes and lopsided smile that calms me the second I look at it. Maybe it's me that's changed. After all, my feelings for him have all dissipated by now.

"Hey, Ben," I say, with my hands clasped awkwardly in front of me. I'm desperate to break the tension between us.

We've never *not* talked for this long before, and I desperately miss him. "How, um, how are you doing?"

"I'm doing okay," he says, setting his phone aside. He shoves both his hands into the pockets of his jeans. I don't know whether he's telling the truth, but I wanna believe him. "I'm not staying long. Elle just wanted a ride."

"It's okay," I assure him. "Stay as long as you want."

Ben's mouth curves upward. His eyes scroll the length of me. "You look good, Blaire."

"Thanks. It's probably the top, though." My fingers pinch my new crop top, which I bought a few days ago with Jax. All this while I'd been splurging on everyone else, it was time I did something for myself. I even replaced my dirty Converse shoes with a pair of new ones.

"No, I mean, you look radiant. Happy," Ben corrects. "I haven't seen you like this . . . ever."

"Yeah. It's kinda weird. But I really am. Happy."

"That's good. You've always sucked at that," he says, smiling but this time, he allows the contentment to reach his eyes. He doesn't have to say anything else. I can't do much to alleviate his pain, but I can see how much he's trying to be okay. The effort shows me that we're going to be fine one day. Just not today.

"I'm gonna go," he mumbles as he registers the time on his watch. "I'll be back in an hour to pick Elle up. You think you guys will be done by then?"

"Should be." I look over my shoulder briefly to find Elle and Nina still enthusiastically engaged in conversation. Something about Kim Kardashian's Met Gala look floats into my ear. I whirl back. "If anything, I can drive Elle back, no problem."

"Cool," he says. A part of me is desperate to talk to him about Portia, but it could probably wait. It doesn't feel like a conversation fit for a dress fitting. With another long glance at me, Ben then turns to Elle. "Hey, Elle, I think I'm gonna leave."

"Then, leave!" Elle yells back.

Ben rolls his eyes, but grins anyway. When he leaves, I return to Elle, whose attention is fixated on the rack in front of her.

"All right. Let's see what we're working with here," Elle orders, raking through the pieces herself. "Oooh. Blue is a good choice. It'll bring out Blaire's eyes for sure."

"Right?" Nina coos.

"Or how about red? That would make a statement." Elle pokes her head between two pieces, zeroing in on a long, sleeveless red dress hung on another rack at the far corner of the store. "Or black! It's classic. Very *Mr. & Mrs. Smith.*"

"Agreed." Nina's eyes spark with excitement. "I'll search the other racks for some black pieces to add to your rack, Blaire, and then you can choose."

"Oh, find some red pieces as well!" Elle exclaims.

God, it's gonna be a long day.

***

It takes a hot minute to slip into the dress because of how tight it is, and when I do finally get it on, my shoulders sag with relief. It's a beautiful, beaded royal-blue off-the-shoulder dress, with a little flare past my hips and a less-than-modest side slit, allowing my right leg to poke through. I don't want to stare at myself for too long because it makes me uncomfortable. I feel awkward. I probably look awkward too.

"Yes," Elle gasps when I push the curtain aside and reveal myself wearing the dress. "Yes . . . this is perfect!"

"This . . . this is too much," I stammer out, feeling overwhelmed with how different my body looks with such fine material hugging me. "I don't—"

She spins me back around so I can look at myself in the mirror. "Shut up and *look at yourself*. Are you kidding me? You're beautiful."

I inhale a sharp breath when I get a real, proper look at myself. My hands slide down my hips, feeling the roughness of the beads. Beautiful has never occurred to me whenever I would look in the mirror. Poverty had chipped away at my ability to feel good about my physical appearance. But now . . . now it's the first time I've allowed myself to indulge in being dolled up like this. I do look amazing. There I said it. Hot, even.

"This . . . this is the one!" Elle clasps her hands together excitedly. "Oh, and you gotta pair it with some cute heels!" She gestures for an assistant to help pull down a pair of two-inch heels. My kind of heels. It still amazes me how some women can wear heels with such a steep arch.

Elle wheels herself toward me and places the heels right next to my feet for me to try. I slip in with ease. Now, I feel like a woman deserving of the red carpet.

The door whooshes open with another customer, but I pay no mind. I stare at myself in the mirror again, a smile growing on my face. I wonder what Jax's reaction would be, seeing me in this. He'd probably say something about preferring to see me out of the dress rather than in it.

"I'm gonna make a loop around the store to see if there are any jewelry pieces that will suit this look," Elle squeals.

My gaze zeroes in on the way the dress hugs my natural curves, watching as my hands smooth over the fabric there . . .

A flash of auburn hair in the reflection catches my attention. At first I think it's Elle, but the hair color is too vivid to be hers. My eyebrows dip low on my face.

No.

It can't be.

Feeling my heart leaping into my throat, I whip my head in the direction of the auburn-haired woman. She pretends to browse the sunglasses shelf, but a flash of her gaze toward me exposes the real reason why she's here. I swallow the lump in my throat and hike up my dress.

"Hey, I'll be right back," I say absentmindedly to Elle and Nina. I doubt they're paying much mind to me, getting sucked into another conversation about Elle possibly interning for Nina before she starts college in the fall. I stalk over to the auburn-haired girl, half-terrified but half-angry that she has the nerve to show up here.

"What the hell are you doing here?" I hiss, low enough that it doesn't catch the attention of the two sales assistants hovering us.

Portia doesn't look my way. Instead, she picks up a pair of vivid blue shades with chrome detailing on the sides, and places them on her face. "Can't a girl do a little shopping?" she muses, checking herself in the mirror.

"She can. But at the exact same place as me? In my neighborhood?"

"We might just have the same taste, Blaire."

I cock my head sideways, not in the mood for her games. "How did you find me?"

This time, she does look up. A snarky smile curls over her mouth when she snatches the shades off her face. "I've been following you."

Fear clamps itself around my throat. *What the fuck? Is she a Bond villain or something?*

"Your social media. God, you have got to see the look on your face," Portia taunts, clutching a hand across her tummy as she lets out a laugh.

I don't like to update much to my twenty-three followers on Instagram, but Elle insisted we take a photo today with the two of us and it was such a nice picture that I just had to share it. I've been trying to take Elle's advice about stopping the whole I-gotta-survive mentality and just enjoy life. I recognize that I'm way too in my head all the time, and I should learn to appreciate the little gifts of life.

"You're going through your cash pretty quickly, huh? What are you doing having a stylist?" Portia teases.

"Just preparing for an event, which is none of your business," I say dryly. "Speaking of, you need to leave."

Portia sets the shades onto the shelf and turns to me. "You and I are not finished."

"I texted you saying that I was out of the game," I tell her. "Besides, not that it's any of your business, but I have something important Saturday that I can't skip out."

I make sure to leave Portia with as few details about the *A Fool's Gold* premiere as I can. She still doesn't know anything about my situation with Baxton, let alone my entanglement with his son, and I'm determined for it to stay that way.

"Well, isn't that a coincidence since we have a little get-together Saturday too?" Portia coos.

I can't afford to keep this conversation going. Not here, while Elle and Nina are around. As far as I know, Elle isn't aware of who Ben's been dallying with when it comes to work, and the last thing I need is to have Nina catch wind of what's happening and tell Baxton.

"Let's talk outside," I mutter to Portia.

Portia's mouth tightens into a sneaky line. Her gaze bounces from me, back to Nina and Elle, then she nods. I force a smile on my face and tell the sales assistant I'll be right outside. They are wary, but let me go anyway. The windows are large enough that they can keep an eye on me so I won't steal the dress I'm wearing.

When we're on the sidewalk, I immediately lose my cool. "What do you want from me?" I snap.

"I want you to keep your fucking *word*, Blaire," Portia hisses.

"Usually I would, but I'm trying to turn over a new leaf here. You know I've been double-minded from the start anyway. At least now with me out of the game, you don't have to worry about that," I state. "And look, I assume, given the tight turnaround, you've probably already done your surveillance, so technically, you don't really need me for this job anymore. You three are very capable of finishing this without me."

"You're right." Portia shrugs. "But I don't want to."

"So, you're just being petty."

"Petty?" She laughs hoarsely. "I have bigger things to worry about, Blaire, than to be petty."

"Then what? You're afraid I'll rat you out?" I say absurdly.

I expected her to refute my accusation, but to my dismay, she merely shrugs. Why did I think for one second she would grow out of her paranoia once she was out of jail? "I may be fickle, but I'm not stupid, Portia. Why the hell would I want to double-cross you?"

"Maybe you think if any of us goes down, I'll be the one who takes the fall the hardest," Portia says, her paranoia evident in her voice. "The cops will want names, and mine will probably be at the top of that list."

"So what? You basically wanna trap all of us in this scheme just so we won't betray you? Is that it?"

"Is that so wrong?" Portia drawls, leaning closer toward me. Enough for a lump to get stuck in my throat. "Consider it a little insurance policy of my own."

Her logic is not unfounded. She had, after all, ended up in jail with a lesser sentence for this exact reason; it stands to reason why she'd be paranoid about it being done to her.

"Don't do this." I beg. "Please."

"Nobody forced you to do this, remember? You came to me looking for a job. So, *finish it.*" Her words are issued like a threat. "You don't even have to take a cut if you don't want to. Just show up. And don't be late." She leans back, straightening her composure. A grin slips back into her expression just as easily as she adjusts her leather jacket. "Tomorrow morning, my place. We'll go over the plans then."

She blows me a kiss and all I'm left with is the sound of her shoes smacking against the sidewalk as she swaggers away from me.

My eyes screw shut and I draw a breath.
Fuck.

THIRTY-TWO

Jax

When Blaire came home from her dress fitting yesterday, she wasn't her usual self.

I tried asking her about it, but she just shrugged my questions off and insisted she was fine, even though she clearly wasn't. When Blaire's sad and won't tell me shit, is when I can't think straight. I've been used to her opening up to me for weeks now, so it's infuriating when she doesn't.

Why doesn't she get it in her head that we're better solving problems together than alone?

By the time I woke up today, she was already out of the house. Later, she popped me a text saying that she wasn't feeling good, so she went to pick up some medication at the pharmacy. I feel more at ease knowing that there's an explanation to her aloofness, but my gut tells me that isn't the only reason.

"You're distracted," Baxton remarks, swirling the coffee in the cup he's holding.

I jolt at the question, immediately reanimating from my stupor. It dawns on me that I'm stuck in a café with Baxton near his house. The place is nice and cozy, with lots of sunlight pouring through the windows. Good pancakes too, which I vaguely remember eating before drifting away in my thoughts. They've taken away our plates now, and my body burns with discomfort, feeling the impatient eyes of customers waiting their turn to occupy our table.

Baxton circles the rim of his latte cup with a finger, sighing. His hair looks almost white under the harsh rays of the midday sun. An hour ago, he'd caught me at the house to run through our schedule for the premiere. Blaire had already left by then, so he had to settle for me as his lunch date. Though he didn't look like he minded one bit; in fact, the prospect of a one-on-one with me after I avoided him for so many weeks was exciting to him.

I love my dad. At least I think I do. I'm sure if someone were to peer inside my heart, there's at least a tiny square inch of space for him, right next to the acres reserved for Blaire.

But there's only so much of him I can take. And today, Blaire's supposed to be my buffer, but as usual, I'm stranded here with him while she's out with the car doing god knows what.

One of Baxton's bushy eyebrows lifts, waiting for an answer. *Well?*

"Sorry. It's just . . ." My hands wrap themselves around my now lukewarm full mug of coffee. "Never mind."

"Is everything okay with Blaire? Is that why she's not here?" he asks, drumming his fingers lightly against the wooden coffee table. His shoulders lift into a nonchalant shrug. "Did you do something?"

I glance up at him, annoyed at his assumption. "Why do you automatically assume that it's my fault?"

He glances back at me expectantly. "Well, is it?"

I purse my lips inward, the corners dragging into a frown. "I don't know."

He shrugs, as if to say, *There you go.*

My face twists into a scowl. "I'm not taking advice from someone who hasn't been in a long-term relationship for ten years," I snap, suddenly wishing I'd thought harder about revealing that I know that little nugget of information.

Growing up, I despised him, but that didn't mean I didn't keep up with what he was up to through tabloid magazines. It's the only reason I ever bought them.

"In my defense, I'm a rather picky guy," he says, albeit a little smugly.

"Or maybe you're screwed up and no woman wants anywhere near that pile of mess," I suggest.

"Me? A *mess*?" He laughs, dismissing the comment. "Is that what they're saying in the tabloids these days?"

"Not that I keep up often, but they also suspect your first marriage was the defining moment."

"Well, that's not technically a lie," Baxton shrugs. "I was married to your mom for thirteen years. Scars like that don't always heal."

He's not serious. There aren't any redeeming qualities in my mom worth mulling over.

"No." I shake my head in disbelief. "I refuse to believe you're hung up on her."

He makes a face and leans forward, folding his arms across the table. "I'm not hung up on her, Jax. But I still think about her from time to time. Apart from her not wanting to support my acting career, she was good to me. And to you. And that was all that mattered to me."

His answer knocks the wind out of my chest.

He doesn't know.

The revelation has my mind whirring.

All these years and he didn't even know? How could that be possible?

My lungs are on the verge of collapsing. My mouth has gone dry and my chest constricts. Everything hurts more than it should.

"Jackson?" Baxton looks alarmed. "Are you okay?"

"Let's talk outside." I squeeze out.

I don't bother waiting for him before propelling out of my seat and walking briskly through the doors. My abrupt exit draws the attention of the girls waiting outside, prompting a reaction from one of them at the front of the line to go "What's up with *that* weirdo?" I don't stop walking until I'm down the block, away from prying eyes.

My body is faint with shock. My hands clutch around my hips as I struggle to control my breathing. Suddenly, it feels like I'm back in that alleyway behind the club, getting my ribs kicked until my breath no longer comes.

Seconds later, Baxton emerges from the café and jogs over to me, a look of confusion and disbelief plastered on his face.

"I can't believe . . ." My eyes squeeze shut, desperately trying to block out the fact that I've been fucking lied to for ten years. "All this while I thought . . . Fuck. *Fuck.*" My voice is thick with frustration. I should've known Baxton had been clueless from the start. I should've *known*.

Baxton rests his hands on his knees, his desperate gaze burning into me. "About what, Jackson?"

"About what happened to me." My face twists with hurt. "What Daphne let the guy after you do to *me*."

Baxton straightens and takes a step back, mulling the implications of what I just said.

"What . . ." He squeezes the space between his brows with his fingers. His voice comes out thin and croaky. "What . . . happened to you?"

My breath is tight in my chest. I don't like reliving what happened during those years. They were memories I'd long buried, along with the people associated with it. I didn't even bring it up to Sienna while we were still dating, and my dishonesty was a huge factor in the breakdown of our relationship. But Blaire knows. She knows everything about me, inside out, and it feels good to be transparent with her. And if Baxton was oblivious of what happened, then he deserves to know too.

So, I tell him. Everything.

About my stepdad, Charles coming into the picture. About how he saw the potential in me fighting and roped me into his underground fight club to reap the monetary rewards off of me. About the times when he would hit and slap and punch and hit me if I didn't produce him a win and lost him money, and how he'd often get the other fighters to join in just for the hell of it. And subsequently, about how I sold him and his fight club out to the authorities just to escape that abuse.

Daphne was livid when she discovered it was me who had

ratted her husband out. She left me no choice, considering that she was aware of what Charles was doing to me. Turns out the money I was bringing in for the club, and subsequently for our household, was more than enough for her to turn a blind eye. And to think I used to pity her, since it was obvious at the time that her reliance on Charles was her way of avoiding all responsibility for taking care of our family after my dad dumped her. But the fact that she was fine about being complicit in my abuse made me realize that she was the bigger monster.

After recalling everything to Baxton, he takes a seat on the bench by the sidewalk, looking like his brain has ruptured.

"I thought—I thought you were in good hands," Baxton rasps, baffled at how this could've happened. "She promised me . . ."

I join him on the bench. Baxton merely shakes his head and buries his face in his hands, regret and shame pours out of him. This is the first time I've ever seen him looking like he's about to cry. I lean back against the bench, hating myself for buying into Daphne's lies. All this while I thought he knew and didn't care. *Daphne* told me he didn't care. That his career was too important for him to come save me.

I laugh to myself at how easy it was for me to believe her, when she'd done nothing to show me she was the better parent. I suppose it was easier to villainize both her and Baxton for putting me in that position than to live with the truth that there was a chance my life could've been better with my dad.

Baxton peers at me. "So that's why you fought in the underground, then? Because he made you do it?"

I nod. "At first. But, after I got out of his club, I knew fighting was what I was meant to do. At least I was doing it on my own terms. But I realize now that even though I'd escaped what he had done to me, I'd unknowingly allowed the fucked-up values he instilled in me to dictate every aspect of my life onward."

My friends. My relationship. My enemies. It was difficult to tell who I was fighting for or against when the lines had already been long blurred for me.

"You shouldn't have had to go through what you went through. Any of it." Frustration simmers in Baxton's tone. "I should've fought harder for you. I tried to reach out when I was in LA, but your mom kept saying that you were ashamed of me, that I'd 'given up on our family' and that you never wanted to talk to me again. I should've seen through those lies. I'm guessing you never saw the child support payments I was paying?"

"No. Daphne said you never left me money. That you told her I had to earn my keep."

"Christ." He gets up from the bench and paces the width of the sidewalk. "*Fuck.*" Hands claw into his blond hair.

"It's fine."

"No, it's not fine," Baxton insists. He's back to being angry again. His nostrils flare, eyes turning molten. "I should've worked harder to be in your life. I should've fought till I had no more fight left in me to give! And I should've *never* taken no for an answer."

"I should've given you more credit too, Baxton," I say, hoping it'll be the peace offering this conversation deserves. There's no way I'm letting him take full blame for this. The point is that he still fought. That there was something there for me after all when I thought I'd been alone.

I was loved.

Someone loved me, even if that love never reached me.

All the muscles in my body ease up.It feels like I'm breathing in new air.

"Jackson . . . I'm so sorry." Baxton utters in disbelief, misery coating his tone and his face when he meets my gaze again. "God, I wish—" He sits back down on the bench beside me and groans. "I wish we didn't waste so much fucking time."

"Ten years. Goddamn." I choke on a dry, miserable laugh.

Baxton lays a hand on my lap, tears shining in the crinkles of his cerulean eyes. "I'm grateful you're here now."

"Took me a while, and with a ton of baggage, but I'm glad I'm finally here." My gaze flickers back to him, softening.

I expect him to crack a smile at that, but misery has taken root so deep inside of him that I'm starting to miss his little quips and nagging advice.

"I, uh . . ." Baxton scratches his head uncomfortably. He looks flustered and fidgety; a far cry from the Baxton that I'm accustomed to, "I gotta be honest, I don't know where to go from here."

I do.

This time, it's me offering a hand out and him taking it.

"The only way is forward," I say, my lips curving into a comforting smile.

He smiles back. The wound that was once separating us finally beginning to heal.

***

When Baxton drops me back home, the car is back in the

garage, which means that Blaire is home. My excitement stirs. I bid Baxton goodbye and head inside. The door to her bedroom is closed, so knock on her door before letting myself in.

"Come in," she calls out.

I slip into her room. Blaire's lying on the bed, facing the other way. She's clutching her blanket, her dark hair splaying across the pillows. I climb into her bed and curl my arm around her waist, nuzzling my nose against her cheek. She smells like home.

"Hey," I whisper.

"Hey," she flips around and smiles lazily at me.

I kiss her on the nose, and she shivers in delight, but when I get to her mouth, she pulls away, followed by a shake of her head.

The rejection nips at me. "What's wrong, darlin'?"

"I think I'm coming down with a cold," she says, sniffling. "I don't feel so good."

"Oh no." Concern pinches my features. "Do you want to go see the doctor?"

She points to the plastic pharmacy bag on top of the bedside table. "You think you're still gonna make the premiere?"

A frown puckers her mouth. "I don't think so, Jackson."

Ah, fuck. She's been talking about how excited she was for the red carpet, and now she won't be able to walk on it. Baxton is going to be disappointed.

"You want me to stay with you?" I suggest. "We can put on a movie while I nurse you back to health. I'll just tell Baxton—"

"No. You should go," she urges me. "It's important to him that you do."

"Are you sure?"

"I'm positive."

"It's a shame," I say, fingering the edges of her tank top. "I was really looking forward to showing you off to the world."

She laughs. "I'm sure there's gonna be other occasions where that can happen."

My eyes search her face again. She sniffs again and she makes a face, like she's annoyed at the bad timing. I stroke her skin again lovingly.

The apprehension prickles under my skin again. And it's not because of her being sick.

Maybe Baxton is right.

Maybe the honeymoon period between us really is over.

"I'm worried about you, Blaire," I say, tucking her hair behind her ear so I can see more of her face. She's a work of art and I'm not gonna miss out on any moment to soak in her beauty. "I feel like we're an ocean away and I don't know how to get to you."

"I'm not an ocean away. I'm right here," she whispers, cupping my face with a hand. She seems so certain of it that it's impossible not to feel okay with that. My overwhelming need to control every situation sprouts in my consciousness, but I shove it away and put it in a locked box.

I need to trust her.

And more importantly, I need to trust that whatever it is she's going through, she'll eventually find her way back to me.

THIRTY-THREE

Blaire

Admittedly, faking a cold so I can skip out on Baxton's premiere tonight was not a good plan, but it was the best I could do given the circumstances.

I dabbed concealer to make my complexion look paler and bought myself a blush stain to smear across my nose. I even got some medicine so it looked like I was working hard to suppress the cold. The only thing I'd been worried about was that Jax would look too closely and discover that I'm lying to him, so I had to make it convincing with my subpar acting skills.

Lying to Jax made my stomach churn. I've never been comfortable with talking to him about my crimes. If I had my way, I wouldn't let him into that world. He doesn't need to be a part of this. I can't afford for him to get too close, since Portia will use whatever ammunition she can against me. There's a reason why I've been keeping my personal life a secret from her.

I'll do my penance, I promise myself as we ascend the Hollywood Hills in a black Subaru van. I'm not going to take a cut of what I steal tonight, and I swear I'm gonna leave all this behind me the second I'm out of this house.

Permanently this time.

Setting a good example for Eden is my number-one priority.

"Keep behind me. And keep low," Portia orders when we step out of the van and pull on our ski masks.

I think I've been on this street before, but I don't remember much about the last time I was here. We're at the back of the house. The walls are tall and covered with vines and surrounded by tall trees and hedges. I can barely make out what's beyond that.

Portia tucks the walkie-talkie into her jeans, on the opposite side of where her holster sits. Then she signals for us to move. I get behind her, while Whiskey gets behind me. Portia gets to work on the pin-and-tumbler lock with what looks like a straightened out paper-clip wire. Ten seconds later, I hear a clicking sound and the door gives way. We pour into the backyard.

The water in the pool shimmers like diamonds under the moonlight. It's a nice backyard. A lot more spacious than mine and Jax's. There's a pretty pergola by the pool, a tennis court, and an outdoor gym with weights and kettle bells scattered across the mats. I sneak a peek at the exterior of the house, lifting my chin high enough to determine that it has three floors, is rather wide and has an Old Hollywood feel to it.

Something about this place makes all the hairs at the back of my neck stand up, but I can't quite put my finger on why.

It's only when we make our way inside the house through the French doors that I notice the framed posters of TV shows and movies that the owner of the house has starred in. There's also a recent addition of a certain rom-com movie playing in theaters next weekend sitting on the cabinet, yet to be hung. That's when it hits me.

I've been here before.

Because the man who owns this house is enjoying his movie premiere as we speak.

All of the air rushes out of my lungs.

I whirl around to meet Portia's gaze, betrayal cutting deep into my bones. But anger is the emotion that takes over because all I see is red. "Is this some kind of sick fucking *joke*?"

How? Is all my mind can think about. How did she *know*? I'd like to think I'd been careful not to reveal my connection to Baxton, knowing full well what Portia was capable of doing with that information.

And I was right.

"A joke? Is that what you think this is?" Portia blinks at me innocently.

She appears unfazed. Her arm extends toward Whiskey to take the duffel bag from her, who also seems to be enjoying my meltdown. *She knew too.*

My heart takes another terrifying plunge.

Did *Ben*?

No. He wouldn't . . . would he? Was he the one who revealed that piece of information to Portia, to give her the smoking gun to further entrap me in this scheme? I'd like to think I know him and that he wouldn't turn his back on our friendship . . . but we hadn't exactly been doing great in that territory. Or perhaps Portia had done the same thing she did to me like Ben—backed him into a corner and left him no choice but to give up my secret.

My chest feels tight. Breathing becomes a challenge.

"You . . ." I point at Portia, retreating backward. I'm so pissed off that my body is trembling from the force of my anger. Somehow, I manage to keep my breathing under control, but the same cannot be said for my hands because I'm this close to wrapping them around Portia's neck and throttling her. "You fucking psycho *bitch*."

We just broke into Baxton's home. The realization repeats in my mind like a broken record, making me nauseous. *This is how I repay him for everything that he's done for me. By* stealing *from him.*

If I don't kill Portia first, I might just kill myself from the shame of it all.

"Can you keep it down?" Portia hisses out. "You're gonna alert the neighbors."

"*I don't care!*" I shriek, my arms flailing about on either side of me. "This is beyond fucked up and *you know it*!"

"What was I supposed to do? I thought we established we'd be honest with each other, Blaire. Then, you had to start keeping secrets from me," Portia coos, like she's the one who got hustled around here, not me. "Besides, you made it so easy to figure out who Baxton was to you. There was no way you could've afforded a crib on *Melrose* on your own. And you've certainly not been careful about who you spend your nights with in that house either."

I force my breath inward. Just like how I'd done surveillance for her, she's done surveillance on *me*.

Portia snorts. "And then we heard about Baxton's premiere. It was a prime opportunity for us, Blaire. Wealthy-as-fuck target, wouldn't be home for hours on end. I mean," she cuts a glance at Whiskey, grinning. "We couldn't *not* do it."

"That day at the boutique . . . you already knew about the premiere. And you still leftme in the dark about this?" Irrational anger surges through me. "This is ridiculous. All because I kept a secret about who I spend my time with? We're not in fucking county jail, sharing a bunk together, Portia. This is the real fucking world!"

"You're right. It is. Which is why you need to get *your* head out of the gutter, because you're so delusional that you think you might actually be part of Baxton's world that you forgot where you once came from." A fresh bolt of anger whips through Portia, her voice rising. She steps toward me, invading the space between us that I so desperately need to keep to maintain my breathing. "Just because you know the guy whose house we're breaking into, it suddenly makes it not okay? How about the other people whose house we robbed before this, huh? They're just expendable, right? When in fact, they're all the same entitled, flashy, care-about-nothing pricks who have way more money and resources than they could ever need. Meanwhile, we're at the bottom begging for scraps." She shrugs. "I think we're just taking what we deserve."

"No. You're wrong." My brows furrow with hardness. "I felt that sense of entitlement before. I'm not making the same mistake again."

"Oh, don't you fucking dare act all high and mighty now, when you were groveling for that stolen money only a few weeks ago." Portia rolls her eyes. I recoil at the indictment, too embarrassed and ashamed to admit that she's right. "Your issues with the world are your problem, and they're going to swallow you whole unless you do something about it. So take charge of your own fucking life, and stop dragging all of us down with you!"

Despite the fear that Portia has instilled in me, the answer has never been more obvious. I'm done being a part of her cruel game. I don't care if she's not going to take no for an answer. She can't force me to do this.

"I'm not going to be part of this, Portia." I glower. "You can rot in hell."

I catch a glimpse of her face crumbling before I turn my back on her and head for the French doors.

But I only make it a couple of steps before I hear the sound of a gun clicking.

"You're not leaving," Portia warns steely.

My heart stops beating.

Fear floods my body like a tsunami.

This is not happening right now. This is not *happening.*

The only sounds punctuating the room are my whimpers, and the vague muffled sounds coming through the walkie-talkie. I'm half-tempted to tell Portia to respond, but I'm also worried that might aggravate her even more and she'll start shooting. I need to be really careful right now.

With my hands raised on either side of me, I turn around slowly. I can't even feel my body anymore. My arms aren't my arms. My legs aren't my legs. All I know is that my feet are twisting me toward the source of the gun because if I don't, I might just leave in a body bag.

My forehead meets the barrel of the gun.

"I don't want to do this, Blaire, but you refuse to comply with what we agreed to and it's *pissing me off*," Portia mutters. "I mean, what happened to you? You used to hustle for what you wanted. Now, you're not just a fucking hypocrite, but a big, fat coward too."

I wince as if she's struck me. I swallow, working hard to form words.

"Portia," I warn carefully. "Put the gun down."

Panic injects into Whiskey's face. "I'm with Blaire on this one," she tells Portia urgently, her hands up in front of her in a similar way to mine as she approaches her slowly. "Let's just . . . let's just all calm down for a second."

"Calm down? You want me to *calm down*?" Anger rises in Portia's throat yet. The gun rattles in her hand as her arm shakes. It moves an inch toward Whiskey, causing her to flinch. "This bitch has been a nuisance since day one and I'm fucking sick of it!"

"Portia, please. *Please*, put the gun down." My voice no longer sounds like my voice. It's weaker. Throatier. Choking with desperation. "Let's talk. All right? We'll talk it out."

I'm hoping if I can diffuse the pressure building up in the room, I can try to talk some sense into her. I doubt she'll listen, but that might buy me enough time to figure out how to get out of this situation without getting a bullet lodged in my skull. If I could somehow get her distracted, I could make a run for it.

"I'm done talking." Her voice drips in icy revulsion. My gaze is still on the gun she's wielding quite carelessly. "You know, I've done *so* much for you, Blaire. I stuck my neck out for you time and time again while we were bunkmates, and then with this, and you keep treating me like I'm some 'crazy bitch' who's determined to make your life hell. But really, it's *you* who can't seem to make up your mind about who *you* are. You act like you despise what you do, but you reap the rewards easily enough. You know why? Because deep down, you like it. You like stealing from them because you're greedy.. Just like all of us. There's nothing wrong with that. And I've made my peace with it. But you never will. And that's gonna jeopardize everything we've worked for. So no, I'm not letting you leave. You'll see this through to the end, whether you fucking like it or not," Portia digs the barrel into my forehead, so hard another whimper escapes me. She bares her clenched teeth at me, growling. "So, once again, and this is the last time I'll ask you, be a good girl and pick up that duffel bag, or *I will pull the fucking trigger.*"

Another wave of fear spikes in my body. My arms and my legs are numb, unmoving.

When her order sinks into my brain, I can only muster a wordless nod. Shuffling to where the duffel bag is, it takes everything out of me just to pick it up. But my hands are shaking so badly the duffel bag slips from my hands not once, but twice.

"Portia," Whiskey starts off, a desperate plea. "You made your point. Put the gun down now, cuz you're scaring not only her but me too."

"You need to *shut the fuck up* and do your job! Let me deal with her!" Portia exclaims. The barrel of the gun is still aimed at me, but it moves an inch closer in Whiskey's direction.

Whiskey notices it too, and she gulps, panic written all over her face. "You're taking things way too far, you know that, right?"

She's just as terrified as I am. Probably thinks Portia will start shooting whoever's within her peripheral just for the hell of it.

Portia snaps her gaze to Whiskey, fury crawling up her body and ripping from her throat in a menacing tone. "Don't you dare tell me I'm taking things too far when she was the one . . ." She starts rattling off to her. I don't hear anything else. The arm holding her gun lowers, just for a brief moment, and my heart quickens. I should seize the opportunity. I might not have another chance like this.

As quietly as possible, I retreat back toward the French doors. I don't look back. I don't want to look back.

Keeping my face angled toward Portia so she won't notice much is amiss, my one hand goes behind me to get a feel for the latch—

Only for it to get crushed when my back bumps against someone's chest.

"What the fuck is going on here?" Ben demands. He's holding a walkie-talkie in his grip as he enters the living room and his gaze zips from Portia, to the gun, to Whiskey then back to me, where the gun is pointed.

I can feel every muscle in his body stiffening.

"Ben," I breathe, never more relieved to see a familiar face.

Immediately, Ben swings a protective arm around me and guides me to the side so most of his body blocks me from Portia. This is the first time in the past five minutes where I finally feel like I can draw a breath.

"I've been trying to reach you guys, but there was no response, so I got worried," Ben's expression is a mixture of confusion and anger. "Portia, why do you have a gun on Blaire?"

"She doesn't want me to leave," I answer for her, feeling more brave than I was before. "Because she thinks I'm gonna rat you guys out."

He swings toward me, confused. "Why would she think you'd do that?"

"Because this is Baxton's place," I whisper sadly.

"What—Baxton? *Your* Baxton?" There's a crack in his voice when it dawns on him. His gaze travels around the living room. Portia merely bats her eyelashes, annoyed about the interruption. "You said this was some random A-lister that I didn't need to know about."

"For fuck's sake." Portia rolls her eyes. She lowers the gun to her chest, her arm relaxing as she balances her weight on one hip. "Like I said before, it's nothing personal! If we treat every break-in job that we do like it is, then we'll never get anything done. I'm sorry, okay? It's just what Baxton represents."

"Jesus fucking Christ, Portia," Ben rubs a hand against his ski mask like he's tempted to rip it off of his face. "Why do you always have to pull some crazy shit like this?"

Portia laughs. "You're overreacting."

"No, *you* are," he snaps back with icy precision. "You have a fucking gun pointed at us! You've always had it out for Blaire since we started doing this together, and now you have the nerve to be a brat about it?" Ben hisses.

"Me? A *brat*?" Portia yells as she recklessly wields the gun around. "I've been holding this fucking operation together since day one and it's *you* three who can't seem to fall in line when the going gets tough!"

A bright flash of light zips through the window, refracted by the curtains.

"Guys—" Whiskey interrupts, but doesn't get very far.

"Put the gun down," Ben steps toward Portia. Anger infuses in his eyes, dark and fierce. He has a hand extended toward her, palm up, like he's trying to tame an animal. His other hand is tucked behind him, signaling for me to *stay put*. "Portia, put it down or you're gonna get someone *hurt*!"

"No, I can't trust you. I can't trust any of you!" she yells, raising the gun again at me and Ben. But her arms are trembling. From fear or from the fact that she's exponentially losing control of the situation, with everyone turning against her, I don't know.

"*Guys!*" A panicked shriek from Whiskey. She's looking at the window overlooking the driveway, hidden by long, billowing curtains. "*Code red!* I hear the front gate opening!"

All of our gazes shoot to the window, then back at Portia. She looks terrified, sweat and fear coating her pale face, but her gun remains raised. This time, the aim isn't just at me. It's on the three of us.

She's really keeping us trapped here.

If we fall, we fall together.

Ben breathes thinly between his clenched teeth. He glances over at me briefly and I plead with him with my eyes, begging him to just make a run for it with me. Fuck Portia. She might shoot at us, but it's better than staying here and waiting to get caught.

But he doesn't join me. Instead, he zeroes back in on Portia.

Careless determination spans across his body.

No. No—

"Don't—" I yell out, but it's too late.

With the last of Ben's patience snapping, he does a Hail Mary and lunges for the gun.

"Ben!" I yell, practically leaping at him.

"Guys, we don't have time for this!" Whiskey's desperate plea pierces the room. "We need to leave *now*!"

Portia screams, wrestling the gun away from Ben's grasp. "Get your fucking hands off of me!" She rasps, but Ben has a firm grip on the gun. He's so close to prying it away from Portia—

A pair of headlights loom closer, dazing Portia. Ben yanks the gun from her and—

A gunshot thunders across the room.

THIRTY-FOUR

Jax

My neck is hot with nerves when the limo joins the line of cars leading up to the front of the TCL Chinese Theatre. Eight huge white tents are erected in front of the coral-red columns, with guests and celebrities alike streaming into the event. On most days, Hollywood Boulevard should be avoided since it's dirty and tacky, with tourists crowding the streets, and peddlers and cosplayers trying to rip the tourists off, but tonight is an exception. A glorious-looking red carpet covers the street, with metal barricades tucking away screaming fans, desperate to steal your attention, and velvet ropes with ushers stationed every few feet to guide you toward the theater.

The interior of the tents are divided in half by a partition that separates the cast and guests from the media people. Sweat prickles my neck when I see the swarm of journalists eager to reel in an esteemed guest and bombard them with questions.

I'm extremely worried I'm gonna say something stupid and have it be turned into a sound bite for social media. My flaws and impulses come as emotional baggage. Thankfully, it's something Blaire doesn't mind helping me haul, but I'm not sure the rest of them would particularly like it if I start unloading.

"Are you excited?" Baxton says, adjusting his bow tie by looking at his reflection through the sun visor. He has a classic James Bond tux on, the most dapper I've seen him since moving here. When he catches me staring at him through the mirror, he grins at me like he's practicing his camera-ready smile. Predictably, he doesn't look nervous, or at least, he doesn't show it. If anything, his grin gets wider when he hears the fans outside chanting his name.

Now, I know where I get my confidence from.

"Excited to have hundreds of cameras right in my face? Sure," I deadpan. My suit feels itchy against my skin and I keep adjusting the cufflinks on my wrist, needing something to fidget with.

"It's a shame Blaire couldn't be here," Baxton pushes the sun visor back into place and adjusts his suit. A Richard Mille watch perched on his wrist gleams under the constant flickering camera lights from outside.

"Yeah," I say miserably. Before I left, I made sure that she had a tall glass of water nearby and that she'd taken her medicine. When I tried to kiss her, she pulled away from me again, worried I might catch her cold, but I leaned in and did it anyway, not wanting to leave without making her feel good.

I did send her a text a few minutes ago, asking if she was feeling any better, but I haven't gotten a reply. Perhaps she's just sleeping the cold off.

I want to be present in the moment. This is an important night for my dad, and therefore it's important to me.

"Blaire did send her regards, though," I tell Baxton, my lips softening into a smile. "And she's really proud of you. Of what you've achieved here."

Baxton's brows curve appreciatively. I hope he knows that those are my words, not hers.

The limo finally pulls up in front of the theater and one of the bodyguards stationed outside yanks open the door. The amplified sounds of fans screaming when they catch a glimpse of Baxton pour into the vehicle. Like I do with any MMA fight, I put on a brave face and wear my charming persona. *Showtime.*

"Ready?" Baxton turns to me.

I nod. "Ready."

We step out of the limo together.

***

The next few hours move by in a haze of flashing lights. After we take a few pictures together, I step aside to let Baxton pose with the female lead of the movie, Tara Sanders. This is the most mainstream movie she's been in yet, so all eyes are on them both.

I let Baxton have his moment, pride settling across my chest and beaming in the form of a wide grin, and talk to other guests. Harvey Dystel is only a few feet away from me, decked out in a stunning all-black tuxedo, and I'm tempted to snap a picture with him just so I can shove it in Blaire's face later. But I decide that I should remain professional in a setting like this.

Instead, I decided to let the press reel me in and answer some of their burning questions. One or two of them had a lot to ask about the post-club drama, and, remembering the media training I'd been given by Baxton's PR team, I already had a few polished answers in mind.

"So, any more shenanigans up your sleeve, Jax?" a blond-haired lady teases as she shoves her microphone at me.

"Not any time soon," I chuckle, playing it off as a joke. "This man's all grown up now. And he's in love."

"Oh, do tell." Interest sparks in her blue eyes. "Who's the lucky lady?"

"I don't want to spoil anything yet, but you'll see her soon enough," I say, keeping it vague. I turn to wink at the camera.

At some point during the night, I'd lost Baxton to his fans. Some of them had his character from *Heartstorm Hospital* printed on their T-shirts and headshots of him ready on the off chance that he'll be giving autographs. And of course he does, whipping out a Sharpie to sign as many as the bodyguards will allow him to before he absolutely needs to get going. I use the spare time to sneak a peek at my phone. Still no response from Blaire. Anxiety prickles my skin.

It's been more than an hour since I left, and still no word from her. Sure, she's not exactly the best texter in the world, but it usually never takes her that long to get in contact with me.

Normally, I hate to be the overprotective boyfriend who can't stand to be away from his girlfriend for a few hours, but I can't shake the weird tug in my stomach telling me that something is wrong. *Really* wrong. I'm struck with the fear that her illness might be much worse than she let on, and she's too stubborn to receive the medical attention she needs.

Baxton finds me again and we head inside the theater together. My legs move, but my head is elsewhere and I hate it. Baxton glances at me worriedly, his bushy brows knitting together. "What's wrong?"

"It's Blaire," I whisper, my shoulder stiffening slightly. "She hasn't responded in a while. I'm worried about her."

Baxton cuts me off by gripping my shoulder. "Go check up on her. I'll let you know how the movie goes."

"Are you sure?" I ask worriedly. "This is your big night. I wanna stay."

"I want you to stay too. But I want to know if she's okay."

I nod, wrapping my arms around him for a hug. He pats me on the back of my shoulder and smiles earnestly. I offer another warm smile. "Congratulations, Dad."

His expression softens. It's the first time I've ever called him that since the divorce, and the word alone nearly brings tears to his eyes. "Thank you, Jackson."

For once, I've never felt prouder to hear him call me that.

With that, I jog out of the theater and call a cab back.

***

"Hey, darlin'," I whisper when I open the door to her bedroom. "You were missed at the premiere . . ."

My feet come to a halt when I realize she's not here. Tissues lay all over her bed, and sheets are wrinkled with the impression of her body, but no Blaire. The water that I had placed on her side table before leaving is untouched.

Panic attacks my chest.

I check her bathroom, then look over the window to check the backyard, but no sign of her.

She couldn't have . . . she would've told me.

My gut feeling forces me to check anyway. I fling open her closet door and rummage through her things, looking for specific items. My stomach drops when I realize I find her ski mask and her black hoodie missing.

My nostrils flare with rage.

She lied to me.

But why?

It's not like I would've stopped her from going. I wouldn't have been okay with it, but I'd be the last person to tell her off, given that I've kept her secret all these months now. Frustration burns a path down my throat. Whatever it is, it probably has something to do with Portia.

If she's not on a job, then where's she right now? And more importantly, is she safe?

I don't think twice about pulling my phone out and punching in her phone number. It rings then goes to voicemail. It must be on silent mode still.

Fuck. Fuck!

What if she finally got caught this time? Or worse, what if she's in serious danger and has no one else to turn to?

I don't waste any time. I leap off the steps to get to the car, swiping a knife from the kitchen on my way out. I don't know what I'm going to find when I see her, so it's better to be safe than sorry. I pull out of the driveway and I'm on the main road in a matter of seconds.

As I wait for the traffic light, I jam my finger on the tracking app that Blaire had installed on my phone. It almost feels like a lifetime ago when I'd linked our devices two-ways. I never thought I'd ever need to use it, but this is an emergency, so I don't give a fuck.

The app pings with Blaire's last detected location. The reading isn't super accurate, so I'm only given the geographical coordinates, but apparently, she's at . . . some house near Lake Hollywood. Okay, that shouldn't be too far.

I hit the gas pedal and set off.

Ten minutes and narrowly avoiding crashing into another car later, I'm on the road where the house should be. I slow the car down and multitask between checking the location pin on my phone and looking at the numbers on the houses. It says 3155 Hollyridge Drive, which is impossible, because that would mean . . .

My jaw locks tight, red-hot anger crawling up my chest and bursting from my arms, prompting me to punch the steering wheel.

She didn't.

Oh, but she did.

But *why?* The question settles itself in my mind. Why would she do that? She loves Baxton. She would die before betraying Baxton in this way. It makes no fucking sense.

And yet, the facts are staring right at me. I'd be a fucking fool to ignore them.

The betrayal cuts a wound so deep that my bones feel the sting.

I can't afford to ruminate on it any longer. *Don't think, just act,* I remind myself and my body moves on autopilot. The house is eerily dark when the gates creak open for me and I park the car in Baxton's driveway. All the windows are covered with curtains, but I can make our vague silhouettes of people moving about. I park alongside Baxton's Tesla, grab the knife I'd stashed under my seat, and brave a steady breath. I've never wielded a knife before, only my fists, but how fucking hard can it be?

My feet barely hit the driveway when a gunshot pierces my ears so loud I think I've been hit in the chest myself.

Perhaps my fists won't do me any good in this situation. Neither will my knife.

Despite that, I hold on to the weapon anyway. I also reach over to pry open the glove compartment for the spare keys that Baxton had given me, but as soon as I do, the front door bursts open, and two masked women sprint as fast as they can out of the house.

"Hey!" I kick the car door open and get out, but it's too late because the two women are headed toward a black van that's parked a few houses away. I can't make out who they are, but the woman who pries the driver's door open glances over her shoulder at me and smirks.

So, that must be Portia.

There's barely any time to digest the revelation before she stuffs herself into the van and drives off.

Was Blaire with her? The other woman didn't look like Blaire. My blood freezes. What if she was the one who got shot?

Holding the knife out in front of me, I run into house.

The first thing I see is the blood.

And lying in the thick pool of it on the marble floor is a disheveled-looking man. His ski mask has ridden up past his nose and he's breathing and panting fast, still dazed from what just happened. He's clutching on to his guts like they're about to spill out of him.

The knife I've been holding clatters to the ground.

My gaze zips from them back to Blaire whose hands are all bloodied up from keeping the pressure on the man's wound. She's no longer wearing her mask, so when she looks at me, all I see is pure misery and desperation and it knocks the wind out of my lungs.

"Jackson, oh thank god it's you!" she chokes out, tears flooding her face. "Please, I don't know what to do with Ben! TELL ME WHAT TO DO!"

THIRTY-FIVE

Blaire

The tears clouding my vision sweep past my cheeks and fall in splatters against Ben's bloodied shirt.

God, *how* did the night turn out like this? How did I end up cradling one of my best friends in my arms, drenched in the blood leaking out of him?

I should've never come tonight. I should have never put my trust in Portia in the first place.

And now, because of her, there's now a hole in the side of Ben's body.

Oh god, and *Jax*. I don't know how he found out I was here, but thank god he found us when he did. I was certain it was going to be Baxton walking through that door and I was ready to accept whatever fate awaited. But with Jax, I thought, maybe, just *maybe*, we could somehow crawl out of this mess. That possibility vanishes as soon as our gazes meet and he gives me a look that fucking decimates me.

That was when it sinks in.

He already knows I've lied to him.

He thinks I'm here to rob Baxton.

He might even think I'm responsible for shooting Ben too.

My eyes slam shut, and more tears dripping down my face.

"Okay," Jax says calmly, finally getting over the shock of this gruesome encounter unfolding before his very eyes. His knife clatters to the ground and he falls on his knees in front of Ben, assessing how bad the wound is. "Tell me what happened," he demands, but the question isn't directed at me. His attention is fully on Ben.

He doesn't trust me to tell him the truth.

Ben appears to have arrived at a similar conclusion as his eyes dart from Jax, then back to me.

"She didn't shoot me," Ben blurts out quickly, coming to my defense. "It was Portia. She tricked both of us. We didn't know . . . we didn't know it was your dad's house. And now, fuck, everything's gone so horribly wrong-"

"It's okay, Ben," I say softly, smoothing the hair away from his face. "I need you to save your breath."

"Right." Jax adjusts himself. "We need to call for an ambulance."

"No!" Ben's arm shoots up to grip Jax's arm in a panic. "No ambulance."

"Ben, you need help right now," Jax snaps.

Ben turns to me. "Blaire, do you know how to sew a wound shut?"

I shrug uncomfortably. "I can sew, but—"

"Good enough," he interrupts again, a desperate edge to

his voice. "Take me to your place, get this damn bullet out of me and we'll call it a day. Jax even brought a knife. You can carve the bullet out of me right now—"

"Ben, this isn't just some minor flesh wound!" I yell, interrupting his delusion. "That bullet might've ruptured one of your organs."

Ben's eyes squeeze shut. He makes a noise of anguish, a sound I've never heard him make before. It sends a bone-chilling feeling down my spine.

"You already know what happens if I go to the hospital with a gunshot wound, Blaire," Ben whispers.

I nod, my body trembling from the possible consequences. If the cops aren't already on their way now, they will be once the hospital calls them. It won't be long till they start an investigation and Ben gets arrested.

"Fuck," I hiss to myself, pushing my hair back with a hand and glancing up at the ceiling. *"Fuck!"*

Jax sees I'm losing it and jerks on my shoulder.

"Blaire, look at me." Jax forces my gaze back to him. "There's a lot of blood."

"I know," I breathe.

"He needs proper medical attention. He won't survive without it."

"I *know*."

My heart is thrashing violently against my rib cage. I can feel every bone, cell, atom in my body, and at the same time, none at all.

"So, we're in agreement, then? I'm calling for an ambulance?" Jax asks frantically.

"I . . ." I stammer. "I . . ."

"Hey, can we stop talking like I'm not here?" Ben cuts a glare between the both of us. "I'll take my chances with Blaire and a needle."

"I'm not comfortable with taking that risk, Ben!" I scream.

"We don't have fucking time for this," Jax mutters, reminding us of the urgency of the situation. "We need to get you in the car ASAP. Let's argue about where we're going later. Can you sit up?"

Ben nods, and Jax and I help haul him up into a sitting position. Ben winces from the pain and I tell him to keep his hand firmly pressed against it. Jax and I get on either side of Ben and we pull him up and drag him into the car. We get him to lie down in the back seat. I join Ben while Jax takes the wheel. We're on the road in a matter of minutes. A chill runs down my spine when I hear the notable sound of police sirens echoing in the distance just as we pull into the main road.

Ben's head is in my lap. His skin is pale and leeched of color, which heightens my anxiety and panic.

He's not going to die. I'm not going to let him.

My head lifts and my eyes flicker to the rearview mirror. Jax glances at me, monitoring our situation it the back. Sweat coats the sides of his face from all the stress. His brows lift in a silent question that only I can understand.

The answer is palpable.

I'm not letting Ben die in my arms tonight. Whatever happens afterward, we'll figure it out.

Slowly, I nod at Jax.

Jax nods back, part in acknowledgement and relief. He makes a hard right turn, aiming for the Southern California Hospital, which should be nearby.

"Stay with me, okay, Ben?" I say pleadingly, curling up against him. "Just . . . stay with me."

"I'm . . . fine," he pants, but he doesn't sound fine. His breaths are becoming more labored and further apart. "Listen, can you not tell Elle about this?"

"Don't worry, she's not gonna hear a word about this until we get you to the hospital."

Ben groans. "I told you, Blaire. We're not going there."

"Yes, we are. This isn't up for debate. I'm not letting Elle lose a brother," I proclaim, my hand brushing against the side of his face. I cupped his face decisively, staring right into his eyes. "We'll figure out the rest later, okay?"

He gulps, but is too exhausted to argue with me. I place my hand over his, putting firm pressure on the gunshot wound. He glances at our hands, then back up at my face.

"Blaire?" he whispers softly.

"Hmmm?"

"I'm scared."

I know he's not talking about his injury.

"It's okay," I coax, despite the fear and uncertainty wreaking havoc in my mind. "Everything's gonna be okay, I promise."

Ben smiles briefly at me before his eyes flutter shut. His face remains unmoving.

"Stay with me, Ben," I plead. But his body has gone slack against me. The hand he'd pressed up against his wound dangles off the edge of the leather seat. "Ben? Oh my god." My hands go around to give his shoulders a tough shake. "Ben? Ben!" I choke out, but he's not responding. He's not *responding*. His skin feels wrong. Cold and dry, like clay. My stomach plummets down to the center of the earth.

With shaky hands, I slide my fingers down his arm and settle on his wrist, at the base of his thumb. Relief floods my body when I feel a weak but steady pulse. That could change any minute now. "He's passed out, Jax! Please hurry!" I scream, my voice so hoarse it's scratching up my throat.

"I'm trying!" Jax hisses, swerving from lane to lane to avoid the cars still dotting the road.

Sweat coats the sides of my face, droplets trickling into my mouth. I keep checking Ben's pulse. Making sure he's alive. *It should've been me,* I think to myself. *He's one of the better ones. It should've been* me *instead.*

Finally, the hospital comes into view. Jax pulls into the emergency department and parks behind an unused ambulance. Everything afterward moves in slow motion. Me leaping out of the back seat to help Ben out. Jax calling for a nurse and explaining to her that there was someone in our car who had been shot. Her seeing the carnage in the back seat and the limp body accompanying it and running back into the building to call for backup. My panicky cries as she hauls Ben onto a stretcher and wheels him off into the emergency room.

"I'll need you both to be in the waiting room later," the nurse says to me and Jax. "The cops are on their way to take statements."

Fear clings to my throat.

Statements lead to arrests. Arrests lead to court hearings. And court hearings lead to prison time. And for what we did at Baxton's house? Ten to fifteen years, easily.

Fuck, I was so *ready* to leave that life behind. I was so ready. And it was already shaping up to be such a beautiful life. It wasn't the perfect life yet, but it sure as hell could've been. Because for the first time in a long while, I had hope. *Jax* gave me hope.

I'm not ready to leave this life behind.

The emergency doors close behind the nurse as she jogs to catch up to the stretcher. My mind is blank. I can feel my body going slack. A strong arm steadies me from behind.

"Come," Jax says urgently, already pulling me out of the building. Away from Ben.

"What . . .?" I say, my voice barely audible. Everything is still a daze.

"I'll get someone to check up on him later. But we can't be here," he decides firmly. "Let's go."

"But . . ."

"You know this is the only way, Blaire."

I look at him desperately. I don't say anything. I can't even think. There are too many thoughts in my head that I don't have the energy to sift through. There are only tears and blood, along with the hopelessness of getting out of this situation unscathed.

Maybe this is the only way.

Jax tugs on my hand again.

This time, I allow him to tuck me into his shoulder and bring me into the car.

I allow him to take me away.

THIRTY-SIX

Jax

Blaire is deathly silent for most of the ride home.

Her window is rolled down and she has an arm propped on the frame, the cold wind whipping through her hair. It tangles up and covers most of her vision, but she doesn't seem to care. It's like her whole body is numb and her feeling the wind is the only thing that's anchoring her to this world.

This night has completely gone off the rails in the worst way possible. My button-down shirt and my pants are soaked in Ben's blood. I doubt there's a way to even salvage them. What was supposed to be a momentous night for my dad is now ruined, or at least it will be once the cops show up at his place and inform him of what happened. At least Blaire is safe. But a shiver zips down my spine at the thought of what will happen to Ben.

I don't say anything, preferring to wait for Blaire to speak.

Instead, I keep my gaze and attention locked on the road. My hands grip the steering wheel hard, itching to get home, to our safe space. Blaire and I were able to get away from the hospital, but that didn't mean our luck would hold. Throughout the drive, I was looking over my shoulder, convinced a police car would appear at any minute.

But luckily for us, the roads are clear. And this time, I'm not flooring the pedal like I was before.

"I wasn't supposed to be there," Blaire says quietly, shattering the silence.

I glance over at her. I assume she means Baxton's house, rather than being in the hospital with Ben. "I know."

"But I don't know if you believe him. Or me," she rasps out, cutting me a wretched look. "*Please* tell me you believe me."

I want to believe you, darlin'. I really fucking do.

"Why did you lie to me, then?" I ask.

"Because . . . I felt guilty." She stares down at her lap, picking away the peeled skin on her thumb. "I wanted to start a new life with you. And Eden. I was going to figure out another way. And then . . ." She closes her eyes, sinking into her seat.

My jaw clamps tight.

"I know it was stupid not to have told you, and I should've. In a way, I was embarrassed. I keep encouraging you to bury the past and be better, but there I was, repeating everything that I promised I was going to leave behind." She screws her eyes shut, drawing a breath before continuing. "When I found out whose premises we were on, I threatened to leave. But Portia pulled the gun on me and next thing I knew, Ben tried to get in the way, and then . . . you know."

I gulp. I don't feel guilty about doubting her, but I do believe it when she says that she had no involvement in the planning of the robbery. It would've fucking killed me. And Baxton.

She has a good heart. I've seen it. Sure, it's a little tainted, but it's beautiful and whole and capable of so many wonderful things.

"I believe you," I whisper after a while. "I just wished you didn't lie to me about it."

"I'm sorry," she whispers back, head dropping to my shoulder, her nose nuzzling the curve of it. "I'm *so* sorry, Jackson."

My hand strokes the side of her arm gently. She whimpers in relief from my returned gesture.

"I'm just glad you're safe," I murmur. "We're gonna figure this out together, okay?"

"Okay."

For a moment, she smiles, like she believes that everything will be okay. And in that split second, I believe it too. But it doesn't last long because her smile fades away, the numbness slips back in, and she sinks into her seat, lost to the silence again.

I'm not going to lose her. Not a damn chance.

I already have a plan formed in my mind; it's not a perfect plan, but we gotta try it. I don't see how either of us will have any other choice. Blaire just needs to trust me on this.

I've just gotten a glimpse of what happily ever after will be like. There's no way I'm letting it slip through my fingers this time.

THIRTY-SEVEN

Blaire

When we reach home, Jax helps me out of the car. He slips an arm around my waist and walks me briskly into the house.

"Come," he insists, stopping only to unlock the door and guiding me toward the stairs. "We don't have any time to waste."

"Why? What's going on?" I'm still a little dazed, not completely broken out of my stupor from falling down the rabbit hole of my own thoughts earlier.

"You need to pack," he orders, grasping my shoulders and spinning me so our eyes can meet. The fear and urgency have darkened his irises. "If we leave in an hour, we'll be on the interstate before anyone shows up looking for you. We'll head east until we find a motel and lay low for a bit. We'll figure out the rest later."

I blink rapidly, unable to digest what he's saying. "You want us to *leave*?"

"It's the only way we can get you out of this mess."

My mind is reeling. Leaving LA . . . I had never once considered it. Not even when life was at its toughest for me on the streets. Despite the city constantly letting me down, I've never felt like I needed to leave it. I don't have much, but I can't just uproot my life. My friends are here. *Eden* is here.

"I can't go," I say firmly. "Not without Eden."

"He can come visit you," Jax suggests. "We'll figure out a way to make it work, okay? I know your brother is important to you, but you need to figure out how to get yourself out of this first." He cups my face in his hands reassuringly. "You will see Eden again. Just . . . not right now. But you will."

"But what about Ben?" I'm growing frustrated. "I can't just leave him to take the fall."

"I don't know if we can help Ben, Blaire," Jax says miserably. "But we can still help *you*. Now, go upstairs and take a shower. I'll start packing. Come on."

He drags me up the stairs and guides me into my room. My insides are screaming at me to tell him that his idea won't work and that I don't want to leave, but I'm so untethered to my own body that I just let him pull me into the bathroom. He sets me down on my feet and helps me run the shower. Steam quickly fills the room, condensation misting my face.

"Are you okay on your own?" he whispers. *God, no.* My body doesn't stop trembling, but I nod, hugging myself tightly. He hesitates, clutching the door handle, before turning back again. "Call me if you need me."

Slowly, I peel off my clothes and my underwear and kick them into a pile under the sink. I climb into the bathtub and sink into it. Water rains down from the showerhead, pelting the back of my head like jagged stones. It's scorching hot . . . I think. I can't feel anything anymore but the tightness clinging on to my chest. I take a few long, deep breaths. One . . . two . . . three. The tightness doesn't ease. Maybe it never will.

My gaze drops to my hands, which are resting on my bent knees. I'm horrified by what I see.

They're painted in Ben's blood, right up to my wrists.

This is the first time I'm able to look at it under such harsh lights. The blood had mostly dried, flaking off as my nails dig into my skin, but for the most part, it's sunken into the creases of my palms. Fear claws at my chest, followed by its familiar friend, panic. Oh *god*. Bile begins to rise up my throat.

I'm disgusted. I'm disgusted with *myself*. My hands scramble for a sponge and I start scrubbing with soap. I scrub and scrub and scrub until my skin is raw and burning. I don't know how long I do it for, but it must be a while because the bathroom is unbearably hot with steam and the mirror is completely fogged up. But I don't care. I scrub some more, the physical pain becoming the only thing binding my consciousness to my body. Suddenly, I feel a jolt in my body, forcing my mind awake.

What the fuck am I *doing* here?

I just abandoned my friend in the hospital.

I left him to take the fall for a crime I participated in.

And I'm planning to skip town to avoid aggravated burglary charges.

The magnitude of what's happening causes my body to tremble and my mouth to choke out an ugly, incoherent noise. My skin is hot to the point of blistering, not from the temperature of the water, but from the pressure building in my chest and crawling up my throat. My vision is foggy, ribbons of gray and black assaulting my perception, overwhelming my mind with immeasurable amounts of unfiltered loudness. Tears begin to flow, melting in with the rivulets of water streaming down my face from above. I hide my face in my legs, but the dam has already broken and everything comes rushing out.

I start sobbing. Uncontrollably.

I'm a coward. What I'm feeling is the oppressive feeling of cowardice.

There has never been any point in my life when I've done anything brave. Not even when I got myself convicted the first time. I've been dodging making the most difficult decisions because it's easier to do the bad thing then stick it out with the good.

That makes me sob even harder.

Snot clogs up my nostrils and I'm taking in lungfuls of air, but no oxygen is going in. I'm left to suffocate in my own hurt and spinelessness, and you know what? Maybe I deserve it. Maybe I deserve for the water to drag me away because I sure as hell ain't doing anything meaningful with my life these days.

"Blaire?" I hear Jax throwing open the door. My eyes are glassy from all the tears that I can only make out a vague silhouette of him. He shoves the shower curtains aside and his expression drops when he sees me in the state that I am. "*Baby* . . ." Hurt cracks his voice. He fishes me out of the bathtub and scoops me into his arms. I curl into his chest, wet and naked, my sobs muffled against the green T-shirt he'd just freshly put on.

I'm still as he sets me gently on the ground in the room

and drys me off with a towel. He's so kind and patient with me—it adds to my guilt. He helps me slip into a shirt, then grabs a pair of shorts from the closet and I shimmy into them. I look up at him and another wave of misery crashes into me.

"I'm a coward." My frail body shudders.

"What? No, you're not. Look at me, Blaire." He tilts my chin to level my gaze with his. "You're not a coward."

"I am," I choke out. "Ever since I got out of jail, I've been terrified of going back. So I've done everything I can to make sure I don't. I let you cover for me the first time I came back after a break-in when you shouldn't have. I ran away from that nurse in that hospital. And now . . . I'm running away again."

"You're just doing what it takes to save yourself. No one can fault you for that."

"But they can," I assert. "And they should."

"I know tonight has been a lot," Jax says, gently smoothing the back of my hair. "But you'll feel better once we're on the road, all right? I don't have everything figured out for us yet, but we *will* figure something out. I promise—"

"I'm not leaving LA," I interrupt.

The realization dawned on me while I was in the shower. I'd be a fool to leave—there's so much more at stake than there's ever been. If I leave, I'll be letting everybody down. I'll be letting *myself* down.

"You're not thinking straight," he informs me. He goes over to my closet and starts pulling out all the hangers, then starts stuffing as many clothes as he can fit into my duffel bag. "Maybe you're just overwhelmed—"

Irritated, I snatch the duffel bag from him, tossing it on the floor, and force him to look at me.

"I'm not leaving, Jax," I repeat, harsher this time. "What if we get caught later? It'll be even worse for me if I leave, and you know it. And you might be in danger too, aiding a fugitive and all. There's no escaping the consequences for me. The nurse from the hospital saw how I looked. I'm fucked either way. And the worst thing is, the cops might implicate you for this too. I can't let that happen. I need to get them the facts before they spin it into something it's not."

He studies my face hard. "What are you saying, Blaire?"

"I'm saying . . ." I breathe through it, finding the strength and courage in me that I'd lost a long time ago. "I think it's better if I turn myself in."

Even I surprise myself with that statement. I don't think I've ever had much of a spine until now.

But as soon as the words are out of my mouth, the decision feels right. There's a clarity in me that has never manifested before. I see it so clearly now.

It's the only way I can help Jax and Ben.

It's the only way for proper justice to be served.

The fear that had once been festering inside my body like a fungus has now withered away. In its place spouts a seed of contentment.

If only Jax could see it the same way.

"I don't accept this. You . . ." He laughs like it's the most ridiculous suggestion to come out of my mouth. "Are you *serious*, Blaire? You do know we're not talking about a month-long jail sentence here, right? If you get convicted, you're heading to prison. *Prison*, Blaire. They'll lock you away for *decades*."

"I know that. But it's the only way, Jackson. I need to do what's right for Ben. For everyone involved."

"You can't . . ." Jax sucks in a tortured breath. "We should be making these decisions together. And *I* say it's a better decision to leave."

"I *can't*. How do you think Baxton is going to feel when he finds out you skipped town without telling him? You can't just abandon him. You have a life here, Jackson, whether you'd like to admit it or not."

"Well, so do you," he argues.

"You're right, I do, but at *what* cost?" I argue back. Jax grimaces. Needing to tame some of the aggression in my tone, I bury my hands in my hair and inhale a breath. "Portia's right about me. I'm a hypocrite. I've done nothing but be selfish, no matter how much I pretend that I'm doing this for reasons other than myself. You warned me about what could happen to me if I continued down this path, and I didn't listen. I was so convinced the world was against me, and that I needed to push back twice as hard to fight back, that it didn't matter what bad things I've done if I balanced it with enough good deeds to make it all worth it. But I realize it doesn't work that way. The bad will always catch up to me. There's no escaping it," I moan. "And I'm *so* tired of running, Jackson. I can't do it anymore. And I especially can't do it at the expense of Ben going to prison."

"But what good will it do if you join him?" he retorts.

"Because it's about making amends for all that I've done," I say softly, my hands going up his chest. I can feel the erratic beating of his heart. He dips his head, burying his nose in my hair, and makes a sad, whimpering sound. I lean into him too and sigh heavily, my cheek grazing his. "I've spent my whole life running away. And when I got sent to jail the first time,

I tossed that second chance out the window and chose the easy way out. I can't do it again. This is my only chance to make things right." I search for validation in his gaze, but his expression remains stoic. I swallow hard. "Look, Jackson, I'm not asking you to be one hundred percent on board with this. I'm asking you to let me do what I need to do."

"How? *How* can I ever be okay with this?" He wrenches away from me. A hand cups over his mouth, stifling the emotions he'd bottled up before rising to the surface. He continues to shake his head. "Letting you go is gonna be the single most heart-wrenching, soul-ripping thing I'll ever have to do. And the worst part is that you're not giving me a fucking choice in this."

"These are *my* mistakes, and I'm the only one who can make things right again," I argue. "I know you want us to work through this together, but . . . I don't see an option where we're together and free from crimes of my past weighing us down. I don't want to do that to you. You mean too much to me for me to condemn you to that kind of life."

He continues shaking his head no, like it's the only word he's accustomed to.

"Screw it," he snaps, his jaw locked tight. He picks up the duffel bag I had dumped on the floor and resumes scooping all the clothes piled up on my bed into it with quick determination. "We'll make our own way."

"Dammit, you're not listening to me!" I yell, giving his arm a shove, hoping he would stop packing, but he just keeps going. "Jax, please stop! You have to let me do this."

"*I CAN'T!*" With a burst of anger, he chucks the duffel bag across the room. Clothes spill all across the floor. He's breathing hard. I'm breathing hard, stunned that he just did that. He paces the length of my bed before sinking onto the mattress, digging his hands in his hair. "Fuck it, I just . . . can't."

Oh, my beautiful, broken soul of a boyfriend.

"Hey, look at me." I drag my feet over to him, my body hovering over his. He wraps his arm around my hips and presses his head against my belly. He looks up at me, his eyes shining like rough diamonds. "Why?"

He huffs out a laugh, despising my question. "Are you really that oblivious?"

"To what?"

"The fact that I'm in love with you."

My lungs drain of every molecule of oxygen.

I peel his arms from my waist, shaking my head. Panic shimmers in my chest.

Jackson Deneris, a man who I once thought was incapable of love, is in love with me.

He rises up from the bed, approaching me slowly. "Blaire, I—"

"Please don't say it again." I shake my head, edging away until my back hits the wall. My knees threaten to buckle from underneath me. "I can't . . . my heart . . ."

"Listen to me. Just . . . *listen to me*," he says, his voice strained.

He tilts my chin up with his index finger so my gaze levels with his.

"Blaire Sullivan," he whispers, softer this time. Light, like a dandelion in the breeze. "I'm so fucking in love with you and I belong to no one else but you."

My hand clutches my chest. It feels like my heart is about

to crumble because it can't sustain the impact his words just made on me.

"You understand that? I've belonged to you from the moment I met you. You own my heart." His voice is low but thick. "But now it feels like my heart is about to combust in your hands, and no amount of pain that I've endured during all my fights combined can ever amount to the sheer agony I'm feeling right now, knowing that the only person I belong to is about to walk out of my life." Slowly, yet seamlessly, I find myself gathered into his thick, strong arms. My entire body is shaking when he finds his next words. "You once said I have to find my own redemption. It hasn't been the easiest thing to do, but I've finally found it. *You're* my redemption, Blaire. It's always been you. And I want a future with you, however that may look. I don't care about specifics. I just want to be with you. But there isn't a future for me if you aren't in it. So, please don't force me to let you go. *Please.*"

I don't say anything. His gaze fixes on mine and the room falls away until there's nothing but the two of us, our souls entwined, and, at the same time, unwinding. If I can't say the words he wants me to say, then I don't want to speak at all.

And he knows this. It's written all over my face.

Jax's entire face crumbles and his head drops in defeat.

"I'm sorry, Jackson. I'm *so* sorry," I say desperately. "My leaving doesn't mean I'm rejecting your love. I just need to practice what I preach. You've finally found your redemption and I've never been more happy for you. But . . ." A sad, broken smile twitches on my lips. "I think it's time for me to find mine."

He nods, pulling away from me, but not before I see the devastation in his eyes. The room is so silent now, and I have no words. There's nothing I can possibly say that'll fix this meteor-size hole I've left in both of our hearts.

I know this is all my fault. None of this would happen if it weren't for me. I've always been afraid of giving my heart to Jax because I thought he was going to be the one to break it.

Turns out, I'm the one who's about to break *his*.

A rough hand smooths over his jaw as he thinks. His gaze flickers back to mine. "Do you have to go now? Can you stay for a little while?" he asks softly. "I'm not ready to let you go yet. I want to spend the time we have left loving you goodbye."

I nod wordlessly, closing the space between us and slide my arms around his shoulders. Then I angle his head to mine so our lips can meet.

We kiss for the longest time, our lips fusing together like we're afraid of what happens to us once we break apart. Jax's lips are pliant against mine, and I plunge my tongue into his mouth, eager to taste him. His fingers trail down my back, fingering the fabric of my T-shirt, until he stops, and his hand glides down until they rest above my waist.

I kiss him harder, clutching his shirt so tightly that my fists leave creases when I let go. I pull away from him a little while, needing to breathe, and we continue to look at one another as the sounds of our breaths fill the air.

"*Blaire*," he rasps my name, desperation lacing his tone. He's staring at me hard, as if he's not sure what he wants, but he's sure enough to know that he wants me to take the lead.

And so I do. I don't know when I'm going to see him again, but I'm certain of one thing: If this is our last night together in a long time, then I want to make it a memorable one.

I step away from him and taking a deep breath, I slip out of my shorts and shirt, allowing them to pool on the floor

I hear Jax inhale a sharp breath. When the towel is gone, I slide out of my pants and step out of them, baring myself completely to him.

"Blaire . . ." His voice trails off as he drinks me in. I tip my nose up. My body comes to life under the heat of his gaze. The hunger in his eyes is evident, but there's also another emotion lingering there too. Doubt.

So, before he can protest, I lean against his forehead, my nose brushing against his as I inhale him.

"I want this," I whisper. "I want you."

"I don't want us to end like this." Jax frowns. "Sex isn't the most important thing to me. We don't have to do this."

"I don't know when I'm going to see you again," I take his hand and guide it, placing it on my hip. "It could be years or even decades. I don't think I can ever live with myself if I don't love you goodbye too."

He covers his face with a hand, debating whether or not he should allow this to happen. I expected that he'd be more than willing to do this, but it boggles my mind how unsure he seems. Perhaps trying to be noble, to not use sex as a way of saying goodbye. But he should know that I'm not a noble woman either. And our connection is so strong when we're together in bed. I want to feel that again, to let it consume me again, for the last time.

Jax still isn't looking at me. His eyes are squeezed shut, the agony spearing him like blades. I don't let his eyes stray away long, though. I fold my lips over his and press against his chest, crushing both of our bodies together.

The last of his hesitation falls away and disintegrates when our tongues clash, and he finally allows himself to succumb to the need of wanting me.

I pull away from him long enough so I can undo the buttons of his shirt and chuck it aside. I help him out of his underwear and pants too, allowing the fabric to pool beneath his feet. Once he kicks them aside, our eyes meet again.

I smile a little, my lips quivering at the sight of his magnificent body. "You're beautiful, Jackson," I murmur, saying it like I'm seeing him naked for the first time again. In a way, it *does* feel like the first time. The anticipation and the longing and the desire is still there, all whirling and lingering. The only difference now is that we both know exactly what awaits us the day after.

I take his hand in mine, lacing our fingers together and slowly guide Jax to my bed. I push him down gently, allowing him to fall back onto the mattress. I climb over him and lean down, covering my lips with his again. We taste and suckle each other, and I'm so hungry that he could feed me kisses all night long and I'd still be dying of hunger. His strong arms curl around my waist, holding me in place.

We take our time with one another. We don't rush. We don't have to. There is no need. We know that the world can keep taking and taking and taking from us, but it'll never have this night. This night is our own. This night will forge in our memories and embed into our hearts forever.

I kiss him back with equal fever, showing him how much I want him, need him, ache for him. I drag my lips down his rough, chiseled jaw, and dipping lower and lower until they make contact with his torso. He groans when I grace with his body with kisses, every single one of them searing onto his skin, leaving invisible imprints.

"God, Blaire," he groans. "This is . . . this is . . ."

Torture. Bliss. Agony. Paradise.

"I know, Jackson," I breathe. "I know."

I touch his lips with the lightest of kisses. We continue to taste and explore one another until the need grows and my whole body craves for him to be inside me. He's already hard, so I break from his kiss long enough to guide him inside me. I take a deep breath as I lower myself down, sinking onto him.

I press my hands against his face and I memorize him as we move together in sync. I want to remember everything about this. I want to remember how his kisses make me feel so loved and cared for. I want to remember how the lightness of his touch can make me lose all self-control.

It devastates me knowing that I'll be separated from him. I'll never get to share my bed with him, spend my time with him, do all the things I've wanted to do with him. I'll no longer be there to bring Eden and Jax together, no longer be there whiling time away with both of my favorite boys.

My days will no longer be filled with hope, happiness, and sanctuary.

My nights will now be filled with loneliness, pain, and misery.

Tears leak from my eyes and fall onto my cheeks, one after another. I make no attempt to wipe them away. I keep moving, keep pressing my hips harder against Jax, trying to focus on the pleasure of it all, the pleasure of giving my boyfriend the one last night we can possibly share together, but the more I think about it, the more my heart clenches with pain.

"Oh, baby…" Jax whispers, noting my change in demeanor. The rest of his body stills as he catches a tear with his index finger and a frown forms on his lips.

"Make love to me, Jackson," I choke out. *"Please."*

Tears are coming down in a steady stream now, beads of them falling onto Jax's chest. He shakes his head and tries to still me with his arms, but I move them away and I'm lifting and pushing down, lifting and pushing down, because I don't want my tears to ruin this, I still want him to feel good, to feel loved, to make him feel like this is not the end even though it clearly is.

My climax hits me sooner than expected and I cry out, clinging onto him as waves of pleasure roll over me like a tsunami. Jax comes soon after, his eyes shutting, allowing himself to lose control, one last time. The last of my energy folds in on itself and I crumble against his arms, collapsing on top of him. We're both breathing hard, the tears are still pouring out of me, and I feel like I'm drowning in my agony.

"I'm sorry," I whisper against his chest. "I'm sorry. I ruined it. I completely ruined it."

"No, you didn't." He thumbs my lips with his finger. "What we did was beautiful."

"But I didn't mean to cry. *God*, I swear I didn't mean to. I just—it was just too much—"

"I know, baby." A tear leaks from his eye too and I catch it.

"I don't know how to let you go either, Jackson. I just don't know *how*. I thought I could be stronger than this, but it hurts too much," I rasp. "Please, *please* tell me how to let you go."

"I don't know how either," he croaks. "I wish I knew but I don't."

Jax's answer decimates me, prompting my cries to turn into full-fledged sobs. He doesn't do anything to stop me. Instead, he simply holds me with a much tighter grip and presses his cheek against the top of my head, then starts to cry, his own tears matching mine.

THIRTY-EIGHT

Jax

Blaire is gone by the time I wake up.

It was hard to fall asleep knowing I had to watch her leave the next day, but I thought I'd have more time than this. We could've had one last breakfast together, or spent the morning lying and cuddling in bed, any final moment of normalcy before she turned herself in. Imagine my surprise when I reached my arm over to feel Blaire's waist, and only found the mattress. The only thing left of her is the impression of her head on the pillow. I feel as though I've been stuck violently against my chest.

No, no, no, no, *no*.

She can't do this to me.

"Blaire?" I call out, desperately clinging to a last ember of hope that she hadn't left without saying goodbye. When silence greets me back, I yell again, so loud the neighbors would have heard me. *"Blaire!"*

I throw the sheets aside and sprint downstairs to inspect the rest of the house. She's nowhere to be found.

Panic swells inside me. I storm back up and search upstairs again. Nothing.

When the realization finally crashes into me that she's really gone, I drop to my knees and release the agony from my throat that rips thought my entire body. I slam the floor repeatedly with my fists, desperately trying to get rid of the overwhelming ache and torment of having the love of my life walk away from me.

Tears soak my cheeks, droplets striking the floor like bombs during a war. My throat is so tight I can barely breathe. This is not how it was supposed to turn out. How did love leave me with nothing but a broken heart and a broken soul? How did love leave me bawling my eyes out like a fucking baby on the foot of her bed, clinging to the last shred of my sanity?

I choke on my own sobs until my nose is clogged up and my throat is raw from screaming. When the last ounce of energy leaves me, I slam the floor one last time before slumping against the side of the bed. My head tilts up to the ceiling as I attempt to catch my breath.

I've never felt more pathetic than I do now. If I were the old me, I'd be laughing at myself for being this shattered over some stupid girl.

But I'm not the old me anymore. And she's not some stupid girl. She's the most extraordinary girl who has ever walked into my life. She's strong, loyal, fierce, and one of the kindest people I've ever met. I didn't just fall in love with her body. I fell in love with her mind, her smile, her heart, and her soul.

This isn't supposed to be how it ends for us. We were *so*

close to getting the ending we deserved. How is it fair? How is she the one facing prison time? I have half a mind to storm the nearest police station and haul her out of there. The only thing stopping me from doing so is what she said last night about respecting her decision to do this. Because she's right; this is a decision only she can make. And as much as it rips my soul to admit it, it's the most practical decision that she's made.

I promised to keep her accountable. I *oathed* it.

I pull myself up onto the bed and sit on the edge, elbows resting on my thighs as I wrestle with Blaire's absence. Usually, a cataclysmic event like this would warrant me slipping back into my old vices again. Open a bottle of Jack and drink until everything is hazy and our relationship is nothing but a long-forgotten dream. But I no longer crave that. For once, I want to feel everything.

I want to be wrapped up in Blaire, both the good memories and the bad.

I'm just about ready to crawl back into bed and sink into the mattress for all eternity when something out of place catches my attention from the foot of the bed. My eyes land on a folded piece of paper. My hands scramble to unfold it, then I begin to read.

Dear Jackson,

You're probably upset that I left. You've probably scoured the entire house looking for me and returned empty-handed.

I'm sorry you didn't get to see me one last time. Making love to you last night was the best and worst decision of my life. Because although it was my last chance to show you how much I care for you, I couldn't bear the pain of not seeing you again after last night. I want to remember you like this—messy blond hair sticking from the sides of your ears, your arms folded protectively around my body, your hands stroking my hair as you wait for me to fall asleep. I want to remember that version of you. Of us. Because that's the version of us I want to come home to.

I'm sorry I walked away without saying goodbye. Apart from the fact that I'm terrible at it, there is also no need for goodbye. Because this isn't the end for us.

Jackson Deneris, I'm in love with you too.

And I will do everything in my power to come back to you.

I don't care if it's going to take years or even decades. I'm getting out of here and I'm coming straight for you, baby. I don't care if you've moved on and you're living what you think is your happily ever after.

Because your happily ever after is with me.

And that sure as hell isn't a promise. Because as you said before, promises break.

That is my oath to you.

Love, Blaire.

I read the letter again, this time, my eyes making sure to linger on every word since I don't know when the next time I'm going to see or talk to her will be. I read it again and again until I've memorized the entire letter and her words sear themselves deep into my heart. The anxiousness rolls off me and my body settles into a state of calm.

She loves me.

She loves *me*.

Fiercely.

She wants to fight for us. I fucking hope she knows I'll do the same for her.

And that is enough to comfort me. That's when I know that whatever comes after with her, we'll be all right. Because we'll *make* it all right.

I fall asleep with the note tucked into the pocket above my heart.

***

It didn't take long for the storm to arrive at my doorstep. It's about an hour later when Baxton, his assistant, and three other men from his PR team have made camp in my living room. Baxton's sullen look and dark under-eye circles are enough indication that he's had a really long night.

Apparently, after the cops showed up at his house, he was called in for questioning, interrupting his afterparty. He spent two hours at the station, but was later sent home, only to be dragged back to the station again in the early morning when they had Blaire in custody. When they discovered Blaire's connection to Baxton, they kept him there for another few hours until his attorney had insisted that Baxton go home and rest. But since he couldn't actually *go* home—with his house still being sealed off—the next viable option was to come here.

I don't mind the company. I'm desperate for updates on Blaire, and all these people around the house keep me distracted enough not to miss her.

Most of Baxton's PR team have dispersed around the house, taking calls from media and news companies. One PR guy is pacing along the hallway, mouthing off at a nosy reporter who is desperate for more details about Blaire's connection to Baxton.

Meanwhile, Baxton is seated on the reading chair, tapping away on his phone screen anxiously. He's wearing a crumpled white shirt that I assumed he threw on before being whisked off to the station a second time, a pair of black joggers, and sneakers with mismatched-colored socks.

"How bad is it looking for Blaire?" I ask, my gaze meeting Baxton's.

Baxton sighs. Heavily.

He sets his phone away and folds his hands together in front of him. "Well . . ." He cocks his head sideways. "Despite me insisting on not pressing charges, the DA is still looking to prosecute, since a shooting occurred during the crime, and this wasn't the first time that Blaire's team had attempted to execute a burglary of this scale."

I clench my jaw. There was no way this case wasn't going to court. Luckily, the story isn't over, as Baxton continues, "But, there's a bit of a silver lining. Because Blaire turned herself in, the DA agreed to a plea deal in exchange for her full cooperation to find the other two suspects connected to the case."

When he explains to me the details of the plea deal, relief floods my stomach. I'd been hoping for a miracle, but I'll be more than happy to settle for this.

"And the press?" I prod.

"Have been alerted about the burglary," Baxton says. "It's

a hard thing to miss, since my house is currently taped off. But the DA has agreed to do everything he can to keep Blaire and Ben's names out of the papers, since it's still an active investigation. I'll do my best to keep her identity out of the tabloids as well."

I can't imagine what Baxton must have felt when he realized it was Blaire who was the one attempting to burglarize his house. And for him to still harbor sympathy for her . . . he must love her very deeply.

"And Blaire . . . she's all lawyered up, right?" I ask.

"I hired the best attorney I could find to help her case."

The irony of the victim supplying the lawyer to the criminal isn't lost on me.

"You know she wasn't supposed to be there, right? It was a trap," I tell my father, my mouth harboring a frown. "She didn't know it was your house."

Baxton's lips flatten into a thin line. It makes me unsure whether his anger has diffused with that information, or intensified. My father shrugs. "Either way, it was going be someone's house. If anything, she should consider herself lucky that it was mine."

I stay quiet. He's right; in that moment, Blaire might have considered herself to be unlucky, being forced into that position, but any other house owner would've been unforgiving in pressing charges. She's blessed to have Baxton fighting on her side.

Baxton's gaze falls back on me again. This time, they hold a world of questions. "When did you . . ." He swallows. "When did you know about her getting mixed up in all of this?"

"I found out about it shortly after I moved in," I say

truthfully. "I'm sorry I didn't say anything. I made a promise to her." It seems like a lifetime ago when that happened. We were such idiots back then, with the both of us ruining our own lives so selfishly. We made a deal to turn a blind eye on one another's affairs, only to unknowingly help one another get better. My gaze swings back up to Baxton, boomeranging the same question back to him. "How about you? Did you know?"

"I knew that there was something more going on with Blaire, but I never imagined . . ." The thought has Baxton shuddering. A rough hand drags down his pained face and his gaze drops to the coffee table between us. "I should've paid closer attention to her. She struggles with asking for help. I should've done more for her, equipped her with more money, got her a job somewhere . . ."

"You know her stubbornness wouldn't have allowed her to take any more of your help," I tell him. "No matter how much you wished you would've done things differently, she needed to learn this all on her own."

"I suppose you're right." He leans back against the chair and purses his lips. "This is going to be a tough few months for everyone involved. Especially the people close to Blaire."

Worry beats in my chest.

I've been so busy thinking about Blaire and what's to become of her, that my mind hasn't stopped to linger on the people she's leaving behind now that she's facing trial. My heart plummets when I think about Eden. I wonder what he'll think about all this. Will his perception of Blaire change? It might, if Laura is the one in charge of the narrative. She's going to spin the story so far from the truth that it'll have Eden second-guessing Blaire's true intentions. And I'll never forgive myself for allowing that to happen.

"I should go," I state, rocketing myself off the couch. "I should be the one to break the news to Eden."

Baxton nods, understanding dawning in his eyes. "He needs you."

"Stay as long as you need," I urge as I jog toward the kitchen to swipe the car keys.

"I will. It's my house after all." Humor gleams in the golden flecks of Baxton's eyes.

I stop at my tracks and turn back, feeling the urge to show him that I'm there for him through this difficult time.

"I hope you're okay, Dad," I say, going over to give his shoulder a firm squeeze. "And I hope this won't get too messy for you."

"I'll be fine. I think Blaire will be fine too." Baxton looks up and smiles, closing a hand over mine to acknowledge the affection. "She's our girl. She's tough as nails. Let's just do whatever we can to help ease her burden."

A smile grows on my face, reinvigorating a renewed sense of purpose inside me.

THIRTY-NINE

Jax

I was worried that no one was home when I pulled up to the Adamses' family home, but as I spot the familiar red Chevy against the side of the house, I decided to park the car at the curb and walk up to the front steps. I press the doorbell, straightening my clothes out before Laura gets to the door. When she appears, her blond hair is clipped into a bun and she has a pink frilly apron over her blouse and trousers. The scent of freshly baked cookies wafts from the kitchen into my nostrils.

"Hi, Laura." I manage a warm, friendly smile despite the tightness in my voice. "Is Eden around? I'd like to speak with him."

She looks me up and down, and her mouth falls into a deep frown. "You're Blaire's roommate," she says, more of a statement than a question as she eyes me with skepticism.

"Yes."

She glances at me again for a couple of beats before resting a hand over her hip. "Whatever you wish to say to Eden, you can say to me first," she says dryly.

So she's gonna pull that card.

"Enticing proposition. But I'd just like to speak to him first. If you don't mind."

"I don't like your tone." The irritation is apparent in her tone.

"If I'm being honest, I don't like yours either," I say sourly. "But what I have to say to Eden is very important."

Laura's expression twists into a snarl. But before she can open her mouth to retort, the sound of someone coming down the stairs prompts her to look over her shoulder. Eden appears at the base of the steps, headphones on and scrolling through his phone. When his gaze is pulled toward the doorway, a look of confusion spreads across his face.

"What's going on?" Eden shuffles toward the door and looks up at his mom, who presses her lips into a grim line.

"Hey, dude," I say with a big smile, dipping my head down to meet his gaze. "How're you doing?"

"Good." His gaze swings around the front porch as if looking for someone else, only to be met with just me. "Where's Blaire?"

My smile wanes. "That's um . . . that's what I came here to talk to you about."

Worry attacks his expression. Even Laura drops the iciness from her face.

"Is she okay?" Eden asks.

"Yeah . . . we just need to talk."

"Like I said," Laura steps in front of Eden to take charge of the conversation, blocking his body with hers. "Whatever you came here to say to him, you can say to me. Is Blaire in trouble? Is she sick?" A note of concern works its way into her voice, a feeling I didn't think she was capable of when it came to Blaire.

I can feel my pulse beating in my neck. Looks like there isn't any way I can avoid telling Eden without Laura being present for the conversation. Besides, her interest is already piqued. And I hate to admit it, but she also deserves to know about what happened.

A sigh is pulled out of me.

"I think it's best if we're all sitting down for this," I mutter.

**

After explaining everything that went down with Blaire and where she is right now, the living room falls into a tense, worrying silence. Eden is the most affected by what he's heard. He's been biting on the loose skin on his thumb for a good ten minutes now; I'm surprised it hasn't bled yet.

The oven *dings*, prompting a sigh from Laura as she gets up from the couch to check on the cookies. As she hurries into the kitchen, I watch Eden as he balances both arms on his legs and leans forward, the headphones perched around his neck wobbling with the movement.

"How long will she be gone for?" Eden asks worriedly.

"With the plea deal, she's going to get two years, with a year of probation," I say.

Eden nods, muscle pulsing in his jaw like he's trying to

swallow the fact. "Okay, that's not that bad. Where's she now?"

I adjust the collar of my shirt. "She's in county jail, waiting for her court hearing." I'd just received confirmation from Baxton while I was on the way over here.

"What? That's too fast," Eden whines.

A loud snort echoes from the kitchen just as a metal tray slams down on the island. Both Eden and my head turn toward Laura, who looks way too smug about the entire situation.

"It's just . . .so predictable." She laughs dryly as she removes the oven mitts from her hands. "Of course she upgraded from theft to *armed burglary*. She just couldn't help herself, could she? I just can't believe I let her buy me dinner with that stolen money. Didn't I tell you before Eden?" Her vicious gaze swings toward her adopted son. "Once a criminal, always a criminal."

I'm quick to come to Blaire's defense. "It's not her fault that life dealt her a shitty hand. She was doing her best."

"Well, she pleaded guilty to get the plea deal, didn't she? If that's her best, I don't want me or my son near any of it." Laura says as she pats her hands on her apron. She moves back into the living room, jerking her head in my direction. "When's her sentencing?"

"The prosecution is looking for the other two suspects first. They have a few leads, although there's nothing concrete yet. They're hoping to wrap up the investigation in a month. Her sentencing will only happen then," I tell her.

"Well, good luck to her. We won't be going," Laura declares.

"Mom!" Eden's head snaps toward her, appalled.

The look she gives him in return is cold and unflinching. "I meant what I said. I'm not going to let you support her behavior. Lord knows we've already done enough of that unknowingly. Starting from today, we're going zero contact with her."

"You can't do that. I *want* to be there. She needs to know that I care."

"Well, she doesn't care about you! Because look at what she did!" Laura raises her voice, so loud my ears ring from the sharpness of her voice. "She ruined her own life! I'm not going to let her ruin yours."

"This is ridiculous! This is not how we should treat her!" Eden's voice shakes with anger. He shoots up from the couch, shaking his head. "I can't believe you would do this. I'm really disappointed in you, Laura."

I swear I feel the ground tremble with the impact of Laura's jaw falling to the floor.

A thousand emotions slash across her face. At the betrayal of Eden calling her *Laura* instead of Mom; at the fact that he'd stood up to her on his sister's behalf.

"Eden!" Laura lambasts. "You do not talk to me like that!"

"No, I don't want to talk to you at all." The resignation is palpable in Eden's voice. And with that, he stalks out of the living room and up the stairs.

It's impossible to wipe the ridiculous grin off my face. I've never been prouder of him than I am right now.

"They never get it," Laura mutters under her breath. Her eyes fall back to me. Her gaze hardens into stone, as if I am the cause for Eden storming off. "You should leave. You've caused enough drama here today."

"Fine," I say through gritted teeth, lifting myself off the couch. I shuffle to the door, with Laura tailing me. Now that she's deemed me as a nuisance, she's eager to get rid of me.

Before Blaire, I used to be a firm believer that people don't change, especially someone like Laura, who holds on to her very black-and-white view of the world so tightly it seems impossible to convince her to see it any other way. But I owe it to Blaire to at least try.

I barely get a foot past the door when I whirl around and pose the question I've been meaning to ask. "Have you ever wondered why she spent all that money on you, Laura? And not on herself?"

Laura blinks at me, momentarily startled by my question. "Because she wanted to bribe me."

"No. It was because she wanted to earn you," I correct her.

"Earn me?" She produces a dry laugh. "Like I'm some kind of prize?"

"Honestly? Yeah. Blaire might not want to admit it, but that's how highly she thinks of you," I explain, and surprise colors Laura's features. "Look, you and I both know Blaire was never gonna match the life you provide for Eden. Hell, even she knew that. All she wanted was to be a part of that life. But you made it *impossible*. You always belittled her, and judged her constantly for her past. She wanted to be the person you wished she was. And yeah, she went about it in the worst way possible, but that doesn't mean her heart wasn't in the right place when she made the decisions she made."

"That still doesn't excuse her appalling behavior."

"You're right. It doesn't. But it shows how much she cherishes Eden. That she was willing to let go of her dream of parenting him in order for him to have a stable and loving family."

Laura remains quiet.

Her expression is defensive, but her mask slips momentarily.

"So what? You want me to *support* what she did?" Laura asks incredulously.

"That's not what I'm asking," I say, feeling my face softening. "But forgiving her would be a good start. And allowing her brother to visit her while she's in prison." Laura purses her lips into a frown. At least she isn't getting defensive again, so I use her silence as an invitation to keep going. "Just like you, with everything she's done, she's done it with Eden in mind. He is the single most important person to her. All she's ever wanted for him is to be happy and fulfilled. But she also knows he can only be that with both you *and* her by Eden's side."

Laura seems to be weighing my words. I step through the door to the front porch and smile at her. She swallows hard. Whatever emotion had flickered in her face within that moment, she masks it before I can even tell what she was feeling.

"Goodbye, Jax," she says quietly before shutting the door on me.

***

The days pass by at an agonizing pace.

With Blaire awaiting her sentencing, there isn't much to do except to wait around to see what happens with the investigation. It wasn't until a few days later when I got word from Baxton that Whiskey had been captured by cops after a speed camera caught her trying to flee the city. And about a week later, they got Portia too, hiding at an abandoned lake house in Oregon. Apparently Blaire had tipped them off to the location since it was one of the secrets that Portia and Blaire had exchanged while they were still cellmates. Portia thought that secrets would allow her to control everyone around her; she probably didn't know it would also be her undoing.

Portia and Whiskey would both be tried separately from Blaire since they had additional charges. Ben would be tried once he was discharged from the hospital, and he would also be given a similar plea deal if he was able to produce the names of all the other criminals that were doing Portia's bidding.

The day of Blaire's sentencing finally arrives. Baxton and I sit in the front row, eagerly anticipating her appearance. Eden and Laura are nowhere to be found.

A little part of me thought I'd gotten through to her. I know Eden must be furious that he's missing this. Hopefully, I'll get to see him again and give him a recap so he feels like he's still in the loop.

When it's time for the guards to bring Blaire into the courtroom, my heart catapults out of my chest and splatters to the floor.

She doesn't look as terrible as I thought. I don't know why I expected to see her with a bruised face or something, but she just looks like her usual self, in the professional skirt suit Baxton had gotten for her. Her hair is pulled into a tight ponytail, and there's a slight flush to her cheeks. I thought I'd be relieved, looking at her now, since I haven't seen her since she'd left me, but my muscles don't relax.

Blaire's eyes scan the people in the courtroom desperately, searching for the one person she's been desperate to see. The devastation is palpable in her expression when she doesn't find Eden.

Oh, darlin'. I'll make it right for you, someday. I promise.

Her gaze draws toward me, and her chest stops heaving for a second. Hope flickers in her irises. I crack a small, reassuring smile.

Today, she doesn't need me to miss her.

She needs me to be her courage.

The judge delivers the guilty verdict and states her prison time, which is two years. Much less than we were expecting, but it still hurts the same. Minutes later, Blaire is put in handcuffs. She whips her face toward me. Instead of fear, I see contentment.

I love you, she mouths to me.

I love you too, I mouth back.

Her sad smile is the last thing I see before she's whisked back out of court.

***

I've made it a priority to keep tabs on Blaire through the week. She is allowed to have visitors starting Monday, so I scheduled a visit and made it my mission to be there at Chino by 10:00 a.m., two hours before I'm supposed to see her. A short bus trip from a parking lot to the prison later, I get my ID checked and pass time in a waiting room for an hour without my phone. When I'm done counting from a thousand back to zero for the third time, a guard finally calls my name and I'm led into the visitation area with a row of designated booths. There's a thick glass wall separating visitors from inmates, and there's already a session happening between a young inmate and an older, bearded man who appears to be his father.

The guard nudges me forward and I settle into my booth—the second-last one at the end. Anxiety rolls off me when the door opens from the other side of the glass door and a familiar dark-haired, brown-eyed girl in blue scrubs shuffles through, with a guard tailing her close behind.

Blaire's face breaks into a ridiculous grin when she spots me waving at her. The guard uncuffs her and she slides into the seat opposite me. We both collectively reach for the telephone receiver.

"Hey," Blaire whispers with a smile. God, is it good to hear her voice again. Sometimes I'm afraid I won't remember what she sounds like.

"Hey," I say with the biggest sigh of relief.

"I miss you," she murmurs.

"I miss you too. How is everything?"

"It's . . . fine. Prison's no walk in the park, but it's not as bad as I thought. I think the county jail might've been worse."

"Are the guards treating you okay? How's your cell?" The concern is palpable in my frantic tone. "I could put more money into your account."

"No, I'm good," she informs me. "I have a good amount to start. Any more and I'll be a target."

"Okay." I'm not convinced, though. "Are you eating? Anyone giving you trouble?"

"I'm fine," Blaire insists. "It's not the best living situation, but I'll survive."

"I know . . . I'm just worried about you."

"I'm sure you are. Everyone's worried. But I'm okay, I

promise," she assures me with a hint of a smile. "How about you? How are you doing?"

"I'm fine. I'm good."

She sighs, her shoulders slumping at my lie. "Jackson."

"Fine." I let out a big sigh, digging the knuckle of my thumb into my temple. "You want me to say that I'm miserable without you? That I miss you so fucking much and I don't know how to function without you in my life anymore? Because I can't, Blaire."

She inhales a sharp breath.

"I can't—" A breath pulls out of me. "I fucking hate this, Blaire. I hate that you're here and I'm there. I hate that I have to learn to live without you in my bed, in that house. And I hate I'm obligated to have conversations with you through a fucking glass wall."

She looks down and closes her eyes. "You're mad at me," she whispers.

"No." I shake my head. "No, baby. I'm not mad. I can't ever be mad at you. I just hate that this is our life for the next two years."

"I know. Me too," Blaire whispers, pressing a firm hand against the glass, leaving a print there. "It's not all bad, okay? We still get to talk. You can visit anytime you want. And you can call too. We've got this, Jackson. Two years will fly right by."

I eye her with skepticism. "Somehow I doubt it."

"It will. Because you'll do so many things with your life, and I'll get to hear all about it." A soft smile blooms across her face. "Do what you've always wanted to do. Go spend time with the people you truly care about, Jackson. And most importantly, make amends. We both know you'll never truly be content until you do."

I shrink inside like a wilted flower. She and I both understand what she means by me making amends. So far I've patched things up here in LA. My dad and I have never been tighter. But there's still one place that haunts me.

I swallow my nerves down. I'd done a lot of damage back in Boston; I'm not sure if making amends will help with anything.

But I should at least try.

I owe it to the people I've hurt. Especially Sienna.

"You sure you're okay with me going back to Boston?" I ask carefully. While Blaire doesn't have a jealous bone in her body, and she's told me time and time again that she trusts me, I doubt anyone is ever really okay with their partner seeing an ex.

"I think I'm okay. You need it. Besides, I don't care if I'm in a cell, I can keep you accountable from in here." Blaire beams.

"I don't doubt that," I whisper, resting my chin on my hand and looking at her tenderly when I add, "I love you, Blaire. So much."

She presses her knuckles to her lips, trying desperately to hide the silly schoolgirl grin that's growing on her face. "I love you too."

"We got this," I promise, and I really mean it. "You get out in like . . . 1,091 days?"

Surprise colors her features. "That's some quick math."

"I googled it on the way over here," I admit and she rolls her eyes.

"Well, 1,091 days is nothing. We got this, Jackson." Blaire lifts her hand and presses it against the smooth glass.

Her determination inspires a warm, optimistic feeling in my heart.

Blaire better be right about time passing quickly. Because I have plans for when she gets out of prison that involve me being very, *very* selfish with her.

My hand slides over the glass, and a grin touches my lips.

"You're right. We got this, baby."

FORTY

Jax

The following week, I decide to take Blaire's advice. I pack a suitcase full of my stuff and head back to Boston. I buy a one-way ticket since I don't know how long I'll be there for, but if it takes me months to work on making amends, then it'll be worth the trip.

Baxton drops me off at the airport. I tell him to keep me updated about the investigation while I'm away and he promises that he'll keep a close eye on Blaire for me.

Deep down, I know I never meant to stay in Boston forever. Something always felt out of place there, and too much has happened there for me to consider settling down there permanently.

LA is my home. Wherever Blaire is . . . that's my home.

But there are some things I need to settle back in Boston first. A person of great importance I desperately need to see.

The one person who has been haunting me for months.

Just the thought of her causes my chest to hurt, as if it'd been compressed by a giant's hand. There are a lot of feelings surrounding her—guilt, pain, sorrow—and they've all been stirring within me for a long time now.

I thought I could escape her. I thought I could put her behind me without seeing her at all. I was wrong.

I need to face her. I need to talk to her again, to settle things between her once and for all. Because the last time we interacted, it was right after the final fight against Kayden and the wound was still fresh and burning.

When I arrive at Caffeinated, I place an order for two coffees at the counter, and sit at a table by the window so I can anticipate when she'll walk in. I sent her a text a few hours ago, asking her if she would meet me today for coffee and she agreed.

Minutes later, I hear the soft *whoosh* of the door opening and my eyes quickly dart up. My heart is caught off guard by the sight of her. Her mess of blond hair is tied into a slick, high ponytail. Her attire—loose tank top, long black pants, and sports shoes—all suggest that she just arrived from the gym. She stuffs the small towel hanging loosely around her neck into her bag. There's a weightlessness to her step that wasn't there before. Usually, she walks around like there's a permanent chip on her shoulder, so this new side of her is refreshing indeed.

Just before she's fully in the café, a hand clamps on her wrist from outside the door and pulls her back. She whirls around and smiles as her boyfriend, Kayden, grabs the bag from her and slings it over his shoulder. He laces his fingers with hers and talks to her in low tones, his eyes serious and focused.

I doubt he's telling her to have a good brunch with me.

As if on cue, his eyes lift and meet mine. When he sees me, a scowl ravages his face.

I grin.

He rolls his eyes.

Sienna turns around to see who her boyfriend is staring at, and when her eyes connect with mine, the corners of her lips tug upward slightly. I wave to her and she nods, then quickly turns to Kayden, and plants a kiss on his lips. When she pulls away and breezes through the door, I hear Kayden shout, "Wait!" as he follows her into the café.

He pulls her back and mashes his lips with hers again. They kiss for a long time, tongues and all that. Kayden slides his hands down her butt, then squeezes, and then his eyes find mine and narrow, like he's warning me *try anything and I'll fucking end you.*

Oh, I don't doubt that you will, Killer.

"You can be a real asshole, you know that?" Sienna grumbles as she peels her lips away from Kayden.

"Sorry, I love you." Kayden smiles sheepishly.

"I love you too," Sienna says begrudgingly. "Now leave."

Kayden kisses her on the cheek one last time before exiting through the door. Sienna rushes over to me.

"Sorry about that," she says apologetically as she slides into the seat opposite me.

"It's fine."

Sienna eyes the steaming cup that I placed on her side of the table. "This for me?"

"Yep. Dirty matcha latte. No sugar."

She takes the cup, lifts it to her mouth, and her expression morphs into one of surprise. She swallows and sets the cup down. "Damn. You remembered," she says, glancing back up at me.

"Of course I do."

It's funny how when you're in a relationship with someone, you memorize everything about them, but all that collected knowledge doesn't just disappear as soon as you've broken up with them. As much as Sienna likes to think I didn't care about her, I still remember everything about her as well as our relationship. Not with a yearning, but with a fondness.

"So, you're back." Sienna purses her lips inward.

"Yeah. For a bit," I tell her. "To be honest, I didn't think you'd notice I was gone."

"It didn't help that you kept popping up in my favorite tabloids."

"I'm guessing you've been keeping up with the Denerises, then?" I eye her amusingly. It doesn't surprise me that news about me and my father reaches here. I'm a decently popular guy.

"Unwillingly," she adds with a sigh.

"Enthusiastically," I correct her.

She shrugs. "I admit, it was a little fun reading about how badly you spiraled."

"Oh, I'm sure you had more than a little fun than that," I murmur. Just because she's a changed person doesn't mean she still doesn't enjoy watching me be out of my element.

"Maybe," Sienna says with a knowing smile. "How've you been, though? Heard you got a girlfriend. What's she like?"

"Yeah. She's amazing. Funny and brave and kind. And definitely a non-bullshit-tolerating girl, who puts a bum like me in his place," I can't help but gush, but the excitement is gone as soon as I remember her predicament. "But . . . I won't be seeing her for a while."

"Oh, that sucks." Sienna seems genuinely sad for me. "Long distance?"

"Something like that," is all I say without getting into specifics. Blaire isn't ashamed of what she did, but I don't need people knowing her business and reading too much into things. I adjust myself in my seat and clear my throat. "But, uh, she's the one who encouraged me to come back. Actually, she's one of the reasons why I wanted to meet with you today."

"Oh?"

"Look, I know my text was vague about why I wanted to meet up, but I swear it's not because I want you back. I'm actually really happy for you and Kayden. Truly." My thumb nervously smooths against the rigid cardboard coffee holder. "I'm here because an apology to you is long overdue. For everything that transpired between us. I know I don't deserve your forgiveness for everything that I put you and Kayden through, but I want to apologize anyway. It wasn't fair to have escalated the fight after Kayden had tapped out, and it certainly wasn't fair to you for what I did afterward. And even though me hurting you was an accident, all of it would have been avoided if I hadn't allowed my ego and anger to get the better of me." I force myself to inhale a breath for courage, and my gaze fixes on Sienna. "You are an amazing woman, Sienna. One of the best people I know. And I'm so, *so* sorry I took that for granted while we were together. You tried so hard with me, to get me to let you in, and I just kept pushing you away.

Maybe if I were a little less immature, or if I'd held on to my ego a little less, it wouldn't have ended the way it did."

Sienna lets out a laugh, like even the possibility of that is absurd. She leans forward and tents her fingers together in front of her contemplatively.

"I appreciate the apology. Really. I've also had a lot of time to think about what went wrong during our relationship," Sienna starts off, her voice strong and firm, but without malice. "We could get stuck on all the 'what ifs,' but in the end, it wouldn't change anything. It won't change the fact that we weren't right for each other. I was too naïve to realize the main reason I couldn't let go of you then was because I needed you to validate my existence, and you were too wrapped up in yourself and too broken from what happened with your stepdad to give me the love I needed. And as a result, we pushed one another's buttons to the point where it got too explosive for either of us to handle. And I especially *hated* that we dragged everyone else down with us. But what happened between us,"—a small smile sneaks up on her face—"I wouldn't change a damn thing. None of it. Because we needed to love one another to realize that it wasn't the kind of love either of us deserved. So . . . I don't hate you. At least, not anymore. I'm tired of holding a grudge against you. All it's done is ruin everything good in my life. And for once, I actually want to be happy."

I blink a few times, equal parts stunned and proud by her maturity. Distance wasn't just beneficial for me, but it allowed for clarity in her life too. I didn't want to be the reason she couldn't move on from the bitterness plaguing her. It would've killed me if I was armed with the knowledge that she couldn't climb herself out of the emotional rut she'd been digging for herself. Her persistence was the reason I fell in love with her in the first place, so I should've given her more credit.

My lips curl into a soft smile and my hand reaches out to clasp on to her arm. "I'm happy to hear that you're happy, Sienna. You deserve the world and so much more. And even though I couldn't give that to you, I'm glad someone else can."

"I hope you know I feel the same about you and Blaire." Her other hand reaches over to clasp over mine. "I can't wait to meet her when she's in the city. And you better not fuck it up."

"Well, that is the plan."

"It's the only plan that matters," Sienna emphasizes, and I nod in agreement.

"Kayden better be following through with that plan too with you," I warn, a protective feeling washing over me.

"Don't worry. I make him work for it every day."

"Glad to know he's still got that fighting spirit," I note, leaning back and folding my arms across my chest. "You know, maybe I should help him test that out in the cage sometime."

A challenging gleam pops into Sienna's eyes. "Actually, I think he'd be down for that." She frowns, lifting a finger. "No underground antics, though. If there's going to be a rematch, we're doing it in a proper MMA ring this time."

Fuck yeah.

"Oh, it's on." I grin.

Sienna shakes his head, as if saying, *ugrh, men*, but fights a smile anyway. After that, the conversation between us becomes light and free-flowing. She updates me on what has been going on in Boston since I left. Ever since getting back together again, Kayden and Sienna are still trying to figure out their relationship. They're still living in Kayden's apartment, but Sienna wants them to move out and start fresh, given the history in their current apartment. They're Looking for bigger and better options, preferably somewhere near BU, where they are both studying.

I ask about her family and she tells me that they're doing fine. Her mom is happily married to her longtime boyfriend. Her dad and stepmom are expecting their first child together and she's really excited about having another brother or sister.

Sienna taps on her phone to check the time and swears when she realizes we've been talking for two hours. "Shit, I gotta bounce," she informs me, gathering her things. "I've have a training session with Jules at 2:00 p.m., so I need to run. Speaking of Jules, perhaps he might be worth visiting while you're still here. I can't guarantee he won't kick your ass, though, but maybe it's worth it."

Julian James, my previous MMA trainer before my ego got too big and I was reckless enough to ruin our relationship.

"I'm way ahead of you. He's on my to-visit list, for sure." I say firmly. "But first . . . I gotta pay a visit to your sister."

Upon the mention of Beth, Sienna makes a face, as if saying *tough luck.*

"Yeah, I know it's not gonna be pleasant, but I live for the torture."

"If that's the case . . ." A wicked gleam manifests in Sienna's blue eyes. "I'll pop a quick text reminding her to rain hell down on you."

"I expect nothing less," I murmur, shooting up from my seat just as she gets out of hers. I chug the last of my cold brew and follow her toward the door.

When we're outside, she ropes me into a hug. I'm so

stunned it takes me a couple of seconds to realize what's happening.

"I'm really glad we met today, Jax." Her cheek rests against my shoulder.

"Me too, princess," I murmur against her hair.

Sienna groans. "There you go again with that nickname," She pulls back just enough for her gaze to meet mine. "Any chance I can get you to drop it?"

I shake my head. "Never. You're always going to be *Princess*. Even if you are Kayden's *Lucky*."

"Nicknames. I'll never understand you men," she mutters as she reels back from my hug and straightens herself up.

***

The next day, I finally pluck up the courage to text Beth.

She doesn't reply to me until later in the evening, where she says that at this point, she still doesn't want to talk to me; not because she still hates my guts, but because she doesn't want to open up the wound again. I tell her I understand, and that I wish her well. And that if she ever changes her mind, she can reach out. I don't want to bother her again, so I leave it at that.

To be honest, I don't think things will ever be the same with me and Beth. And I think that's okay. She deserves to move on from what I did to her, and if not talking to me is her form of closure, then I'm going to respect that.

But I do make sure to squeeze in one last stop before I leave Boston.

The frows of heavy bags and the faded MMA posters and

quotes over the rustic walls of Universal Fighter's Gym are a familiar sight as my eyes roam over them, assaulting me with an avalanche of memories. I was a kid back then, a runaway with a relentless drive to keep fighting in any way I could.

I weave past a few fighters by the benches, gearing up for a round in the cage. By the mats, a few people are warming up while a trainer instructs them on how to tackle a punching bag.

"Well, if it isn't Jax Deneris, the dirtbag of the underground," Julian calls out from his office door. Despite him being a forty-year-old grumpy man, there's no mistaking the spitefulness grating his voice. Which is fair. I have burned many bridges in the past, but this one was the most painful.

Julian James, decorated ex-UFC fighter, Sienna's boss, and my ex-trainer. I was working with him for years to go pro, only to be tempted by the underground and leave him and the gym altogether to pursue it. I hurt him bad when I left, but I'm ready to do what it takes to get in his good graces again.

"Actually," I say, shoving my hands into my pockets, "it's not Jax anymore. It's Jackson now."

He lifts a dark eyebrow. "You changed your name?"

"Changed it back."

He grumbles unpleasantly. "If you're looking for Sienna, she's not here."

"I came here for you."

Julian purses his mouth into a flat line. He doesn't say anything. Just flicks his hand like he's saying *why not*, and leaves the office door open for me to come in. Not much has changed about his office since the last time I was here; the fluorescent lights in here are still way too dim, and the plaques and belts that sit on his shelf are long overdue to meet a feather duster. But the place feels happier somehow. Where the air was usually tense before, there's a sense of ease and calm now.

I settle into one of the seats. Julian grabs two round glasses from his shelf and gestures to the bottle of gin sitting on the edge of his desk. "You want a drink?"

"I'm good."

My response prompts an eyebrow raise from him, and then he shrugs, dropping one of the glasses back on the shelf. "Suit yourself."

Once he pours himself the gin, he slides into his seat, the chair groaning as it accommodates him. I wait for the inevitable sense of discomfort to start tickling my neck, but it doesn't come. For the longest time, this gym was my second home. Still feels like it is.

"It looks like the gym is doing well," I remark.

"Ever since Kayden started training here, people have been looking for a slice of that winning pie."

"That's good. Sienna training here too?"

"She's got tryouts soon. Been coming in about four times a week to work with me."

"She's gonna do great."

"She will."

There's a strong sense of pride in his tone, something that I miss because that's how he used to talk about me.

"You know . . ." My thumb grazes over my lip contemplatively. "I always thought my purpose was to win. Now, I think that my purpose has changed."

Blaire always thought I was meant to be in that cage. And I believe that I am. But now I'm starting to realize that that isn't my true calling. It's something else, but I can't quite put my finger on it.

Julian lays an arm on the table, a serious look on his face. "You gonna quit fighting?"

"No. But I think I want to go pro. For real this time. Do that for a few years. But I never dreamed further than that. Now I think my end goal is something different."

Julian grunts, like he understands what I mean.

"Was that the same for you?" I ask, gesturing to the office space surrounding us. "I mean, how did you know running a gym is what you wanted to do?"

"I didn't, really." Julian shrugs. "I guess at some point in my MMA career, I kind of realized that this can't go on forever. I could keep fighting, but what else is there left to fight for when you're only fighting for yourself?"

An odd feeling sprouts in my stomach at his words.

"That's when I had the idea for UFG," he finishes, circling the rim of his glass with a finger. "I no longer felt like I wanted to be in it for the glory. I want to be a part of other people's fights. Whether they win or lose. That's why training you, and now Sienna, are some of my greatest accomplishments."

Suddenly, it's as if everything has locked into place. A settled feeling floats down onto my chest, and the noise in my brain has quieted down.

"*That.*" I point to him. "That's what I want to work toward. I had a taste of it in LA, when I was teaching a few homeless kids MMA, and I loved it. Fighting for myself was great. I think it'll always feel great. But I don't want to do it forever. I think I have skills that'll help other people more than they will ever help me."

From a young age, I'd been conditioned to fight only for myself, and that was what I was best at. All that mattered was how I could benefit from the situation. I always thought that being selfish was me being in control. I've never been more wrong.

Being in control is knowing when to relinquish it for the betterment of the situation. Being in control is to flow with the tide, and to still know that you're going to be okay at the end of it.

"You know running a gym is hard work right?" Julian argues. "You have to get in a couple of belts first to build your reputation. And even if you somehow get the gym running, business is gonna fluctuate depending on the season and the quality of fighters you have."

"Yeah. It's gonna be hard. But I can do it."

Julian laughs, smoothing a hand over his scruffy jaw. "You know, usually your cockiness is extremely grating, but in this situation, it might actually be needed. You need a lot of guts to take that leap."

Delight dances across my face. *And that's when I'll fight the hardest.*

"Thanks, Jules," I say, shifting my weight forward in my seat. "And look . . . I'm sorry about bailing UFG for the underground. It was a shitty move."

A heavy breath gets stuck in his throat. He tents his fingers together in front of him contemplatively. "I accept your apology, Jackson. It's about time you came to your senses."

"Whoa, really?" I'm a little taken aback about how easy it was. "You don't think I'm all bullshit?"

"Well, are you?"

"No."

"Figured as much."

"How?"

"You came to me first. Which you never do, because you had everyone chasing you." He jerks his chin toward me. "Well, come on, then. Is it because of a girl?" When I grin, he relinquishes another dramatic sigh. "It always is."

"I think you'd like her, Jules. She's the best thing that's ever happened to me."

Julian raises his glass in recognition of that fact. "Then, you owe it to her to make your life count."

I smile, knocking a light fist against his glass in cheers to that.

I take Julian's advice to heart. When there's no barrier between us any longer, Blaire will get to see the man she always wanted me to become, the man who is no longer held down by his past and his mistakes, the man who will be undeniably loyal to her.

I'll wait for her. I will. I'll count down the days, minutes, and seconds until I can have her in my arms again and when I do, I'll make it all worthwhile.

FORTY-ONE

Blaire
Two Years Later

"Sullivan, roll it up."

The door to my cell wrenches open and Dreena leans against the frame, her fingers curled around the loops of her pants. She's always smug for no particular reason, like she's hiding a secret that nobody else knows, even though she's notorious for spilling them to us.

What we're doing today, though, isn't a secret.

When someone's going home, everyone here makes it their business too. If you're on good terms with everybody, you'll get treated better during your last week. If they hate you, it's gonna be the worst. Luckily for me, I'd been careful not to make any enemies here, so my send-off was uneventful.

At least I'm tight with the people that matter, namely my bunkmates, Lisa, Cam, and Paula. As a parting gift, the girls

PERFECT RUIN

from the salon helped dye and cut my hair. I let them take charge since I didn't have any preference other than the fact that I wanted something fresh and new. Now, I have beautiful shoulder-length hair with pink tips. I wonder what Jax will say about it. He'll probably say something about me looking like a rockstar's girlfriend, and the edgy nature will likely turn him on.

Dreena nudges me out of the cell and down the stairs. It's surreal, walking down these hallways for the last time. I've been dreaming of this day ever since I got sent here. I had a calendar hung over my bed to count the days down.

An unfamiliar feeling spreads across my chest, something I haven't felt in two years: pure, unabashed excitement, like a kid about to jump into a ball pit. It's been two years since I've seen the outside world. Two years since I've glimpsed a sidewalk or the beach. Two years since I last smelled grass, let alone fresh flowers. Suddenly, I wonder how the plants are doing in the garden behind Baxton's spare home. I wonder if I even remember how to make a compost.

Dreena is present for the entire checkout process. I take my mattress, sheets, and uniforms to the laundry room and dump them, then devour my last breakfast here. After changing out of my scrubs and into normal clothing, I head to the office. The paperwork is endless, but each minute that passes and every signature I scribble has my heart racing with nerves. When everything is signed and my property has been checked, Dreena ushers me toward the gate.

"I hope I don't see you around anymore," Dreena says with a grin.

"Trust me, you won't." I grin back. As much as I hate to

admit it, I'll miss Dreena. She was one of the good ones. She never participated in any violence toward inmates. She made life here a little easier to stomach and I'll always be grateful for that.

"Ready?" she asks, her hand tugging on the ID card slung around her neck that unlocks the gate in front of me.

I hold my breath and nod.

We shake hands and she opens the gate for me to exit. My stomach is in knots. Jax did promise me last week that he would come get me when I got released, but what if he changed his mind? Anxiety prickles under my skin. For two years, I've been in stasis, while the rest of the world has continued in motion. Jax is running an MMA gym now in LA, where he teaches homeless kids on the weekends. Baxton just got nominated for an Oscar for his supporting role in a Martin Scorsese film. Eden's in seventh grade now. Everyone has moved on with their lives. What if they've all moved on from *me* too? How do I fit into their lives now that I've been gone for so long? Is there still a place for me here?

What the hell am I going to be walking into?

I'm so terrified that my legs refuse to move.

My body is trembling. My knees are weak. I'm spiraling. I've been too focused on getting out that I haven't stopped to think about what comes after. I can't fuck this up again. I *can't.* I've let too many people down before.

"Hey." Dreena pulls me out of the sinkhole of thoughts by placing a hand on my shoulder. "You're good. It's okay to be nervous," she says tenderly. I look at her, inhaling the courage she's giving me.

This is normal, I remind myself. Feeling scared about what happens next is *normal*. I calm myself down. At the very least, I'm in control of what happens with the next phase in my life. I need to learn to trust myself again, to stay out of trouble, and learn to do the right thing.

"They're waiting for you outside," Dreena mentions.

They? Plural?

"You've got a good family out there," she adds with a smile, and it immediately puts me at ease.

I inhale another deep breath.

Okay, I'm ready.

As if she's heard my thoughts, Dreena swipes her ID over the door. It makes a beeping sound and she pushes the gate open.

Five different sets of familiar eyes fall on me. All of them equally relieved to see my face.

My gaze immediately zeroes in on Eden, who's hurtling toward me and tackles me into a hug.

Good lord, he's so tall now. It was hard to tell during his visits because he was usually seated in the booth waiting for me before I got to see him. He's tall, but lanky, his long arms circling my shoulders and pulling me into his chest. His voice is gruffer now, as most thirteen-year-old boy's voices would be.

"*Blaire*," he chokes out, so relieved that he squeezes me a second time, nearly knocking the wind out of me.

I laugh against him, tears leaking from my eyes. "Oh god, Eden." I bury my head against the crook of his shoulder.

There are so many things I wanna ask him. During his last visit, he casually mentioned he's seeing a girl, and before he could tell me who it was, our time was up and I was forced to return to my cell. I'm also dying to know how teaching Jax guitar has been going. Despite Jax's account of the lessons going smoothly, I'm well aware that Jax isn't the easiest person to teach.

Eden steps back from me, grin wavering. "Look, I want to tell you so many things, but I also know you need time to settle down, so when you're free, maybe the three of us can get dinner?" His brief glance at the woman standing beside him suggests that she's the third participant of the dinner party.

My gaze drifts to Laura. Two years ago, frustration would spread across my chest like wildfire with just one look at her, but this time, a different feeling arrives. And I'm happy that it does.

It took a long time for Laura to warm up to me again after hearing about what I did, and while I was disappointed that she and Eden weren't at my hearing, she did make it up to me by bringing Eden to see me every month. The first time they were at the visitation area was a week into my sentence and I couldn't believe my eyes. Laura also allowed me to call whenever I could, so Eden wouldn't have to wait another three weeks to talk to me. I was so sure my relationship with Laura was broken beyond repair, so I wonder what changed her mind. I guess Eden had eventually gotten through to her. Whatever the reason is, I didn't deserve it, but I sure as hell am grateful for it.

"Laura," I whisper.

"Blaire." She nods at me, a barely there smile.

"It's a surprise seeing you here."

Laura slides an arm around Eden. "If it's important for Eden to be here, it's important for me too."

"Thank you so much for letting him visit me so much," I say gratefully.

She smiles again, light coming into her eyes and creasing her face. "A brother always needs a sister."

I'm so relieved I could cry.

"Perhaps we could discuss visitations again over dinner?" Laura asks.

"Of course, Laura," I whisper back.

A young woman in a wheelchair behind Laura clears her throat and I laugh, jogging over to throw my arms around my best friend. "Ellesmere!"

Elle groans, shrugging in disgust. "I told you to stop calling me that," she says as she peels herself away from me by wheeling herself backward. She stands out amongst the sea of beige and gray of the building, sporting a pink crop top and a plaid midi skirt. Her blond hair is swept into a half-up, half-down ponytail, and eyeshadow glitters on her eyelids. Despite the color on her, she's never looked more mature and confident. I'd been worried that Ben's sentence would have left her as a husk of herself, but I'm glad to know that I was wrong.

"How are you? And how's Ben doing?" The burning question slips out of my throat.

"I admit, it's been a little hard without Ben." Elle smiles, but it's a sad one. "I've been good, though, juggling school and having a part-time job has kept me busy. And Baxton's been helping me and my dad get through, financially.

"Really?" I didn't know her family and Baxton had a relationship now, but at least Elle's family is doing okay with his help.

"Yeah," Elle says, looking up at Baxton and nudging his side with an elbow. "He's a good guy."

"Baxton," I say, turning to face him. I fold my arms across my chest in amusement. "Ever the philanthropist."

He rolls his eyes at my comment. "Just trying to keep your friends safe."

That does it for me. My eyes water again with tears, threatening to spill out.

"Congrats on the Oscar nomination," I whisper when Baxton's arms go around me. "I better be in your speech when you win."

"I'll remember that," he replies, his lips curling upward. He pats me across the back before releasing me. "I won't keep you long. I believe there's still one last person who's dying to see you."

I nod wordlessly. Baxton steps to the side. My heart is beating so fast when my eyes connect with Jax.

God, he looks so *good*. His blond hair is swept to the side, a loose wavy strand falling down his widow's peak, and despite the harsh fluorescent lights lining the area, the golden flecks in his eyes are still ever present. The white shirt he has on hugs the powerful muscles cresting his body. He's gotten even buffer in the two years we were apart, most likely because he's training to get back into the cage again. At least, that's the plan. Tryouts are next month, and aside from making weight for his MMA class, he also needs to refine his skills again. But there's no doubt he'll make tryouts. He's the most ambitious person I know when it comes to the sport.

Jax steps forward, laying a hand on Baxton's shoulder to pass through.

I don't know why I'm so nervous to be in his presence. I

just saw him last week. We talked. We laughed. We were both beyond excited for this day to come.

"We'll give you guys some space," Eden says with a knowing smile, accompanying Laura, Elle, and Baxton out of the building.

I don't hear them leave. All I hear is the loud thumping of my heartbeat pulsing heavily in my mind and my ears. It's clear Jax is just as nervous as I am. He's breathing hard, his lips curving into an uneasy and uncertain smile.

"Jackson," I somehow manage to squeeze out. A desperate plea.

And that's all he needs to close all remaining distance between us, weave his fingers in my hair, and kiss the hell out of me.

He kisses me like a man dying of thirst and I'm the only source of water. He kisses me like he's been infected by a life-threatening disease and I'm the only thing that can cure him. He kisses me like I'm the ocean and he's the sand on a beach and we've spent our entire existence meeting but never meeting, and today is the only day time stands still and the fates allow us to draw ourselves together.

His hands dance across my back, his knuckles brushing against my shoulder blades, down my arms, and finally resting them on my hips. I let out an embarrassing moan, and he tightens his hold around me, deepening the kiss.

"Wow." By the time we release one another, I'm gasping for breath. "That was one hell of a kiss."

"Seven hundred and thirty days, darlin.'" Jax smooths my hair and grins. "Best believe there'll be a lot more where that came from."

My heart tugs at those words. *I can't wait.*

He lifts his arm for me to take. "Ready to go home, baby?"

I nod, locking our arms together. "I'm ready."

And this time, I really mean it.

***

After saying goodbye to everyone, Jax drives me back home. We're not in Baxton's old car anymore, but rather a black Ford, which is an interesting pick for my boyfriend. I don't know why I picture him in a sports car or something. Jax holds my hand tightly the whole drive home, squeezing it every few seconds. Finally, our life together can begin.

The familiar Melrose street comes into view, and my heart picks up. I wonder if the house still looks the same. Memories whizz by me when we pull into the driveway. I had the best summer of my life here. I would've been gutted if Jax had moved out. Thankfully, he didn't.

Jax jogs over to my side and helps me out of the car. He produces the key and opens the front door. The smile growing on my lips threatens to break my face. It looks exactly the same as it did when I left, with a few minor improvements. The furniture is all the same, except for a few more picture frames adorning the mantel, most of me, or both of us. I hadn't realized that Jax was such a photographer. I didn't even realize a photo was being taken for most of these; he was always so discreet with his phone like that. I stroll over to pick up a frame containing a picture of me holding his hand while we sit in a booth of a restaurant in Santa Monica. I have my chin resting on my arm, and I seem to be looking away, eyes shut, with a smile on my face like I'm enjoying the moment.

"That one's my favorite of you," Jax says, casually leaning against the back of the sofa . "Everything is just as you left it. I didn't want to touch a single thing."

"Baxton really is okay with you still living in this house?" I say as I set the frame down.

"I don't see what problem he would have, since technically, he doesn't own it anymore."

My face scrunches up with confusion. "What . . .?" The knowing grin gracing his face drops the conclusion into my head and I gawk at him. "You *bought* it? You didn't tell me about this."

"I wanted it to be a surprise," he tells me, dragging me toward him and tugging a stray lock behind my ear. My knee wedges between his legs. "I couldn't possibly see myself living anywhere else but here."

"How could you afford it?" I whisper, suddenly terrified that he spent his entire life savings on this. All I know is that during the two years I'd been in prison, Jax had been working hard from the ground up here in LA, training with this guy called Hunter at his MMA gym Rocketfuel and fighting in every amateur MMA competition he can. But those amateur fights aren't paying him enough, and I don't want him spending all his money on a piece of property, no matter how sentimental this place is.

"Now, before you think I blew all my savings on this, I didn't all right?" Jax answers my thoughts briskly. "For a while now, Hunter was looking for someone to co-run the gym with him, since he's getting too busy with his other businesses, and asked if I'd be willing to come on board. I said yes, and now, I'm helping him run the business."

"Wow," I say, my lips curving upward again. "I'm so proud of you, Jackson."

"Thanks, darlin'," he murmurs, resting his forehead against mine. "You should come by one day. I want to show you around. We're open ever day except Thursday nights. We reserve that time for the kids."

Jax's commitment to the kids from the family resource center has always been something that was important to me. I'm happy to hear that it's just as important to him too.

"Also, don't hate me, but . . ." Jax scratches his head, unable to hide another grin forming on his face. "I made another investment."

"Don't tell me you bought another house."

"No. It's a different kind of investment," he mentions cryptically, prompting a perplexed look from me. He pulls away just enough to slip a hand in his pocket to pull something out. "Here. I wanted to give this to you while we were in the car, but I thought I should wait."

Jax hands over what looks like a crumpled white envelope. I open it and pull out its contents: a printed letter and a bank card. "A debit card?" I look at him, all confused. "I have a bank account, you know."

"I know, but I took the liberty of making another savings account for you," Jax mentions, smoothing a thumb over my jawline. "A few people chipped in with the money. Baxton, me, Elle, and even Laura. It should be enough money for what you've always wanted to do, go back to school."

My heart drops out of my rib cage.

"What?" I sputter.

"Go back to culinary school, Blaire," Jax murmurs. "Be who you've always wanted to be. Make your dad proud."

Uneasiness trickles down my spine like drops from a leaky faucet. My gaze falls on the letter and bank card in my hand. This time, my eyes scroll through the contents of the letter and I nearly gasp when I see the amount that's been credited into the account.

"I can't take this, Jackson." I shake my head, my hands trembling. "This is too much."

Jax refuses to hear any of it. Instead, he closes his hands over mine, tucking the debit card tightly into my palm. "Like I said. It's an investment. We're investing in *you* because we love you and we know you have what it takes to make it," he whispers, prompting a fat tear to roll down my cheek. "You've been carrying your own burdens for a long time now. Don't repeat your past mistakes, Blaire. Let us help you. You don't have to be alone anymore. You've got people you can count on now."

Through my tears, I nod. Jax is right; being stubborn is what led me to this life in the first place. If I'm truly determined to break the cycle, I need to recognize that flaw and turn it into something that can really help me.

I'm done being in survival mode.

For once, I want to see what it's like to actually live.

"Oh, Jackson . . ." I cup his face in both my hands and brush my nose against his. "I love you so much."

"I love you too, Blaire," he tightens his hold around my waist, pressing our bodies together. I haven't been this close with anyone in so long that it should feel foreign, but it doesn't, my body melting into his. "Thanks for coming home to me."

"Thanks for waiting for me," I whisper back.

Our mouths meet in a deliciously featherlight kiss. No tongue, no urgency, time stretching out in front of us forever. We kiss as if a single second had never passed between us. The only time our mouths are apart is when we're catching our breaths, and then we're back at it again, Jax's mouth crashing over mine. This time, there's nothing exploratory about this kiss. It's pure, unabated hunger. I hear myself moan, and Jax swallows the desperate sound with another greedy kiss, his large hands clamping on my hips desperately to tether our bodies permanently together.

My heart pounds, knowing where this is going. Heat pools between my legs, and I blush intensely, not used to being turned on like this. There have only been a handful of times where I'd taken care of the need while in prison, but having my hand down my underwear while constantly surrounded by three bunkmates has admittedly been a lady-boner killer for the longest time, so I didn't do it often. Now that I have the privacy I've been craving, I'm suddenly afraid that this might be too much for my body to handle.

I'm even more terrified that while I've been waiting to have this moment with him, it's a different story with Jax.

I inhale a nervous breath. "I know I said if you really wanted to . . .with other people, you could, but have you . . . um . . . have you . . ?"

Understanding dawns in Jax's eyes. "No," he says adamantly, allowing his fingers to fall down my spine. "I told you I didn't need the option then. I meant it."

Surprise slams into my chest. "So, no sex? For two years?

Really?" Jax grins, but nods in confirmation. A laugh tears out of me. "Jackson Deneris, a reborn virgin. Who would've thought?"

"How about you?" I watch as his fingers graze down my arm. "Any pretty inmates do it for you?"

"Never. No one could hold a candle to you."

Jax peers back at me, but his hands are elsewhere, creeping up my shirt. "Is that so?" I'm desperate to get a feel of him too. To explore the hard planes of his chest and trace each sculpted pec with my index finger.

You can tell I've thought about this for *ages*.

He watches me with lust-filled eyes. "So that means we're both kinda rusty here."

"Insanely."

"Well, you know what they say, hmmm?" Jax hauls me up, allowing my legs to wrap around his hips so he can take me upstairs. I giggle, looping my arms around his neck. "Practice makes perfect."

EPILOGUE

Jax
Four Months Later

The crowd surrounding the cage is much bigger than Julian and I ever anticipated. In fact, it's bigger than any crowd I've ever fought in front of while I was in the underground. And there are still people desperately trying to squeeze their way in through the front doors of the gym.

From the cage side, Julian is looking stressed as hell, pacing back and forth at the front. I bet he's thinking about whether insurance will cover a stampede in his gym.

Suddenly, flying back to Boston for this is starting to look like a big mistake.

"You sure you still wanna do this?" Kayden asks, bouncing around the cage with a slight smirk on his face. His dark hair is slick with sweat as he jogs from side to side to warm up.

A little too late to back out now, isn't it? I gesture frustratingly around us, trapped in the cage with him.

Tonight was supposed to be a small, friendly match. Just the two of us and some of our friends and family. The whole gang is here, apparently; Sienna's friends: Daniel, Alex, Cara, and Evans, as well as Kayden's brother, Brent. And of course I brought Blaire, and even flew down Baxton and Eden too, since they were also eager to see how this long-standing rivalry between me and Kayden resolves itself. Blaire's caught them up to speed with all the drama, and apparently, Eden's got his money on Kayden. That bastard.

Still love him to death, though.

Anyway, I don't know how word got out that Kayden and I were having a rematch, but it did, and now we've got the whole city holed up in the basement of UFG right now, and, to be honest, it's kind of terrifying, with half of the crowd yelling for me to end Kayden, and the other half yelling for my blood to spill.

"You got this, baby!" Blaire yells excitedly from below, with an arm slung around Eden.

I jog over to her and blow her a kiss. She's wearing a replica of my fighter's robe, the black and gold gleaming underneath the newly installed stage lights. Her short hair is pulled into a half-up, half-down do, the pink highlights a welcome distraction. At the back of her glistening silk robe, in bold white font spells DEADBEAT'S GF. A little cheesy, but I'm still adamant on showing everyone that she's mine.

Standing beside Blaire, Baxton beams proudly up at me. I grin back at him, grateful to have my dad by the sidelines for once, supporting me in the way I've always longed for.

Meanwhile, Kayden's got a little corner of his own. Sienna's also wearing her own version of Kayden's signature red robe, branded with her LUCKY nickname. On either side of her are Brent and Evans both holding GO and KILLER! signs respectively.

From the other side of the cage, Sienna beckons Kayden over, and he crouches down as she tells him something. Whatever it is, it must be good because he nearly doubles over, roaring with laughter. She laughs as well, happiness spilling out of her. I've always known Kayden to be the stoic one, so Sienna bringing out a lighter side of him is a refreshing change.

Shouts of "Killer" and "Deadbeat" reverberate throughout the UFG basement, as the referee holds his hand up, getting ready to signal the start of the match. At first, Kayden and I opted for Julian to be the referee, but he insisted that he didn't want anything to do with it because he didn't want to "play favorites."

Me. It was obvious he was talking about me.

"I want a clean fight, boys, you got it?" the referee says carefully, gaze ping-ponging between me and Kayden. "That means no hair-pulling, no eye-gouging, biting or spitting, and no throat or groin strikes of any kind. Disqualification may occur after any combination of fouls or after a flagrant foul at my discretion."

I fight the urge to roll my eyes. He talks to us as if we're still playing dirty, when Kayden and I had cleaned our acts up a long time ago.

We tap gloves and fall into our stances. I slip easily into mine, but Kayden seems to flow into his. I can tell he's kept up with training in the years since we last fought. His body settles into the stance like it's his natural state, a part of him. Organic. Kayden still has a shadow of a smile on his face, but his eyes gleam with anticipation, I'm not certain, but I think I catch a flicker of doubt glaze over them.

A grin slashes across my face. I can win this.

"Three . . . two . . .one!" The referee drops his hand as the bell rings out. *"FIGHT!"*

I explode into motion, punching straight for his center frame. Kayden blocks. Once. Twice. But I'm faster the third time, feinting right, I shift my weight forward and spin into a kick. It connects, and I feel the air leave Kayden's lungs. In an instant he closes the distance, using the small window where I'm still slightly off-balance from the kick to wrap his arms around me trying to force us into a grapple.

You're not going to get me the same way again, I grunt, fighting back.

We trade blows. He gets some body shots in and I counter. I get some hits in and he blocks. We disengage, falling back and circling one another, each confident in his own abilities, sizing the enemy up.

But this fight is different; we're not enemies, at least not anymore. I've even come to consider Kayden, well, not a friend, but someone I've grown fond of.

It's not life or death for me anymore.

A match is just a match. The outcome won't affect me as soon as I step out of that cage.

But that doesn't mean it won't make me feel a fuck-ton better if I step out with a victory.

Kayden makes his move, charging into a full-on tackle. I brace, but he fakes me out, and then hits. My timing is off, muscles straining as my body fights against the pressure. It's a full-on contest of strength. He tries to trip me, but I push my weight forward and wrap my arms around his waist. With a heave, I lift Kayden off his feet, catching him off-balance as he manages to trip me.

We both crash onto the floor.

Hard.

I roll, trying to lock Kayden into a choke hold, but he slips out. We both struggle, a flurry of motion in the cage as we wrestle. Kayden ends up smashing me against the side of the cage and puts me in an armlock. The angle is weird, and I'm yelling and writhing in pain. If I can keep calm, I have a small chance of getting out. The angle is slightly wrong; I might be able to twist and get out from under him. I *could*.

But from the corner of my eye, I spot Sienna. Her eyebrows are furrowed low on her face and she bites down on her lip anxiously. *Come on, come on, come on*, her mouth repeats the words.

She wants this win for Kayden.

She *needs* it.

My face contorts with pain as Kayden pushes my arm down. I can squeeze out. Use my legs as leverage and pull myself out. I can do it. *I can do it*.

But . . . I don't want to.

With a yell of agony, my hand reaches down on the mat and I tap out.

The gym erupts into a set of cheers so loud it shakes up the floor.

Kayden helps me off the mat and we bump fists. *No hard feelings*. We both nod in tandem. Because there truly aren't.

I watch silently as he turns away and runs toward Sienna,

who leaps into the cage. She jumps into his arms and he swings her around, laughing and roaring with victory.

Right on cue, the net above us drops a rainstorm of balloons, and confetti pours down. I cast a glance at Julian in the crowd. *Nice touch, Jules.* He shrugs with a hint of a smile.

"Hey, it's okay," Blaire says, her arms going up my shoulders to console me. "You did your best."

I lean into her ear, trying to hide my grin. "You wanna know a secret?"

"What?"

"I let him win."

Blaire chokes on a laugh. "Sure you did, baby."

"I did!"

"Yeah, and I let Harvey Dystel cop a feel. Both of those statements are what you call lies."

I brought a hand melodramatically to my chest. "That hurts."

"You know what I mean." Blaire smiles, gently dusting the flecks of blood from my face. "I'm just saying maybe it's what you think. Maybe he won fair and square, and you're just a little bitter about it."

I glance over her shoulder. Sienna and Kayden are all wrapped up together, gazing at one another as they hold up the belt for the crowd to go nuts. Her smile when she looks up at him is infectious.

I hope her happiness never goes away.

"You're right, darlin'," I whisper to my girlfriend. "Maybe I'm just bitter."

"It's okay. You're still a champion to me," Blaire whispers back, kissing my nose. "Always."

I break into a grin.

And when I catch Blaire's chin with my hand and fit my lips over hers, the world has never felt more right.

ACKNOWLEDGEMENTS

The Perfect series has been my life's work. When sixteen-year-old me published the first chapter of *Perfect Illusion* on Wattpad, I had no idea it would lead me down a path of international recognition and success, spawning four award-winning books and a movie. As a small-town girl from Malaysia, the scale of it is still unfathomable to me. Now, at twenty-five, I'm eternally grateful that younger me took that first step to click "publish"; it shows that anything is possible when you set your mind and heart to it.

Concluding the series with Jax's story felt right to me, since he was the last loose thread that I felt like I needed to tie up. He has appeared so much across the series that it felt full circle to end with his story. It warms my heart that he and Blaire have found healing in one another; and I'd like to think that they integrate well into the Perfect series friend circle.

I'd like to thank everyone who played a part in my journey shaping the series. Firstly, a huge thank you to Deanna McFadden and the Wattpad Books team for believing in the series. To Rebecca Sands, my editor—thank you for being patient with me and for playing a huge part in morphing the series into something I'd always dreamed it could be. To Shannon Whibbs, my lovely copy editor, who helped carry this story all the way to the finish line.

To my parents, who have always encouraged me to turn my hobbies into something more. I wouldn't be doing what I'm doing today without their endless love, care, and support. To Nicole, who always entertained my crazy book ideas and beta-read every chapter I ever gave her. You're the real MVP. Also, to Irwin, who helped me breathe new life into the published version of the series. I love you. Shout-out to Matthew Noszka, who played the role of Jax so perfectly in the *Perfect Addiction* movie adaptation that it helped shape Jax's redemption arc for this story. And lastly, to the fans. You know how much I love and appreciate each and every single one of you. Without you, this book wouldn't even exist, since it was you guys who petitioned for Jax's story to be told. You saw something in him that I never thought twice about, and now, we have a redemption arc for him, which is crazy!

To those of you who have stuck by the series since it was barely a draft on Wattpad, thank you so much for your never-ending loyalty and support. I'm so glad I got to be a part of your lives. It still blows my mind when people tell me that the series was such an integral part of their reading experience when they were younger. I love you guys so much, and I hope you're satisfied with the conclusion to the series.

I hope to see you soon in the next book or series that I write.

Love, Claudia

ABOUT THE AUTHOR

Claudia Tan is a new adult romance writer. She graduated from Lancaster University with a BA in English Literature and History. Her massively popular Perfect series is a two-time Watty Award winner and has accumulated over 160 million reads on Wattpad. The series has also been published in French by Hachette Romans. Book two, *Perfect Addiction*, was released by W by Wattpad Books in 2022 and has been adapted into a major motion picture with Wattpad WEBTOON Studios and Constantin Film.